because of the camels

BRENDA BLAIR

Siwa Publishing
Austin, Texas

Siwa Publishing
P.O. Box 6029
Austin, TX 78762
siwapublishing.com

Printed in the United States of America
10 9 8 7 6 5 4 3 2 1

Library of Congress Cataloging-in-Publication Data is available for this title.
ISBN 978-0-9850470-0-9

Text design and composition by Silver Feather Design
Cover design by Silver Feather Design
Maps illustrated by JT Schwable

To my mother, who taught me the joy of language

Matagorda Bay, Texas

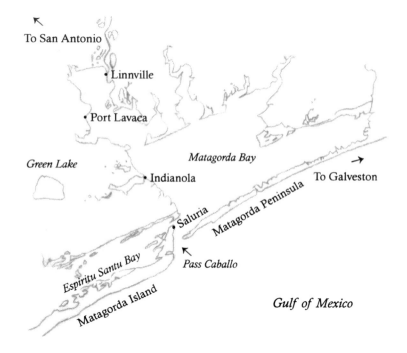

Central Texas

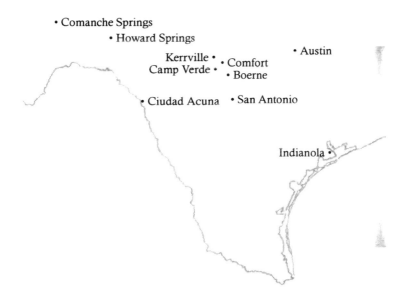

- Comanche Springs
- Howard Springs

Kerrville • • Comfort
Camp Verde • • Boerne

• Austin

• Ciudad Acuna • San Antonio

Indianola •

T HE FIRST MENTION OF the camels was entirely inconsequential. As far as Elizabeth was concerned, it portended nothing whatsoever.

The news arrived in an unpretentious envelope with a foreign stamp and two lines of indecipherable script. The sender's name was legible: Major James Babcock. Although correspondence from her mother's favorite cousin arrived predictably near holidays and birthdays, a letter at this time of year was most unusual. A piece of mail so out of the ordinary hinted at unforeseen events or a dramatic family story. She should have been more attuned to the letter's possible implications. On any other day, she would have wondered at its contents, tried to determine its point of origin, and sought to uncover its secrets. But today's post contained more enticing items that overpowered her natural curiosity. The newest editions of *Godey's Lady's Book* and *Peterson's Magazine* fired her imagination, while the strange-looking letter was relegated to a mere afterthought.

Clutching the fashion magazines, Elizabeth skipped up the steps to her parents' stately mansion and nonchalantly passed the letter to Antoine, the butler. She and her friends moved to the shaded porch and spread the journals across a low table. They hunched over the pictures, giggling and gossiping, their cheeks flushed from the summer heat and from the excitement of their deliberations. In anticipation of next year's May Day festivities when they would make their social debut, they were already plotting what to wear. Captivated by the prints of shimmering gowns, they envisioned themselves attired like princesses for a spring night of magic. As they exclaimed over one design and then another, the afternoon passed like a butterfly flitting by, delightful and happy. Engrossed in the merits of pagoda sleeves and flounces, Elizabeth failed to notice Antoine until his shadow loomed over the magazines. He had to clear his throat to get her attention.

"Oh, Antoine. What is it?"

"Excuse me, Missy 'Lizbeth, but your mama says it's time."

"All right. Tell her I'll be right there."

Reluctantly Elizabeth escorted her friends down the wide staircase to street level, promising to let them know what her mother thought of her favorite gown. Keen to find her mother, she dashed back up the stairs past Antoine, who was obliged to step aside to avoid a collision. On the other side of the veranda, Sylvia McDermott sat in a wicker armchair with an assortment of books and letters scattered about her feet. When she heard the thumping enthusiasm of her daughter's footsteps, she set aside her reading.

"Hello, dear. Have you had a nice visit?"

"Yes, and I think I've found the dress." She thrust the magazine onto her mother's lap, opened to a page marked with a bent corner, showing a particularly tempting illustration.

"Let's see. That one? It's a bit décolleté. Isn't that suitable for someone older?"

"Mama, I thought the point of May Day was for us to be grown ups!"

"I suppose so. But you're only fifteen."

"Please, Mama! I'll be sixteen by then."

"Well, that style might look good on you. Let me think about it." Sylvia held the magazine with one hand. Her other hand rested beneath it, cradling the unexpected letter. "I've a note from Cousin Babcock."

"I saw it. What does it say?"

Sylvia had the habit of reading her cousin's letters aloud in order to acquaint her children with their Philadelphia relatives. Elizabeth usually appreciated these recitations, because Major Babcock described people in such lively language that she could visualize their appearance and mannerisms. He always conveyed cordial greetings to her and her brothers, even though he had never met them, a thoughtful gesture. Today, however, her mind was elsewhere, and she hoped her mother would offer only a brief summary.

"My cousin has been given a special assignment by Secretary of War Jefferson Davis to buy camels for the US Army! He's to bring them here to see how they'll hold up in our western deserts. The letter was posted from Tunis, and his next stop is Egypt. I've been looking in these books to see where he's going. I've found Cairo. See? There." As her finger hovered over a map, Sylvia looked up to catch her daughter staring at the *Godey's Book.*

"Elizabeth, did you hear me?"

"Sorry, Mama, what did you say?"

"I said that my cousin is going to bring camels to Texas. Can you imagine that?"

"No, Mama, the only thing I know about camels is the story of the three wise men."

Sylvia smiled. "I've combed our library for anything about Egypt or camels." She gestured at the stack next to her. "Not much here. I guess I'll have to order something."

"Good idea, Mama, buy some books."

When Sylvia McDermott married, she brought with her a portion of her father's substantial library, and taking advantage of Galveston as a port town, purchased books often. The bookseller informed her the moment a shipment came in and gave her first access to the newest volumes. Because Elizabeth shared her mother's voracious appetite for the written word, the two women routinely passed their afternoons reading for pleasure or in pursuit of Elizabeth's studies. But this afternoon Elizabeth wiggled in her chair, unable to stop thinking about the May Day festivities. Images of colorful gowns gliding across a dance floor distracted her from listening to her mother.

"He hopes to bring the camels to Indianola some time next year. If we're lucky, he may be able to stop in Galveston."

"That's nice."

Elizabeth's remote tone effectively ended the conversation. Sylvia folded the letter and tucked it back in its envelope, overjoyed that in several months she might receive a visit from her cousin. Having not set eyes on Major Babcock in years, she wondered how he might have changed and tried to picture his adventures in the Orient. Although not quite able to believe the part about the camels, she nevertheless wished that he might acquire them successfully and arrive in Texas safely. Neither she nor Elizabeth had any idea that Major Babcock's enterprise a world away would completely alter the trajectory of their lives.

Many years later the two women sat together on a different veranda trying to reconstruct the camel story. Between them lay the contents of a small metal box: a ball of rough brown yarn, a blue and white glass bead, a rabbit's foot, and a silver goblet wrapped in blue velvet. Next to the box stood a gold-framed daguerreotype. Precisely etched, the glossy image depicted a young girl astride a kneeling camel, surrounded by three young men dressed like cowboys. Elizabeth held it tenderly, examining each of their faces with a wistful smile.

To the odd assortment, Sylvia added a stack of letters, on top of which was the first correspondence from Major Babcock. Sylvia had to remind her daughter of that letter, because Elizabeth had completely forgotten.

ACQUISITION

H ASSAN TOUCHED HIS BROW to the ground and rose to find his heart was pounding. He took a deep breath, knelt and bowed again, resting his forehead on the cool silk of his prayer mat. He repeated the words, but could not capture the solace that the Friday prayers usually brought him. Next to him Alhaji Mustafa also bowed, rose, and recited the prayers. Hassan welcomed this weekly communion with his maternal grandfather, a well-known scholar. He appreciated the one-ness in the uniform motion and the repetition of prayers that had sustained his family for generations. Sometimes, if he concentrated especially hard, he would feel the presence of his ancestors and would be overwhelmed with a joyful sensa-tion of connection to those who had preceded him.

Today, however, all Hassan felt was impatience for his grandfather to announce his decision. So momentous would the decision be, and so outrageous the request from a nineteen-year-old, that his father had deferred the matter to Alhaji Mustafa. The discussions had been going on for two weeks. He had visited his grandfather nightly, gently and re-spectfully putting forth first one argument and then another in response to his grandfather's questions. He had begged his mother to intercede on his behalf, but she said her heart would not permit it. He had approached Alhaji Mustafa's wife, his grandmother Ara, who indulged him beyond reason and whom he loved with the total devotion of a babe in arms, but she gave only enigmatic answers.

The prayers were lasting interminably. All around him the city was alive, but Hassan was so absorbed that he did not see the sun rise like a smoky torch over the ochre walls of the mosque. He barely scented the freshly baked bread wafting from household ovens throughout the city, bread like his grandmother made for him on Fridays. He failed to hear the rooster crowing or the cries of babies waking hungrily. He ignored the blossoming beauty of the sun as it came to fruition and was deaf to the muezzin calls to prayer. One day the memory of these images, sounds, and smells would be a source of strength and comfort, but today they only irritated.

Today his thoughts were filled with sailing ships and foreign tongues. His mind's eye saw the bustling port of Alexandria, overflowing with vessels, people and cargo of every size, purpose, and costume on earth. He focused on the recently arrived ship the *Supply* from the United States of America, an untamed country across the ocean. The Americans had come to buy camels, and he had the possibility to accompany the camels to that alien land. Such an opportunity felt like a gift from God. Surely his grandfather must agree.

The prayers ended and his grandfather turned to look at him, gazing as if standing on a faraway mountain. Hassan lowered his eyes, his blood beating in his temples. At last Alhaji Mustafa smiled. "Come, let us go."

Hassan quickly rolled his prayer mat and his grandfather's, pausing ever so briefly to admire the woven strips of color and to feel the smoothness of the silk. Hassan was proud of having a mat that matched his grandfather's. Alhaji Mustafa had given it to him on the occasion of his birth, and it was Hassan's most treasured possession. Its manufacture was Asante, from south of the Sahara, acquired by his grandfather on a visit to that faraway place. At this recollection, Hassan felt a surge of hope: his grandfather had traveled extensively as a young man.

Hassan followed his grandfather from the mosque, keeping respectfully silent. The walk home seemed endless. Every few steps Alhaji Mustafa stopped to exchange words, offer a greeting, or pronounce a blessing. There was Muhammad the shopkeeper who sold the best olives in the whole of Alexandria, Alhaji Samir the copper dealer whose beautiful wares were polished each day and caught the glittering rays of the midday sun, Salah the beggar who always received a coin from Alhaji Mustafa, and Tariq the fruit seller who offered Hassan's grandfather a gift of the tastiest dates in his shop. No fewer than three men approached Alhaji Mustafa and asked to speak with him in private, glancing at Hassan as they stepped away. Embarrassed by these secretive conversations, Hassan feared that these men were influencing his grandfather's decision.

A harsh bleating forced Hassan to dodge a female goat and several kids skittering across his path. The goats had been frightened by a donkey cart, piled high with amphoras of olive oil and topped with bunches of dried herbs. All the pedestrians had to press together to allow the cart to pass. Hassan felt as overloaded with frustration as the cart was with goods. He was about to shout an insult to the young boy astride the donkey when he felt a touch on his shoulder. He turned to see his grandfather smiling.

"My son, smell that delicious fragrance." Choking back his exasperation, Hassan meekly agreed that the aroma was pleasant.

When the hubbub subsided, Hassan noticed that they were near Auntie Fatima's house. For Auntie Fatima, Friday was filled with personal rituals, most important of which was participation in prayers at the mosque. Wearing hijab and flowing robes, she strolled to the women's section to join her voice to those who praise God. These sojourns sometimes drew criticism because her clothes, although always meticulously correct in design, included the richest fabrics in a seemingly inexhaustible supply. There was hissing speculation that Auntie Fatima's Friday faithfulness was less due to piety than to her desire to display her wealth. But because she was Alhaji Mustafa's relative, the undercurrent of complaint never erupted into open rebuke. Every Friday after prayers, Auntie Fatima returned to her home, drank a glass of cool water, surveyed the preparations in her sitting room, and waited for her distinguished cousin.

Hassan spied Auntie Fatima inside the door of her house, dressed in black silk embroidered at the edges with silver. Usually, he would leave Alhaji Mustafa at this juncture and return to taste his grandmother Ara's freshly baked bread, but today there was no escape. Struggling to contain his annoyance, Hassan glanced skyward and caught a shadowy movement on the second floor. He felt his stomach tighten as he realized that someone was watching him. Suddenly all concerns about his future dissipated and his only interest lay in the possibility of seeing Auntie Fatima's granddaughter.

When Auntie Fatima invited Alhaji Mustafa inside, it was Hassan who agreed. "Grandfather, wouldn't you like to take some tea and rest awhile?"

Alhaji Mustafa nodded gravely, but his eyes were twinkling. "My Cousin Fatima's hospitality is always a pleasure."

Auntie Fatima inclined her head. "And I always appreciate a visit from my distinguished Cousin, especially when there are so many events in the world that you can explain to me." She flashed a piercing look at Hassan.

As he crossed the threshold out of the blazing sun into the cool of Auntie Fatima's marble entry hall, Hassan didn't know which thought consumed him more: the joyous prospect of seeing Sula or the dangerous possibility that Auntie Fatima was scheming something that would affect his grandfather's decision.

From the shadows of the elaborate wooden lattice that covered Auntie Fatima's upstairs balconies, Sula had seen Hassan and Alhaji Mustafa make their way toward her grandmother's house. Even taller than Alhaji Mustafa, Hassan had thick black hair and strong eyebrows. His clothing hung elegantly from his broad shoulders to below his knees. The pale blue cloth complimented his dark skin and eyes. Sula knew that some people found Hassan's color unattractive, but to her, the glowing auburn tones in his complexion made Hassan more appealing, as a darker cup of coffee often has a richer taste. Some detractors said his curls gave him a Jewish countenance, while others flatly stated that he resembled a Nubian. He naturally had a hint of his grand-mother's African hair, but he also bore Alhaji Mustafa's aquiline nose and Roman forehead. What does one expect of a family that has lived for generations at the crossroads of the world? As his shining brown eyes flashed in her direction, Sula couldn't help smiling.

Sula's only chance to see Hassan would be while serving the men their refreshments. Her contact with him had not always been so limited. As children, they had spent many hours in Alhaji Mustafa's courtyard under an old grape arbor, playing together and whispering their dreams. Hassan looked after baby Sula, five years his junior, and she in turn was always making a trinket for her elder cousin. A few years ago, all that had changed as Hassan became increasingly disinterested. Sula's mother replied to her complaints with a wry smile and the admonition to be patient. Now at fourteen, Sula grasped her mother's intuition, for the bond between herself and Hassan was reviving. However, because they had entered into that mysterious world of manhood and womanhood, they were bound by numerous strictures on their behavior. Sula rarely saw him. Today Auntie Fatima had specifically requested her presence to help serve Alhaji Mustafa, and Hassan was here, too. Surely these events were not a coincidence.

Auntie Fatima knew everything that happened in Alexandria, gathering news from every possible source. She questioned servants, neighbors, friends, and workers; she overhead conversations with her husband's guests; she collected tidbits from her children, nieces and nephews; and she watched and listened to what transpired on the street in front of her house. Her capacity for predicting the outcomes of significant events—marriage, divorce, neighborhood alliances, and family feuds—was unequalled. Her greatest pleasure was having more information, and sooner, than anyone in her acquaintance. With snippets of chitchat and innuendo, Auntie Fatima wove a complex web of protection for her family.

Within a few hours of the docking of the *Supply*, some four weeks ago, she knew that Americans would be calling on the Viceroy to buy camels. She immediately began to speculate on the possible repercussions for Hassan's father,

Yusuf, who supervised the Viceroy's horses and camels. One always had to look out for petty jealousies, demonstrated through a thousand slights, affronts, and carefully modulated insults, designed to sting but not to cause attention to the one doing the stinging. When she learned that the foreigners were staying at the Hotel Isis, she paid a social call on a woman who had a shop next door.

"The sea voyage takes two months?" Auntie Fatima was shocked. "What else can you tell me?"

"Two adult men and a boy stay at the hotel. The boy is related to the leader. The other man wears a sour expression and is often feverish. The captain sleeps on the ship with the sailors. Not one of them can speak Arabic, but they have hired an interpreter, Ali ibn Jamal, you know, the one who worked at the British Embassy."

At once Auntie Fatima summoned Ali, who by good fortune was a friend's son. He told her that the Viceroy's advisors were divided. "Several are opposed to the Americans because they are too much like the English. Nobody trusts the English. This faction wants to delay them or even refuse to supply the camels."

"And the other view?"

"They think helping the Americans could be an advantage against the British. They want the Viceroy to sell good quality animals to cement an alliance, charging a duly high price of course."

When Auntie Fatima wondered what the Americans thought of all this, Ali reassured her. He had not informed them of the raging conflict, because they had not asked. "This morning I heard of a compromise. The Viceroy will authorize the export of ten camels, but of poor quality. Yusuf will be instructed to send the best camels into the countryside."

Auntie Fatima was appalled. Surely the Americans would perceive the insult, and then in order to save face, the Viceroy would blame Yusuf for offering inferior animals.

"There is more." Ali had saved the tastiest morsel for last. "The Americans have asked for three men to accompany the camels to America. I will go as interpreter. The second will be someone experienced with camels. The third person proposed is Hassan ibn Yusuf ibn Mustafa."

Auntie Fatima gasped, utterly stunned. Not Hassan, not to be sent away on the ocean to someplace where the name of Allah is not even called. And how would he return? Another long and dangerous voyage? What if some calamity befell him in that uncivilized place? Auntie Fatima felt faint. She thanked Ali and dismissed him, begging him to keep her informed.

Auntie Fatima immediately began hatching the plan that was now unfolding in her drawing room. While her guests sipped their tea, she led the conversation through the formal greetings and listened intently while Alhaji Mustafa dissected a fine point of the Imam's commentary. She summoned Sula to bring goat kebabs, marinated olives, stuffed grape leaves, and fresh dates. Sula greeted Alhaji Mustafa and Hassan demurely, nevertheless daring to lift her eyes to Hassan's. Distracted by the delicate scent of her perfume, Hassan nearly forgot to return her greeting. When Sula presented another tray of delicacies, he complimented her on the baba ganoush and asked if she had prepared it.

"No, no, the recipe is Auntie Fatima's, but I did help in small ways."

Auntie Fatima smiled. "One day soon, I will teach you my special recipes, Sula, so that you can serve them in your own household."

Hassan stared at Auntie Fatima. Was she implying that Sula was soon to be married? Why had he not heard of it?

"Hassan, I'm sure you would enjoy resting in the garden while I visit with your grandfather."

"Certainly, Auntie." Hassan rose, baffled by Auntie Fatima's enigmatic smile.

Sula caught her breath and left the room. Hassan followed her into the courtyard, mesmerized by the way her long skirt flowed around her hips and thighs. She moved like a woman! Hassan had seen her naked as a toddler, but that had been years ago. Suddenly he found himself imagining her naked again. Glancing at the servant who stood at a discreet distance, Sula sat daintily on one end of a bench beneath a fig tree. Hassan perched on the other.

"Sula, it's been too long since I have seen you."

"I couldn't believe it when I saw you walking with your uncle. You looked so tall and strong. I thought, 'Could this be my cousin Hassan? He looks like an important man.'"

Hassan laughed. "You are no longer a child yourself. It's good to see you."

"Can you guess what Auntie Fatima is up to? She really wanted me here today, even though she knows my mother likes me at home helping her."

Hassan's brow furrowed. "I don't know."

"Maybe she will ask your grandfather if we can be allowed to visit each other as we used to."

"Sula, you know that is not possible. But I don't want to waste time speculating about Auntie Fatima. She is always up to something. Let's talk of other things."

Hassan took her hand in his, and Sula felt a shiver like the touch of a breeze when stepping out of the bath. They spoke softly, amazed that the courtyard was so peaceful when just outside the street was dense with boisterous activity. Here in the tranquil garden, as in the old days, they began to dream. Suddenly, Hassan jumped up. Before Sula could ask him to explain, he was running across the courtyard.

Meanwhile, Auntie Fatima worked her plan. "Cousin, I believe you are refreshed?"

"As always, your delicacies give a man a glimpse of what life will be like in paradise. But I know that this elaborate display is meant to prepare me for some news or scheme that you have concocted." Alhaji Mustafa smiled indulgently.

"I can hide nothing from you. I think it is time to plan for Sula's future."

"My dear Cousin Fatima, since they have been born, we have been planning for our grandchildren's futures. Sula is still a young girl. There is plenty of time to find her a suitable husband. I am considering Suleiman, the teacher at the madrassa."

"I'm sure he is a most suitable prospect, but I am also concerned for Hassan's future."

Sure that Auntie Fatima was leading him somewhere, Alhaji Mustafa decided to play along. "I couldn't agree more. Hassan has developed into a fine young man, well educated in the Qur'an. Through assisting his father he has learned to manage both animals and men. I have been thinking he should expand his education. He is bright enough to become a scholar."

"Dearest cousin, Hassan is not only intelligent, but handsome. I have already received several informal inquiries from prominent families with lovely daughters. I have been circumspect with them, as I have not known how to reply."

"Thank you for this information. I will consider it."

"Alhaji Mustafa, you force me to speak frankly. Do you not think it is time for Hassan and Sula to be betrothed? Their affection is obvious, and we can put an end to the meddling of others if we announce their plans to marry."

Alhaji Mustafa burst out laughing. "How long have you been plotting this?"

Auntie Fatima lowered her eyes and spoke softly. "Honored Cousin, you are the spiritual leader of the family, and your wisdom far exceeds what I, a poor woman, can imagine. But when it comes to matters of marriage, I do have some meager experience, and I would like to humbly make a few observations. Sula has blossomed into womanhood. Stories of her beauty have started to circulate. Hassan is a man now. He should be assuming his responsibilities and settling down, not roaming about."

Alhaji Mustafa's thoughts raced as he realized that she must have heard about Hassan's wish to travel. Putting on a serious face, he looked at Auntie Fatima intently. "An American ship has come to purchase camels from the Viceroy. These Americans know nothing of camels, so someone will accompany them to teach their people. Hassan has requested permission to go."

"Eeeiyaah!! Surely you aren't going to permit this! Who will guide him through the dangers in these foreign places among infidels? What would be the point of such wandering? How could it possibly be good for him?"

"Stop, cousin. You are talking like a woman who sees only home. Have you forgotten that I myself traveled across the Sahara to Timbuktu, Djenne, and even to Kumasi? Can you pretend that my wife Ara would be here if I hadn't gone away? Hassan would not even be born if I had not traveled! You forget yourself. Decisions such as these are made by men. Hassan is a man, and he can take any voyage he chooses."

Hassan burst in from the garden, followed closely by Sula, in time to hear his grandfather's pronouncement. Alhaji Mustafa stopped short. Unexpectedly, he had given consent, and so it must be. Hassan managed to repress a smile, but he could scarcely stand still.

Intensely disappointed that her strategy had backfired, Auntie Fatima escorted her cousin to the door. She leaned toward Alhaji Mustafa and whispered quickly. "There is something I must tell you. It is rumored that the Viceroy's council is divided on these camels, and some are suggesting he should sell the Americans inferior animals. If the Americans discover this...."

"My beloved cousin, you are a torment and a delight. How can a woman acquire such knowledge about the workings of the Viceroy's court? Thank you for your hospitality."

"Thank you for honoring us with your visit. Please convey my warmest affections to Ara."

Sula felt the room close in around her. Hassan would leave her again, just when she felt she was getting him back. "Hassan, please tell me what is happening."

Quickly he recounted his plans to go to America with the camels. Seeing her bewildered expression, he considered for the first time how this separation might affect them. Impulsively, he pulled Sula towards him and pressed his face next to hers. "Sula, one day the whole neighborhood will rejoice at our wedding and we will have many children."

He stepped back and hurried to join his grandfather. In a split second they were out in the bright bustle of the street. Alhaji Mustafa, looking grave, strode purposefully home, his greetings noticeably briefer than prior to the visit with Auntie Fatima.

My dearest Annabelle,

As I sit here in a veritable inferno of desert heat, I am forced to wonder why I ever allowed myself to be convinced that this harebrained scheme would meet with any positive result. I understand why Secretary Davis would, in theory, be enamored of the possibility of employing camels in the Great American West. I can even comprehend why Major Babcock, who has a relentlessly cheery disposition, might conceive of the notion as intriguing. But frankly, I find that the latter's enthusiasm begins to border on romantic fantasy — the exotic East, and all that — and his unfailing optimism threatens to become an impediment to our success.

We have been in pursuit of camels longer than the time allotted for their acquisition. We are in possession of only one Bactrian and two dromedaries, having had to discharge a diseased one on arrival here that we purchased in Tunis. The Viceroy issued a decree that no camels could be exported from Egypt, a blatant manipulation, as camel caravans can be seen coming and going throughout the city. Then he changed his tune and promised us ten camels, but his emissaries continue to offer an assortment of pathetic excuses for not securing them. Major Babcock fervently believes that the Viceroy's camels shall be our salvation. I am certain that after interminable intrigues and delays, we shall still find ourselves wanting. Major Babcock insists we must adapt to Egyptian ways. I wonder if he has lost sight of our purpose.

I contemplate whether duty may compel me to write directly to Washington, even though such an action might be construed as insubordination. Perhaps you could discreetly relay a few of my observations to your father.

I do not mean to burden you with my concerns. I miss you. Lying here sweltering, glued with my own perspiration to this most unsuitable bed, I imagine lying on crisp, cool, sheets savoring the scent of your smooth skin and,...ah, if I continue in this vein, I shall write things that should not be written. My dear, I think of you daily and miss you with all my heart.

I must desist. Soon I shall once again go to the camel market with Major Babcock and that obstreperous nephew of his. Would that our two youngsters should not develop such tastes and comportment. But that is a story for another letter. They are knocking.

All my love, in haste,

Your devoted husband,

Winston

Alexander Babcock burst into Lt. Winston Halter's room at the Hotel Isis. "Good day, Lieutenant. Major Babcock is waiting outside in the carriage. Shall we be off?"

Lt. Halter barely concealed his disdain. "Mr. Babcock, I see that you are maintaining your penchant for native dress."

Alex glanced down at his leather boots, caked with mud, and his soiled breeches, topped off with a loose Egyptian shirt. Following Lt. Halter's gaze to his head, he concluded that the Lieutenant must object to his fez.

"This? Yes, I bought it last evening. Don't you think it's remarkable? Although I do like my turban as well." Remarkable was not the term Winston Halter would have employed. He found the ensemble ludicrous.

"If you insist on parading the streets dressed like that, at least you could clean your boots. Do I detect an odor of camel dung?" Lt. Halter wrinkled his nose.

"Sorry sir, I suppose that's possible. I went this morning to investigate a small camel market in the old town. I thought that since we were going to look for camels again this afternoon there was no point in cleaning my boots yet."

"Surely your uncle didn't authorize you to go unaccompanied into the city?"

"No, sir. I went with Ali the Interpreter. Apart from our failure to see any decent camels, it was enjoyable. We stopped at a local coffee shop and learned about predictions for this year's rains and Nile flooding. You see, last year was drier than normal, so therefore this year...."

"Never mind. Let us not keep your uncle waiting."

Appalled at the liberties that Major Babcock granted his unruly kinsman, Winston Halter knew instinctively that he would have to muzzle his tendency to criticize. He had numerous other points of contention with Major Babcock that were far more relevant to the outcome of the mission. The acquisition of camels was his absolute priority for the moment.

Lt. Halter joined Major Babcock in the carriage, while Alex leapt up front and squeezed onto the seat with Ali the Interpreter and the driver. The boy's choice to sit there, though lacking propriety, at least spared Lt. Halter from proximity to the aroma of camel. He checked his jacket pocket for his two handkerchiefs, neatly folded together and soaked in lavender that he held in front of his nose when visiting the camel sellers. Satisfied, he relaxed enough to converse with Major Babcock.

"Good afternoon, Major."

"Good afternoon, Lieutenant. How are you? You seem a bit more rested today."

Winston sighed. "I cannot for the life of me understand why we must engage in these fruitless excursions, especially in the heat of the day. We have not found one decent camel for sale in our last four outings, and we are still waiting to hear from the Viceroy. Don't you think it's about time we abandon Alexandria and look elsewhere?"

"You are far too easily discouraged. We've been told repeatedly that even the best letters of introduction aren't enough here. People must get to know us before we can conduct business. There is another reception tomorrow night given by a close associate of the Viceroy, and I feel confident that a good showing there will speed up the delivery of our camels."

"Not another reception! I find these events to be singularly unpleasant. I'm sick of the artificial formality. There's no alcohol and nothing but lamb or goat meat. I crave some fine wine and French canapés, followed by a juicy steak.

Really, what can possibly be gained from attending yet another of these charades?"

"Much, I hope, and Alhaji Ibrahim Muhammad's receptions are reputedly a good deal livelier than others."

"Really, Major, I fear that the sole purpose of these receptions is to distract us. Secretary Davis said nothing about attempts at international diplomacy. We are not obligated to curry favor with these people, and we must not exceed our authority. We've sent Gwynne Heap to Smyrna, and I'm sure he's acquired a sizeable contingent of camels by now. Even if we secure all ten of the Viceroy's animals, we will still be short of the full complement. Why not go to Smyrna now?"

Major Babcock bristled. He was in charge of the mission and resented Lt. Halter's implication that he was mishandling his command. He noticed that Lt. Halter was sweating profusely beneath his wool jacket and that his hands trembled.

"Lt. Halter, no one would like a rapid resolution to our mission more than I. We simply disagree about the best approach. I have noted your objections, but for the time being, we will wait for the Viceroy's response. Your presence is required tomorrow evening. By the way, I see that your color has not returned to normal. Why don't you stay here and rest? I see no reason for you to go out now. Far better for you to be fully recovered by tomorrow."

"Very well." For once, Winston Halter was unable to think of an acceptable retort.

After several hours, Major Babcock and Alex returned from their search totally discouraged. The only camels available were old, mangy, and completely unacceptable. Ali the Interpreter avoided the issue, saying only, "Perhaps the next camels will be better."

Back in his room, Alex fingered a book of Arabic, trying to devise a way to help the mission. He went over the vocabulary again. Every night during the sea voyage, he had memorized basic words and deciphered some of the script. Now that he was hearing the language, he was able to pick out phrases, confident that he would soon be able to understand what was going on. Whether he would ever be able to pronounce those guttural sounds was another question, but he was determined to try. The more information he could give his uncle, the better. Tomorrow night at the reception, he would see what he could find out. Alhaji Ibrahim Muhammad, a legend in Alexandria, owned half the docks and warehouses, controlled extensive property and ran a good portion of the olive trade. Alex suspected that if Alhaji Ibrahim Muhammad wanted the Americans to have camels, they would get them.

Grandma Ara watched Alhaji Mustafa pacing back and forth. She was distraught by his decision for her favorite grandchild who reminded her of her husband as a young man. Except for their height, the resemblance was not outwardly physical. Seeing them seated, one would not assume that the dark, curly-haired youth was the grandson of the blue-eyed, patrician elder. But once they moved, their carriage and gait were a match. Ara had noticed this when Hassan was a toddler. She smiled at the recollection of the moment years ago when she had mentioned this to her husband.

"Your grandson walks exactly like you do."

Alhaji Mustafa had laughed out loud. "Are you saying that I move like an unsteady child who changes his direction all the time? Do people notice when I walk to the mosque?"

"No, your walk suggests confidence and purpose that inspires deference and respect. Watch little Hassan. His walk is the same."

Worried that she might never see Hassan's walk again if he went to America, she prayed silently that her husband would revoke his permission. In fact, Alhaji Mustafa was second-guessing his decision, afraid that he had taken the wrong position because of a frivolous conversation with Auntie Fatima. On the other hand, he had made his choice following the Friday prayers, so perhaps the hand of God had been guiding his voice. Hoping that this evening would enlighten him, he called Hassan to join them.

"My son, Alhaji Ibrahim Muhammad has done us a great service by inviting us to tonight's reception. We must take care how we carry ourselves. You are to observe quietly.

Do not attract attention. Stay by my side or move discreetly on the edge of the gathering. Listen and learn about the
Americans and their mission, then report everything to me.
I will determine its relevance for our family. Abdullah will
meet us there to help with translations."

"Yes, Grandfather." Hassan readily agreed, fidgety to
get going and meet the Americans.

Grandmother Ara straightened Hassan's robes, smiled
warmly and touched his cheeks with both hands. "Blessings
be upon you and may your evening go well, Inshallah."

In a carriage in front of the Hotel Isis, Lt. Halter and
Captain Turner sat resplendent in their dress uniforms,
satisfying Major Babcock that they would make a suitable
impression. Alex Babcock sported a clean white shirt, an
emerald green brocaded vest, and a black frock coat with
a horizontal cravat, starched and tied below his shirt's high
collar. Most astonishing to Lt. Halter, Alex was thoroughly
washed, including his blond hair, which when clean, had a
gentle wave. Ali the Interpreter had donned a long navy kaf-
tan, not new, but freshly pressed, and even the driver wore
clean clothes.

Near the edge of town in a plush suburb, a crowd of carriages stood in front a rambling mansion that resembled a
Roman palace, adorned with palm trees and fragrant flowers.
Peacocks strolled on the lawn. Alex estimated at least a hundred men in attendance, all dressed in exquisite costumes.
He followed Captain Turner, Major Babcock, and Lieutenant Halter into the house only to be quickly separated from
them and engulfed by a group of younger men who had an
air of good breeding about them. At home, Alex would have
called them the "up and comers".

Without Ali the Interpreter, who had remained with his
uncle, Alex had no idea how he was going to communicate.
He wasn't confident enough in his Arabic and felt it unwise
to reveal that he understood anything at all. Much to his
surprise, one of the men knew some English. Three others
knew French, and although Alex's French was a bit rusty,
the conversation evolved into bits of Arabic and English su-
perimposed on a French base. After exchanging pleasantries,
the Egyptians remarked that Alex, like the city, must have

been named for Alexander the Great. They peppered him with questions about crops grown in America, the climate at different seasons, risks of the sea voyage, and the estimated profits on a variety of Egyptian goods that Americans might buy. Knowing that Alexandria's prosperity for centuries had been linked to commerce, Alex did his best to answer, but he really wanted to steer the conversation to camels.

"Let me tell you about the Great American Desert. It is not like here. You have your Nile River to provide water for those who live near it. We have only small streams that run dry most of the year. The only plants growing are cactus and thorny shrubs. Can the camels eat them?"

He had done it. An animated discussion ensued about the appetites and virtues of camels as well as the vagaries of handling them. The conversation was so fast and multilingual that Alex had a hard time keeping track of what was happening as the group disintegrated into lively two-way debates. It looked as if Alex might be forgotten until he was addressed by a man who had been speaking English earlier.

"Hello, I am Abdullah. Pleased to meet you."

A younger man with him added in very halting English, "I am Hassan. Pleased to meet you, Alexander. As-salaam alaikum."

Perhaps a dozen years older than Hassan and Alex, Abdullah was a relative of Auntie Fatima's deceased husband. After working for the British as a young man, he had quit to help with his family's camel herd and olive groves. He was honored to accept Auntie Fatima's request to translate for her distinguished cousin. Because Alhaji Mustafa was engaged in an intense Arabic exchange with a visiting mullah from Khartoum, Abdullah was free to assist Hassan.

Alex spoke simply, allowing time for Abdullah to translate. He was pleased when he recognized a few words of Arabic. "Do you live in Alexandria?"

"Yes. Where is your home in America?"

"Virginia. I have two sisters. I am the youngest. And you?

"I am the oldest. I have one younger brother and one sister. What is Virginia like?"

"It is a beautiful place, green, with rolling hills, large rivers and small streams, neat farms. It is different from here. But you might not like it. In the winter it can be very cold."

To the translation, Abdullah added in Arabic, "I think he might be exaggerating about the place to impress you. The British used to talk this way about their home, too." Alex grasped enough Arabic to get the general drift, but waited for Hassan's reply.

"It sounds like paradise. Will the camels go to Virginia?"

"No, the camels are needed for the West. It's a vast wilderness, mostly desert, teeming with hostile natives. We have people living across the desert, and it's very hard to get goods and information to them. We think the camels can help."

"A camel can carry much weight. They are strong and can go a long way without water."

"You sound like you know something about camels."

Hassan replied in Arabic. "My father is responsible for the Viceroy's camels."

Abdullah looked disapprovingly at Hassan and changed the translation. "My father works with camels." But it was too late. Alex had understood enough.

"Does your father work for the Viceroy?"

Before Hassan could continue, Abdullah interrupted. "Excuse me, we are being called by Alhaji Mustafa. He is Hassan's grandfather and a most respected scholar." Alex looked at Hassan, who smiled broadly.

Alhaji Mustafa studied the young American who approached with Hassan and Abdullah. The youth looked to be about the same age as Hassan, and they were about the same height, but never had Alhaji Mustafa seen flaxen hair of such silken texture. When he learned that this blond boy was the nephew of Major Babcock, whom he had already begun to appreciate, he felt that Hassan might be in good company on the voyage to America.

Late in the evening, after limitless food, drink, music, and entertainment, their hosts escorted the Americans to their carriage. On the way back to the hotel, Lieutenant Halter, who seemed a tad inebriated, offered his comments. "Well, Major, for once we were served some excellent wine."

"Yes, I found it a lovely evening."

"I wouldn't go that far. We were treated well, and Al-haji Ibrahim Muhammad was genuinely hospitable. But frankly, I believe we were lied to all night long about the camels, international affairs, and everything of substance."

Captain Turner did not want further discourse with Lt. Halter. That left it to Major Babcock to reply.

"You always notice the risks and problems. So tell me, how were we lied to?"

Lt. Halter became more energetic, slightly slurring his words. "Every time we asked about the camels, someone either changed the subject or made an excuse. I have never heard such nonsense. 'The camels are grazing outside of Cairo.' 'The Viceroy is searching for the best quality beasts.' We are no closer to having the promised camels than before."

"I'm inclined to agree that there were undercurrents we couldn't follow. But Alhaji Ibrahim Muhammad introduced us to a number of people close to the Viceroy, and I think we should have a favorable outcome before long."

"For heaven's sake, Major, you always see the world through rose colored glasses. We could be here for months. I say we give them a deadline, and if we don't have the camels in good order by that time, off we go to Smyrna."

At this Captain Turner revived. "Perhaps Lt. Halter is right. A deadline might help."

Major Babcock was exasperated and tired, his enthusiastic assessment of the evening threatened by Lt. Halter's withering attitude. "Let's discuss this tomorrow. We've arrived at the hotel. Good night, gentlemen."

Lieutenant Halter and Captain Turner went straight to their rooms. The moment they were out of sight, Alex blurted, "Wasn't that the most fantastic evening? The clothes, the food, the company. Uncle, my Arabic is getting better, and I could follow little bits of the conversation."

"Yes, Alex, contrary to what Lt. Halter thinks, I felt that it was worthwhile. Alhaji Ibrahim Muhammad is clearly a man of great influence. I found him charming and gracious, and I believe his sentiments were genuine."

"I liked him, too, Uncle. What did he say about the camels? Will we get them?"

Major Babcock's spirits lifted while talking with Alex. Although others had questioned his decision to bring his nephew along on this mission, at moments like this, he was sure he had made the right choice. "These things do seem to take time. I have a feeling that tonight's event involved two factions within the Viceroy's household."

"Oh blazes! The Viceroy's household! I almost forgot to tell you! When you were talking with that scholar, Alhaji Mustafa, did he say anything about his connection to the camels?"

"What? No. He's supposed to be a very learned man. Quite respected. He speaks no English, though."

"Well, have I got news for you. Do you remember Hassan, about my own age?"

"Yes, Alhaji Mustafa's grandson."

"His father is the official responsible for the Viceroy's camels. Hassan and I agreed to meet tomorrow for coffee. His friend Abdullah will come along to translate."

"My, my, Alex, you have done very well. Let's see what you can find out tomorrow."

Alexandria, Egypt, July 20, 1855

My dearest Annabelle,

These moments of correspondence with you do soothe the anxieties which come upon me in this wretched place where I lie bathed in sweat, listening to the incessant racket from outside. Five times a day we hear the piercing cries of the muezzin calling the people to prayer, and whatever they are doing, they stop dead in their tracks. Of course the many Christians and Jews who live here carry on normally, but the Mohammedans pause to pray, and at least for those minutes, the din diminishes somewhat.

Last night we attended a reception at a luxurious home. Carpets of the finest weave covered the floors and extended out the front door to welcome the arriving guests. Unfortunately, not all went well. Captain Turner and Major Babcock proceeded first, as protocol would dictate. Imagine my surprise when Major Babcock launched forth in Arabic in an effort to greet our host. It seems he had asked our interpreter to teach him a few greetings. He was quite proud of himself when our host smiled and answered in Arabic. I was mortified. We are here representing the United States of America, and instead of putting forth a strong image, we cater to these Egyptians at every turn. What an embarrassment when we learned that our host spoke impeccable English!

The locals have the habit of crowding close when speaking to you. The press of people nearly suffocated me, as the men were perfumed with rose water and various exotic scents. The heady atmosphere nearly made me swoon. When I tried to slip out for some fresh air, someone always seemed to be with me. In any event, a steady stream of people came to our host to pay their respects, and he always introduced the most important ones to us. Though I still find Major Babcock insufficiently assertive in these matters, we may soon have the camels.

Winston Halter took a break from his letter to wash his face. In the mirror he saw the perfect image of an American Yankee: tall, straight, square jaw, and slate gray eyes, complete with a slightly arrogant smile on his thin lips. What on earth was he doing here? His prior assignment in Washington was a desk job handling inventory and materiel. His most adventurous duties had been occasional visits to loading docks or warehouses to check the accuracy of reports. A trip as far afield as New York was always followed by a delicious dinner at a fine restaurant or at the home of a friend. He had never had any desire to travel.

His father-in-law had arranged this deployment. His words still echoed. "Son, we must position your career carefully." Lieutenant or no, he was still a desk clerk. Unless Winston did something original to gain attention, his future was not promising. A post with the Camel Corps was certainly original, and he had had no choice but to accept it. Sighing, he noticed that he was already damp around his temples. He returned to his letter.

We dined today at the hotel. When we dine on board ship, I savor the American-style fare. I regret my earlier castigations of the ship's cook, whose productions please me more than the stews and aromatic dishes that we are forced to consume here. I confess that my inability to determine what I am eating greatly reduces my interest in eating it.

My fever has subsided, and I have rather more energy, a good turn of events, because we are summoned to another meeting this afternoon. Here I sit, ready to carry out diplomacy on behalf of my government, in an effort to secure camels to import to the Great American Desert. It does seem rather preposterous when one considers it dispassionately. Wishing that I shall soon be in your most pleasant company, I remain,

Most affectionately yours,

Winston

Washington, DC, Office of the US Secretary of War

C ONSISTENT WITH HIS USUAL routine and methodical nature, Clerk Habberford Smith opened the daily post and reported the contents item by item.

"Correspondence from Major James Babcock, sent from Tunis almost four months ago. He was heading for Alexandria, where he hoped to acquire the bulk of his camels. He apologizes that finding healthy camels has been more difficult than he expected but notes that the cost of the voyage thus far remains well within budget. He sends his personal regards."

Jefferson Davis, Secretary of War, leaned back in his wide leather chair and surveyed the members of his senior staff assembled around the oval oak conference table for the morning briefing. He wondered whether they would engage in their usual debate. Major Greeson responded true to form.

"Aw, not that again. Don't you gentlemen think we've spent about enough time foolin' with foreign ideas? We've got citizens scattered throughout Texas and on to California that need protection. We're wastin' resources on crazy notions about camels when we should be buildin' more forts and enhancin' the strength of the cavalry."

"My dear Major, we all know that you are a cavalry man yourself, and we would expect you to advocate for your branch of the service." Colonel Simon Cole could not abide the pompous blowhard. He knew that Major Greeson bred horses and wanted to sell his steeds to the Army. "Congress in its collective wisdom saw fit to appropriate the money for this project, and $30,000 is not a sum to bankrupt the War Department. We must think expansively, as befits this great nation of ours. Camels may be just the thing until the railroads are built."

Since the end of the Mexican conflict in 1848, the War Department had directed substantial attention to linking California with the rest of the country. Ever since gold was discovered in 1849, a stampede of Americans had attempted to cross the vast continent, although no good way of doing so had been found. The northern route required crossing the mountains before winter set in or disaster was assured. The Donner Party experience in 1846 still frightened many into taking the southern route through Galveston and San Antonio. But that trek held equally terrifying prospects. Crossing the desert was dangerous. Horses and mules died of dehydration with remarkable alacrity, and the Army had insufficient experience to know where water could be found. All transport had to include calculations for carrying water and food for the animals, lest travelers be stranded to face certain death. Local Indian populations, none too pleased with incursions into their hunting and grazing territories, hectored the Americans with rustling raids as well as more serious attacks that included kidnap and murder.

Railroads held great promise, but Congress had not yet agreed on a transcontinental route, and construction would take time. Seeking more inventive approaches, Jefferson Davis had been intrigued by reports of the effectiveness of camels. He had urged Congress to allocate funds to test their usefulness, and finally, he had succeeded. But the appropriation, victory though it was to him, was only the beginning.

Major Greeson replied in his languid Southern drawl. "My goodness Colonel, for a military strategist, your argument is remarkably lackin' in practicality. I have served with Texans, and I can assure you that they would no more give up their horses than their pistols. A Texan's horse is an extension of himself. He will never sit in a carriage or a wagon if there is an opportunity to ride horseback. Can you picture our western army ridin' on camels to defend against Indian attack? Surely you jest. As to the question of railroads, perhaps your personal perspective is interferin' with your objectivity?"

Colonel Cole had railroad investments from which he stood to make a healthy profit if Congress selected the Northern Route. He hoped that the camel cavalry might distract Jefferson Davis from proposing the Southern Route. Counting on his son-in-law, Lt. Winston Halter, to provide any relevant information about the mission's progress, Colonel Cole suspected that the camel importation was a wild idea that would not come to fruition. Nevertheless, because Secretary Davis viewed the camels as his pet project, Colonel Cole thought it prudent to sound favorable.

"Well, Major, the matter of the railroads sits before Congress this very session, and we can all agree that progress must continue. If the Northern Route is selected, I can foresee using camels in the Southwestern desert."

"I declare, you are simply refusin' to see the reality of the situation here. No self-respectin' man is goin' to go ridin' around on the back of a camel, lookin' like some kind of heathen Arab!"

Secretary Davis had heard enough. "Gentlemen, this importation of camels is an experiment, as you may recall. The objective is to investigate the animal's usefulness for transportation of goods and armaments, as well as," and he glanced at Greeson, "their possible use as cavalry. Armies in other countries have employed camels to great advantage. The British are apparently quite pleased with their camel corps in the Crimea. By all reports, the military advantages afforded by the camels are excellent. As to their adaptability to our needs, we'll have to wait and see."

"Yes sir."

"Excuse me, gentlemen." They turned to Clerk Smith. "There is a second letter in the packet, written ten days after his arrival in Alexandria. Major Babcock attests that the British have engaged many fine animals, resulting in a shortage. He anticipates getting some from the Viceroy's stock, but expects further delays."

"At least that confirms our intelligence about the British, but the delay is regrettable, most regrettable." The Secretary was frustrated. Having waited over three years for Congressional approval for the project, he now wanted the camels acquired expeditiously. Westward migrants were clamoring for greater protection. His disappointment was deeper than he let on.

The silence was broken by a knock on the door and the entry of a uniformed guard. "Please excuse the interruption, sir. A messenger has arrived from Fort Laramie telling of Indian attacks and requesting reinforcements. He's gone to clean up and will be here directly."

Jefferson Davis turned to his War Cabinet. "Gentlemen, I think we have more immediate problems to consider. Mr. Smith, address a reply to Major Babcock. Instruct him that this Office expects a timely purchase of camels and that we look forward to a more positive report in his next correspondence."

GALVESTON, TEXAS, NOVEMBER 1855

E LIZABETH MCDERMOTT LET HER hand graze lightly over the rainbow of fabrics laid out before her. She and her mother were seated behind a curtain at the rear of the store, a privacy that allowed them time to consider their options without the prying eyes of other shoppers. Mrs. Witherspoon routinely extended this courtesy to certain families, especially those with daughters approaching their first May Day ball. She had witnessed many an otherwise sensible girl, overwhelmed by the possibilities before her, devolve into a puddle of tears. The embarrassment of the moment was worse for the girl if the whole town gossiped about her.

Mrs. Witherspoon had become adept at orchestrating these sessions. She was scrupulously silent about her own opinions while folding and unfolding the samples as often as her customers wished. The girls were permitted to wrap the fabrics around themselves before a mirror, scrutinize multiple choices at once, reject them all, and then begin again. Tea and cookies were offered. In the warmer months she hired someone to fan the ladies and set out a bowl and pitcher in case her customers should begin to perspire. Accompanied by mothers, sisters, aunts, and friends, the girls fussed and fretted, giggled and frowned. Preferences flew in the air, colliding and falling until only one or two remained aloft, while Mrs. Witherspoon waited for a final choice. She remained vigilant lest grueling conflicts erupt between mother and daughter over color or texture or price. Fortunately, price would not be a problem today, as per Quentin McDermott's instructions. To prevent anyone from having a dress like Elizabeth's, he had authorized purchase of the entire bolt of cloth.

Seeing her daughter's hand pause repeatedly on one particular selection, Sylvia began to pay closer attention.

"Elizabeth, you still have months to decide, and Mrs. Witherspoon gets new shipments regularly."

"Yes, Mama, but if we see the right one, we should buy it."

"Let's take a break from thinking about May Day and plan for Christmas. We'll both want new dresses, especially if Cousin Babcock arrives in time for the holidays."

"I hope he can. I've been looking at some of your books. Did you see the one that has sketches of camels?"

"No, you'll have to show me. By the way, I've ordered a new *History of Ancient Egypt* that should be arriving soon. It's supposed to have color plates of the pyramids and temples."

Mrs. Witherspoon pulled back the curtain. "Excuse me, Mrs. McDermott. Mr. Balkins heard that you were here and sent over this parcel along with today's post."

"Thank you, Mrs. Witherspoon."

While her mother opened the parcel, Elizabeth stroked the fabric again, captivated by its cheerful canary color.

"Look, Elizabeth, it's the book we were just talking about. What gorgeous illustrations!"

Elizabeth sank into the book. Lost in the pictures, she imagined what it must have been like to live thousands of years ago. She was startled by her mother's huge sigh.

"What is it, Mama?"

"A letter from my cousin, written in Egypt. He has been delayed. He won't be here for Christmas, and we may not see him until next spring. I'm so disappointed."

Elizabeth could see that her mother had lost heart for shopping. As the women prepared to depart, Elizabeth begged Mrs. Witherspoon to hold their top choices in reserve. Her mind was already made up. She would enter the May Day ball in a swirl of sparkling yellow.

On Board The *Supply*, November, 1855

A LI THE INTERPRETER STOOD in silent reflection on the deck of the *Supply*, at last wending its way toward Smyrna. He still felt buffeted by the wild ups and downs of the past few weeks. The Americans had almost left Alexandria without any camels. He doubted whether he would ever understand exactly what had transpired.

The confusing chain of events had begun after Alhaji Ibrahim Muhammad's reception, when the Americans received word that the Viceroy had released the promised ten camels. Their joyful anticipation was soon dashed as they beheld decrepit specimens instead of the choice animals from the Viceroy's personal stock. Lt. Halter had wandered over to inspect the beasts more closely.

"Look at this camel. It's the one we purchased in Tunis and sold the moment we landed here, the one that kept getting the itch!!"

"I'll be damned!"

Ali would never forget the look of utter disgust on Major Babcock's face as his eyes widened in disbelief. The Major touched the offending animal as if forced to feel the diseased skin of a leper. His consternation was evident across the language barrier as he scowled, paced, and muttered. Outrage echoed in his voice. Ali had never seen him so angry.

"Ali, would you kindly inquire as to the origin of this camel? No, never mind. We must issue a complaint to the Viceroy's office. You are dismissed for today. Please report to the hotel in the morning."

Mortified, Ali stood stranded as Major Babcock leaned out of the carriage to give him a few coins for transportation. The Major had never behaved in such fashion.

Ali knew that this situation had become too weighty for him. He did the only thing he could think of, and God be praised, it had been the right thing. He went straight to the home of Alhaji Ibrahim Muhammad, where he begged to be seen on an urgent matter. In a sumptuous waiting room, a servant brought him a moist cloth to wipe his hands and a pitcher of hot sweet tea. Admiring the inlaid silver teapot and sipping slowly, Ali began to calm down and collect his thoughts. After a suitable interval, Alhaji Ibrahim Muhammad entered the room, poised and gracious, and politely inquired into Ali's health. In the presence of this cool wisdom, Ali's confidence returned, and he explained everything in detail: the horrid state of the proffered camels, the unusual but justified anger of the Americans, and most importantly, the fact that they were going to the American Consul to register a protest.

"Thank you, Ali, you have done well to come to me. If the Americans issue a formal diplomatic letter, a response will be required." He had spoken quietly, but Ali could see the annoyance. "I will see what I can do."

While Ali translated the official letters that went back and forth for weeks, Alhaji Ibrahim Muhammad arranged to provide the camels from his own personal stock at prices below market value, thereby helping everyone to save face. Naturally, the Americans knew nothing of this.

A few days ago, with departure finally imminent, Ali had received an unexpected invitation from Alhaji Mustafa. "You are most welcome in my home, Ali. Is your family well?"

"Praise be to God, yes, and yours?" Ali was sure that more than one person listened from behind a screen.

"Yes, thanks be to God. Ali, I have interest in matters about which you possess unique and valuable knowledge. I met the Americans at Alhaji Ibrahim Muhammad's reception, but you have spent more time with them and know them better. What kind of men are they?"

"Major Babcock, the leader, is completely devoted to the project. It is more than an assignment for him. He is passionate. For him, it is a thing he does for his country."

"What do you mean?"

"The Americans have an idea of country, a kind of abstraction. Perhaps this idea arises because they are such a young nation. I don't know how to explain it. They feel a personal attachment to their country."

"Ali, I have traveled widely. I can assure you that everyone feels attached to his homeland. Please explain."

It was not prudent to discuss lofty subjects with a scholar, but Alhaji Mustafa was so easygoing that he seemed to pull the words from Ali's mouth. "Most people love a landscape, people, food, and daily life. For the Americans, their love and loyalty extends to ideas. They believe they have found a new way of governing. They are proud and wish others to copy them. I would say they are naïve. Everything they do, they are convinced must be good. Major Babcock says that the camels are important for American expansion to the western part of their country."

"Expansion?"

"I am sorry, sir, I have found only one map, and beyond the eastern sections, it shows nothing. Nothing at all. I have no idea what to make of that. The Americans have described both mountains and deserts."

"What about the other men?"

"The Captain is serious and works hard to prepare the ship for the camels. Lt. Halter reminds me of an Englishman that I once worked for who could find joy in nothing. And there is the boy Alex, about the age of your grandson."

"As you know, I have granted permission for Hassan to go to America. Because you are the most experienced with foreigners, it is to you that I entrust my confidence. If these Americans fail, anything could happen. With an ocean between here and there, you might not be able to return easily. I am considering revoking my permission."

Ali heard sighs of relief from behind the screen. "Sir, the wisdom is yours, not mine. If you choose for Hassan to

go, I will do my best to watch out for him, and if it please
God, we will return to you in about one year's time."

Alhaji Mustafa sat immobile. Ali scarcely breathed as
he waited for the elder's response. At last Alhaji Mustafa
inhaled deeply and issued his determination.

"Then you shall be in God's hands." From behind the
screen, shrieks escaped but were quickly stifled when Alhaji
Mustafa looked in their direction. "We will pray for you
every day of your absence. May you all return to us in good
health at the appointed time, Inshallah."

Ali sighed. What was done was done. He, Abdullah and
Hassan were now on the American ship heading to Smyrna
to acquire more camels before crossing the vast Atlantic
to America. Of the three, Ali was the only one vertical.
Abdullah and Hassan lay prone, leaving their bunks only to
be overcome with nausea. Ali prayed that they would adapt
to sea life soon. He glanced up to see Alex Babcock calling
and waving frantically.

"Ali, can you come help us here? One of the camels
doesn't look quite right."

Ali dashed off, hoping that it was nothing serious, because he did not know as much about camels as either
Abdullah or Hassan.

Smyrna, February 20, 1856

My dearest Annabelle,

*After passing a bleak Christmas and New Year here in Ana-
tolia, we depart tomorrow. Alas, we have determined to take
the most direct route to Texas instead of stopping along the
New England coast. Nevertheless, we have finally acquired
the camels. At long last, I can foresee the prospect of being back in your most delightful company. I cannot believe
that so many months have passed, with yet the sea voyage
remaining. I have sent a letter to your father, requesting
that I be discharged from this mission at Indianola. Someone should come to Washington to report in detail, and I*

have neither skill nor desire to remain with the camels any longer than necessary,

While we dawdled in Egypt, with the appalling result of nearly causing a diplomatic breech, the man that we sent ahead, Gwynne Heap, was more successful. We now have a full complement of 33 camels, and this last lot contains by far the best specimens.

I fear you would find the ship's appearance chaotic and congested. Although the vessel has been fitted with special holding pens, the decks are crowded with camels and five Arabs brought along to care for them. To be quite accurate, they are not all Arabs. Three are Egyptian Arabs, one Turk, and one Armenian. They are gradually sorting themselves out, but occasionally loud disagreements occur among them and we are at a loss to know what is happening. Arabic appears to be their lingua franca, but when they mix in words of English, we get a hint of what is going on.

In appearance and temperament, the cast in this petty drama is a rather motley collection. Ali's primary skill is interpreter. Abdullah is purported to be the most knowledgeable about camels, which of course remains to be seen. These two once worked for the English. There is a boy Hassan, who has taken up with Major Babcock's nephew. We picked up the other two in Smyrna. Erdem the Turk appears to be a decent saddle maker. I rather appreciate him, because he is quiet and seems to know his place. Pertag the Armenian is more outgoing and interacts well with the crew. I believe he shall turn out to be the most capable of the lot.

Another man, called Alhaji something, who speaks English, Arabic, and Turkish, is the one we should have with us. Captain Turner has promised to engage his services on the second voyage. (They are all so confident that there will be a second voyage.) Alhaji is an honorific greeting, referring to a person who has made the pilgrimage to Mecca. Among Mohammedans, one is expected to visit that city at least once in one's life to perform various ritual obligations. Most of the distinguished members of society that we met were called Alhaji. This Alhaji seems to lord it over the camel men who have not been to Mecca. Much to my amusement, our seamen call him Hi Jolly, a clever way of mocking his arrogant ways. He naively thinks it affectionate. The Egyptians seemed content to leave him behind.

As we begin our voyage across the Mediterranean and into the open ocean, Captain Turner has put forth detailed orders regarding care for the beasts. (I append a copy as this may be of interest to your father.) Four soldiers, who were specifically assigned as camel crew, will supervise the animals and disembark with them in Texas.

Today all thoughts turn toward our imminent departure. A quiet apprehension has settled on the Arabs as we anticipate weeks at sea. We Americans have already made the voyage, but for the Arabs, this shall be quite a new experience. Pray for the Lord's blessings of calm weather as we traverse the ocean once more. At sea one is always reminded of man's inherent weakness. "What is man that thou art mindful of him" is especially called to mind.

Your devoted husband,
Winston

Galveston, Texas, March 1856

S TANDING IMMOBILE WAS NO easy task for Elizabeth, especially when her girlfriends were chattering. The seamstress had already chastised her more than once, and it would not do for a complaint to go home to her mother. Whether because of the spectacular spring weather or the mere anticipation of the coming events, Elizabeth was a bundle of twitching excitement. She anticipated two marvelous days: her birthday next month when she would turn sixteen and then her presentation to Galveston society at the May Day ball.

"Miss McDermott, could you please be still? Face forward, please."

"Yes, ma'am. I'm sorry."

In the folded mirror, Elizabeth saw herself in triplicate. The dress fit snugly at her waist, flattering her shape, but the neckline didn't sit right. The hem failed to hang evenly and needed to be adjusted. Knowing that her gown had to be perfect, Elizabeth did her best to remain motionless. She pondered her long dark curls and decided she would have to do something different. This style made her look too childlike.

"Suzy, don't you think I'll have to put my hair up for the May Day ball?"

"Of course. Lucille said she was wearing hers down, but she won't in the end. Have you seen her dress? I hear it is a peachy color, which in my opinion, goes poorly with her complexion. She'll look washed out."

Rosemary chimed in, "But your dress, Elizabeth, that color! Didn't they call it saffron?"

"No, I think it was lemon."

"It's striking with your dark hair. When William sees you, he won't have eyes for anyone else, and Caroline will be so jealous. Quiet, here comes your mother."

"Hello, ladies, how is the fitting coming along? I trust you were giving Elizabeth advice, rather than gossiping about the boys who will be coming to the ball?"

"Mama, we have to figure out who should be on our dance cards. Don't tease us. You were young once."

"Yes, but that was a long time ago." Sylvia McDermott thought these girls looked very young, but she anticipated that within a year or two most of them, including her daughter, would be married. Sylvia and her husband had already begun scrutinizing the sons of the Galveston elite much as these same families had been examining her daughter. She laughed easily with the girls.

"You're very cheerful today Mrs. McDermott. You seem almost as excited as we are."

"I am excited, but for a different reason. I've received a letter from a dear cousin who may be coming to visit us."

"Cousin Babcock? He's finally coming?" Elizabeth turned sharply, and the seamstress let out a sharp gasp.

"Elizabeth! Pay attention to Miss Johnson and keep still."

"Sorry, Miss Johnson. Sorry, Mama. But please tell me."

"Let me give you young ladies something completely different to talk about. The US Army is bringing a shipload of camels to Texas to make a new kind of cavalry."

"What? Camels?" Even the dressmaker stopped to stare, pins sticking out of her mouth like odd teeth.

Elizabeth giggled and clapped her hands, causing Miss Johnson to groan. "Sorry, sorry. They're coming from Egypt, right?"

"Egypt? Really, Mrs. McDermott?" Rosemary was intrigued.

"Yes, my cousin is leading the expedition. They've been to Egypt and to other places in the Orient to buy the camels. He should have quite a few stories to tell."

"Does he say he's seen the pyramids?"

"No, the letter is brief. The camel ship plans to land at Indianola. If it all works out, they'll stop here first and we might get to see the camels. Instead of cluttering your minds with ribbons and gossip, try to imagine that if you can!"

Before she left, Sylvia admonished the girls to obey the seamstress and concentrate on their fittings. Elizabeth fell silent, thinking about the Egyptian history book that her mother had bought for her. Maybe Cousin Babcock could tell her whether the monuments and temples were as magnificent in reality as in their representations.

All at once it dawned on her that her mother had not specified when Major Babcock was expected in Texas. More than anything she hoped that he would not arrive at an inopportune time. She could not bear for an untimely visit to upset her plans for the May Day festivities.

Kingston, Jamaica, April 1856

My dearest Annabelle,

I hope you are not overly concerned by my silence since Smyrna. We encountered the most ferocious gales that forced us to make for Jamaica. Captain Turner proved an able commander, but the camels and their attendants were ill to the point of incapacity. The camels were well battened,

but most would not eat. We arrive with one more camel
than we started with; four were born but three died. Given
the tempests we endured, it is a satisfactory outcome.

We have been in Jamaica for some days to replenish our
stores. Captain Turner also thought it prudent to allow
the men shore leave to vent their excess enthusiasms before reaching American soil. During this time we have had
the unfortunate experience of being perceived as a traveling
circus. Some four thousand residents of Kingston felt it necessary to wander near the ship, and Major Babcock could
not resist showing off the camels. He even invited certain
dignitaries to come on board to see the animals close up.

One most intriguing visitor was an American called Mrs.
M.J. Watson, a businesswoman who was quite vague in de-
scribing the nature of her commerce. I became suspicious
when I overheard her remark that the smell of the camel ship
could mask other aromas. In my estimation this woman is
involved in the illegal slave trade from Jamaica to Texas. I
mentioned to Major Babcock the risk to the credibility of our
camel project if such a woman were to import camels as a
cover for human cargo. He dismissed my observations and
my worries. He is impossibly naïve.

Major Babcock fears the camels have been at sea too long.
I have been at sea too long as well. After we discharge our
cargo, I hope to return to your gracious company.

Your devoted husband,

Winston

GALVESTON, TEXAS APRIL 1856

FROM THE GULF, GALVESTON floated and shimmered like
a mirage in the desert. The sea and the land were in-
distinguishable, as if one could sail a ship directly up to the
front porch of one of the gleaming alabaster houses. It was
easy to believe that any of the pedestrians strolling along the
street could turn and walk straight out onto the water. The

buildings appeared to hover as though they lacked foundation or substance, having been conjured out of thin air. Like
miniature ivory sculptures, the houses were surrounded by
shades of green palm trees and lush tropical vegetation that
gave the whole city a fairyland appearance. Alex had read
with skepticism the fantastic descriptions used by Texas land
speculators to attract European settlers to Galveston. Now
he would concede that even the most rhapsodic tales failed
to do justice to a sunlit view of Galveston from the Gulf.

Major Babcock found Alex on deck with Hassan. "Almost there. I'm really looking forward to seeing my cousin
Sylvia."

"How are we related, Uncle?"

"No relation of yours, actually. She's from the other
side of the family. My goodness, look at that port!"

Sometimes referred to as the New York of Texas,
Galveston thrived on shipping. Its highly navigable harbor,
the best between Pensacola and Vera Cruz, was accessible
through a broad passageway at least twelve feet deep that
was not prone to the silting or shifting sandbars that clogged
other rivers along the coast.

"The city must be very rich."

"They say that the citizens pay no taxes."

"No taxes?"

"Yes, imagine that. The town makes enough money
from port duties. Alex, do you remember a Monsieur Savi-
gny whom we met in Paris? His consular delegation had to
petition the French government for an increased budget to
entertain at the level expected of Galveston society."

"And your cousin Sylvia is part of that society?"

"It would seem so. Her husband's business is shipping
and banking. They met in Philadelphia while he was up
north in 1838. You know our family: Yankee, Episco-
palian, and abolitionist. Here comes this Southerner, a
Methodist and a slaveholder, wooing their daughter. You
can imagine. Her parents finally approved the marriage,
only to have him take her away to Texas. At that time
Galveston was a barely settled outpost, most famous for
the pirate Jean Lafitte. It was swampy, fever stricken, and
far from civilization. The whole family was heartsick. But

from her letters, it seems my cousin has enthusiastically embraced her life here. I suspect she found Philadelphia somewhat constricting."

Alex nodded at that. Having grown up in the City of Brotherly Love, he wondered whether he could return to his hometown where everything seemed ordered and predictable.

"In any case, Sylvia is now in her eighteenth year of marriage, nearly as established as the town itself. Alex, tonight will be a business dinner." Apart from the family reunion, Major Babcock hoped this dinner might provide important intelligence about sentiments in Washington toward the camel experiment. Quentin McDermott had mercantile interests not only throughout Texas and the Gulf Coast, but also in New York and Washington. If they could get him interested in the camel project, his voice in Washington might carry weight against those who disparaged the effort. "But I'll bring the family to the ship tomorrow and you can meet them then."

"All right, Uncle. Hassan and I would rather explore the town anyway."

"I imagined as much. By the way, Lieutenant Halter has a fever again. Perhaps you could see if he needs anything from the chemist. Most likely he'll want you to post another letter to his wife."

"Yes, Uncle. I'll do that. And good luck tonight."

Soon after the *Supply* arrived at Galveston harbor, a well-dressed slave named Samuel presented Major Babcock with an invitation for himself and Captain Turner to dine at the McDermott home, preceded by drinks in the afternoon. The rather formal note, penned by his cousin Sylvia, contained a statement of her great anticipation of their visit. Major Babcock quickly composed a warm acceptance. Both he and Captain Turner, accustomed to a standard of living associated with the higher classes of the eastern seaboard, were curious whether the stories of Galveston's extravagance were true.

Samuel returned with the carriage precisely at five o'clock. "Miz Sylvia says to show y'all some of the town, if it please, sah."

"That would be splendid."

From the port, they proceeded south toward the Gulf on Second Avenue and after one block turned right onto Strand Street. Here they found substantial brick banks, mercantile houses, and shops on a tree-lined street that ran the length of the town directly to the Episcopal Church. The carriage followed a series of broad straight streets to a neighborhood of large, multi-storied houses, all slightly elevated to protect from flooding, a necessity because the highest point on the island was only five feet above sea level. They stopped in front of one of the grandest of these homes, enclosed by wrought-iron fencing designed with scrolls and fleur-de-lis. The two-story frame building, painted in delicate pastel colors, was surrounded on all sides by a covered veranda decorated with the same intricate wrought-iron railings and posts. They climbed eight wide stairs to a mahogany doorway that opened into a substantial hall stretching from the front right to the back of the house.

The door was opened by a tall, dark-skinned slave, dressed in a brass-buttoned red jacket with a starched white shirt. Sylvia McDermott stepped past Antoine to take Major Babcock's arm and welcome him into her home. Petite and curvaceous, she wore a pale blue crinoline dress that complemented her sparkling red hair, swept up in the latest style. Major Babcock grinned. He remembered his favorite cousin with bright red braids and a pinafore. He also recalled her days as an eligible maiden, flashing her gray-green eyes at all the potential beaux selected by her parents. He was pleased to see that after so many years and three children, she still cut a lovely figure and had a vibrant smile.

"Cousin, Captain, do come in. We're so happy you could join us."

Elizabeth hovered behind her mother, anxious to have a peek at this favorite cousin. She had met very few relatives among the many guests who frequented her parents' active social circle. She wondered whether Major Babcock would be as friendly in person as he was in his letters. She noticed the kindly way he looked at her mother with his cheerful dark eyes. He smiled through his mustache and bushy beard, and in spite of his formal top hat, he seemed jocular. Elizabeth at once felt that he was family.

"Allow me to introduce the children. This is our daughter, Elizabeth, and our sons, Ezekiel and Zachary.

"My, my, Sylvia, you've done very well. Excuse me, my young cousins, but may I inquire as to your ages?"

Elizabeth stepped forward quickly and confidently. "Of course, sir, I am sixteen, and most pleased to make your acquaintance." With that, she curtsied, smiled, and nodded to her brothers.

Ezekiel stepped forward. "Pleased to meet you. I am fourteen, sir."

"And I am twelve." Zachary lost his sober demeanor. "Sir, is it true that you have camels on your ship?"

Everyone laughed, and Captain Turner replied. "Yes, would you like to see them? I'm sure we could arrange a visit tomorrow."

"Oh! Really? Yes!" Zachary stammered in his excitement. "That would be terrific." He then remembered his manners. "Thank you very much."

"All right, then, boys, you are free to go."

Sylvia did not allow children at the dinner table but wanted Elizabeth to participate this evening as a kind of dress rehearsal for the upcoming May Day festivities. Elizabeth had feared the dinner might be stuffy, but based on her first impression of her mother's cousin, she was taking a more favorable view. Besides, her mother's beaming happiness was infectious.

"Gentlemen, shall we? We have invited a few friends for this occasion. They have already begun with a mint julep out on the veranda. Let's join them."

Sylvia led them from the hall left across the parlor toward the large covered porch on the west side of the house. The parlor room had twelve-foot ceilings with full-length windows draped in wine-colored velvet, propped open to catch the sea breezes. In spite of the bright sun outside, the temperature inside the house was cool and pleasant. The veranda was large enough to hold several chairs, settees, and small tables. Two immaculately uniformed slaves stood at attention next to a large bowl of punch, pitchers of tea and water, and an assortment of the finest Irish whiskeys and French brandies. A third slave replenished silver trays with delectable appetizers. A different pattern of wrought iron narcissus and iris adorned the low banister around the space, which was shaded by a parallel veranda on the second floor. A lush garden of oleanders, hibiscus, and other flowering plants framed a view of the sunset.

Their host, occupied in a lively conversation with one of his guests, turned to greet the new arrivals. Major Babcock had never met his cousin's husband and had only her letters to give him a sense of her married life. He perceived immediately why Sylvia had been attracted to her husband. Quentin was over six feet tall, with wavy brown hair, mustache and beard. He carried himself erect, like someone used to having his orders obeyed instantly. Formidable was the word that came to mind. But tiny wrinkles at the corners of his eyes betrayed a penchant for laughter and sociability. In spite of a fondness for good food, whiskey, and cigars, he was in remarkably good physical condition for a man over forty. He had none of the portliness that obtained among his guests, who had perhaps indulged in too many luxuries.

Quentin McDermott boomed, "Welcome! Welcome to Galveston!" He greeted Captain Turner with a firm handshake and embraced Major Babcock in a warm bear hug. "Ah, the world-traveling cousin. Major Babcock, you are most welcome. Our home is yours."

"The pleasure is all mine. Allow me to say that I have always known you made an excellent choice in a wife. I can see now that Sylvia made an equally fine choice of husband."

"Ha ha! Well said, Major. And for my part, I can already appreciate why my darling wife is so fond of you. Let me introduce you to our other guests."

The man's charm was infectious. Major Babcock warmed to him immediately. He reminded himself, however, that there were important matters to attend to before the evening was over. He had heard that Quentin McDermott could be a ruthless and cunning businessman, but perhaps this disarming friendliness also explained his success.

Sylvia slipped in between her guests. "May I present our illustrious guests. These two gentlemen have just completed a successful mission to the Mediterranean to bring camels to Texas. We are most pleased to have them among us to-night."

The guests chorused. "Hear, hear!"

"Quentin, dear, will you continue the introductions while I see to the refreshments?"

Quentin smiled at his wife. "Sylvia is correct, as usual. Let's get our guests something to drink and show them some proper Texas hospitality."

One of the guests raised a full glass. "Indeed, Quentin. Not like you to keep someone waitin' for a drink."

Quentin waved his arm to embrace the whole assemblage. "May I present Mr. Michel Menard, founder of our fair city, and his wife Rebecca; Mr. Sebastian Smith, lawyer and reporter for the *Galveston News,* with his wife Annabelle; Mr. Byron Hurlinger, my esteemed business partner; and Mr. Gail Borden, formerly Collector of Customs here in Galveston, but lately an inventor of beef biscuits and condensed milk."

Michel Menard chuckled. "Don't worry, Mrs. McDermott won't be servin' us any of Mr. Borden's culinary delights tonight!"

"I should think not!" Gail Borden agreed. "But I shall give you samples to test during your experiments with the camels."

"Ever the entrepreneur," chided Byron Hurlinger. "It would serve you right if they fed that stuff to the camels."

Major Babcock rose to the occasion. "We are interested in any new ideas about moving or feeding our Army. I hope to hear more about your inventions."

"Oh dear, now we'll have to protect you from endless descriptions of the contents of beef biscuits." Quentin McDermott skillfully redirected the conversation to another topic.

Judging from the array of hors d'oeuvres, including fresh oysters, tropical fruits, and canapés that came forth from the kitchen in seemingly endless quantity and variety, the Galveston elite were used to a level of comfort to equal or exceed anything in New York or Philadelphia. After so many months at sea, Major Babcock and Captain Turner were thrilled to be spending their first night back in the United States in the midst of this lavish hospitality.

As the sun dipped below the horizon, its parting shot lit the sky with such gorgeous hues that the guests stopped talking for a moment to absorb its wonder. Although the house was lit with the incredible luxury of gaslights, the slaves brought candles to provide soft light on the veranda. When Antoine informed Mrs. McDermott that dinner was served, the group repaired to the dining room, where an ornately carved maple table was set with gold-rimmed porcelain, polished silver cutlery, and cut-crystal goblets. Seated in a place of honor to the right of Quentin McDermott, Major Babcock thought that the evening so far had been perfect.

Approximately half the crew of the *Supply* had been granted shore leave. Although most of the men had their minds set on a bar and brothel of fine reputation, Alex, Hassan, Pertag and two of the Americans decided to walk around town. Never had Hassan seen streets that were so clean and orderly. Alex said the straight lines reminded him of Washington, the nation's capital. Dazzling white, the Galveston streets were paved with crushed seashells. Twice daily a specially outfitted water wagon sprayed the main thoroughfares, thus controlling the dust that plagued towns with dirt roads. Fascinated by the shells, Hassan thought that something like this could be done in Alexandria.

"I like the sound of these—what do you call them?"

"Shells. I don't believe I've ever seen streets paved with shells before."

"Yes, shells under my foot. It makes a nice sound." Hassan was trying hard to communicate in English.

"Really? I find it annoying. Listen to this noise. I tell you, Hassan, I would rather be able to sneak up to my girlfriend's window unnoticed than to have the whole town know where I was going from the sound of my boots on these shells."

"You would go to your girlfriend's window?" Hassan was rather shocked.

Alex, laughing, reminded Hassan that he didn't have a girlfriend at the moment.

The five men made quite a picture. The soldiers proudly wore their US Army uniforms to distinguish themselves from ordinary seamen. Hassan had bought some American-style clothes in Kingston, including a new broad-brimmed hat. In freshly laundered civilian clothes, he and Alex looked like locals, while Pertag stood out in his brightly colored fez. Even for a port town, they were an odd group.

The men passed a park where a German band serenaded families lounging under the shade of live oak trees over picnics of sausage, potato salad, and beer. Hassan was amazed to see so many people with hair like Alex's, the color of wheat fields on a sunny day. In this part of town there were fewer slaves, less English spoken, and simpler clothing. Still, everyone looked well fed, with children laughing, running and dancing to the oom-pah sounds of German music.

After listening for a short while, they headed across town to the coast. Even though they had just spent weeks at sea, they were drawn to the beach, and lovely indeed was the beach at Galveston. The seabed in this part of the Gulf coast descended into the ocean at an extremely gradual angle, producing a beach that was long, flat, and calm. One could walk out a great distance and still be in shallow water, without any fear of undertow or dangerous currents. The sun began to set as the men walked along the water.

Hassan paused. "Alex, it's time for prayer."

The others knew the Muslim prayer rituals and did not intend to wait around for Hassan. They strolled down the beach while Hassan walked to the water's edge, washed, and went back to drier ground to unroll his prayer mat. Alex remained at shoreline, entranced by the sunset that splattered pastel colors across the sky.

On ship it had been relatively easy for Hassan and the others to pray five times a day, and they had settled into a comfortable rhythm. At first the Christians on board were perplexed by the work stoppage, but they got used to it. In return, the Muslims took care to be respectful of the ship's Sunday services and the Bible reading group that one of the sailors organized every Wednesday. However, during the stopover in Kingston, Hassan had rarely managed to pray, and he was determined to find a way to be more faithful. His grandfather, Alhaji Mustafa had described situations when compromises were allowed, but he wanted to do his best. Galveston was so gorgeous that he wanted to thank God for his many blessings and for being allowed to see such beauty.

Alex, too, was praying silently as the water lapped near his feet. He thanked God for safe passage, for his new friend Hassan, and for the stunning colors in the sky that shimmered like spun silk. The colors melted into subtle variations, then flashed with gold and auburn as a few thin clouds caught the sun's rays from different angles. He stood still, absorbed, while the figures of Pertag and the two sailors receded into the distance.

Hassan, facing east with his back to the sunset, caught the reflections of the dying day as the high whisper clouds faded to dusky plum. He knelt, touched his head to the ground, rose, and repeated the movements. The peace of the prayers came over him, and he felt close to his grandfather, who certainly would have liked this place. Alhaji Mustafa would have known elegant words to describe the beauty, would have recited a sura that captured the feeling.

As Hassan rose again, someone slammed into him from behind, pushing him down so that he landed with his face in the sand. Breathing hard, he rolled over, thrust his legs upward against his attacker, rolled again, and shouted, "Alex!" But Alex was upwind, and Hassan's call was lost in the sound of the gentle waves. A second man grabbed him from behind, and Hassan was quickly immobilized with both hands tied behind his back.

"Well, well, what do we have here? What's yo' name, boy?"

Bewildered, Hassan replied with his full name. "Hassan ibn Yusuf ibn Alhaji Mustafa."

"Sounds to me like he don't even speak English."

Still on the ground and a bit dazed from his fall, Hassan was at eye level with the worn boots and frayed pant legs of his fat and filthy attacker. The man's gut hung over a worn leather belt; his shirt looked like it had seen many too many days of sweating in the Texas heat; and his hair was long and stringy. The man's face was round, with heavy eyebrows, a crooked nose, bad teeth, and a scraggly beard.

Not yet afraid, Hassan was totally repulsed. He was offended that such a creature had touched him, especially while he was at prayer. As he lifted himself off the ground, he was kicked in the ribs.

"No sireee, Slim, he looks to be one o' them escaped slaves."

"Sure looks like it, Josiah."

His second attacker, Josiah, was the one who was thin. He looked undernourished, sinewy, but gave a somewhat neater appearance than Slim. Josiah's mustache and beard were clean. His clothes were more intact than Slim's, apart from a rip under one armpit. Perhaps it had been torn during the scuffle, whereas it seemed that Slim's clothing must always be in tatters. Josiah's tiny eyes made him appear untrustworthy.

Hassan lay in pain, uncertain whether Alex had seen what was going on. He knew that the others had gone down the coast, probably too far away to come back and help. Perhaps Alex had followed them and was also out of calling range. Suddenly alert, his body tingling with the sensation of danger, Hassan felt completely alone. He would have to use his wits because fighting would be useless.

"Boy, who you belong to?"

Hassan groaned as if hurt worse than he was.

"I say, who you belong to, boy? Stand up here and let's get a look at you." When the two attackers pulled Hassan up to his knees, he saw that Slim held a gun.

In his best English, Hassan replied, "Sir, I belong to no one."

Josiah let loose a belly laugh. "Well, you don't say, a 'free' nigger. This is better'n Christmas. We can take him to the port and sell him to that fella buyin' slaves for his cotton farms up the Brazos. He's leavin tomorrow mornin'. We get paid, he's gone, and no one's the wiser."

"Yeah," Slim paused, "looks to me like he's ours to sell." Both men laughed again.

Hassan ventured to turn his head slightly while the two men were laughing and thought he caught a glimpse of Alex running towards them. He decided his best course was to distract his attackers.

"Sir, I do not know what you mean. I am Egyptian."

This sent the two men into uproarious laughter. Alex ran up, plowing into Slim who toppled over onto Josiah. Hassan got to his feet and tried to kick Josiah while both men were tangled up on the ground. Seeing a rider going by, Alex shouted at the top of his lungs for help. This was a risky move, since the rider could have been a friend of the attackers, but Alex saw no other choice.

The man dismounted and drew his pistol. He walked calmly toward the melee of the four men and fired a shot into the air. "Break it up, now."

"Howdy, Deputy Lassen." Slim's voice had a sarcastic edge.

Alex breathed a sign of relief. "It's good to see you, sir, but watch out, he's got a gun."

"Boy, I can see that. Who are you? Are you off one of the ships that came into port today?" Deputy Lassen's tone was accusatory.

"Yes, sir, off the *Supply*, me and him, sir." Alex was breathless and almost stuttering.

"You know the rules about sailors stayin' near the port?"

"Yes, sir, but we are not sailors, we are employees of the US Government, bringing camels to serve the War Department. We were taking a walk on the beach when these two men attacked my friend. I came to his rescue just before we saw you."

"Isn't that a tall tale? Slim, Josiah, what's your story?"

Deputy Lassen made it his business to know the names of the riffraff that hung around the port at Galveston. Many men earned their living loading or unloading ships, packing goods for the newly arrived German immigrants, taking cargo inland, and doing odd jobs. Some of them also engaged in petty thievery, gambling, and smuggling goods or slaves. Slim and Josiah had come into the area a few weeks ago, a bit down on their luck, but so far hadn't caused any problems.

"We found this here nigger all alone on the beach, on his knees and lookin' mighty peculiar. We figured he ain't no sailor."

"So you're claimin' this runaway, if I get your meanin' boys?" Slim and Josiah nodded, relaxing a little, and all three men smiled.

Alex suddenly distrusted Deputy Lassen's intentions. "He is most definitely not a runaway. He is an Egyptian citizen, and we're off the *Supply*, like I said."

"A what citizen? Son, I can see plain as day that he ain't no citizen of Galveston. And I also see that your little disturbance is upsetting the ladies on their evening promenade. We'll head on down to the courthouse to discuss this."

"How about taking the ropes off him at least?"

"Boy, you are cheeky." Deputy Lassen gave Alex a hostile stare. "We got us a runaway slave in violation of the laws of the City of Galveston. Havin' him tied up like that saves me the trouble." All three men chuckled again.

Hassan, who had remained completely quiet during this interchange, recalled a story that Alhaji Mustafa had once told him. His grandfather had crossed the Sahara and was far from home when he had been captured by a group of Mossi warriors. Bound and surrounded by angry people, his grandfather had had no idea what was going on because he spoke only a few words of Mossi. Alhaji Mustafa had decided to watch carefully and silently. He had allowed his traveling companion to engineer their escape. Hassan had no choice but to watch and be patient, like his grandfather. He would trust Alex and the law officer to lead the way out of this mess.

Desperate, Alex tried to sound severe. "Sir, you are ill advised to mistreat a crew member of the *Supply*."

"Are you sayin' he's a free nigger? Can he talk? Hey boy, can you talk?"

"Of course he can talk, but he speaks Arabic, and it's ridiculous to call him a Negro. He's Egyptian. Our Captain is dining right now at the home of Mr. Quentin McDermott. Let's go over there and straighten the whole thing out."

"I happen to know for a fact that Mr. McDermott is a stickler for enforcin' the law. I wouldn't disturb him over a silly matter of a slave, especially not while he's eatin'."

"Hassan is not a slave!"

"Boy, do not toy with a representative of the law. You go get your Captain if you want. We'll be down at the courthouse, holdin' our guest in jail while we sort things out." Pushing Hassan in front of them, the men turned to go.

Hassan whispered to Alex in Arabic, "My prayer mat." Shoved again by Deputy Lassen, he staggered as he was marched toward town.

Momentarily stunned, Alex seemed paralyzed by the crunching sound of boots on the shell paving as the three men walked away with Hassan. Then he scooped up Hassan's prayer mat, grabbed Hassan's brand new hat lying beside it, and sprinted toward the McDermott home.

Tiring of the political discussion at the dinner table, Elizabeth McDermott was pleased when her mother changed the subject. "Do tell us about Egypt, Captain Turner."

"We spent quite a bit of time there. Our efforts to acquire camels came square into conflict with local views about the United States and England. We were forced into idleness for many days."

"Ah, but Captain Turner was never idle," interjected Major Babcock. "He was constantly on board the ship, supervising construction of special quarters for the camels. I personally believe this is one of the reasons that they arrived in such good condition."

Sylvia persisted. "But surely you were able to visit the Great Pyramids?"

"Yes. We had business in Cairo, so profited from the occasion to visit them."

"Do tell us more, please."

"They're enormous beyond one's capacity to imagine, constructed of gigantic hewn boulders. The formations are estimated to be thousands of years old and were used as burial sites for the pharaohs. From Cairo, one rides out to see them on a camel. What a marvelous day we had, seeing one of the wonders of the world and having our first camel ride!"

Mr. Smith, the journalist, had many questions. "Do you believe that people could have built such wonders? Or were they perhaps an act of God?"

"Without question, humans built them. Thousands of people worked on them. Captain Turner devoted several evenings to calculating the number."

"I tried, but each block is of a scale that I was unable to figure how one would move them and stack them, let alone how many people would be required."

Mr. Smith pressed the point. "Who were the builders? Although Egypt is in Africa, I always believed they weren't Africans."

"Agreed. I cannot imagine Africans constructing such sophisticated monuments."

Elizabeth spoke up. "Excuse me, Mama, but I have a book that might help."

Quentin took over before Sylvia could respond. "Captain, you will have to pardon our daughter. Never have I seen a female child so passionate about books." He said this affectionately, but Major Babcock got the impression that Quentin was unhappy with his daughter's behavior.

Elizabeth curtsied as she left the table and soon returned with the book. "Excuse me for being so bold, Cousin Babcock, I mean Major Babcock. I thought this would be interesting."

"My dear Elizabeth, I am your cousin, and I give you leave to call me so."

"Thank you, Cousin. I've been reading this book on the history of Egypt. See these pictures from the walls of ancient tombs? Don't those people look dark-skinned? I'm so confused. I always thought the ancient Egyptians were white people like us."

Captain Turner responded. "It's true that Egyptians are more swarthy than fair, rather like an Italian or a Spaniard, but they are white." He smiled at Elizabeth. "However, they lack the pale translucence of yourself and your mother." Both ladies colored a high pink. "Nor do they blush so lovely."

"Well," said Mr. Hurlinger, "we cannot assume that the people of today resemble the ones who built the pyramids. Those people most probably died out from disease or conquest, leaving the pyramids as a monument to their civilization."

Major Babcock rejoined. "I don't know. Some of today's citizens must be descendants of the original Egyptians. We certainly met some refined and sophisticated men on our trip."

"As well as a few who were boorish and rude!" added Captain Turner. Everyone laughed.

Elizabeth was satisfied with her role in the evening, in spite of her father's earlier remarks. Her book had sparked a lively debate, which she had thoroughly enjoyed. Nevertheless she was still befuddled about who had built the pyramids and continued to ponder while the conversation drifted to less interesting subjects.

Antoine the butler, who stood immobile at the entrance to the dining room, had caught a glimpse of the pictures in Elizabeth's book. Silently he drew his own conclusions. "Dark folk built the great Egyptian pyramids, but these white folk will never say so. Gotta tell Samuel and Esther 'bout this." Antoine was startled by a loud knock. At the door he found a disheveled young man, who looked distraught.

"Good evening, sir, may I help you?"

"My name is Alexander Babcock, and I need to see Major Babcock. Right now." Having run all the way from the beach, Alex was still panting.

"One moment, sir. Please be so kind as to wait here in the parlor." Antoine prided himself on the polite English constructions that he used with guests. Miz McDermott appreciated having a cultured household, though guests sometimes thought he was trying to treat them as equals. He always spoke in a differential tone to compensate.

Sylvia's eyes widened as Antoine whispered the message. Her husband, who knew her every expression, noticed immediately. "Sylvia, what is it, please?

"A caller for Major Babcock. He said it's urgent. I'll see to it, darling. Cousin, would you care to come along?"

Major Babcock rose quickly and followed Antoine and Sylvia into the parlor to find Alex pacing furiously. On the pretext of returning her book to the library, Elizabeth excused herself from the table and crept to a spot in the hall where she could overhear the conversation without being seen. She deduced that this must be the Major's nephew. In a rush of words, Alex recounted the incident.

"Hassan was attacked on the beach, nearly kidnapped and taken into slavery. We fought until an officer of the law came by, but instead of helping, the Deputy took Hassan to jail!"

"Whoa! Calm down. You're not making sense."

"Uncle, I explained that Hassan was an Arab and an Egyptian citizen. I doubt if these people had ever heard of Egypt or Arabs. The two were rough characters, and the lawman was not much better. We have to rescue Hassan."

"Alex, what had he done?

"Nothing, absolutely nothing. He was on his knees praying when he was attacked. I didn't see it until after he was down. They claimed he was a Negro and an escaped slave. It's outrageous!"

Sylvia interjected. "Do you know that it's illegal for free Negroes to enter the State of Texas? We've had lots of trouble with this. African or mixed sailors are prime targets. All non-white sailors must spend their shore leave aboard ship or in jail. Your man's attackers were trying to make some easy money by calling him a slave."

"I don't understand, Sylvia. Hassan is an Arab. His skin isn't fair, but he's certainly not a Negro."

Alex shifted impatiently from one foot to the other while Major Babcock and Sylvia McDermott deliberated.

"I'm afraid your employee's situation is rather grave. The price of slaves has gone sky high. Once sold, a person will always be considered non-white and a slave."

"The timing is awkward. Sylvia, we need your husband's support of the camel project in Washington, and we were about to turn the conversation to that topic. Having one of our camel men in jail is not a pretty subject to introduce right now."

"Uncle, the only thing that prevented Hassan from being given over to those slavers was the name of Mr. McDermott."

"We must tell my husband. Someone will have to go to your crewman, because anyone who appears to be a Negro may not speak for himself in legal matters."

Alex chafed. "Shouldn't I go directly to Hassan?"

Major Babcock considered a moment. "Let's describe the problem to Mr. McDermott and then I'll send you to the courthouse. This is a delicate moment."

The look that Major Babcock gave Alex contained every lecture about behavior, moderation, and patience that Alex had ever heard in his life. He glanced down, smoothed his rumpled clothing, and took a deep breath. "Yes sir."

An astonished Elizabeth eased back to her chair in the dining room just before her mother returned.

"Excuse me, Quentin. Gentlemen and ladies, we have another guest and a bit of a conundrum that could use the wisdom of this assembly."

Alex was introduced and replied formally to each person. It seemed to take forever. Then he was introduced to Elizabeth. Not expecting to see anyone his own age, certainly not a girl, Alex stared at her cascading black curls and bright azure eyes, an arresting combination. The slight flush that rose from her ivory complexion highlighted her pink lips that now were smiling at him. He looked away only when his uncle started speaking.

As succinctly as possible, and with no small degree of embarrassment, Major Babcock explained the situation. All eyes turned to Quentin McDermott.

"Let's have our dessert, and then perhaps we can amuse ourselves with a visit to the courthouse. I imagine it will all be straightened out by then."

Alex fidgeted, thinking Major Babcock would never reply.

"My nephew states that the kidnappers plan to sell our employee as a slave. Please understand that the young man in question is not only one of our camel drivers, but also the son of a prominent family in Egypt. The US Government has committed to protecting his safety. May I dispatch my nephew to the courthouse to monitor the situation?"

"Of course. Antoine, tell Samuel to get my horse. In the meantime, we can finish up here." Quentin was not in the least interested in interrupting his evening.

Alex bowed and bolted for the door. Captain Turner twisted in his seat.

"Excuse me, Mr. McDermott, but as Captain, I must see to the fate of one of my men, and I would prefer to do so forthwith."

"Yes, Quentin, and I should like to come as there may be something newsworthy here," Sebastian Smith added, "and my familiarity with the law may be useful."

Quentin sighed, already regretting the dessert, coffee and cigar that would have marked the end of a most enjoyable evening. "All right, then, let's go."

Antoine held the door to the carriage for Quentin McDermott, Captain Turner, Major Babcock, and Sebastian Smith to climb in. As Samuel took up the reins, he locked eyes with Antoine, who had briefly described the reason for this unusual outing. Curiosity consumed both men.

When Sylvia suggested that the ladies retire to the parlor for the meantime, Elizabeth pulled her mother aside. "Mama, I have to go with them. I have never in my life seen a real Egyptian."

"What a thought! Have you taken leave of your senses? It would be quite unseemly for a young lady to be embroiled in something like this. That boy is in jail. You most certainly cannot go. You'll see the Egyptians along with the camels when we visit the ship tomorrow."

"Yes, but Mother, I really want to go. Perhaps I could take a basket of food to the prisoner. Who knows how long he might be stuck in that jail, and he is a ward of Major Babcock, isn't he?

Sylvia was not fooled for a minute. Elizabeth was equally as curious about Alex Babcock as she was about a real Egyptian. "No, you'll stay here and act as hostess to the ladies."

When Mr. Hurlinger and Mr. Borden realized that they had been left alone with the female guests, they decided to go to the courthouse as well. Mr. Hurlinger called his coachman, Benjamin, to bring the carriage around while he informed Sylvia. He professed a lack of confidence in a good outcome to the situation, considering how much everyone had imbibed. Deferring to the wisdom of this view, Sylvia let her guests depart.

Elizabeth saw her opportunity. She grabbed a chunk of bread and some fruit, tossed them in a basket, and slipped out the side door where she prevailed upon Mr. Hurlinger that she was to carry refreshments in case the proceedings ran long.

His captors shoved Hassan into the jail, a solid brick building with two cellblocks. Tonight being a Saturday, there
were already several occupants who had earned their keep
during excitements at the bars. The white cell held two ine-
briates and a pickpocket. The second cell's resident was a
frightened dark-skinned boy, who appeared to be a couple
years younger than Hassan.

Deputy Lassen motioned to the second cell. "Put this
boy in there."

The jail attendant, Luke, looked quizzically at Deputy
Lassen. "This here is a white boy. Why we puttin' him in
with the nigra?"

"Look again, stupid. He ain't no white boy. Slim and
Josiah found this boy on the beach, a full mile away from
port, givin' all evidence of bein' a runaway."

"But Deputy, if he's a runaway and these two have
claimed him, why are we keepin' him?"

Slim grinned. "Luke's right. All you gotta do is let us
take him. Give us leave, and we'll take care of everythin'.
We might could provide somethin' in return for your con-
sideration."

A percentage of a deal like that would certainly be
worthwhile. Deputy Lassen had been running low on cash
lately, and he surmised that a fellow like this would bring at
least $1200, maybe even $1500. If his share was only $100,
it would be easy money.

"I know, damn it. But that kid's goin' for Quentin Mc-
Dermott, and he ain't one to be crossed. I can't figure him
gettin' mixed up with the likes of this boy, but we're gonna
wait awhile in case he shows up."

Throughout this conversation, Hassan stood stock still
in the middle of the room, his hands tied behind his back,
observing his surroundings and trying to clear his head that
still ached from being smacked into the dirt. Luke walked
around and around him, staring.

"He don't look like no nigra. Look at that nose. Why
his nose is longer and straighter than yours, 'course I guess
yours is flat and crooked from gettin' broke once or twice."

This was too much for Josiah. "Luke, shut up. Look at the color of that boy's skin. He's at least an octoroon, could be quadroon or mulatto. Look at that nappy hair."

Much as he would have liked to let Slim and Josiah take the boy, Deputy Lassen realized that the situation had gotten out of hand. Three people were now watching from the doorway to see what Luke's ruckus was all about.

"Put him in with the other boy, and lock the door."

Luke persisted. "Can he talk, boss? Why don't he say nuthin'?" Luke stood close enough for Hassan to smell the rank odor of tobacco and whisky on his breath. "Well, is you a nigra?"

Hassan stood as straight as possible. "I am Arab."

Luke shrieked. "An Ay-rab. Well, I'll be. This is the first Ay-rab we've ever had in this jail."

"Enough. Get in that cell."

Hassan was upset, but not really frightened. He believed that Alex would soon return with Major Babcock to straighten everything out. Hassan had the confidence of youth and of position. He could not fathom that anyone would dare to hurt, let alone kidnap, the grandson of Alhaji Mustafa. And yet, there was something disconcerting about his predicament.

Back home in Egypt, status was determined by what family you belonged to and who you knew with power and influence. If you came from a slave family, you would be a slave. But that was not based upon the color of your skin, the curl in your hair, or the straightness of your nose. Had Luke actually thought the shape of his nose was important? He remembered a conversation with Alex, who had explained that some people categorized everyone by how much African they had in their parentage. He thought it an odd concept then, and even more so now. He supposed by their reckoning, with his African grandmother, he would be considered a quadroon. Did this put him in danger?

Out of the question. His grandmother protected him, as did her ancestors. Grandma Ara had explained that ancestors watch over us and help us in times of trouble. "We pray to God for matters of consequence, but we cannot bother God with every little thing that comes along in our lives. That is where the ancestors come in. They can influence the small currents of luck that flow across our paths. They protect us from those who wish evil against us, and they can bring us good fortune." Grandma Ara was famous in the neighborhood for being able to ask for advice from the ancestors, and she had helped her children many times. She kept a small shrine in one corner of the house where she occasionally left offerings of food for the ancestors and spoke to them about the needs of the family. Alhaji Mustafa accepted this, as it did not interfere with her adherence to Islam.

Hassan did not know much about his Grandma Ara's background, but to him she seemed like a princess. She came from an important kingdom across the Sahara, and his grandfather Alhaji Mustafa had performed some great service in order to win her. When he got home, he would have to find out the details of these stories. Tonight his grandmother could not possibly cause him any danger. As he sat quietly in the jail cell, he called upon Grandma Ara to give him patience and wisdom.

As his jailers continued their banter, Hassan missed much of the content. The tone, however, was crass, boorish, and hateful. Instead of trying to comprehend the meaning, he drew inward and gradually separated from the chaos around him. He felt his grandmother's presence, along with her ancestors, and gained a sense of security that belied the facts of his situation.

"Come on, Deputy Lassen. How long are you gonna wait? I tell you, if he's gone, he's gone. There won't be that much fuss, and we'll soon be back with a nice bit of gold for your trouble."

"I sure would be happy to let y'all have him. These uppity niggers do irritate me. Look at him, sittin' there so straight and cocksure, like he ain't never had hisself a proper beating."

Luke, in his feeble-minded way, kept asking questions. "Do you suppose that's the Ay-rab way of doin'? Bein' uppity, I mean."

"Jesus, Luke, can't you keep quiet?"

At that moment, Alex rode up to the courthouse, leapt off Mr. McDermott's mare and strode into the room. "Hassan."

The sound of Alex's voice snapped Hassan out of his reverie. He wistfully felt his ancestors fade from his consciousness but was still surrounded by their strength and guidance.

"What is Mr. Hassan ibn Yusuf doing in jail?" Noticing a few onlookers near the courthouse door, Alex decided to be provocative before as many witnesses as possible until his uncle arrived.

"Boy, you are startin' to annoy me." Deputy Lassen snarled. "We're holdin' him as a runaway."

"Deputy, I urge you to choose your words carefully. This man is innocent until proven guilty under the laws of this country. Have you harmed him in any way?"

Alex turned to Hassan and whispered in Arabic. "You all right?" Hassan nodded.

Fortunately, they didn't have to wait long. Once having decided to forego his cigar for the sake of calming his agitated guests, Quentin McDermott wanted an end to the matter. The riffraff that had been hanging around the courthouse door stepped back to let the McDermott carriage unload its distinguished-looking passengers. Slim, who had been leaning against the wall with his foot on a chair, and Josiah who had been slumped on the desk, quickly stood up and tried to look respectful. Luke remained in the corner with his broom, while Deputy Lassen stepped forward. Quentin took charge.

"Evenin', Deputy. What's goin' on here?"

Deputy Lassen explained the dilemma as best he could while Mr. Smith took detailed notes.

"The dispute seems simple enough," asserted Mr. McDermott. "Captain, does your employee speak English?"

"To a degree, yes."

"Then we'll ask him a few questions. If what he says matches what you've said, then he'll be free to go, if that's all right with everybody." Quentin looked around and saw that no one would countermand him.

Hassan was released from the cage and stood directly in front of Mr. McDermott, who noticed with some displeasure that the young man stood erect and looked him in the eye. Very few people, white or black, held themselves so confidently in front of Quentin McDermott, especially when he was angry or had been interrupted as he had this evening.

Hassan had studied the Americans, with some tutorial from Alex. He knew that they valued a strong handshake and direct eye contact. At home, if he had been addressing his elders, he would have diverted his eyes as a sign of respect. With his grandfather, Hassan always cast his eyes away, spoke softly when questioned, and waited to be asked before speaking. He had learned that the Americans preferred someone who was more open, more aggressive. This was not Hassan's nature, but he had practiced. Now he greeted his shipmates confidently with a smile, shook hands firmly, and looked directly even at Major Babcock and Captain Turner. He only hoped he would remember to be respectful when he got home.

Hassan had noticed that the blacks here were far more polite than the whites. They spoke softly, cast their eyes down, and waited quietly. He had been impressed, thinking that these people had maintained their culture from Africa, an accomplishment to be proud of. But he noticed that the whites never treated the blacks with the same respect. Gradually he realized that this was a sign of subservience. Blacks were expected to show deference to whites, but the whites were capable of every sort of rudeness without any qualms whatsoever. He decided to try for a middle ground, polite but not obsequious.

"Now then, son, what is your name?"

Hassan understood the question easily and replied carefully, "Sir, I am Hassan ibn Yusuf ibn Alhaji Mustafa."

Deputy Lassen had never in his life seen a Negro in jail respond in such a prideful way. Maybe the boy was an Arab after all. No American slave would be so stupid.

"And where were you born?"

"Alexandria, Egypt."

"What are you doing here in Galveston?"

"I am from the *Supply*. I care for camels."

"Are you a slave?

"No."

Quentin McDermott turned and looked at the assembly, including those peeking in the courthouse windows. "That seems to take care of it. This boy is not a slave but an employee of the US Government. He doesn't belong in jail."

Deputy Lassen's position would be tenuous if he drew the ire of a man like Quentin McDermott. But he also had a protector, Collector of Customs Harvey Parkson, the richest man in Galveston, who supervised the collection of tariffs from ships passing through the port. He was particularly adamant about the comings and goings of colored people. Deputy Lassen was pleased when Collector Parkson arrived.

"Greetings, Quentin. What seems to be the matter here?"

"Evenin', Harvey." Quentin smiled even as he fumed over the presence of his closest rival. "I'm surprised you're workin' so late on a weekend. Let me introduce you to Captain Turner of the *USS Supply* and Major Babcock of the Army. Seems we have a case of mistaken identity with one of the Captain's crew, but we've just resolved it."

"That may be, but I'd like to review the case. Deputy Lassen, may I hear your report?"

During Deputy Lassen's recitation, Mr. Hurlinger entered the courthouse attended by his coachman, Benjamin. Elizabeth McDermott followed with her basket, sheltered by Mr. Hurlinger's broad frame. Luckily, her father, Major Babcock, and Captain Turner had their backs to the door. Facing them, and fully in view, were Alex and the Egyptian. Alex spied her immediately and nodded ever so slightly, causing Elizabeth to blush. Then she saw the Egyptian and was transfixed. Never had she seen such a handsome person. She grasped that the Egyptian was about to be released and breathed a sigh of relief. Her father had prevailed. Then she heard Collector Parkson.

"Thank you, Deputy. If this boy is free as you say, then we have another problem. No free Negroes can come into the State of Texas."

Transfixed, Elizabeth watched her father struggle to maintain his composure. "Listen, Harvey, we have established that this boy is an Arab, not a Negro. The law doesn't apply to him."

Ever oblivious to protocol, Luke piped up. "I been studyin' him. At first, I was sure he was white, but now I figure him for mixed. I mean, look at him."

Furious that Luke would dare to address him directly, Quentin McDermott mocked. "Shall we call that visiting phrenologist to examine his cranium and tell us whether he is bright or dull, and whether is white, black or Arab? Shall we have him take a look at you, too, Luke, while he's at it? No, he is an Arab, and that's that."

The assembly laughed, and once again Elizabeth felt relief.

Luke missed his cue, as usual. "But Mr. Parkson, why don't we ask him?"

Mr. Parkson grinned. "For the record, boy, what are you?"

Hassan hesitated. He wanted to shout that he was the scion of one of the best families in Egypt, that his grandmother was strong, beautiful, and yes, an African. But then his grandfather Alhaji Mustafa's voice came to him. "Grandson, you must accommodate to the customs of the local people. You may find yourself in danger, and you must read the situation with great care. Do not react the way you would at home. Become a strategist. See the implications of today's words and deeds for tomorrow's consequences. If pressed, show strength, even if you do not feel it."

Hassan stood tall and looked directly at Mr. McDermott and Collector Parkson. "Sirs, I am Hassan ibn Yusuf ibn Mustafa from Alexandria, Egypt. My father's father and his father's father are an important family. I am not a slave. I do not belong in this jail."

"But do you have black blood in you?"

He would not deny his grandmother and her ancestors who protected him. He was determined to honor them. Yet, if he confessed to having African roots, he might be in this prison for the rest of his stay. If this law applied to all of Texas, he might be unable to disembark with the camels at Indianola. Or he might be taken into slavery. He breathed deeply.

"Sirs, I try to be polite. I come from a good family. I come from Egypt. I work for the United States. I do not like your question. I will say no more."

"That is the most impudent response I have ever heard." Mr. Parkson spied Mr. Hurlinger's slave Benjamin. "You there, come here." Benjamin lowered his head and walked slowly forward. "Step up here. Now gentlemen, look at these two next to each other. That slave is lighter. The so-called Arab is a darkie if I ever saw one."

Elizabeth retreated one step further, hoping that her father had not seen her, while she maintained a clear view of the Egyptian and Alex. The Egyptian stood serenely, but his eyes were not glazed over. He was calmly watchful. Alex's eyes darted from speaker to speaker around the room. He often glanced in her direction. Afraid that he might draw attention to her, she ducked behind another spectator and tried to avoid his gaze.

"Excuse me." Because Sebastian Smith usually avoided disputes among the mercantile families, all parties looked at him in surprise. "We have established that this boy is not a slave, being of foreign birth and newly arrived in this country We are now trying to determine his status under the law regarding free men of color. Deputy Lassen, did you interview the suspect before these other gentlemen arrived?

"Yes, sir, I did."

"And Mr. McDermott, did you also pose questions to the accused?"

"Of course, I did."

"And we just witnessed your inquires to the boy in your official role, did we not, Mr. Parkson?

The Customs Collector assented.

"Well, then it is quite plain that he is an Arab. No person of color is allowed to speak for himself during any official inquiry. Yet each of you asked the boy several questions, which you would not have done had he been a Negro. Therefore all of you judged that the boy is an Arab."

Quentin let forth a deep belly laugh. "Count on you, Sebastian to remark the legal point that every one of us missed."

A deep red color crept up Mr. Parkson's neck in the space between his collar and his beard. Elizabeth, at the precise angle to observe this, shivered, but she soon realized that the Customs Collector had been checkmated this time.

Mr. Parkson seethed. "Regardless, it would be more prudent, Captain Turner, if your 'Ay-rab' crewman was confined to the ship."

"My men will see to it."

Mr. McDermott addressed his adversary. "Harvey, can you join us for a cigar? A new shipment arrived today from Cuba, as I'm sure you know."

Mr. Parkson's smile was forced. "Thank you kindly, but I'll test your cigars another time."

"Suit yourself." Quentin kept his own smile firmly fixed. At that moment, he turned and saw Elizabeth. He walked briskly to her side. "Elizabeth, my dear, what brings you here?"

The flash of anger in his narrowing eyes terrified her, but she looked upon this as a kind of a test. Pretending she had only been there a few moments, she replied steadily. "I brought refreshments." She was careful not to say "for the prisoner" as he had just been released and she didn't want to start the argument all over again. "Mama is busy with our guests, so I volunteered to bring them."

Quentin did not believe her for a moment but went along with the charade. "How thoughtful of you. Well, fortunately the matter has been settled without long delays." He took his daughter's elbow, a bit too firmly in Elizabeth's view, and headed to the carriage.

Alex watched this exchange, incredulous. Not only was Elizabeth beautiful, but she was also graceful under pressure. He had no idea why she was in the courthouse, so clearly out of place, nor what she carried in the basket. But she had handled herself smoothly, and Alex was enchanted.

Captain Turner escorted Hassan outside. At the doorway, he found two of the *Supply*'s seamen and ordered them to go with Alex and Hassan to the ship. "Hassan, your shore leave is cancelled, but the rest of you are free to go once Hassan is safely on board."

After Major Babcock and Captain Turner were settled in the carriage, Samuel snapped the reins, thinking he would have a lot to talk over with Antoine that night.

Hassan walked beside Alex, wordlessly. He had been attacked on the beach, smashed in the head, dragged to jail, interrogated by idiots and humiliated in front of his Captain. For this, no one had apologized.

TEXAS  SOIL

MATAGORDA ISLAND, TEXAS, MAY 1, 1856

STILL AND QUIET SAT Jeremy Blackstone, just like the Gulf of Mexico stretching before him. The water reminded him of a piece of homemade glass, not perfectly smooth, but lustrous and shimmering. It almost seemed that he could reach out and run his hands across the surface, feeling the minor imperfections in a windowpane. For the past three days, the only change in the water had been subtle shifts in shades of blue. Jeremy averted his eyes from the brightness. He was attuned to this stretch of Gulf. He knew that this stillness would persist at least several hours, but that a stiff wind would likely follow. The lighthouse towering before him was the pride of Matagorda Bay, and Jeremy's job was to keep a lookout. On a day like today, with no breeze, Jeremy need not perch up top but could sit on the porch of his caretaker's lodge and whittle, letting his mind wander. Although deeply tanned and wrinkled, he was healthy for his fifty-three years, and he was content with his quiet life at the lighthouse. His grandson, however, was profoundly bored.

Nathaniel Aldous Wilkers had been up in the lighthouse since early morning. Jeremy looked up as he heard the clanking of his grandson's feet rapidly descending the metal stairs. Nate rushed across the open yard to the caretaker's house, handed the spyglass to Jeremy, and pointed to a barely glimpsed ship out on the horizon.

"Grandpa, that ship is still out there. It must be the one we've been waitin' for, but how long is she gonna lie there doin' nothin'?"

Jeremy kept his thoughts to himself. He knew which ship Nate was waiting for. "Yup, it'll be a little while yet before we see her in the bay. No wind right now."

Nate took the spyglass for a better view and sighed. "You're right, Grandpa. She's just sittin' there!"

"Son, they'll send a signal when they're ready. You might as well wait. The wind will pick up, maybe later to-day, possibly not until tomorrow."

Nate fidgeted. That was so typical of his grandfather. "Let everything come in its own time," he always said. Nate saw the world very differently. At eighteen, Nate wanted action. He had plans. He dreamed of Galveston, a port that every sailor described with excitement in his eyes. Even more appealing were the stories he heard about San Anto-nio, an established town at the crossroads of the country. He would have to leave in order to make his way in the world, but he wasn't sure which way to go: the sea or the land. He knew a lot about sailing, but was coming to the conclusion that he did not want to spend his life at sea. For-tunes were being made in cotton, but he owned neither land nor slaves and couldn't figure out how he would get either. Maybe this ship would bring an opportunity.

With the spyglass fixed to his face, Nate studied the ship. Captain Van Steendam, the government official across the bay in Indianola, had been expecting the *Supply* for some time. There were supposed to be camels on board. No one had been able to describe quite what these beasts were like, so Nate was determined to be the first to see them.

"I'm going over to Saluria to see if there's any news about the ship. Bye, Grandpa."

Nate turned abruptly and headed for his horse. With a smooth motion, he hefted the saddlebags that he had load-ed with overnight gear in anticipation of this moment. As he tossed them high, they arced into the air and onto his horse's back, landing with a dull thud. Something about the movement and the sound caught Nate in his throat. This ordinary act had suddenly become filled with implications. No longer the kid from the lighthouse, Nate was about to be somebody else.

Nate stood deeply still for a moment and realized that he was unwilling to disclose his plans. He feared his grandfather's caution. Hesitation would kill his resolve, would threaten to trap him forever at the edge of the water when a whole continent lay behind the bay. He needed to be impulsive, willful, and most of all, without encumbrances. He intended to tell his grandfather once the plan was set, but now he had to go. He needed to be his own man in this. That ship and those camels would come to mean something important, of that Nate was sure.

"Grandpa, I may not be back for some days. I have my gear with me. Gotta go." Nate turned, mounted, and headed away from the tedium of a windless sea.

Jeremy smiled at his grandson, but didn't reply. How he and Nate had come to be minding a lighthouse on the Gulf Coast was a simple story of survival. Jeremy believed that no matter what happened in life, you had to keep going. It was best not to think too much. But in spite of himself, he sometimes thought about Linnville, about the Comanche raid of 1840 that had killed his wife, daughter and son-in-law. Remembering it, even all these years later, he sometimes forgot to breathe. Yet, miraculously, his two-year-old grandson had escaped the massacre. When a few men had called for revenge and mounted a raiding party—a hopeless cause, as the Comanche rode hard and fast into the hill country, and if chased, into Mexico—Jeremy picked up the baby Nate and became quiet in his determination that this child would survive.

With nothing left of Linnville, Jeremy put one foot in front of the other, moving down the coast to Lavaca and on to Indianola. His grief clung to him, like a stubborn mule that would not move. It held him down and contained him in a world of grey images and conjured memories. The sadness cloaked him, and when people saw his face, they turned away. Anger might have cured him, but he feared his anger. Giving vent to such fury would release demons that he might not be able to control. It was Nate who saved him. Inexplicably to Jeremy, who had no appetite, the child was hungry. When Jeremy would have spent days without sleeping, his nights rent by memories of the devastation at Linnville, the baby needed rest. He crawled into Jeremy's lap to sleep, thereby bringing peace and drowsiness to both of them. Nate laughed as only a toddler can. So Jeremy extricated himself from the pull of his grief, turned aside from the temptation to rage, and concentrated on keeping Nate alive. It was hard to believe that had been sixteen years ago.

Ever since Linnville, Jeremy had become a watcher. Mostly he watched the sea and the bay and the weather. He also watched for cheaters, liars, diseases, and danger. But first and foremost he watched his grandson, and he knew what to expect. His grandson was getting restless, and the lighthouse was no place for him now. Just as a whooping crane migrated to the Gulf Coast in winter and then felt the urge to fly north at springtime, so Nate would have to leave Matagorda Island.

Jeremy knew it, because he had been exactly the same way when he left his Tennessee home at seventeen. He had married the only daughter of a poor farmer in Alabama, but then had left her and their little girl for months at a time. The routine of domestic life would weigh on him, and he would have to be going. The going was part of the rhythm he lived by. Then came the day when he gave Melissa unexpected news: Jeremy Blackstone, supreme wanderer, had decided to settle down. They were moving to Texas! Melissa had laughed out loud. She knew a number of people who were GTT—gone to Texas—but she never figured to be one of them. They settled in Linnville, upriver from Matagorda Bay. Melissa thrived there, making friends easily. Their daughter Abigail, then fifteen, married the blacksmith's son and made Jeremy a grandfather at age thirty-five. Amazing everyone, especially himself, Jeremy found an unlooked-for tranquility in his new domestic circumstance. He liked how he came to know the small differences in their lives. He felt somehow satisfied with this stability that in the past would have crimped like a shirt one size too small.

Still, from time to time, he had missed the gambling, drinking, and storytelling that went with the road. He would fabricate an excuse about needing supplies and head up to Galveston, as he had done that summer of 1840. During an evening of whiskey, poker, and old friends, a patron at the saloon mentioned the Comanche attack on Linnville. There he was again, thinking about Linnville. He had to stop that.

Anyway, the thought proved his point: Nate had the rambler's itch, and he came by it honestly. The signs were as plain as day. Nate was spending more time over on the mainland, running imaginary errands and staying longer than needed. Even though Indianola was twenty miles across the water, the grandson of the lighthouse keeper had no problem hitching a ride with the pilots who sailed Matagorda Bay. And Jeremy had no trouble finding out exactly when and where his grandson had crossed over. Very few people in any part of the Bay were not in some way indebted to Jeremy Blackstone, and everyone knew of his devotion to his grandson. Possibly Nate had taken a shine to Herman Blauvelt's daughter, Evangeline. More likely, Nate was frequenting the Government Depot. Jeremy's eyes followed his grandson's departure, noting the ease with which he rode the horse and sensing the boy's excitement. Yes, it was clear that Nate needed to go. Where or how that would happen, Jeremy didn't know. What he did know was that he would go with him.

He accepted that Nate would have to live his own life, but in no way was Jeremy ready to let him venture off without protection. If Nate planned to move, then he would have to be moving, too. Sitting pensively in his rocking chair, he caressed the smooth armrests that he had carved himself and thought of the many times he had drawn comfort from both the carving and from the sitting. This chair he knew could not come with him. It was the first indication of the import of his decision. With purpose, he rose and climbed the steps of the lighthouse to have his own look at the *Supply*.

On the *Supply*, the crew and the camels were restless. The lookout scanned impatiently for signs of a steamship from New Orleans while the humid, windless air increased the sense of frustration. Men passed time playing cards or sleeping, anxious to have the journey completed. Some wanted to be rid of the camels, while others longed to return to sea. Major Babcock had gone ashore to post reports to Jefferson Davis along with a stack of letters from Lt. Halter to his wife and a large bundle of missives from the crew. He also hoped to meet Captain Van Steendam.

The endless waiting and forced idleness annoyed Alex. "I swear, I'm fed up. I wish I could have gone ashore with my Uncle. At least then I'd be doing something."

"Why must we wait?" asked Hassan. The three Egyptians, Alex and two soldiers lounged on deck with their backs resting against several kneeling camels.

"They say that Matagorda Bay on the other side of that pass is less than five feet deep in places. So we have to wait for the Fashion, which draws less water, to lighter the camels. I guess that's pretty normal for these parts."

"Lighter?" Hassan's English had improved so rapidly that almost any general conversation was possible. Technical terms, politics, and slang expressions were still a mystery, and rapid exchanges left him bewildered, but when it came to bantering with Alex, he did just fine. Alex had also improved his comprehension of Arabic, and he rather enjoyed having an insider's perspective of the goings on among the camel crew.

"That's what they call it: lightering. Most ships can make it through the pass, but a flat-bottomed boat has to take the cargo to the wharves. Even then, it's so shallow that they can't make it to shore. The wharves stick way out into the bay." Like elongated tentacles probing the shallow waters, some of the wharves extended as much as a half mile.

"So we have to get the camels onto the *Fashion* first?"

"That's right. That's why we're waiting."

"Look Alex, there's Major Babcock!"

The Major's return was greeted with whoops of joy and groans of disappointment. Some of the crew had several letters from home, while others came away empty-handed. Lt. Halter's bounty exceeded all the others, as it seemed he had weekly correspondence from his wife. With a sly smile Major Babcock distributed the last item: a bound leather satchel marked "Special Handling" sent by the US Consul in Alexandria. The Egyptians were nonplussed. They whispered among themselves, and then Ali the Interpreter stepped forward.

"With our greatest appreciation, Major Babcock." He accepted the packet with a dramatic bow, stepping backward to rejoin his countrymen. The sailors laughed and clapped while the Arabs smiled and retreated to a corner to investigate the contents.

As men stole away to their bunks or otherwise sought privacy to read their mail, a peculiar silence descended over the ship, punctuated only occasionally by a laugh or exclamation. Major Babcock's letters from the Secretary of War's office were disappointing: brief responses to prior reports, and most regrettably, no orders regarding the future service of Lt. Halter. The only good news was confirmation that Captain Turner would go for a second shipment of camels. Among the Major's personal correspondence was a letter from Quentin McDermott that must have been sent by express steamer immediately after their departure from Galveston. Guessing at its contents, he put it aside to read later.

The three Egyptians crouched over their prize. Ali, whose shaky hands exposed his scarcely contained excitement, carefully opened the satchel. Inside was a large decorated pouch made of the softest camel hide dyed in hues of beige, amber and cocoa. It contained three smaller pouches, each sealed, with a name burned into the leather in Arabic script. Someone had paid dearly to send these letters.

Abdullah and Ali each had two letters in their packets: one from their families and a more formal note from the palace encouraging them to act with all propriety on behalf of the Viceroy. Hassan's pouch contained four: from the Viceroy, his father, his grandfather, and Auntie Fatima, who, not content to be appended to anyone's letter, had hired a scribe to write her own. Hassan smiled at the thought of

Auntie Fatima negotiating with the scribe, requiring him to rephrase her thoughts, most likely insisting that he recopy the whole thing flawlessly, and then haggling over the price. He would read her letter last. He felt sure that Auntie Fatima would convey something from Sula, even in an oblique way. He began with his father's letter:

To Hassan ibn Yusuf

In the name of Allah, I greet you, my son. Your mother calls your name with great affection, as do your brother and sister. We hold you daily in our prayers. When I am required to inspect the Viceroy's camels, I often think of you. I wonder how our "ships of the desert" fare on a real ship. I hope those that are pregnant give birth well and that the young survive.

You must rely on Abdullah's knowledge of camels. You must listen to Ali for advice on how to carry yourself. You must learn well, and then come home to us as quickly as possible. We all pray for your rapid return to the arms of your family, Inshallah.

Wishing you health and many blessings,

Your father, Yusuf

Hassan took a moment to savor images of his parents and younger siblings, guessing what they might be doing at this very moment. He salivated with an intense craving for his mother's lamb stew, rich with aromas of cinnamon, nutmeg, and onion as he opened his grandfather's letter.

To Hassan ibn Yusuf

In the name of Allah the Most Merciful, I greet you. I send you best wishes from your family, friends and neighbors, all of whom pray that this message finds you well. Alhaji Ibrahim Muhammad arranged to send these letters through the American Consul. We take this as a blessing upon you, your companions, and your voyage.

Your grandmother counts the days until you come home. Every Friday when she makes bread, she sets aside a portion for you. Concern for your welfare occupies her prayers five times a day without fail. Yesterday I told her that her devotion to you might threaten her spiritual health. I attempted to sound authoritative, but she saw through my teasing. She insists that nothing is more important than your safe return.

Auntie Fatima pesters me every week for your news. I explained that you would be gone a year and might be unable to send letters. She reminded me that my years of wandering had nearly killed her. She brought her own letter already sealed!

Friends at the mosque question how I could permit you to go to the land of the infidels. Most of them are too young to remember my own travels, but there is a difference between my voyages and yours. Among the peoples of Africa, I encountered many Believers. You, my grandson, are destined for a country where Believers may be rarely found. The Qur'an teaches that Jews and Christians, as Peoples of the Book, know truth and must be respected, even though they do not realize that their truth is incomplete. I caution you that some followers of Jesus are convinced of the rightness of their way and unwilling to listen to others. Do not engage them too vigorously in debate. Rather show the wisdom of the teachings of Islam by your actions. Hold to your faith while allowing them to hold to theirs, and pray that they might some day be enlightened.

Remember your origins and walk proudly but not arrogantly. Do honor to your family in all things great and small. Your grandmother joins me in sending our most affectionate greetings. May the blessings of Allah be upon you.

Alhaji Mustafa

His grandfather's letter left Hassan weak. He became once more a small child, nestled in the crimson embroidered cushions on Alhaji Mustafa's rug-covered floor with his head in his grandmother Ara's lap, contented, warm, and without a care. The love and laughter of his grandfather's household enveloped him in an aura of well-being. Until this moment, he had not realized how much he missed his family. Rereading his grandfather's advice, he was amazed at its accuracy, written as if he already knew the trials that Hassan had experienced. He would strive to exhibit the self-control he had observed in his grandfather and be an admirable representative of the family. Now more than ever, he was glad that he had not dishonored his grandmother in the Galveston jail.

He turned to the letter from Auntie Fatima, noticing that his heart rate elevated when he broke the seal.

To Hassan ibn Yusuf

In the name of Allah, I greet you. To the dear grandson of my most esteemed and respected cousin, Alhaji Mustafa, we pray daily that your health blossoms like the spring flowers and that you prosper like a bountiful harvest even though you travel in the land of the infidels.

Hassan laughed out loud at Auntie Fatima's florid prose. He wondered whether this language accurately reflected his Aunt's own words or was an exaggeration created by the scribe. How he wished he could have eavesdropped on the production of this letter.

We long to see your visage gracing our doorways again. When that day comes, we shall prepare for you the finest dishes in the land. The entire family, especially my grandchildren, long to enjoy your companionship. As fitting tribute to your return, we shall offer a grand feast in your honor and hope that such a celebration marks a new phase in your life, one that keeps you close to home.

I hold you fondly in my heart as I held you in my arms in your infancy. Now that you are a man, we pray for you to be strong. May you return to us as soon as possible, Inshallah.

With deepest affection,

Auntie Fatima

There it was, a clear reference to Sula! Auntie Fatima was telling him that Sula was looking forward to a marriage feast. No interloper was taking her from him. Although confident that his grandfather would fend off other suitors, he was happy to read the words directly from Auntie Fatima.

Many among the crew had also finished reading and now passed the time penning replies to loved ones at home. Eager to post them, they became cranky. To be so close to their destination and unable to reach it amounted to a kind of torture. Alex and Hassan went back to watching the flat seas.

"You know, Hassan, at this rate we almost could have stayed in Galveston. I certainly would have loved to see that May Day celebration."

Hassan laughed. "Or is it Miss McDermott you really want to see?"

"You must admit that she is uncommonly beautiful, and I like the fact that she reads and thinks for herself."

"I do not understand, Alex. Were you not ashamed to see her in the jail? Why would her father allow her to go there?"

"Her father didn't allow it. Didn't you see how angry he was? I bet she had a lot of explaining to do that night!"

"It was bad thing for her to come there."

"Yeah, I suppose. What Elizabeth did was unusual, but not that serious."

"In Egypt, a woman can not go where men belong."

"Really? What about your Auntie Fatima? She seems pretty independent."

"Haha, yes. She is very independent, but she is also an old woman. If my Sula..."

Alex laughed. "So it's your Sula you're thinking about. Afraid she is out of the house instead of waiting for you to come back?"

Hassan was spared the need to reply by the lookout's cry. "It's the *Fashion!*"

The sailors ran cheering to their posts, and as if to compensate them for their frustrations, the wind picked up as well. At last the ship was moving toward the Pass.

On the way to Saluria, Nate stopped to look through the spyglass. A bit sooner than his grandfather had predicted, a gentle breeze disturbed the waters and, as the wind rose, the waves became more rhythmic and determined. With sails now puffing full, the *Supply* cruised toward Pass Caballo at a reasonable speed. In his peripheral vision Nate caught a glimpse of smoke, and focusing his telescope, recognized the steamship coming from the direction of Galveston. Then it all made sense. The *Supply* had been waiting for the *Fashion* to lighter the camels.

He snapped the reins and urged his horse to the harbor, where he found his buddy Amos Prudeau preparing to launch a rowboat. Of an age to be Nate's father, Amos was a pilot from Galveston who had been obliged to slip down the coast in search of other employment after accumulating one too many gambling debts. He had taught Nate much about the ways of the water: how to spot the shifting sandbars that were a mortal danger to ships, how to tell when a storm was coming, and what inlet to hide in if you didn't want to be found.

"Hello Amos, I knew you'd be the one to go for the *Supply*. You're going to make history today, the pilot who brought camels to America!"

Amos was not at all surprised to see Nate, who had talked of little else for weeks. Nate had his mind set on these camels being something special, and Amos surely hoped his young friend would not be disappointed.

"Yup, it's the camel ship, but seems to me you're a little late with the news, Nate. One Major Babcock passed through earlier."

"Wish I'd known that. What did you find out?"

"Not much. He crossed to Indianola with Drew Johnsville who says the man is a Yankee and couldn't stop talkin' about camels with anyone who would listen. Said they would lighter today and brought a note from Captain Van Steendam for me to do the piloting."

"Great." He paused.

Knowing Nate's unasked question, Amos laughed out loud. "Of course you can come. But you'll have to act like my apprentice and keep your trap shut. No talkin' out of you 'cept maybe 'yes sir and no sir.' You got that?"

Nate nodded vigorously and jumped into the rowboat with Amos. Shortly, they came alongside the *Supply*.

"Permission to board, Captain?"

His inquiry was answered promptly. This was the moment that everyone on board had been waiting for: the first step to landing the camels in Texas. After brief introductions, Captain Turner released the wheel. "Mr. Prudeau, the ship is yours."

So monotonously calm for the past few days, the waters of the Bay began to simmer and shift as the wind picked up. Amos piloted the ship successfully through the channel at Pass Caballo and alongside the *Fashion*. Marking the change in the waves, he hoped this lightering could be quickly accomplished.

Nate couldn't believe his luck to get a glimpse of the camels before anyone else in Texas. He did his best to appear the studious apprentice pilot, but he couldn't keep his eyes off the animals. On the upper deck, several sat in a kneeling position with their legs folded under their bodies, strapped to prevent them from sliding about. Their midsections had a large curved hump, the sight of which caused Nate to question where one would put a saddle. Their long necks led up to a somewhat horse-shaped head, though thinner with relatively small ears and oddly formed nostrils. Others stood below decks, so tall that their furry heads rose above the upper deck through openings in the floor. No two appeared to be the same: they were blond, dark brown, or even black, most with one hump but some with two. Astonished, Nate noticed a baby camel. Scurrying about the animals were handlers every bit as strange as the camels and were speaking languages that Nate had never heard.

To Nate's further amazement, the first camel selected for offloading was placed in a harness, rigged with a clever pulley system. The pulleys would raise the camel until it was completely free of the deck of the *Supply*, suspended from the end of a horizontal frame like a yardarm. Once the camel was lifted, the arm was designed to rotate over the *Fashion* and then gently lower the camel onto the smaller ship.

Major Babcock chose Tullah, a female known for her generally calm disposition. He hoped that her easy-going nature and her special responsiveness to Abdullah would enhance the likelihood of success. Hovering by her side, Abdullah spoke to Tullah gently, rubbing her nose and knees while three sailors turned the crank on the pulley system. Gradually, she lifted a few inches off the deck, while Abdullah stroked her neck and maintained eye contact. Although a bit confused by the sensation of weightlessness, Tullah nevertheless rested quietly in the harness, as Abdullah continued to stay close. Major Babcock circled the camel and rechecked the pulleys for the hundredth time.

"Careful, careful. Raise her nice and easy. No jerking."

The wind continued to rise, and the rocking waves for which the Gulf coast was infamous started their relentless motion. Nate could see trouble brewing before the first camel was elevated even a foot off the deck. When she was high enough to clear the deck railing, the men rotated the arm over the waters of the Bay, up above the *Fashion* that was now close alongside the *Supply*. The men below began to have their first sight of a camel as bits of her came into view. A most startling view it was: large dangling feet, ungainly limbs, and a long furry neck.

"Will you look at that? She's as big as two horses."

"And those teeth look like they could chop your arm off with one bite."

"Wonder what she weighs."

"Can't say that I've ever seen such an ugly critter."

"If she looks to come crashing down on us, I don't plan to be the one underneath her, that's for damn sure."

"Yeah, and there's a whole shipload of them. Let's get goin' so we can move 'em and then be rid of 'em."

"At least this one looks pretty quiet. I bet my horse wouldn't take so well to bein' hung about like that."

Despite the ingenious design of the pulley system, once the camel was rotated at right angles to the *Supply*, the displacement of weight caused the ship to tilt slightly toward the *Fashion*. Just then, a wave pitched the ship further and the camel swung out over the *Fashion*. The *Supply* slid into the trough, sending Tullah flying back. With the rocking of the waves, the camel became a gigantic pendulum. Even for Tullah, this was too much, and she let out a piercing scream. Nate and Amos later swore that the sound was ghoulish.

The arc sketched by the suspended camel grew wider and higher with each change of direction. Tullah screeched, bellowed, and protested. She struggled to free herself from her bindings. Astounded, Nate watched the camel handlers and seamen as they danced around trying to adjust the pulleys to stabilize her. Nothing worked. The *Fashion* was also rising and falling, usually at odds with the motion of the *Supply*. Amos cursed at the wheel while Captain Turner shouted commands on deck. The chances of successfully lightering the camel onto the *Fashion* seemed almost nil.

Major Babcock was horrified. "Get her back on board, get her back! We can't risk having her injured like this. It's far too dangerous. Get her back! Now!"

"Too dangerous for *her*? We're the ones in danger!" The sailors on board the *Fashion* also grumbled and swore. "Yeah, get us out from under that beast!"

Chaos reigned on the camel ship. Tullah's shrieks had upset the other camels, some of which started howling, too. Several strained at their bindings and attempted to rise. Everyone was shouting. The soldiers and camel men were running from one camel to another, in an effort to prevent one from breaking loose. Meanwhile, Tullah was still in the air.

"Pull the lines in. Rotate that arm back! Lower her gently. No, not now, she hasn't cleared the ship's railing yet. Yes, now. All right."

Tediously, carefully, interminably, the pulleys wound tighter and the camel was successfully brought back on board the *Supply*. Major Babcock was aghast that they had almost lost Tullah and was too distraught to decide what to do next. Captain Turner paced back toward the wheelhouse, while Hassan and Ali rushed to help Abdullah ease the camel onto the boat. The look of disgust etched on Lt. Halter's face conveyed his opinion to any who cared to know.

Tullah was particularly upset by her ordeal, and she had scraped a long wound on her left leg. Her rapid breathing worried Abdullah. He and Hassan soothed and coaxed her while gently releasing the harness. She stood shakily before being escorted back into a resting position onboard. Abdullah was beside himself trying to figure out how to mollify Tullah and tend to her wound. When she finally took some oats and water, he was satisfied that she had survived without serious damage. The camel men hovered over the other camels until their heart-rending noises slowed and eventually ceased. Nate was mesmerized.

When the Captain of the *Fashion* came on board, an animated discussion ensued. Watching the two Captains and Major Babcock, whose color was rising, Nate could see that Amos was frantically trying to extricate himself from this impossible situation. Keeping one eye on his friend, Nate focused the other on Alex. He had noticed Alex the moment he boarded, and although curious, had been too absorbed with the camels to pay much attention. While the debate among the captains raged, Nate tried to guess who Alex was and what he was doing on the camel ship. When Captain Turner declared that there would be no further lightering attempts today, Amos turned quickly and signaled to Nate, who would have to wait to answer his questions about Alex. Nate followed Amos as they left the ship abruptly.

Amos cursed, "I'll be damned if that wasn't the worst mess!"

Throwing his weight into the rowing, Nate knew better than to say anything. He guessed what Amos would be touchy about being blamed for problems with the camel ship. Although sympathetic to his friend, Nate was enthralled with the camels. He thought them marvelous and couldn't wait to come back to the ship tomorrow. Nevertheless, he, too, worried about how to get the animals lightered.

GALVESTON, TEXAS, MAY 2, 1856

THE SUN WAS BARELY breaking the horizon, but Elizabeth could hear her parents arguing. Their voices rose and became strident, then dropped to a whisper. Vaguely, she wondered what they were upset about, but she really couldn't care less. Her head was filled with echoes of music, tastes of champagne, colors of ball gowns and memories of flirtation from last night's May Day celebrations. She smiled and rolled over, intending to stay in bed until noon. Whatever was bothering her parents was not her concern. At the thought of William Quig, she giggled out loud. Soon after pulling the covers back over her head, she fell fast asleep.

Pacing anxiously back and forth in her room, Sylvia McDermott cried, "Move to San Antonio? You can't be serious!"

"Perfectly serious, my dear. I know it appears impetuous."

"Impetuous! It appears as if you are deranged. How can we possibly do this, and in only a few days' time? It's simply not feasible, even if it were a wise choice."

Quentin McDermott allowed his wife quite a bit of latitude to express herself, but he was rapidly losing patience with this discussion. His mind was made up. "The last two fever seasons have been particularly deadly, and it's always worse at the coast. I want you and the children away from here. Also, I have business in San Antonio, and I want you to set up a house for us there. Of course we'll keep this house, but I need a domicile in San Antonio. And, I tell you this only because I trust that you will repeat it to no one." He paused for her to nod her assent. "It's politics. I foresee the possibility of war and want us to have a refuge if it should come to that."

Stopped in her tracks, Sylvia sank to the bed. "Could it come to that?"

"I believe so. Not this year, but within the next few years maybe. A good number of Texans wish we'd never joined the United States and would be happy to separate again."

"But, Quentin, Texas statehood has been good for us. The past ten years have brought a bounty beyond our dreams. All your businesses have thrived."

"Yes, we've prospered, but others have not fared so well. Competition has increased since statehood. Outsiders from Atlanta, New Orleans, and even the northeast are running local folks out of business. You may remember that Jasper Priestly closed his shop a few months ago."

"Jasper Priestly had no more business sense than a mouse, and he drank what little profits he made."

"I know, but a Philadelphia-based company has taken over. In the days of the Republic, it would have been someone with roots in Texas. These northerners are a different breed altogether."

"Careful, darling, you're talking to a northerner by birth." Smiling, Sylvia tried unsuccessfully to lighten the mood.

"Yes, dear, but I was referring to business matters. The economy of the northern states is based on industry, while ours relies on agriculture. The relationship can be mutually beneficial or can become unbalanced as the nation grows. We have reason to fear northern companies taking over. They don't understand our way of life."

"What do you mean exactly?"

Quentin sighed again. This was becoming a long explanation just to get Sylvia to start packing for the move to San Antonio. But he appreciated his wife's lively curiosity, so he persevered. "Life isn't easy for our farmers these days. It goes without saying that a successful cotton plantation requires slaves. There's not enough natural reproduction, prices are going up, and fresh stock is needed. We both know that slaves ships come to Texas from the Caribbean, even though the trade isn't legal."

"Isn't legal and hasn't been for fifty years!"

"Sylvia, the point is, under the Republic nobody paid any attention. Everybody saw the economic need. But there are more US government patrols now, which means greater risk and still higher prices. On top of that, people worry about the abolitionists."

Sylvia sighed. "Oh, Quentin, not that again. Surely that's not enough to fight a war over."

Sylvia's brother in Pennsylvania was vehemently opposed to slavery, and although she had doubts about the institution, she had become a slaveholder when she married Quentin. She had agonized, rationalized, and then gradually accepted slavery as part and parcel of her life. Nevertheless, the politics of slavery risked dividing her from Quentin, so she studiously avoided the subject. She assuaged her lingering guilt by making every effort to treat her house slaves well, fully aware that she had no control over what happened at Quentin's inland plantations.

"Yes, I'm afraid it might be."

"But even if there is war, it could be years away. Surely we must stay here to let Elizabeth get settled. Another year should see it done."

Marriage for Elizabeth was one topic that Quentin McDermott did not wish to address. His daughter was precious to him, and he was determined to see her well situated. He had been less than thrilled with at least one of the potential suitors who had approached their daughter at her debut last night, but he would not trouble Sylvia with that now.

"I've been planning this move for some time, but I didn't want to spoil the May Day celebrations. Sylvia, you know

I want the best for Elizabeth, but there's no need to rush it. She's only sixteen."

"Well, Jackson Quig's boy, William, has taken an interest. He's grown into a handsome lad and plans to join his father's business. He gets along nicely with Elizabeth, and we've known his parents for years. I would hate to miss an opportunity."

"I know these things are of monumental concern to you, but compared to the other points I've made, this one is not as pressing."

"You say there's no rush for Elizabeth's sake, and yet you're rushing us out of town. This all seems too precipitous. Why must we go now?"

"Because I do not want my wife and children at the mercy of just any caravan going into the interior. You can travel with your cousin and the camels."

"My cousin? How can you know that it's possible for us to go with him?" She scrutinized her husband, and he flinched. "No, Quentin, you didn't! You've already spoken to him about it. I can't believe you would tell him before telling me!"

"Sylvia, my darling, I had to propose the idea to see if it was feasible, and indeed, the Major is willing to oblige."

Sylvia thought fast. She sensed the change in Quentin's tone that signaled a final decision had been rendered. Anything she said or did now she would have to live with for a long time.

"Who will go with us?"

"I thought you might want Antoine and Esther. I'll keep Rebecca at the house, and Moses will continue to deliver provisions. The other house slaves can go to the Brazos plantations."

"All right then, but I'll also need Samuel and Agnes, and we can't leave Esther's two children. We should have at least two men with us, and I want two women to manage the household. What about Precious? Samuel is quite fond of her."

Quentin sighed. It would be easier to travel with fewer people, but Sylvia was right. The household would need to be set up properly. "Everyone you mentioned except

Precious. That's one too many. You must take the minimum that you need."

"I can tell you that Samuel isn't going to take this well."

"Sylvia, my God. I don't care whether Samuel takes this well or not. If you have any doubts about him, he can go to the fields with Precious, and you can have Moses or someone else."

"No, I need Samuel. He works well with Antoine. Please, send Rebecca to the fields. Keep Precious here with you, and she and Samuel can be together after we return from San Antonio."

Quentin sighed more deeply. His wife imagined that she was planning a marriage for her slaves. It was a tricky business, letting slaves feel that they could have a normal life. Their disappointment was all the greater if they began to conceive of certain privileges as their right. Better they should understand from childhood that life was dictated by others. In the end, he supposed that giving in to Sylvia on this was a small compromise.

"All right, my dear. Precious stays at the house."

"Quentin, as long as we've been married, you have never surprised me with something like this, nor have you been so secretive about your business dealings. It worries me."

"I know. But you must trust me in this. As soon as I can tell you more, I will do so. Sylvia, I need you to be strong, for the sake of the children."

Sylvia promptly went downstairs and summoned Antoine. Surprised to be called to the kitchen so early in the morning, he suspected trouble. He cast a surreptitious glance at Esther, who shrugged. She had no more idea than the man in the moon what was coming. It was plain as day that Miz Sylvia was all in a tizzy, with a look in her eye that meant long hard work for everyone.

Esther stood thinking. It was not that Miz Sylvia shirked, and Esther appreciated that. No, the mistress was not afraid of a little sweat and elbow grease. It was the never-ending nature of what might be coming that daunted. All the usual chores of cooking and cleaning had to be done without fail, no matter how many supplemental tasks might be assigned. They had known mornings like this when Miz Sylvia was in the mood for spring cleaning. But something felt different today.

In less than a minute Miz Sylvia had made her wishes known, and Antoine was dispatched to the carriage house to search for every trunk and valise that the McDermotts owned. No explanation had been offered, but there was an urgency in Miz Sylvia's voice that Antoine had not heard since one of the children had come down with whooping cough a few years back. He felt his empty stomach tighten with anxiety.

Esther's instructions were to make a special breakfast for the children, and then to take an inventory of all the cooking supplies and utensils. As she scrambled eggs, sliced the bacon, and whipped together the biscuit dough, she felt a great unease. Massa Quentin came bounding downstairs, grabbed some coffee and exited the back door. His mumbled greeting was a far cry from his usual banter. He often took his breakfast at the worktable in the kitchen, where he would chat cordially with Esther while she cooked and served him. Cordial is exactly what he wasn't today.

In an effort to keep her mind off unanswerable questions, Esther started mentally to create the inventory that Miz Sylvia wanted. Of all the slaves, she alone was literate. Despite the law prohibiting slaves in Texas from learning to read and write, Miz Sylvia had taught her, having convinced her reluctant husband that an ability to read lists would allow Esther to oversee the others. Quentin believed that literacy was insidious in a slave community, and though it might be useful for Sylvia's household management, he thought it reckless. This was one of those deviations he had permitted on condition that neither Sylvia nor Esther should speak of it to anyone. Esther had agreed, but in the quiet of the evening she taught the ABCs to her children, Sally and Mabel.

"Three fry pans: two big and one small; four pots; one Dutch oven; four iron biscuit molds." Esther was engrossed, when an unwanted thought assailed her. "Why does Miz Sylvia need an inventory of the kitchen?" Unable to conceive of a plausible answer, she was so distracted she almost forgot to salt the eggs.

As Antoine shuttled back and forth, working with Samuel to heft the trunks onto the side veranda in a neatly stacked row, Esther pulled him aside. "Antoine, my mind is troubled. What you think they doin'?"

"Looks like they plannin' to move. You heard nuthin' else?"

"Nuthin'. But she set breakfast in the drawin' room and sent Agnes to wake the chillun. Massa Quentin already gone to town. I don't like this. Sounds like trouble, trouble."

"Samuel and them askin' all kinda questions, too. Everybody scared."

Esther served the family in the drawing room and retired to the kitchen, where she stood waiting to be called and straining to hear what might be said. Miz Sylvia spoke so quietly that Esther couldn't follow. Then suddenly Elizabeth wailed as Zeke and Zach shouted, "No, Mama, no!" All manner of whining was interspersed with shouts of, "So soon!" and "Please, no!" Elizabeth began sobbing loudly.

Antoine passed by the back door again, and Esther whispered. "She say somethin' 'bout movin' to San Antonio. Lord deliver us!"

"San Antonio! My God, Esther. All of 'em? When? And us?"

"Seems soon, but I ain't made out nuthin' else."

For Antoine, Esther and the rest of the slaves, the next few days were a hurricane, fierce and unrelenting. Fatigue flooded them like a rising tide. There was no shelter.

The children didn't help matters. Knowing that their father would tolerate nothing less than complete cooperation, they struggled to be quiet and agreeable at dinner. The price of that effort was wild outbursts during the day, mostly directed at the slaves. Zeke and Zach were as unpredictable as leaves in the storm. One minute they would feel inspired by the adventure, excited to see San Antonio and intrigued by the camels. Then they would think of being away from friends for the whole summer and possibly even longer. Afraid of their father's wrath, they complained not to their parents, but to Antoine, Samuel and Agnes. They shouted and abused. Even Esther, normally a favorite, was not immune.

"Lord almighty, those boys like to kill me. I ain't had no respect from them since their mama told 'em 'bout movin'. They wasn't raised this way, and it sure is a trial to me to see 'em like this." Esther wiped her forehead as she looked up from the kitchen utensils she was packing.

Antoine replied, "They feelin' their roots bein' ripped up, Esther. They don't know what's comin,' and they can't say they's afraid. That's how it is with boys."

"I know, but my roots bein' ripped up, too. I was born into this family. All thirty-two years of my life, I been with them, and my mama before that. Massa Quentin used to mind me sometimes when my mama was cookin'. He always looked out for me and mine, like he fixed things for me and Henry and our babies."

"I only been at the house a few years, but I'm as worried as you, Esther. Listen, you gotta hide your upset. Miz Sylvia tryin' real hard to hide her upset, too. You help her in that way, and I know she'll try to help you."

"Thanks, Antoine. You have a good way of calmin' a person."

"Esther, you're the rock here."

Esther sighed again. "Missy 'Lizbeth is havin' a rough time, too. Ain't nobody in this house in their right mind."

"Ain't that the truth!" Antoine shook his head and went back to work.

"Esther, come here at once!" Sylvia shouted at the exact instant that Elizabeth also called her.

Esther sighed, ran part way upstairs, and called, "Sorry, Missy 'Lizbeth, your mama's wantin' me. I'll be right along." She dashed back down, arriving breathless.

"No, no Agnes!" Agnes shrank as Miz Sylvia raised her voice. "Wrap each piece of crystal separately, in soft cloths. Then you can put them into the carton. Make sure you use enough straw padding. They must travel well, and nothing must break!"

Agnes was terrified. The louder Miz Sylvia spoke, the less Agnes heard. She was practically paralyzed with fear. What would happen to her? This was the only life she knew. She could not be a field hand. Moses had told her what it was like to work cotton and live in shacks.

"Esther, you must explain to Agnes how to do this and she must do it right. I know she's slow, but there's no time for dallying here. Agnes, pay attention to Esther and make sure you don't break anything!" Sylvia departed abruptly and went upstairs to see how the boys were packing.

Agnes looked down to see her hands shaking. Yes, she was slow. She knew that. She tried to understand what was happening and could find no way.

"Agnes, you mind Miz Sylvia, now. You know what you s'posed to do? Yes? Good, now get to it."

"Esther, you never talk to me like this before."

"Agnes, you fool. Nuthin' like this ever happen to any of us before. Now you mind what you're told. Whatever Miz Sylvia ask, you do it, and you do it just so. Understand?"

She nodded, tears forming in her eyes.

"None of that, Agnes. Don't let Miz Sylvia see that. Everyone cryin' round here ain't gonna help none. Now you wrap those glasses. Be quick and be careful."

Alone in her room, surrounded by the detritus of the whirlwind of the last two days, Elizabeth was as confused as she had ever been. She could not believe her father was doing this to her, the day after the social season had begun. She had plans for Sunday picnics, outings to the beach, and at least two dances in the next month. It seemed as if her life divided into before and after. Before her father had decided to send them away, her life had been piano lessons, sewing, reading, and most of all, preparing for the May Day celebrations. She had been thrilled with the day, walking into the room on her father's arm, hearing her name called. Her dress was perfect. The off-the-shoulder cut had been alluring without revealing, and the pale yellow contrasted with her ebony hair. People looked at her as if they thought her beautiful.

How she had loved the dancing! After gliding to the waltzes in the arms of one handsome boy, she was released into the arms of another for a rousing polka. Elizabeth had commanded the rapt attention of several admirers who filled her dance card rapidly, and a couple of young men had tried to cut in for a second or third dance. Although she had dutifully danced with the unpleasant boys who approached her simply because she was Quentin McDermott's daughter, she also managed to have more than one circuit of the floor with her favorites. Her mother had praised her, saying she had behaved flawlessly.

It had been the first day of her future as a grown-up woman in the most exciting society she could imagine. Everything was as she had dreamed it since she was a little girl. Elizabeth burst into tears. Now she was living in the "after" part of her life, an inconceivable postscript. She failed to put words to it. Clothing lay strewn across the bed; her piano music was stacked in a corner along with a selection of books; and her mother had just told her to reduce the number of dresses she planned to take. She had no idea what to expect, but she knew very well what she felt: emptiness, loss, and fear. What she most felt, she suppressed with all her strength. She must not show anger.

Her parents had become like bizarre and unpredictable imposters in the house. Her usually gregarious father left early and remained absent until dinner. His evening conversation consisted in grilling each family member as to the progress that had been made during the day. No one dared to ask him questions. Elizabeth badly wanted to know why he was not coming with them to San Antonio, but her father offered no explanation. Her lively mother became meek and obliging, answering her father's questions in a perfunctory tone. During the day, she kept up a banal undercurrent of meaningless chatter that Elizabeth thought was meant to encourage, but had the opposite effect. She seemed to be play-acting according to some expectation that Elizabeth failed to comprehend.

Elizabeth followed sullenly in her mother's wake. She sorted and packed and rearranged according to her mother's instructions. In between chores, she accompanied her mother on an untold number of tedious farewell calls. After each visit, Elizabeth became more melancholy and more annoyed. On one of these sorties, her mother complained briefly of a shooting pain in her neck and shoulders. Only then did it occur to Elizabeth that her mother's aloofness might be her way of coping with everyone's looming apprehension, that perhaps her mother was grappling with her own riotous anxiety. Although Elizabeth vowed to be more accommodating, she remained testy and unable to keep from making sharp remarks.

The only enjoyable thing she could do was brush her mother's hair. Every evening since Elizabeth had been a toddler, she had been brought to her mother after Esther or Agnes had helped her wash and prepare for bed. Quentin McDermott had never seen his mother, aunt or sisters brush each other's hair. That had always been a maid's job in his household, but he could see that Sylvia cherished this intimacy with her daughter. Observing his wife seated with the tiny girl's thick black hair flowing through her fingers, watching her pull the brush in smooth rhythmic motion, he sensed Sylvia's contentment and was glad. When Elizabeth was a little older, she had asked to brush her mother's hair, too, and the ritual became firmly established in the family.

Elizabeth clung to the evening hair brushing as the single moment of calm in their chaos. She wished her mother would talk about their plans. Surely at sixteen, she was old enough to be her mother's confidante during this unsettling time. Her mother brushed in silence. Elizabeth wanted to complain about her father's decision. Instead, so as not to upset her mother, she stuck to simple questions.

"Mama, what can you tell me about San Antonio?"

"I've never been there, but it's inland, so there's no bay and no ships. It's a very old city, settled by the Spanish more than a hundred years ago. You will meet people whose families have been there for generations. I am told that the women are beautiful, with dark hair and eyes, but fashions will likely be different. Most of my information comes from Mrs. Eberly. She used to live in Austin and San Antonio."

"Tell me more about Mrs. Eberly."

"Mrs. Eberly owns one of the best hotels in Indianola, and we'll be staying there. She's successful in business, but more than that she is a hero of Texas, or I guess I should say heroine. She's known as the heroine of the Archive Wars."

"The what, Mama?"

"It was in 1842, when you were just a toddler, and the Republic of Texas was only six years old. That conniver Sam Houston tried to sneak the official archives out of Austin. The old thief. He said he was taking them to 'safekeeping', but everyone knew that once the archives were out of Austin, he could move the capital wherever he wished. Mrs. Angelina Eberly happened to spy them at the evil deed and fired a cannon to warn everyone. Because of her, the archives stayed where they belong and Austin is still our capital."

"Oh my goodness! Mrs. Eberly knows how to shoot a cannon?"

"Apparently she knows a great many things. Your father thinks very highly of her. That's why he has entrusted us to her care. She has also arranged for a house for us in San Antonio."

"Ooh, Mama, what does the house look like? I know it's only for a summer, but will it be similar to our house?"

"That I doubt. The architecture in San Antonio is completely different, supposedly with a Spanish flavor. Maybe we can ask Papa to describe our house at dinner tomorrow night. He has been to San Antonio three times."

"Do you really think we'll get to travel with Cousin Babcock and the camels?"

"Your father says so. Imagine that, we'll be part of the first camel caravan in the United States!"

"Yes, it's almost like we'll be part of a circus parade!" At that thought, both women laughed, and their worries receded for the moment.

MATAGORDA ISLAND, TEXAS

E ACH OF THE NEXT two days, Amos and Nate boarded the *Supply* and listened to the officers debate the wisdom of lightering. Amos told the Captain straight out that he would not serve as pilot as long as this stiff wind blew and urged him to avoid any place along the coast that would be plagued with the same persistent wave patterns. At last it was decided that both the *Supply* and the *Fashion* would run for the Balize at the mouth of the Mississippi, nearly all the way back to New Orleans. There they could transfer the camels to the *Fashion* in protected water. Eager to be done with this assignment, Amos Prudeau maneuvered the *Supply* back out through the pass, skillfully avoiding the sandbars and shallow areas.

Major Babcock motioned Alex to join him on deck, where he stood in serious conversation with Lieutenant Halter.

"Alex, Lieutenant Halter has volunteered to remain here to help Captain Van Steendam prepare for the camels. He may need assistance, and I have proposed that you accompany him to render whatever service he may require. We need all the sailors and the camel crew to stay with the ship."

This was absolutely that last thing that Alex expected or wanted: to be stuck with Lieutenant Halter with no one else around. And for how long? But something in his Uncle's tone suggested that no objection would be accepted.

"Certainly, sir."

"Good. You will both descend now with the pilot, who will arrange for your conveyance to the mainland. After we lighter the camels, Captain Turner will take the *Supply* to the Mediterranean for the second camel shipment, and we should be back with the *Fashion* within a fortnight."

Alex sat quietly in Amos Prudeau's rowboat, watching the *Supply* retreat as they moved towards Matagorda Island through the never-ending swells. Even though he had lived on or near the ship for the better part of a year, it was striking to see her from below. He suddenly felt small and alone. He had been so excited to reach Texas and to see the camels safely to their staging area. But here he was, with two strangers and the least agreeable member of the crew, bobbing along to shore while the camels, his uncle, Hassan, and everyone who mattered sailed off into the Gulf.

Amos Prudeau pulled hard on the oars, frustrated beyond measure that he was now saddled with responsibility for these two. Since it was dusk, he would have to find lodging for his charges tonight in Saluria, but early the next day, he would get them passage to Indianola.

Amos looked over at Nate, who tugged the oars steadily and without complaint. Of medium height, muscular, with long brown hair and small dark eyes that hinted at a quick wit, Nate worked hard and carried his own weight. He was not as quiet as his grandfather, but did not trouble a man with unnecessary talk. The boy was trustworthy.

Amos could not help but compare Nate to Alex. Although Alex appeared to be at least nineteen or twenty, he was clearly ill at ease. Taller than Nate, he somehow seemed less fit. He clutched his bag in his lap and had a skittish look about him. Amos wondered if he feared the open water. Unlikely. The lad had just completed a sea voyage longer than Amos had ever done. It had to be something else. He guessed that Alex was in the habit of having access to authority and someone to protect him. Amos took him for a sissy.

Lt. Halter was a typical Yankee, aloof and somewhat discomfited. Amos paid him no mind, other than to give him the attentions befitting his rank. He had the feeling that Lt. Halter was not one to be crossed, so he would give the man no reason to be offended. Two Yankees, both rich. He would be well rid of them.

Nate was also studying their passengers, especially Alex. Nate had not planned for anyone like Alex to be involved with the camels. Would he be a hindrance or could he help in some way? Major Babcock was Alex's uncle, which meant a high-class upbringing, certainly in comparison with his own. Feeling a twinge of resentment, Nate knew he would not tolerate slights or arrogance from Alex. When they approached the beach, Alex jumped out to help drag the boat ashore. Surprised that Alex had not waited in the boat with Lt. Halter, Nate thought he might have to reassess his first impression. But he had little time to do so, because the Lieutenant was already barking commands.

"Mind the baggage! I don't want it getting wet."

Amos, Nate, and Alex struggled to unload Lt. Halter's luggage. Unlike Alex, who had brought only a lightly packed bag, the Lieutenant had brought all his possessions, consisting of his sea trunk, a large carpetbag, and several satchels full of papers.

"There now. That does it. And where will I be spending the night, if you please, Mr. Prudeau? I can see it's too late to attempt a crossing to Indianola."

Amos barely suppressed his irritation. "Right this way, sir. We'll see if Miz Arnoth has a place for you at her inn. It's small but clean. We'll take the bags and send someone for the trunk." He hefted the bag onto his shoulder and marched off. Lt. Halter grabbed his satchels and hurried behind. Neither man noticed that Nate and Alex were not following.

Alex had quickly deduced that a town this size would have only one inn and figured he could find it on his own soon enough. Besides, he wanted to keep a distance from Lt. Halter. Hoisting his own bag out of the rowboat, he set it on the beach and turned to Nate.

"We weren't properly introduced. I'm Alex Babcock."

"Nate Wilkers." They shook hands.

"I'm trying to figure out what's going on here. You seem to know quite a lot about the place. I wonder if we could get some grub."

Nate was flummoxed. He had no thought to linger with Alex, but perhaps there was some useful information to be had. "All right, as soon as we get rid of this trunk."

They waited in silence for a while before Alex started the conversation. "Say, Nate, while we were stuck out in the Gulf, we saw a lighthouse. The whole of the Texas coast is as dark as moonless midnight, except for Galveston and here."

"First light was four years ago."

"And what about the paint? Most lighthouses where I grew up are white. Those stripes are something."

"Yup, red, white and black horizontal. Painted them the first year. With all the white sands around here, it stands out better in the daytime."

"Really good looking, and tall, too."

"Fifty-five feet." Although Nate was fed up with life at the lighthouse, he was nevertheless proud of it and of his grandfather's role in building it.

"It looks taller than the one at Galveston."

Nate frowned. "No, Galveston's is taller, but ours was first lit. Do you want to see it?"

"Oh yeah, can we do that?"

"Sure. We can stay there tonight, and you can meet up with your Lieutenant in the morning."

"Stay there?"

"My grandfather is the caretaker. I live there."

"Hey, that's great."

Nate spoke to the boy who came with a wagon for Lt. Halter's trunk. "Take this to Miz Arnoth's place and tell Amos that the other passenger is stayin' with me. Thanks."

They retrieved Nate's horse. Alex swung up behind him, and they set out toward the lighthouse that towered over the tip of Matagorda Island. Across Pass Caballo, Matagorda Peninsula stretched its narrow finger toward the island, as if trying to reconnect to its severed self. The Gulf of Mexico displayed a turquoise vista, and inside the pass, Matagorda Bay opened the gateway to Texas. The luminescence of the water on all sides beautified the flattest landscape that Alex had ever encountered.

Atop the lighthouse, Jeremy Blackstone watched the sea. The tossing waves broke mildly on the beach below but gathered into confusing angles and altitudes as they converged on Pass Caballo. Rising in frothy peaks, they crashed into each other with spray flying in all directions. Lit by a low-angled sun, the spray briefly became a curtain of tiny lights before sinking, extinguished, into the roiling indigo below. Jeremy didn't move. Each of the crashing waves brought a different outcome. Each one offered a different light, color, and direction. And yet they were the same: indistinct, repetitive, and pointless. He was convinced that without Nate, his life would be pointless. He stared at the waves, all the same yet all different. Some droplets of water, trapped in a kind of centrifugal force, went round and round in the same spot, while others broke free to strike the land or return to the sea. He knew that Nate must have the freedom to strike land or lose himself in the wider ocean.

After years of defining his life by how much Nate needed him to survive, Jeremy was coming to understand that now he needed Nate. White clouds streaked high across the sky from the southwest. Delicate as the tracings of a feather brush, their soft design belied the strong winds they signaled. Jeremy sighed. Both the *Supply* and the *Fashion* had left the bay, probably unable to lighter the camels. Perhaps that was an omen. Perhaps Nate would not really leave. But he knew that this weather was not an omen, merely a gift of time, a delay to be used wisely.

Jeremy startled to see Nate returning with someone riding behind. Nate had never been one to bring home strays.

Deliberately he descended the spiral staircase. "Howdy, boys. Grub's on."

Inside the caretaker's cottage, Jeremy wordlessly whipped together a cornbread batter and poured it into a cast iron cauldron of stew that had been simmering for hours. Covering it with a heavy lid, he turned to set the table. Instead of the simple split log table and sparse furniture that one might expect, the room had a polished hardwood table with turned legs and claw feet. That had been Hilde's doing. More than two years since Hilde died, Jeremy still ached. He stifled those thoughts and regarded the boys.

Nate almost immediately regretted having brought Alex here. His grandfather's silent attentions seemed cold and appraising, dampening the excitement he had felt during the day. In a voice slightly too loud, Nate launched into the introductions.

"Grandpa, this is Alex Babcock from the *Supply*. Alex, meet my grandfather, Jeremy Blackstone."

"Pleased to meet you, sir. And an honor to visit the lighthouse."

"Figured you was from the *Supply*. You boys can bed down here tonight."

"Thank you, sir. It's been a long journey."

Jeremy nodded. Something about Jeremy's quietness put Alex off. His own natural ebullience subsided as if a fog had rolled in. Alex sensed no hostility but was completely unused to a lack of conversation, particularly after all the noise and closeness of the ship. He already missed his uncle and Hassan.

"Alex was askin' about the lighthouse." Seeing that his grandfather wasn't going to say anything, Nate sighed and continued. "Congress set aside fifteen thousand dollars for two lighthouses. Five years later, when the cast iron finally arrived from back East, we put the sections together and Grandpa lit up the reflectin' lamps four days before Christmas. Then the feastin' started. That was somethin', wasn't it Grandpa?"

"Sure was, son. Sure was some Christmas that year."

Jeremy smiled with the recollection, and then the smile faded. His second wife, Hilde, had cooked for days, preparing for the dignitaries who came for the illumination. After the formalities, the party had moved into Saluria. Jeremy let the 14-year old Nate wander around with his friends while he and Hilde ate, drank, and danced all night, taking a break for some rollicking good sex. He should be happy to remember that night, but all he felt was loss.

Hilde had been among the wave of German immigrants that started arriving in 1844. Their enthusiasm for Texas collapsed upon realizing that no lodging was ready to receive them nor was transportation available to the promised lands. Sanitation and food were scarce, disease prevalent. When Hilde discovered that Jeremy paid Mrs. Blauvelt to care for Nate, she convinced him that he needed a wife. Over time a real affection grew between them, and Hilde provided him an anchor of steadfastness that he defined as love. Her laughter brought an end to his grief. She taught both him and Nate how to read and figure, and together they built a life. As if to spite Jeremy's joyful confidence in his rebuilt existence, Hilde succumbed during the fever season two years ago. Once more, and against the odds, Nate survived.

Jeremy cut the corn batter that had now baked into light, moist dumplings and placed a chunk on each plate. Next to it he ladled a rich stew of beef, carrots, onions, potatoes, and herbs from the garden that he had kept after Hilde died. He had always been a cook, fending for himself on the road and then feeding Nate, but he had learned a great deal from Hilde. Tending Hilde's herbs brought him a measure of peace in the moments when he most missed her.

"Son, did you see them camels?"

"Gosh yes, Grandpa, and amazing beasts they are, too, but they couldn't lighter 'em. Too much swell in the bay today. They decided to make a run back to the Balize and do the lightering there."

"So far?"

"Grandpa, it's got to be dead calm water to do this. You see, they swing 'em into the air to offload."

"Swing 'em into the air?" Jeremy's skepticism was so palpable that both boys burst out laughing, and Jeremy joined them.

"Tell me while we eat."

"Sir, this is delicious!

Alex forgot his reticence and Nate his desire to be secretive, as they outdid each other in recounting scenes from the afternoon. Jeremy listened closely. He ascertained that no one in Texas as yet had any favorable impression of the camels. Amos Prudeau would be annoyed that he had been put in a potentially compromising position, and the seamen on the *Fashion* would surely regale everyone up and down the coast with descriptions of the unlikely creatures.

With a little whiskey, Alex relaxed completely and told tales of Tunis, Constantinople, Alexandria, and Cairo. He spoke of Hassan only in connection with the other Arabs and Turks. Not a single word did he utter about the incident in Galveston.

In the middle of the conversation, Jeremy stood up and walked toward the lighthouse. "Nate, you know where the blankets are. Checkin' the lights. Might stay up there awhile. Not sure about this wind."

The next morning, after a breakfast of fried eggs, biscuits, and gravy, Nate and Alex made ready to leave. "Take two horses, boys. I'll pick 'em up at the dock later."

"Thank you, sir. I sure do hope the camels will be all right. I'll be happy when I see them walking on Texas soil. Thanks again for the excellent grub."

"You're welcome."

"Grandpa, there's some things I need to take care of over at Indianola."

"No mind, son. I'll expect you when I see you." Earlier that morning, Jeremy had noticed that the locket containing a likeness of Nate's mother and father no longer hung on his bedpost. But his grandson had not yet revealed his intentions.

As the two lads rode off toward town, Jeremy was fixed to the spot, pondering. He wasn't one to plan. More often, he was comfortable letting situations unfold on their own. He was in no mood to make decisions, especially ones that could have life-changing consequences. But Nate was up to something with the camels, so he would have to divine what to do before it was too late. Possibilities slowly began to take shape. Every one of them required him to leave the lighthouse.

A fussy wind was still blowing off the Gulf. Time would help him decide. It would be ten days, maybe two weeks before the *Fashion* returned with the camels. He would wait a spell for the newcomers to settle in over at Indianola and for Nate to work out his thinking. Then he would go visit Captain Van Steendam at the Government Depot.

Saluria was even worse than Lt. Halter had expected. The walk through town, if one could call it a town, revealed a few single-story buildings that barely rose above the sandy patches separating the street from tide pools and swamp. He surmised that one stiff wind could blow the whole place away. There were a couple of docks, a few drunken seamen, and an overall air of desolation. Sea salt covered everything. A pathetically gaudy sign was the only thing that distinguished the inn from the other nondescript buildings. The pilot Amos Prudeau escorted him to the door of the inn and promptly disappeared.

Mrs. Arnoth, chubby, disheveled, and wiping her hands on her apron, welcomed him. The inn of which she was so proud consisted of a single room below for sitting and eating, with its mirror image above for sleeping. The upstairs room held one raised platform covered in straw mattresses, relatively clean, but obviously heavily used. Residents set their boots at the foot of this mass bed and crawled onto it. When Mrs. Arnoth asserted that the bed could accommodate ten men, he inquired about a private room.

"Sorry, Herr Kapitein." Mrs. Arnoth called everyone who had the slightest appearance of shipboard authority a captain, and it always came out accented in her native German. "Jah, only this room, but you sleep here, on the end platz, and it will be gute."

Lt. Halter had mixed feelings about immigrants. He knew the country needed more settlers to stave off the Indians, but Mrs. Arnoth's German accent annoyed him.

"Come, come, Herr Kapitein, I give you nice soup for supper."

Reluctantly, Winston faced reality. There was nothing for it except to sleep on the communal bed. Luckily, fate had provided only three bedmates, and he managed to retain the coveted end position. He grudgingly admitted that Mrs. Arnoth's cooking, though simple, was hearty and delicious. A full stomach plus the whiskey he shared with Mr. Arnoth improved his negative impression of Saluria.

When at last he retired, two of his three companions were already snoring in a syncopated cacophony of grunts, whistles, and gurgles to equal the creativity of the best composers. The volume of these intonations could have raised the dead. Restraining a desire to kick the noisemakers, Winston sat on the low wooden footboard at the end of the wide sleeping platform and removed his boots, which he left neatly on the floor. He climbed into his corner position. Aided in ignoring his co-habitants by the quantity of alcohol he had consumed, he began to doze.

As he was drifting off, one of the sleepers suddenly burped, jerked and reversed himself on the bed diagonally. With his feet now perilously close to Winston's head, he swung his arms and groped for the chamber pot. He flopped on the bed, kicking and wriggling, and lunged for the pot that tipped over and rolled to Winston's end of the room. Clattering on the floorboards, the chamber pot knocked over Winston's carefully arranged boots. Mercifully, the pot was empty of any substantial contents.

The two other occupants, now revived, grumbled and rolled around, trying to avoid the flailing legs of their companion. Diving headfirst off the end of the bed, the nameless bedmate retrieved the wayward chamber pot, blasphemed loudly, and pulled it closer. He then heaved most of his supper and whiskey into the vessel, with only a little spilled on the floor. The stench of vomit overwhelmed the room. The other two cursed their friend, and one of them punched him.

"Look what you've gone and done. I swear I ain't gonna drink with ya no more if ya cain't hold it. Goddamn, it stinks in here."

The perpetrator wiped his mouth on his sleeve. Proud of his accuracy, he declared loudly, 'I got aim, ain't I? Even drunk, I got aim!" He belched deeply, rolled over and within a few minutes resumed his rhythm in the trio of snores.

Winston pulled his knees up and squeezed tighter against the wall in the corner, keeping his back to the others. Then it started to rain. He shifted position to avoid the drips from the leaky roof only to find himself closer to the bad breath of the nearest sleeper. Apparently untroubled by the rain, the other three slept on, letting the rain provide the staccato to their snoring melodies.

As he remembered it all this morning, Winston shuddered. Not even Mrs. Arnoth's home-cured bacon and freshly-baked biscuits could change the reality: he had been unceremoniously dumped ashore by Major Babcock. Morosely, he wondered whether being left behind was a form of punishment. Maybe he should have modulated his comments about the lightering fiasco. Perhaps 'incompetence' had been a poor choice of words, but he could not keep silent when the Major's blind enthusiasm for the camels led to faulty decisions.

His thoughts spiraled downward. He had been assigned to help Captain Van Steendam complete the Major's plans for the camels on land. What if those preparations were as badly conceived as the lightering? He would be obliged to correct any poor planning that he discovered, but what if the Major objected upon his return? Perhaps the Major was testing his loyalty, a sentiment that eluded Lt. Halter when it came to the camel project generally and to Major Babcock personally. He reconsidered each fact. In the end, he concluded that he was reading too much into the situation. His embarkation was likely just another of Major Babcock's spur-of-the-moment actions.

"Another biscuit?" Mrs. Arnoth tried desperately to please her despondent guest.

"No, thank you." He mustered a polite reply, but no smile.

"We have plenty. Please another one?"

"No, thank you."

"You feel fine, Herr Kapitein? You not like eggs?"

"I'm fine, thank you. I would like more coffee, please."

"Jah, jah, coffee is gute."

Winston's head throbbed. He feared that he might be coming down with another fever, but then decided the cause could be cheap whiskey and lack of sleep. Despite his queasy stomach, he forced himself to tackle his breakfast with more earnestness, causing Mrs. Arnoth to smile benevolently. She watched as he ate a piece of bacon and tasted his eggs. At about the third bite, however, he paused so suddenly that Mrs. Arnoth jumped.

Lt. Halter had remembered Alex. Last night a messenger boy reported that Alex was with the pilot's apprentice. He was glad that he hadn't shared his primitive accommodations with Alex, but he did have some measure of responsibility for the Major's nephew. He settled the bill and headed for the dock, hoping to find Alex and yearning for a better hotel in Indianola. A persistent itch led him to imagine that his clothes were infested. He longed for a proper wash.

Although it was early, the sun was already converting last night's rain into a soupy, humid mix. Fog clung to the low-lying areas like a series of steaming cauldrons. Alex wiped the sweat from his forehead, adjusted his hat, and frowned as he watched Lt. Halter coming toward him. He had seen that look before. Never had Alex met someone so skilled at taking a good situation and making it bad. Unconsciously, Alex started to turn away from the Lieutenant, but realizing his duty, stepped forward as nonchalantly as possible.

"Good morning, sir. I hope you are well-rested."

"Not at all. The accommodations left a lot to be desired. Mr. Prudeau said we should report here for the first packet to Indianola. Ah, there he is. That must be our ship." Lt. Halter didn't even bother to inquire how Alex had slept, and that suited Alex just fine.

Amos Prudeau would not usually pilot this small schooner that ran between Saluria and Indianola. But for the past week he had been helping his pal Drew Johnsville, whose horse had surprised a rattlesnake, reared, and thrown him hard, injuring his right arm and leg. Bad luck to be hurt like that, so Amos had been lending a hand. Nate left Alex with Lt. Halter and went to greet his friends.

"Mornin' Amos, Drew."

"Mornin' Nate. I was just tellin' Drew here about our Yankee passengers. Bet he's lookin' forward to some lively conversation with 'em, ain't ya, Drew? I can tell ya'll, I'll be mighty pleased when they're on the other side of the bay. No tellin' what they might ask for next. What did you do with the boy? Got a message you was takin' him to the lighthouse. That true?

"He wanted to see it, so I took him. Grandpa said we should bed down there, so we did, that's all. He ain't that bad. Told some good stories about the camels."

Laughing out loud, Amos teased. "Never seen anyone so obsessed with critters he ain't set eyes on 'til yesterday. As for me, I'll be happy if I never see them animals again. The noises they made! My god, it was the sound of Hades itself."

Drew chuckled. "Yeah, I ran into some of them boys from the *Fashion*. They stopped in here before headin' back to the Balize. Bad dispositions, they said. Not an animal you'd like to stake your life on. And where do you put the saddle? Can't be ridin' one of them things bareback!"

Amos and Drew were both laughing now. Nate lowered his eyes and started to breathe deeply.

"Alex says that on land they're fast, and they can carry heavy loads. Maybe they're just what we need to fight Indians and open the way to California."

Amos knew of Nate's temper and that he hated to be the laughingstock. Amos started to back away from the subject of camels, but Drew continued.

"What? Do I hear you startin' your sentences with 'Alex says'? You takin' a fancy to northerners these days? I can't figure which is worse, animals from hell or sissies from New England." Drew's laughter began to draw others who came around to listen. "Nate here says he's gonna ride these camels to fight Indians. Maybe he's gonna be part of a travelin' show along with the bearded lady and the two-headed goat!"

A flush of anger started to bloom on Nate's cheeks. "Well, Jefferson Davis himself wants these animals tested. Imagine if we could get goods to the forts in half the time it takes now. The army could wipe out the Indians in no time."

Amos hoped that Drew would notice Nate's rising emotion, but Drew kept on. "This army depends on horses and mules and that's it. I'm tellin' y'all, if I ain't on the water, I'm stickin' with my horse."

With a sly grin, Nate saw his chance. "You mean the one that threw you last week?"

Amos smiled as everyone laughed. He worried about Nate's sensitive nature. Sometimes Nate couldn't take a joke, but this time he had gotten the better of Drew, and Amos was glad to see it.

Drew clapped Nate on the back, laughing in return. "All right, but I've sure got my doubts about them camels. What do they eat, anyway?"

The conversation was interrupted by the arrival of Lt. Halter and Alex. Lt. Halter didn't speak as he strode onto the ship and pointed where Alex should set his bags. Nate flashed a look at Alex who shrugged his shoulders. As soon as they could, the boys left Lt. Halter and went to the front of the boat.

The bay was a mysterious place with patches of mist refracting pale blue, turquoise, and deep green. The transparent water was so shallow in some places that they could see the bottom, covered with crystalline white sand interspersed with delicate grasses and darting fish. It seemed as if they could reach over and scoop up the fish with their bare hands. To the port side, the shallowest areas sported thicker stands of native plants that marked the conversion of the open water into a series of tide pools, inlets, and newly formed islands. Hundreds of plovers, avocets, and shore birds of every variety hovered near the marshy areas, while gulls and terns flew overhead. Turtles rested on an exposed rock, and a raccoon busily cleaned its supper at shoreline.

Alex was dazzled by the abundance of life. In a quick, sleek movement, what appeared to be a log slithered into the water, giving him his first close-up look at an alligator. They enjoyed the sight of a pelican's speedy dive to catch its breakfast, admired the delicate motions of a snowy egret landing at the water's edge, and inhaled the salty air. To starboard, the slightly deeper open water was ruffled by a gentle breeze. Nate, whose sharp eyes were used to the bay, was the first to spy a pair of dolphins that cavorted toward the ship before dashing away. Gradually the misty flumes evaporated to reveal a liquid blue sky with a fully formed sun already flashing bright reflections on the water. Squinting against the brightness, they watched as Saluria receded and the wharves at Indianola came into view. The light played hopscotch on the water while gulls flew overhead. Alex found it heavenly, and once again he said a little prayer of thanks.

When they disembarked, Nate left Alex and headed straight for the Government Depot, hauling his overstuffed bag and scarcely saying goodbye to Amos and Drew.

Drew shook his head. "You think he told his grandpa?"

"Hell, he ain't even told us, not proper. But a man don't carry a bag like that just to go to town for a spell."

"Nope. You think he'll really do it? Go off with the camels?"

"Sure looks like it. But they ain't here yet, and he may change his tune when he sees 'em up close."

"How you figure his grandpa's gonna take it?"

"Hard tellin'. Jeremy Blackstone ain't no fool. He's probably figured out somethin's up."

Alex had for so long anticipated stepping onto the Texas mainland with the camels that he was acutely disappointed to have landed without them. Wishing he were going with Nate, he summoned the strength to deal with a cranky Lt. Halter, who impatiently motioned for help with his baggage. Alex secured and loaded a carriage while Lt. Halter watched without lifting a finger. Unable to hold back a grimace, Alex reckoned that two weeks with Winston Halter would feel like eternity. Reluctantly he accompanied Lt. Halter to the hotel, acutely aware that he had no idea what would happen next.

Mrs. Eberly could see immediately that her new guest was a gentleman who had been traveling a long time. His clothes were of impeccable quality, but rumpled and last year's fashion. She watched him descend from the carriage with mincing steps to avoid the mud and horse droppings. While she liked a careful man, she detested a prissy one. As of yet, it was unclear which kind of man this new guest would be.

The second guest who descended was scarcely more than a boy. He leapt down from the carriage with only a quick glance at where he was landing, yet managed to avoid the most serious puddles. His head was in constant motion, scanning left and right, up and down the street as if trying to memorize every feature of every building, person and animal. A spunky lad. The two did not act like relations, so she searched for another connection between them. She caught a hint of scorn as the elder man turned to see the younger one following. The boy seemed oblivious. She was curious whether both would require lodging.

The elder guest paused at the base of the hotel steps to consider the building. Mrs. Eberly loved this moment, when a guest of breeding grasped that he was entering a refuge of style and luxury. Festooned with potted plants and flowers, the covered veranda was furnished with two rocking chairs on one side and a table with four chairs on the other that gave an immediate sense of comfort. The veranda topped six steps, painted navy blue and trimmed with white, a fitting match to the sea and sand that constituted the entire geography of Indianola. Mrs. Eberly waited at the top stair. She stood at the precise spot where the angle of the sun and stairs created a backlighting to accent her figure without letting her face be clearly seen. Her dress was simple but, had they been women, her new arrivals would have recognized the latest cut.

The slave Malvina, holding a tray of glasses and ice, stood just inside the hotel, invisible from the street. It was a point of pride that at any season of the year Mrs. Eberly could offer her guests the extravagance of an iced drink. That Mrs. Eberly came to have iced drinks in this tropical climate was the culmination of logistics and careful planning. Imported from the north in winter, the ice rested throughout the spring and summer in Mr. Wellbourne's warehouse encased in layers of brick and sawdust that were several feet thick. Mr. Wellbourne's enterprise also provided ice to the other hotels in town, but her arrivals would not know that. Mrs. Eberly signed an annual contract and paid in advance, assuring that her ice was the cleanest, clearest, and if such a thing were possible, coldest. Moreover, neither ordinary ice chunks nor shaved ice would suffice. Last year she had devised a new plan to import trays of ice in the shape of flowers, hearts, and diamonds. When packed thoroughly with the enormous block sent to Mr. Wellbourne, her fanciful ice cubes survived unmelted. Malvina stood totally still, waiting for her part in the coming scene. She stepped back from view as the two men mounted the stairs, and the first stage of the ritual began.

Mrs. Eberly smiled warmly, extending a bejeweled hand. "Good morning, gentlemen, I am Mrs. Eberly. You are most welcome."

"Lt. Winston Halter, Madam, from the *USS Supply.* I am most honored to make your acquaintance and to have the privilege of visiting your excellent establishment. It comes well recommended." He noted that Mrs. Eberly, who had looked so imposing from below, was not more than five feet tall and older than she first appeared, perhaps in her mid-fifties.

"The pleasure is all mine, Lieutenant." Mrs. Eberly smiled gently and then turned her head ever so slightly toward her second guest.

"Ah, this is Alexander Babcock, also in the employ of the United States. He's a civilian." Lt. Halter hesitated as he searched for words to describe Alex further.

Never one to wait, and certainly not for Lt. Halter, Alex stepped forward and bowed low, removing his hat with a flourish. "Pleased to make your acquaintance. You have a beautiful place here, Ma'am."

Unable to suppress a smile, Mrs. Eberly replied graciously. "Thank you, Mr. Babcock. Gentlemen, may I offer you a drink while we discuss your accommodation requirements?"

In early May, it was already hot and humid in Indianola, so chairs had been arranged on the veranda in the shade with a view directly onto the bay. The table was set with a white linen tablecloth, Adams flow blue china from England and silver cutlery from Philadelphia. A bouquet of brown-eyed susans stood in a cut crystal vase. A plate of sweet pastries waited under a gauze cover that protected them from flies. Malvina had risen early to bake the kolaches according to a recipe from a Czech immigrant who had passed through last year. The chairs were elaborate wrought iron, adorned with cushions covered in floral chintz.

When summoned, Malvina appeared with an ornate silver tray, three crystal glasses, a Meissen porcelain teapot, and a large silver bowl filled with ice. With silver tongs, she lifted several ice pieces into each glass. Pouring sweetened tea over the ice, she topped off the presentation with a slice of lemon and a sprig of mint. After setting a glass in front of each person, she slipped back into the house, out of sight but within earshot. As expected, both Winston and Alex were astonished. Winston's serious countenance gave way to a true grin.

Alex slapped his knees. "Why, Mrs. Eberly, I think you must be the most amazing woman that Texas has ever seen. Iced drinks on a day when walking across the road is enough to roast a man! It's a miracle!"

"Madam, I am truly astounded at the delicacy of these ice shapes. Beautiful! Your thoughtfulness is most appreciated. Ice, indeed. Thank you!" Lt. Halter smiled again. In over a year of close company with the Lieutenant, this was the first time Alex had ever seen him look remotely contented. Even when he received letters from his wife, he would be happy for only a moment before becoming melancholy again. Mrs. Eberly's ice had melted his frosty countenance. Alex smiled at the irony.

Mrs. Eberly nodded demurely, fanning herself gently with a green silk fan. "Gentlemen, you are most welcome. I am pleased that you are able to refresh yourselves. "

"You may well appreciate our gratitude for these amenities after our long voyage. We thank you most heartily."

"I look forward to hearing about your travels. I regret that we did not toast your arrival with something stronger. Were it a bit later in the day, I would have offered you a whiskey with your tea. I'm sure you'd like to sample some this evening. We serve the best from Tennessee and from Ireland, to suit your preference. I dare say you'll find it more to your taste than the local concoctions."

Winston grimaced. "My dear Madam, I've had experience with the local concoctions over in Saluria. I will earnestly follow your suggestion of an alternative."

"You had to sleep last night in Saluria! The folks are kind, but there are times when one wishes for more tangible comforts. Isn't that so, Lieutenant? Please tell me more about your plans."

Winston Halter was charmed. This woman was stately, cultured, and a most engaging hostess. For a moment, he forgot that he was supposed to be on a mission to make arrangements for the camels. He wished them every conceivable delay as he contemplated rest, relaxation, good food and conversation.

"We're with the Army's mission to test the possibility of a camel cavalry."

"Camels! Yes, of course. Captain Van Steendam has been preparing corrals for them. I thought he would have alerted me of your arrival. I apologize for not being prepared. I shall be most interested to hear your stories."

"Yes, Ma'am, allow me to explain. We were unable to lighter the camels, so the *Supply* has returned to the Balize in search of calmer waters. It may be two weeks before they return."

"What an honor to have you, Lieutenant! Let's put you into one of our front rooms with a bit of morning and evening breeze. I'm sure you'll find our other guests most agreeable. We have a family in transit to Fredericksburg and a businessman from New England who stays with us every year for several weeks. We tend to avoid the rowdy set that you might find in other establishments."

Before Mrs. Eberly could continue, Lt. Halter asked, "Now Alex, what sort of accommodation should we find for you?"

Mrs. Eberly was taken aback, as it appeared that Lt. Halter wanted Alex to lodge elsewhere. She wondered again at their relationship.

Alex took the initiative. "Mrs. Eberly, I do not require the standard that Lt. Halter merits. Would it be possible to have a small room at the back, perhaps? I don't mind sharing if that is more convenient."

Mrs. Eberly cast an appraising eye on Alex Babcock, finding him diplomatic and quick-witted. "Why, certainly, Mr. Babcock. I propose one of our two downstairs rooms near the kitchen. Three beds to a room. There is an entrance in back, in case you wish to come and go without marching through the parlor."

"Yes, Ma'am, that sounds about perfect."

"Well, then, gentlemen, let's get you settled."

Malvina started moving toward the group a split second before Mrs. Eberly could call her. Alex stepped from the table, smiled at Malvina, and said, "Excuse me, ma'am." Malvina lowered her eyes. She never could get over the different ways that guests treated her. She didn't trust the way some Northerners tried to treat her as equals. Keeping her eyes down, Malvina motioned for Alex to follow Mrs. Eberly and said nothing.

Alex deposited his bag in his room and left by the back door. The hotel filled the entire width of a long narrow lot, except for a driveway that led to a stable on the left at the rear. Attached to the stable, a sizeable room served as storeroom and also as a bunkhouse for male slaves traveling with their masters. Straight back from the hotel stood the kitchen. To the right, facing the stable, a small, rough cabin could be used for storage or to house the female slaves of visitors. In the central yard, a large live oak shaded the cistern. Like Galveston, Indianola depended on captured rainwater. Mrs. Eberly had erected a complex system of gutters and pipes that led into the cistern and a pump to retrieve the water that would be carried by bucket either to the kitchen or to the guest rooms. Malvina was already at the pump getting water for Lt. Halter's bath.

Alex went off in search of the Post Office. Major Babcock had given him the previous day's energetic production of letters from the crew, as well as the Major's own urgent replies to the War Office. Getting those dispatched would be his first priority. After that he'd look for Captain Van Steendam at the Army Depot, where he expected he'd also find Nate Wilkers.

INDIANOLA, TEXAS, A FEW DAYS LATER

AN EXHAUSTED ELIZABETH MCDERMOTT slumped in a chair on Mrs. Eberly's veranda, incredulous that she was temporarily homeless. She felt numb, an emotion preferable to the fury that consumed her otherwise. It was hard to believe it had been less than a week since her father had laid upon them the burden of this move, a week that felt like an entire lifetime. The hotel appeared nice enough, but Elizabeth could not comprehend that her life would now take place in a room shared with her mother. As for Indianola, the town stretched along a single road that hugged the coast, nowhere near as grand as Galveston. When Mrs. Eberly explained that Major Babcock and the camels had not yet arrived, a disappointment fell upon Elizabeth like a crushing weight. She wanted to cry, but when she saw her mother fighting to maintain a dignified countenance, she bit her lip. Fighting back tears, she realized that they could be marooned here for weeks.

With her gaze fixed to the street in front of them, Elizabeth was the first to spot Alex. Covered from toe to waist with splatterings of dried mud, he strode confidently toward Mrs. Eberly's hotel. Elizabeth liked the way he moved, but his hair, covered by a dirty hat, was matted and in need of a wash. She scarcely recognized him.

Alex had been busy during his brief time in Indianola, thanks to Nate's introduction to Captain Van Steendam. In contrast to Lt. Halter, whose habit of demanding information and taking notes annoyed the Captain most thoroughly, Alex answered questions rather than asking, was willing to lend a hand anywhere, and relished any assignment that kept him away from Lt. Halter. He especially liked exploring the countryside, as he had today. Seeing Mrs. Eberly seated on the veranda with new guests, Alex smiled to think about the ice blocks that she would present with such panache. Intending to slip around back, he was surprised when Mrs. Eberly called him.

"Mr. Babcock, your presence is requested please."

"Yes, ma'am."

Alex pulled off his hat and knocked it against his knees
to remove some of the grit. He reeked of horses, and although that was normal in Texas, he did not feel it appropriate for meeting strangers. He approached the veranda from
the side and made no move to mount the front staircase.
Standing the full six steps below, with the sun in his eyes, he
made out the silhouettes of four people.

"I believe our new guests are acquaintances of yours."

Alex started to speak and then stopped, his eyes opening wide. Sylvia McDermott joined the laughter at his startled expression but could not keep a hint of melancholy
from her voice.

"Hello, Alex. I imagine you are as bemused at seeing us
here as we are at being here."

"Hello, Mrs. McDermott, it's a pleasure, I assure you.
Elizabeth, Zeke, Zach." He nodded at each in turn, his bewilderment plain for all to see.

Elizabeth smiled, nodded, and glanced down at him
with glassy eyes. Her brothers jumped up and leaned over
the veranda's railing, bursting with questions. "Why aren't
the camels here, Alex? When are the they coming?"

Mrs. Eberly interjected. "My goodness, young gentlemen. Can't you see that Mr. Babcock is fresh from the
road? Alex, won't you come up here and join us for some
lemonade?"

"Oh, no, ma'am. Much as I admire your lemonade, especially on a day like today, I fear that I'm not, hmmm,"
he searched for the right word, "commodious for present
company." Frantically, he ran one hand through his disheveled hair.

"Mr. Babcock, a Texan can enjoy civilized company
while evidencing his manly pursuits. The ladies won't mind
one whit, and it's a good example to the young men. I will
brook no further objections. Malvina!"

Alex climbed the steps and sat at the table between Sylvia and Zachary. He was perfectly positioned for an unob-
structed view of Elizabeth with the light on her face. As the
others chattered around him, everything seemed to be moving slowly. His brain must not be working right. Elizabeth
McDermott was here in Indianola, sitting in front of him.

He studied every aspect of her and still could not discern whether or not she was happy to see him.

Watching from her customary post, Malvina had already prepared another glass along with additional ice. Alex thanked her and grabbed the glass a bit too hastily, downing at least half the lemonade in one gulp. Embarrassed, he turned to Mrs. Eberly.

"Excuse me, Ma'am, but I guess I had a powerful thirst."

"By all means, have as much as you like. You've been working hard these last few days."

Mrs. Eberly observed closely as her guests explained to a confused Alex Babcock how they happened to be in Indianola. She knew her old friend Quentin McDermott planned to expand into San Antonio, but she was surprised by his sudden request to accommodate the family, especially since he was not coming with them.

"I'm sorry that my cousin isn't here." Sylvia sighed. Fatigue shadowed the soft skin below her eyes.

"Well, ma'am, we had some trouble with the lightering, but Major Babcock should be back within a week or so. We're all impatient." Alex proceeded to explain what had happened.

Elizabeth's stupor gradually faded as she listened to Alex. Something about him put her at ease. He was clever and humorous, a great storyteller. Soon she was entranced by his tales, as well as by the way his hand gestures augmented his words. His description of the failed lightering left her breathless, and for the first time in days, she stopped thinking about her own predicament.

Seeing that the mood had improved, Mrs. Eberly suggested that the new guests find their rooms. She then sent Malvina to sort out the slaves.

Under the live oak behind Mrs. Eberly's hotel, Antoine stood bone tired, his exhaustion as much emotional as physical. Wearily, he assessed the great upheaval that had befallen him. From his exalted position as butler and chief domestic servant in one of the richest households of Texas, he now stood barefoot with a bedraggled group of ordinary slaves. His crisp white shirt, fitted jacket and dark pressed trousers were packed in a trunk, and his status was marked by simple cotton pants and a loose shirt. He was appalled at how little he knew. Faced with incomparable uncertainties, he longed for the predictable rhythm of his life in Galveston where routines were established and duties clear. The order that defined his existence had turned topsy-turvy with no warning and little explanation. All he could do was go through the motions: lifting, carrying, packing, and running errands from before dawn until past midnight. The sheer effort wore him out. The worry was beyond anything he had ever known, and he grieved for those who had been sent to the plantation. People looked to him for answers, but he had none. The discontent in the household became a living being that shadowed him, making every burden heavier and each task more difficult.

When they had boarded the ship for the passage to Indianola, the sudden inactivity had come as a shock. After arranging the luggage, Antoine sank to the deck, inert. He felt like a pot of molasses that if poured would be too thick to flow. He had no need to move about the ship and no right either. He and the other slaves slept where they sat on deck among the cargo, exposed to the elements. They made themselves as comfortable as possible and waited. Tense muscles relaxed, and Antoine dozed.

Once the ship reached open water, his body betrayed him. The treachery came on him slowly, as an indistinct upset in the pit of his stomach. Gradually, discomfort rose in his chest as if a foreign entity had taken up residence and wanted to escape. Soon his insides were gurgling and his foul-smelling belches embarrassed him. He rose to distance himself from the others, and in the briefest moment he was retching over the side of the ship. A strong and healthy man, Antoine could not remember when he had last thrown up, but there he was, sick as a dog, and he remained so during the entire trip.

His intermittent sleep, stolen between bouts of nausea, came in the form of nightmarish visions of his father's passage from Africa in the holds of a slave ship. As a child, he thought his father's stories were meant to frighten him into obedience. Antoine had not given them much credence. He could not believe that humans had been shackled in closed

quarters, in a space barely the size of a body, surrounded
by urine, feces, and vomit. But feeling the pitch and roll of
the ship, he began to know what his father had endured. He
vowed to remember more of what his father had told him,
once he was feeling better.

This morning, when he stepped onto Indianola's solid
ground, his stomach settled and his body returned to him a
measure of stability. As the fog cleared from his head, the
precariousness of his situation affronted him with full force.
He had been so complacent in his life in Galveston. Now
he realized he had not one iota of control over what was to
become of him.

Antoine marveled at the number of trunks and chests
that were piled on the back porch of the hotel, thinking this
did not look like a temporary move. Esther, Agnes and the
children had already gone out back to the kitchen where
they met Althea, an older woman who cooked for the hotel.
They learned that she had been purchased only the year before, that Malthus was the stable hand, and that other slaves
were hired as needed. Miz Eberly made most decisions personally, and if not, a slave called Malvina was in charge.

The McDermott slaves were distressed by the absence of
proper slave quarters. Althea slept in an alcove in the kitchen
and Malthus bedded down by the door of the stable. Malvina
was the only one who slept in the hotel, in a tiny space used
for an office. Antoine and Samuel would likely have to bunk
in the stable, with the women and children sleeping in a crude
shack. Life here was going to be much less comfortable than
in Galveston.

Antoine looked around at the forlorn group huddled
together. No one spoke, the unease palpable. Esther looked
drawn and tense, barely standing upright as her two children
leaned against her. No one sat. The ground was too wet from
yesterday's rain, and they dared not sit on the steps. Samuel
stood apart, trying to conceal the anger and despair that hung
over him with the loss of his beloved Precious. Agnes, swinging her arms aimlessly back and forth, looked lost and confused. The gloom was broken by the appearance of Malvina
on the top step of the back porch. She surveyed the group
with disdain. She had a stately beauty, golden-colored skin, a

straight nose, and bright green eyes, but coldness hung about her. Esther had seen that haughty look before in mulattos and quadroons, so she braced herself for what came next.

"Ya'll get outta the yard. Men in the stable, women over here. Miz Eberly ain't said yet 'bout food, but when she does, kitchen's out back."

Antoine stood to his full six feet, straight and with his shoulders back, to indicate that Malvina was not the master of him or his companions.

"Good afternoon. May I make introductions?"

The girls tittered. Everyone knew Antoine could talk like a white man, but they'd never heard him do it except in jest or when greeting McDermott guests. This time they could see that he was in earnest. He wanted Malvina to know that she would not get away with rudeness.

"I am Antoine, Miz McDermott's butler. This is Samuel, coachman. Miz Esther, cook. Miz Agnes, assistant cook." Agnes squirmed, as no one had ever called her that before. "The children, Sally and Mabel."

He nodded to the others, turned and walked toward the stables with his head held high. The women and girls followed his example as they marched toward the storage room. No one looked back at Malvina. They did hear the door slam as she went back into the hotel.

INDIANOLA, TEXAS, MAY 14, 1856

S AMUEL WOKE BEFORE DAWN to find Alexander Babcock saddling a horse. He quickly rose, tossing on a shirt. "Anythin' I can do for you, sah?"

Samuel was willing to put forth a little extra effort to engage Alex, who was a particularly good source of information. The slaves had found no good way to get news. Most of the hotel guests had no discourse with them, and the easy give-and-take that used to characterize the McDermott household had diminished. In Galveston, when he or Antoine drove Miz Sylvia on errands, they chatted with other slaves to keep abreast of important happenings, and Esther garnered information from her trips to market. Through conversation and reciprocal small favors, the slaves learned of social events, family strife, business dealings, and political matters that their masters never dreamed they knew about. Samuel and the others were respected participants in a complex network of obligations and relationships. Here they were appendages to a transient family, and no one told them anything. He hated the interminable waiting, not knowing what was coming next. It felt like watching meat over a fire that was too low, rotating over and over, never roasted, never ready to eat.

He was particularly annoyed with Malvina, who was worthless when it came to sharing information. She carried herself superior to the others, scarcely deigning to look at them, let alone providing helpful knowledge of the goings on. Malvina never offered a scrap of gossip. Samuel couldn't abide her airs. Alex, however, would talk to anyone.

Alex munched on a fresh biscuit. With so many guests at the hotel, Esther and Agnes had already started preparing breakfast, providing Alex the good fortune to grab some bacon and a hot mug of coffee at this early hour. Unlike Samuel and Antoine, who had too little to do, Esther and Agnes had no shortage of work helping Althea in the hotel kitchen. Samuel figured that Miz Eberly must be offsetting the family's lodging costs with the savings, because Esther and Agnes weren't getting any hire wages. There was one good thing. With Esther in the kitchen, he and Antoine were eating nearly as well as they had in Galveston. After Alex left, he would see about getting a biscuit and coffee.

"Sorry, Samuel. I didn't mean to wake you, but I have to be at the Government Depot before sunrise."

Alex was dressed in breeches and a cotton shirt, and he carried his hat and work gloves. No city clothes for him today. Samuel liked the way Alex could do for himself. "You plannin' on ridin' out somewhere again today?"

"No, the camels are coming. The *Fashion* should be steaming through the pass at first light."

"The camels finally here! That's good."

"Very good. I expect you'll be bringing Mrs. McDermott and the family to watch. Once we get the animals used to being on land again, we'll start testing them. In a few weeks, we should be on our way west."

"A few weeks?" Samuel had expected them to go as soon as the camels landed.

"Perhaps less. It all depends on how they do. They've been cooped up on the ship a long time. The first one we bought nine months ago! You know, Samuel, these animals really are easy-going. I can't imagine horses putting up with that kind of confinement. I just hope they aren't too upset by the unloading. By the way, Lt. Halter should be following me to the wharf soon. He's taking his breakfast in the dining room first. Me, I can't wait for that."

Samuel kept a carefully straight face. Lt. Halter had his routines, and he kept to them with a disciplined devotion. Despite being a northerner and reputedly an abolitionist, he treated the slaves as poorly as any white man. Samuel had learned that everything had to be exactly the way he wanted it or there would be retribution. Fortunately, it was easy for the McDermott slaves to stay out of his way, but he'd overheard the Lieutenant's harsh words to Malvina.

"I'll git Lt. Halter's horse ready."

"That would probably be a wise idea." Alex couldn't contain a slight smirk.

Alex led his horse to the front of the house and mounted quietly so as not to wake anyone. The golden glow coming from the room shared by Mrs. McDermott and Elizabeth told him that a lamp had already been lit. "Good," he thought. "They won't be late for the excitement."

Elizabeth sat facing the window, eyes half-closed, as her mother brushed her hair. In her mind's eye, she tried to picture how the camels would be unloaded. Alex had said there were over thirty of them. Surely it would be too dangerous to let them walk, but how could you get a camel off a ship? Maybe the Egyptians would speak to them in their own language and that would help.

"What is it, dreamy daughter?" Elizabeth had let out the faintest of sighs, caused by the thought of the fine-looking Egyptian that she had glimpsed in the Galveston jail.

"Nothing, Mother. I was just trying to figure out how they will unload all those camels."

Sylvia's melodic laugh filled the room. She was happy that her daughter's attention had been drawn toward the anticipated camel landing. She, too, was grateful for the diversion. They had been at Indianola for a full week under the competent surveillance of Mrs. Eberly, who hovered over them in matronly fashion anticipating their every need. Sylvia appreciated these attentions and wondered whether she would have such a well-respected ambassador to help her adjust to life in San Antonio. Her husband had planned the first phase of this move quite well, but she was galled by her ignorance of his plans. Daily she tried to practice patience. He had sent only one package containing two letters. Mrs. Eberly's no doubt detailed arrangements for their lodging and sustenance. Her own letter disappointed her enormously. Composed with a nonchalant tone that she found inappropriate to the occasion, the letter revealed nothing of substance. She hoped the next one would be more complete.

The ladies switched places, and Elizabeth brushed her mother's thick, auburn hair. Sylvia relaxed into the motion, but could not clear her mind.

"Mama, my turn to ask, what is it? You've wrinkled your brow. I saw it in the mirror."

"You are too perceptive by far. I was missing your father, that's all."

"I miss him, too. Wouldn't he be excited to see this day?"

"Yes, but he did get to see the camels in Galveston."

"That was wonderful. But now we will see them up and walking. They will open the route to California, fight the red Indians, and supply the army. They are the future!"

"Why, Elizabeth, you sound just like Alex Babcock!" Sylvia chided deliberately. She had observed that Alex had an interest in her daughter and wanted to discern whether Elizabeth harbored reciprocal feelings. Elizabeth gave no indication of her emotions.

"Well, Mama, you have to admit that he has been telling us marvelous stories over dinner."

"Yes he has, but now it's off to breakfast before the big day when we'll see for ourselves."

By the time Sylvia had marshaled her three children, finished a substantial breakfast, organized a picnic lunch, decided that both Samuel and Antoine should accompany them, and given instructions to Esther and Agnes, the sun was well above the horizon. Even Lt. Halter had long departed by the time they all piled into the carriage.

Before they reached the Government wharf, they heard the commotion. Nearly every man, woman and child in town had congregated, and more were flowing in. Perched on buckboards, hanging from second story windows, and squeezing around each other, they strained to see what was happening. Newly arrived German immigrants came on foot from the tent camps, teamsters and wranglers rode in from all directions, and anyone with a skiff or a rowboat moved alongside the *Fashion* or parallel to the wharf for a closer look. Antoine was the first to see the chaos. Holding the reins tightly, he tried simultaneously to negotiate a safe passage through the throng and to imprint this scene on his memory, in order to tell Esther, Agnes, and the children. He was used to the congestion at the port of Galveston, a beehive of comings and goings with people speaking all sorts of strange languages. But here, the mass of people all focused on one space that shifted as some people retreated from their positions while others inched forward. Above the masses, he could see a furry head that must be a camel. He also saw horses rearing.

Mrs. Eberly had arranged for her guests to have a privileged view of the day's events. They left the carriage with Antoine and Samuel and snaked through the crowd toward Mr. Ashbeth's place. Passing through the well-stocked general store, they mounted the staircase to take seats on his upper balcony where they were perfectly situated to watch the spectacle.

The first to step through the door and onto the porch, Elizabeth shrieked, "Oh, Mama!"

Heedless of manners, Zeke and Zach shoved their way past the ladies. "Look at that! I ain't never!"

Even Mrs. Eberly uttered, "My goodness," while Sylvia was speechless.

Below them to the right, three camels were milling about in an open space near the wharf. Their attendants, one to a camel, tugged on their leads in a somewhat vain effort to keep the camels a reasonable distance apart. None of them looked anything like the docile creatures that Alex Babcock claimed them to be. They danced and leapt about while the handlers tried to cajole them into submission. One exuberant camel ran back and forth, kicking and snorting. A handler ran parallel, patting it on the side and speaking to it in a foreign language. Gradually its pace slowed. Another camel settled into a prancing gait, tossing its head back and forth. The bells adorning its halter added a musical note to the uproar. Eventually it slowed to a walk and seemed ready to be fitted with a hobble. Its handler looked satisfied as he led her away. A third camel trotted around a handler that was barely able keep ahold of the tether. The handler spun in place while the camel raised great dusty circles around him. Suddenly the camel broke its circle to lunge toward a spectator who had drifted too close. It kicked, sending the astonished and frightened crowd hopscotching in retreat. No one had expected the show to be dangerous.

From the safety of the balcony, Mrs. Eberly dissected the scene. "I am at a loss to say which is more exotic, the animals or their handlers. Look at that hat. It's shaped like a chopped-off cone. Whatever would he do in the rain? I'm sure the next time we see that fellow, he'll be wearing a proper hat with a brim."

"Yes," added Sylvia, "and look at the loose pants he's wearing. They almost look like underwear, except for the bright red sash wrapped around his waist."

Zeke chimed in, "That can't be practical."

Zach added, "No, and it almost makes him look like a girl."

Sylvia countered, "Yes, but he is certainly strong. See how he's managed to keep his camel away from the crowd."

"It looks like the handlers are as brutish as the beasts. I can't yet discern any plan to this unloading!" Mrs. Eberly leaned forward to see better.

Pointing excitedly, Elizabeth cried, "Mama, isn't that Cousin Babcock, over there speaking with Lt. Halter?"

"Oh yes! How wonderful to see him. I am sure that with his guidance, everything will go well. Still, it looks a frightful mess at the moment."

"Look, Mama! Here comes another one! Look how they do that!"

Normally, a ship would unload goods onto wooden cars set on rails that ran the full length of the 250-foot wharf. The rails assured stability as mules pulled the wagons to the shore. Today, however, a different contraption traced its way from the ship. Larger than a typical wagon, it was lower to the ground with higher walls. Rising above these walls was the head of a camel. The car was pushed by three muscular slaves who had been hired out by their owners to Captain Van Steendam for today's purpose. Two other men walked in front, speaking to the camel and controlling the speed of the vehicle.

"Look, look!" shouted Zeke. "There's Alex, at the front of that car! Who's that with him?"

Elizabeth caught her breath. In spite of his American clothes, it was the Egyptian she had seen in Galveston. Beneath his hat, his curly hair shone the color of polished onyx. Elizabeth wanted to run her fingers through it.

After some study, Mrs. Eberly determined that the effort was more organized than she thought. "At last I see the order in this. The men on the ship choose a camel and load it onto that ingenious carting device. When it reaches the end, Lt. Halter records pertinent details on the official record. Then a handler takes over until it gets used to having solid ground under its feet."

Elizabeth noticed a makeshift holding area, surrounded on three sides by wagons. The first camel to reach Texas had been passed off to Nate Wilkers. She didn't know quite what to make of Nate yet, but Alex got on with him well enough. Nate tied the first camel to the side of a wagon, where it stood quietly. Much calmer now, it seemed content to await the arrival of its kin. Then, to Elizabeth's surprise, it knelt down as if for an afternoon siesta.

From their less advantaged view down by the carriages, Antoine and Samuel sympathized with the three dockworkers, shirtless and sweating. The sun was blasting, and the camel car looked heavy. Back and forth they went, pushing the empty car toward the ship, waiting for the loading, and pushing it back again, as one by one the camels came ashore. As if the hard labor wasn't bad enough, from time to time the animals on ship, on shore, or in transit would utter an ear-splitting wail.

Antoine sighed. "I wish Agnes, Esther and the girls could see this. I'll be rememberin' it for a long, long time."

"Precious, too. Wish she could see. I wonder what she doin' today." Samuel's sad eyes turned to Antoine. "Ain't a minute goes by that I don't pine for her."

"I know, Samuel, but you gotta be patient."

"I dunno. Somethin' goin' on here that we can't figure."

"Maybe these camels have somethin' to do with it."

"Maybe. Hey, Antoine, see them camel-men? Look kinda Mexican, don't they?"

"Yeah, but they ain't. Alex says they're from Egypt and Turkey."

"Egypt, I heard of in the Bible. But turkey? That's for eatin'!" Both men laughed out loud.

Out on the wharf, Hassan and Alex, drenched with perspiration, labored side by side. They eased a camel onto the cart, guided the cart to shore, kept the camel relaxed, and ran to lend a hand if one of the camels onshore became unruly. The intense physical effort and mental concentration helped Hassan to keep his turmoil at bay. His joy at seeing Alex was tempered by a severe reluctance to be in Texas. His experience in Galveston still haunted him.

Hassan feared that they would be held as virtual prisoners at the camel camp as he had been confined to the ship in Galveston. He faced the day with anxiety.

For reassurance, he reminded himself that Alex had stood by him in Galveston, but Alex apparently had no thought for Hassan's concerns today. When he boarded the *Fashion*, Alex greeted Hassan heartily, but briefly, before going straight to Major Babcock and then to the camels. The only news Alex conveyed was that the McDermott mother and children were in Indianola and would be joining the camel caravan as far as San Antonio. Hassan noticed the look of complete rapture on Alex's face when he mentioned Elizabeth McDermott. Deep in thought, Hassan glanced up as the camel car reached the waterside.

Alex called. "Hassan, stop daydreaming. We're ready to unload Perguida. Look sharp."

"Why do you want to look sharp? Is someone watching?"

Alex reddened. "You know too much, my friend. Just get Perguida out. Abdullah is ready for her."

Hassan was baffled by the tumult that engulfed the entire shoreline. Having lived all his life among camels, he had not expected the townspeople to be so fascinated, nor so ill mannered. People were pushing and shoving, pointing and shouting. He couldn't believe the way they clustered around the camels at every point. While he and Alex walked up and down with the camel car, rowboats shadowed their progress along the wharf, their occupants calling out remarks, both kind and unkind. He was glad that he was responsible for the camels rather than for the raucous crowd.

Not only did the onlookers shout out their opinions about the camels, they freely included the camel handlers in their insults. Many of the worst were directed at Abdullah, who had insisted on wearing his fez and scarlet belt. Normally he would not have chosen those items for work that would be dirty, but he was determined to make a good impression. At the moment his strategy was backfiring. Whistles and catcalls rained down upon him.

Among the crowd, Amos Prudeau and Drew Johnsonville sauntered over to the makeshift corral to watch the show. Though uncomfortable being this close to the camels, Amos wanted to keep an eye on Nate, who had been put in charge of this part of the operation. Captain Van Steendam, anticipating correctly that the spectators might pose more problems than the animals, wanted his older, experienced men on crowd control. Nate had been delighted to get this job. He nodded to the pair, and then did his best to ignore Drew.

"So you didn't get the chance to pilot the arrival of the century, hey Amos? You could have made history. Guess you'll be regrettin' this when it comes time to tell your grandchildren."

"Naw, just as well I missed it. After the last try, I ain't fond of them beasts anyway."

"They do stink. Why'd we have to set ourselves up so close to 'em?"

"What did you have in mind, Drew? You plan on sittin' up on the balconies with Miz Eberly and the fancy folk? I know. You'd like to be standin' with one of them German lasses. Ah, that's it! By all means, let's go over there, and you can look at the girls instead of the camels."

"That Etta Schmidt sure is a pretty one."

"Yeah, and her pappy's got a mighty fine shotgun!"

Drew shouted loud enough to be sure Nate could hear. "What about Evangeline Blauvelt? She's almost of a marryin' age, ain't she? Hey, Nate, what about Evangeline? You know anybody has his eye on her?"

Nate tried to pay attention to the camels. The last thing he needed was taunting from Drew Johnsonville. He wondered what made Drew always want to provoke a man. He had once posed this question to Amos, since Amos and Drew were friends. Amos had replied, "Drew is a man you want on your side in a scrape. He's mean, even with his friends. That's the only way he knows how to be. But he'll stick by you. Let him be, and you'll be glad you did."

Nate turned his back to Drew and made the rounds again. There were now eleven camels in the corral, all restrained, and some kneeling quietly. At first he had been terrified by their size and energy. Each camel behaved differently when released from the camel car. The unpredictability of their antics added to the difficulty. Nate watched each camel closely and studied how each handler responded. He concluded that the handler wearing the outlandish pantaloons and funny hat was nevertheless the most able. Nate liked a man who knew what he was doing, and he would forgive the foolish clothing. The most normal-looking handler was the least skilled, judging by how often Alex and the others had to help him out.

Nate had a good view of the McDermott family suspended above the fray on the balcony. They were every bit as spellbound as the crowd below, gesturing, shouting, laughing, criticizing and praising the actors in the theater below. He tried to get a good look at Elizabeth, the one that Alex was sweet on. She was taller than her mother and Mrs. Eberly, a bit flat-chested for Nate's taste, but she had a pretty face and beautiful dark hair. He couldn't see what color her eyes were.

"Why Nathaniel Wilkers, what are you looking at up in the sky when there's someone right here for you to cast your eyes on?"

It was Evangeline Blauvelt, saucy, buxom with dunn-colored hair and dark brown eyes who strolled right over to him and planted a kiss on his cheek, in the middle of the camels and in view of everyone. Before he could react, she had bounced her way right past him and joined a group of her friends, staring too intently at the camels.

Someone cried, "Look, a baby!"

Crooning sounds of "oooh" and "aaah" arose from every woman present. Nate followed their gaze to see a tiny young camel coming off the wharf. Immediately upon release, it ran to one of the others, which most took to be its mother. Not usually one for showmanship, Abdullah decided to parade the mother within the cleared space. The baby, its tether still held by Ali the Interpreter, promptly trotted behind. Seeing an opportunity to make a positive impression on the crowd, Major Babcock marched into the middle of the circle, bowed to the people, and formally announced:

"I present to you the first camel born into the US Camel Corps. Its life began during our voyage at sea, and it was named in honor of this great nation. Ladies and gentlemen, please welcome 'Uncle Sam'!"

Wild applause and cheers broke out. Lt. Halter shook his head in disapproval, but Nate was enchanted, as was nearly everyone else. The enthusiastic reaction of the crowd helped Nate to feel completely vindicated in his belief that the camels would save the west for America. More than ever, he was sure that somehow he would be a part of it, and he vowed to adopt the baby Uncle Sam as his personal mascot. Smiling from ear to ear, he took the guide rope from Ali and gently led his new charge into the camel pen.

Jeremy Blackstone rotated the roasting pig again. On the spit since early morning, the pork had turned a crispy brown and smelled of sage and rosemary. Wilma stood silently nearby chopping vegetables. A plump woman, she wore a sleeveless sack dress, soaked with sweat rolling down her neck and onto her ample bosom. A determined frown darkened her otherwise pleasant face. An experienced cook, she cut quickly and quietly. Only her heavy breathing betrayed how hard she was working in the stifling heat.

The men employed by the Government Depot were entitled to a ration of food as part of their pay. One of their own usually did the cooking, but on holidays and the occasional Sunday, Captain Van Steendam arranged a special meal though Mr. Blauvelt, who hired out his slave Wilma. Although allowed to keep half her wages, Wilma didn't see much chance to ever accumulate enough money to purchase freedom for her children. When she was lucky enough to get a hire job, she spent her earnings for food or clothing. She wanted her children strong and healthy. She just hoped they wouldn't be sold away from her before they could stand on their own.

Wilma liked the assignments at the Government Depot because she knew exactly what to do. Today was different, though, because she was working at the camel corral outside of town at Green Lake. Without the pleasing familiarity of the Depot kitchen, the working conditions were not ideal. A rough shelter stood half-open, little more than a hearth with a partial roof. A worktable made of lumber scraps, a couple of cauldrons, a ladle and a knife were its sole furnishings. Fortunately, Mr. Blauvelt had sent along additional cooking utensils that would be returned to him along with Wilma. Each soldier had his own plate, cup, and cutlery, but today Mr. Blauvelt had sent extras to provision the men from the ship. He always offered the free loan of such items. As might be expected, most new soldiers outfitted themselves with purchases from his shop.

Confident that she was a good cook, Wilma preferred to be left alone to do her job. Her logical mind held an organized plan to have everything ready by evening. Usually Captain Van Steendam provided the supplies and left it at that, except on holidays, when he often asked his wife to bake a pumpkin pie or a pound cake. This day, however, the Captain's wife was everywhere underfoot.

Wilma didn't know which annoyed her most, Mrs. Van Steendam's intrusion or Mr. Blackstone milling about. Everyone knew him, and she had nothing against the man. She'd seen enough of him to find him a decent sort, for a white man. Rumor had it that the lighthouse keeper had been in town regularly for the past two weeks. His boy Nate had made camp in the Government Depot, running up and down with the new kid, Alex. Wilma had seen them once when they came to the lumberyard on an errand. What a pair. One of them tall, pink and sunburned, with sunflower hair like the German immigrants; the other one tanned and compact. Nate was like his grandfather, no wasted speech nor excess motion, but Alex was a talker. No wonder the grandfather was checking up. He sure did care for his grandson. Still, she didn't like Jeremy Blackstone in her kitchen. Too many cooks.

"Wilma, go and fetch more onions," called Mrs. Van Steendam.

"Yes'm." She hurried to the bag of onions.

Mrs. Van Steendam hustled about the kitchen. Tiny droplets of perspiration coated the few hairs that escaped her chignon and her apron was spattered with grease, but she was composed and presentable. "Mr. Blackstone, do you have any idea how many are comin' now?"

"Ma'am, I figure we've got at least ten of our own, plus maybe five from the ship."

"And what about those foreigners? Surely we must feed them, too?"

"Yes, ma'am, that would add another five. We'd best figure on at least twenty."

"That's good, because I planned for twenty-five. Thank you so much, Mr. Blackstone. Would you mind fetching us some more firewood?"

Jeremy nodded and crossed the yard past the large new structure with extra high ceilings that had been built for the camels. Approximately ten surrounding acres provided room for the camels to exercise. Hitching posts stood throughout the grazing area, and troughs for hay and oats were positioned at intervals. He thought the corral rather cleverly devised. Because lumber was expensive and Captain Van Steendam frugal, he had staked out a space that took advantage of existing hedges, trees, fences and cacti. He ordered his men to dig up and move prickly pear to fill gaps in the perimeter. With a bit of nurturing these heavy, spiny plants had grown to form an enclosure that was dense, tall, and impenetrable. The Captain had tested the fence by riling horses in the paddock to see if they would crush the plants or try to leap out. The animals avoided the cactus and did no damage to the corral.

"Look at that," thought Jeremy. "That's the kind of doing that makes this country great." Because some of this preparation was Nate's, Jeremy was proud.

Sgt. Stacy Bly came riding hard into the compound looking for Mrs. Van Steendam. "Ma'am, Cap'n says to tell you we've started marchin' toward the corral."

"How's it going, Sergeant?"

"Better'n at first. They've settled a bit and they're pretty good at followin' in a line. They're makin' quite a parade. I gotta go back and clear all horses from the route. None of 'em can abide the camels."

"All right. We'll be ready when the men get here."

Covering the dishes to fend off a swarm of flies, Mrs. Van Steendam looked over the spread laid out on the table: roast pork, beans, corn bread, and collard greens. A good hearty meal, well prepared. A bolt of gold from the lowering sun added a visual allure to the agreeable aromas. She had decided there would be no pies today. Maybe on Sunday. Wilma watched carefully, and when she saw that Mrs. Van Steendam was satisfied, relaxed onto a short, three-legged stool to await the men.

The camels arrived in a stately single file, led by one of the camel handlers. The only sound was their soft feet on the ground and the tinkling of the small bells that decorated some of the camel gear. One after another they strode into the corral and calmly starting eating. Soon, several formed into groups and knelt down. Mrs. Van Steendam found them beautiful.

The five foreign workers and four soldiers from the ship, along with Nate Wilkers, Alex Babcock, and Major Babcock had spaced themselves along the route, and one by one they assembled in the corral along with the camels. Bringing up the rear, Captain Van Steendam's men were responsible for keeping back any curious citizens who followed the procession out to Green Lake. Once in the paddock, the local soldiers put up their horses and headed straight toward the table. Praising the food effusively and thanking Mrs. Van Steendam, they sat down a respectable distance from the camels and tucked into their meal with gusto. The last person to arrive was Lt. Halter, who rode up in a carriage and remained seated.

Jeremy helped Wilma serve the men while listening intently to talk of the day. Most of the men had no better opinion of the camels than the first impressions he had heard from Amos Prudeau. By contrast, Major Babcock was as excited as a man can be. It was clear that the Captain didn't necessarily share the enthusiasm.

"Well, Major, time will tell. Now we need to see to your accommodations. Mrs. Eberly has invited Mrs. Van Steendam and myself to join you and Lt. Halter for supper at the hotel."

"Do thank Mrs. Eberly for her kind offer, but I should remain here with the camels on their first night, at least for a few hours."

"Major, leave your men to handle it. My boys will show 'em where to bunk. I believe you have relations waiting for you."

"Gracious! My cousin Sylvia's here. I noticed her and the children watching the day's events from a balcony. By all means, let's go. Alex, come now."

While tempted by the idea of dinner with Elizabeth, Alex wanted to be with the camels. "If it's all the same to you, sir, I'd like to stay here."

Major Babcock was relieved. Although he had some confidence in the other men, he trusted Alex implicitly. Mrs. Van Steendam had long since removed her apron, washed up, and donned a fashionable bonnet. She and Major Babcock joined Lt. Halter in the carriage, with Captain Van Steendam riding along side.

Wilma sighed. Now she could serve the remaining men, clean up her kitchen, and bed down in a corner for a few hours before making breakfast. She had to admit that Mr. Blackstone was a help, and he knew a lot about what to do in a kitchen. With only a few left to serve, Wilma breathed easier. Sgt. Bly, Alex Babcock, and Nate Wilkers were served, smiling and contented, and then came trouble.

The first foreigners wouldn't touch her beautiful roast pork, and an animated, incomprehensible discussion broke out. The last one took a good serving of all the food, strode away from the others, and sat down to eat. The remaining four talked among themselves and continued to point at the food. Wilma had never seen such behavior in the face of a fine meal. Her temper started to rise, and she was about to say something when Jeremy shot her a look that clamped her mouth tight.

Alex rushed over to the foreigners. All conversation ceased when Alex started speaking softly to one of the camel men in a foreign language, with assorted English words thrown in. Nate was dumfounded. Other men left their plates to approach the group, and the attentive silence intensified while Alex and Hassan whispered urgently to each other. When Wilma accidentally dropped a spoon, the sound reverberated like a clanging symbol. People began to regard Alex with a mixture of awe and suspicion. They heard the word "pork" and "no" repeatedly. Alex spoke to Jeremy.

"Excuse me, Mr. Blackstone, do you happen to know whether pork fat was used to prepare these delicious dishes?"

Wilma couldn't contain herself. "Are y'all askin' if I use bear grease or somethin' poor when I fix food for y'all? Course not! Them beans is simmered with pork rind, there's pork lard in the cornbread, and a ham hock cooked with them greens." Her voice was becoming shrill.

"Wilma."

Jeremy said it only once and without raising his voice. Wilma looked angrily at him, but she shut up. Much as the men may be skeptical of both camels and foreigners, they would not tolerate a slave speaking up like that to a white man. Wilma realized, almost too late, that Jeremy had saved her from a serious rebuke, maybe even the loss of the opportunity to be hired out. Wringing her hands, she kept her eyes to the ground.

"So everything has been prepared with pork?"

"Yup."

"Sir, I wonder if there might be any other food available. These men cannot eat pork, according to their religion."

A moment of stunned silence was followed by hoots of laughter from Capt. Van Steendam's men. "What religion would that be? The religion against good eatin'?!"

Wilma stared at the foreigners. Sgt. Bly looked around nervously, trying to determine what to do. He'd been left in charge, but he'd never faced this kind of thing before. The four Americans from the camel crew on the *Supply* stepped close in support of Alex.

"These men are Mohammedans. That's their religion, and it does not allow eating pork."

A cacophony of guffaws and shouts greeted this statement. "You mean they're not Christians?"

A solder waved his hand. "I got an idea. Maybe you should ask Miz Goldberg to cook for 'em. They don't eat no pork neither."

Another soldier pointed to Pertag. "What about him, over there? He's chowin' down just fine."

"He's not a Mohammedan." Alex tried to keep things calm and simple.

"So what he is then?"

"He's a Christian." Alex wished he weren't the only one trying to answer these questions, but he did appreciate the men who stood behind him. Nate, still flabbergasted, stood off to the side near his grandfather.

"What kind? Catholic or Protestant?"

"Orthodox, Eastern Orthodox."

"Ain't they a kind of heretic?"

"I don't know." Alex wondered how he managed to get into the position of amateur theologian.

"But what about these guys? They won't eat pork, so are they Jews?"

"No, they're not Jews. They have their own Good Book, the Qur'an, like our Bible, and it tells them they can't eat pork."

Alex was quickly becoming exasperated, but he could see that he had to try to answer the questions or risk further problems. In spite of his calm tones, the mocking threatened to turn to indignation or even anger. The men shouted questions on all sides.

"What are you saying? They don't follow the Bible?"

"Are they saved, then?"

"Wait, didn't the Mohammedans fight against Christians during the Crusades?"

In spite of his impatience, Alex tried to respond. "That was hundreds of years ago. A lot has changed since then. Christians and Mohammedans live side by side, peacefully. I've seen it myself."

As voices rose and fell, Hassan stood stock still, as he had in the Galveston jail, watching Alex, feeling helpless and furious. And hungry.

Jeremy carefully noted each man's pose and demeanor, assessed the levels of hostility and observed how they egged each other on. Scanning the group of foreigners, he saw from their continued whispering that they were struggling to be calm, but he could see their irritation building. His eyes locked ever so briefly with Nate's, before he spoke quietly.

"Nate, go on over to Miz Habberson's place. You'll likely find Amos Prudeau and Drew Johnsville there, and I know they pulled in a fine catch today. Ask 'em to make some fish stew, and then you bring it back right smartly."

"Yes, sir."

"On second thought, bring the catch to me."

Nate ran for his horse, thinking his grandfather was clever. He would do the cooking himself to make sure no pork was used.

Alex spoke up. "Mr. Blackstone, could we have your leave to check on the camels? It could take us a bit of time before we'd be able to eat. I'd be grateful if you'd keep this for me near the fire."

Jeremy nodded, and the soldiers returned to their places, still mumbling, but no longer stirred up. Reluctantly Alex handed over to Wilma the most delectable smoked pork and beans that he had ever tasted. Shamed by Alex, Pertag also left his plate and joined the others at the far end of the camel pen.

Sgt. Bly squirmed. He was relieved that the crisis had passed, but also troubled. Shouldn't Alex have asked him rather than Jeremy Blackstone? Wasn't he in charge? He tried to work out whether he should be offended. Army life was usually straightforward and his place in the chain of command clear. But tonight everything seemed out of order. He wasn't at all comfortable with these new fellows. He went back to his food, which tasted somehow flat.

Later that evening, with spices from the savory fish stew lingering on his lips, Hassan reviewed the events of the day with Ali and Abdullah. The good food had improved their mood, but their emotions were still in conflict. Recollections of both joy and anger dashed in and out of memory, vying for dominance. There had been several acts of kindness. Seeing Hassan hatless with sweat clouding his vision, a young man had offered him a bright red bandana, his first gift from an American. In the full heat of the afternoon, a distinguished African-looking man had brought a jug of cool water for the men to share. Alex explained that it was Antoine, a slave of Mrs. McDermott. Another time, the palest woman Hassan had ever encountered had peeked shyly from behind a huge sunbonnet and offered them each a sweet square pastry filled with cherry jam. In some ways it had been a king's welcome, with the people cheering, waving, and shouting encouragement. This really was a historic event, and they felt privileged to be part of it.

But the camels' behavior had created bad impressions, even though it was understandable that the animals would be a bit wild after being at sea for so long. Pertag in particular had been unable to control the camels. His poor performance today was the latest in a string of disasters. On the *Supply* Captain Turner had taken Pertag for a camel expert and deferred to his recommendations. Pertag had bound the first two babies born on ship in a kind of swaddling cloth that rendered them unrecognizable to their mothers. Both had died. A third infant had succumbed when Pertag's negligence allowed an adult camel to roll on it and crush it. Captain Turner blamed all the camel handlers for this death. Again today, Pertag's incompetence made them all look silly. They were at a loss what to do.

The three Egyptians also worried about the taunts, jeers, and harsh words from the local people. Hassan believed that some of it was fear. Ali blamed ignorance. Abdullah, unable to find a good reason, was the most upset, especially about dinner. His English employers in Alexandria had always met his dietary requirements. Ali, who had more experience with non-Muslims, urged patience and reminded everyone that once Alex had explained their food restrictions, a good-tasting meal had been served on short notice.

"Let's see what we are offered for breakfast. What if they cook everything in pork fat?" Abdullah remained skeptical.

"Then we may have to compromise." This launched a lively debate between Ali and Abdullah that drew Erdem into the discussion as well.

Not in the mood for religious interpretation, Hassan stayed aloof from the argument by investigating the shabby lean-to outside the new camel stable. The structure would not keep them dry if it rained. Hassan had expected better accommodations. Most of the Americans had cots inside the larger shelter, in a partitioned area that served as a bunkhouse. He did not wish to believe it, but maybe Abdullah was right. Maybe they were being treated inhospitably.

Alex returned from checking on the camels and sat down beside Hassan. Both were too tired to speak, and neither knew where to start. Their dilemma was solved when Nate Wilkers appeared, bedroll in hand. He had surrendered his cot in the bunkhouse to one of the men from the ship. Nate approached cautiously, uncertain of his standing

with Alex now that the camel men had arrived. Normally
Alex told stories about everything. No campfire would burn
long enough for Alex to finish telling tales, and Nate had
listened to plenty of them. Yet, in all this talk, Alex had not
let on that he was close to the camel handlers, and he had
certainly had not let on that he spoke their language.

Alex got up and shook Nate's hand. "Howdy, Nate.
Quite the day we had, huh? Can you believe it? Camels in
Texas, and we were here to see it! Look at them all snuggled
into their corral, acting like they're right at home." Laughing, he turned to make introductions. "Nate, meet Hassan
ibn Yusuf. Hassan, this is Nate Wilkers."

Hassan rose and extended his hand. "Pleased to meet
you, Nate.

Nate stared. The foreigner spoke English, heavily accented, but definitely English. He found himself stuttering
his reply. "Pleasure's mine, uh, Hoss?"

"Hassan."

"Glad to know you."

Hassan was enjoying Nate's surprise. Alhaji Mustafa
always stressed the importance of learning the language
when traveling in a foreign country. Hassan wished his
grandfather could see the look on Nate's face.

"Nate, you did well today! I saw you with the camels. It
is like you have been around them all your life."

"Thanks. You and Alex did a great job with the camel
car." Nate hated to feel foolish, which was exactly what
he felt now. If these men could speak English, then they
had understood the abuse hurled at them during the day as
well as the whole discussion over supper. His ears reddened
at the thought. Had Alex been deliberately keeping this a
secret from him? Alex spoke the Egyptians' language and
they spoke English. Nate couldn't believe it. "Say, Hassan,
how did you learn English?"

"I learned on the ship. Lots of time to practice."

"And that's how I learned Arabic. I only speak a little;
it's hard to learn. But I can understand a fair bit. Sometimes
it's easier for Hassan and the others to speak their own language."

"You sure kept that under your hat, Alex."

Hassan looked curiously at Nate. "What did he keep under his hat?"

Both Nate and Alex burst out laughing. After they'd explained it to Hassan, he found it so funny that he called the other camel men. Soon everyone was engaged in a hilarious exchange of expressions from several languages. Nate actively contributed German idioms that Hilde had taught him. At last, the men prepared to turn in. The four Muslims lined up for their last prayers of the day, and Alex was grateful that the men in the bunkhouse didn't see them. Inspired by Hassan's devotion, Alex knelt to revive his childhood routine of praying before bed. Nate, who had never been much for religion, crawled under cover and was asleep before the others were done.

When he opened his eyes at dawn, Nate thought it must still be evening, for the scene before him had changed little from the night before. There stood the four men, repeating the bowing motions of their prayers. Momentarily befuddled, he checked the sky, where puffy pink clouds confirmed that it was just before sunrise. The reality of daybreak was reinforced by the roasty smell of Wilma's coffee wafting from the kitchen. Nate studied the foreigners in amazement, wondering if they had been doing this all night. Nearby Alex dozed, and Pertag snored unapologetically, completely oblivious to the prayerful murmuring. Though tempted by the coffee, Nate was reluctant to get up. When he stretched, he noticed some stiffness in his back after yesterday's efforts yanking the camels. Nevertheless, he was happy with his situation. The camels - his future - were right beside him in the paddock. Rolling over to catch a few more minutes of sleep, he gazed lazily toward the camel pen.

"What the hell?!"

He shouted and leaped up. Alex jumped up behind him and both men sprinted toward the section of the camel enclosure that had been built up with prickly pear cactus. There stood Adela, Amisa, Perguida, Tullah, Ayesha and Gourmal munching on the fence!

"Holy shit!"

Sgt. Stacy Bly came blasting out of the bunkhouse. The Texans and the soldiers from the *Supply*, half-dressed and groggy, fell out of bed and followed at a run. The camel handlers interrupted their prayers and dashed to join them. The inexperienced Texans tugged at the camels, whose tethers became entangled as they bunched together around the cactus. Having no desire to quit their contented chomping, the camels responded with kicks and angry braying. The Texans, now furious, pulled even harder on the tethers, irritating the camels more.

Abdullah urgently conferred with Hassan, Alex and Sgt. Bly. The Americans had built the fence without knowing a camel's preference for spiny plants like acacia. Untroubled by stabbing spines, a camel's mouth is designed to graze on plants that no other animal will touch. In fact, these prickly pears were a luxurious meal. There would be no chance whatsoever of shooing the camels away from the cactus fence without someone getting hurt. The animals would have to be coaxed.

Sgt. Bly was worked up. "What the hell are we supposed to do? I can't tell y'all how many hours me and the men spent puttin' them cactus there, and I ain't about to watch all that work get eaten for breakfast."

Like Stacy, the other men who had built the corral were irate. One man struck Amisa on the nose with a stick, and she responded with a serious sideways kick that missed him by a hair. Perguida spat on another man, who reached for his holster. Alex knocked the man aside and frantically waved the other Texans away from the camels. Earning Alex's gratitude, Nate called out, "Get back! Y'all get back! Let the handlers calm 'em down."

Slowly and carefully, they started to ease the camels away from the cactus. Hassan, Erdem, and Abdullah had the best success at extricating the animals one by one from their morning appetizers. They passed them to Ali, Alex, Nate and Pertag who hobbled them near the feed troughs filled with fresh oats and hay. Willing at last to accept this alternative breakfast, the animals began to settle down. By that time, a significant portion of the fence was gone.

As Alex counted the animals to make sure they were all present, a shot went off. Several hundred yards away stood a male called Mahomet, his huge body silhouetted against a fireball of morning sun, languorously chewing on Paul Diefendorf's cactus fence. Mr. Diefendorf held a shotgun aimed squarely at Mahomet's broad body.

"That was a warning shot, and y'all can see how much good it did. Moved him a couple feet. I ain't havin' no circus animal eatin' my fence, so y'all get him outta here or I swear to you, I'll shoot him right now!"

Hassan, Abdullah, Alex, and Nate hurried out of the corral toward Mahomet, but much to their surprise, Jeremy Blackstone was already on the move. Before they could reach Mahomet, Jeremy strode right between Mr. Dicfendorf and the camel.

"Howdy, Paul."

"For Chrissake, Jeremy, what are you doin'? Git outta the way. That dern animal is about to ruin my garden."

Jeremy reached his arm slowly toward the shotgun and looked steadily at his friend. "Paul, listen to me. Somebody's gonna get hurt if you're not careful. Besides, that animal is government property, and if you kill it, you'll most likely have to pay for it."

"What the hell? Pay for the camel? And whose gonna pay for my garden?" Grousing, he lowered his shotgun. "Damn it, Jeremy, it ain't right for them animals to be wanderin' all over. You see this here bullwhip at my feet? That's Whacker. I swear to you, if that camel or any of 'em comes anywhere near my fence, they'll be gettin' a talkin'-to from Whacker. Am I makin' myself clear?"

"How was anybody to know these critters would eat prickly pear? It won't happen again."

"Better not. Them beasts are foreign, and they plain do not belong here. Say Jeremy, what the hell are you doin' over here away from the lighthouse anyway?"

"Nothin' much. Visitin' Nate. How are your tomatoes doin'? Let's have a look." Jeremy then engaged Paul Diefendorf in a lengthy conversation about the best way to grow every vegetable in his garden.

Abdullah approached the camel with a ball of oats and water, one of Mahomet's preferred foods on the *Supply*. Calling softly, he gently pulled the rope and turned the camel's head toward his outstretched hand. Alex, Hassan and Nate

held back to let Abdullah work. Once distracted from the
fence, Mahomet obediently followed Abdullah toward the
compound. With a sigh of relief, Abdullah skirted the corral to enter by the front gate away from the tempting cactus fence. So focused was he on settling Mahomet that he
scarcely noticed Sgt. Bly sitting alone with a mug of coffee,
scowling and deep in thought.

Indianola, May 16, 1856

My dearest Annabelle,

*The camels have landed, though I cannot say that the event
went smoothly. Your father will undoubtedly manage to ob-
tain a copy of the official account sent to Secretary Davis. Let
him cast a jaundiced eye on that document. I can assure you
that Major Babcock's description fails to adequately portray
the chaos. The Major referred to the males as "pugnacious"
and mentioned "prancing and cavorting" of the animals. Such
understatement! What occurred was nearly a rout. Only the
quick intervention of Captain Van Steendam and his men
prevented a complete disaster. The animals are now secured
in a camel paddock outside of town and are beginning to take
more nourishment. They still are weak from their voyage.*

*The larger question is this: can these animals ever be suitable
for the US Army? The locals view them as sideshow creatures, and quite frankly, I cannot picture any red-blooded
Texan sacrificing his horse in exchange for a wobbly saddle
on a camel.*

*Major Babcock recently wrote to the Secretary requesting
patience. I would not have addressed Mr. Davis thusly, but
the Major lacks caution. He asserts his views aggressively,
yet naively. He insists, not only to the Secretary but to any
who will listen, that the camels number too few and that
the extant group should be used to inaugurate a breeding
program. The absurdity of the US Army running a camel
ranch seems to escape him. The beasts are to be tested, not
farmed. I shall be most curious to see what comes of this,*

though lately the Major has become cagey and neglects to inform me of the nature of his correspondence.

Please convey my warmest greetings to your father. I believe, indeed I fervently wish, that I may receive orders to return to Washington before the camels move inland.

Your devoted husband,

Winston

GREEN LAKE, NEAR INDIANOLA, TEXAS

THE FIRST SUNDAY AFTER the camels landed, Elizabeth was over the moon with excitement. Straightaway after church, she and the entire resident population of Mrs. Eberly's hotel paraded out to Green Lake to see the camels. Anticipating a multitude, Major Babcock had established a viewing area. Under a gigantic live oak, Elizabeth and her family joined the crowd that came in seemingly endless profusion. Dressed in their Sunday best, whole families tumbled from carriages and wagons lugging large baskets of food. Some spread blankets on the ground in a random patchwork of color. Others laid out hay bales to serve as tables and as galleries upon which they climbed to get a better look. The wealthier among them were accompanied by slaves who unloaded chairs, tables, plates, cutlery, crystal glasses, and a plethora of roast chickens, vegetables, and cakes. The less well off came jammed together on buckboards or in groups traveling on foot. Mr. Blauvelt, ever alert to an opportunity, set up a shuttle service between the immigrant camp and Green Lake. For those who arrived without benefit of picnic, enterprising Mexicans sold pinto beans wrapped in corn tortillas and golden fried sopapillas, while competing German vendors offered grilled sausages and slices of fruit pie. The men pulled out flasks of whisky and lit cigars, all the while debating the virtues of the camel project. A carnival atmosphere ensued.

Hoping to present a flattering image of the camels, Major Babcock called for Ayesha, Tullah, and Perguida, three of the most accommodating females, to be fitted with riding saddles.

"Let's acquaint the local citizens with our camels. Erdem, Pertag, and Ali, you keep the rest of the herd away from this area. Alex, Hassan, and Abdullah will offer camel rides. Abdullah, please show the crowd how to mount a camel."

Squeals of delight arose from children and adults alike as Abdullah caused Tullah to kneel and climbed on. When he tapped her side, she rose slowly, her knobby knees seeming to thrust in all directions. A child screamed, sure that Abdullah would fall. Then, as Tullah unfolded her front legs to stand erect, a chorus of "Bravo!" burst forth from the crowd. While Abdullah marched his camel stoically back and forth, Major Babcock offered explanations and answered questions for a full fifteen minutes. Finally one of the bystanders objected.

"Hey, when do we get to try her out? My son here wants to be first!"

That ended the educational session, and people scurried into three lines. Although Elizabeth would have loved the chance to ride a camel, her mother cautioned against a public display.

"No, child, you must wait. When we travel to San Antonio with the camels, you shall surely have an opportunity to ride one."

"Yes, of course, Mama, we'll have them all to ourselves soon."

The camel rides provided Elizabeth with a superb excuse for studying both Hassan and Alex as long as she wished. Although Alex had a little more trouble making the camels rise and kneel at his command, his charm worked wonders with the townsfolk. Keeping up an easy banter, he spoke endlessly about the camel's strength, gentleness, and many virtues. She admired his way with people. Hassan was much quieter, perhaps because of the language, but displayed a kindly patience as he helped the children climb on and off the camels. Elizabeth imagined riding first Alex's camel, then Hassan's. The thought of touching Hassan's hand, as might occur if he were to help her onto a camel, sent a shiver up her arm.

Careful not to let her mother notice, she stole more glances at Hassan and memorized every detail of his movements.

Two hours later, Major Babcock called a halt for the day, promising more opportunities the following Sunday. The public had been enchanted. Major Babcock was ecstatic, as was Alex, who had thoroughly enjoyed showing off the camels. Though tired, Hassan hadn't minded too much, as he loved to see the children smiling, but Abdullah felt humiliated.

Soon most of the townsfolk had seen the camels at least once or twice. During the week, women of the leisure class, often attended by their slaves, came to pass the afternoon reading, snacking on savory tidbits, and admiring the exotic scene. Passing ranch hands and itinerant merchants detoured out to the camp for a look. Some would gawk for half the morning, while others sauntered through, one brief peek being sufficient. They praised, guffawed, marveled and criticized in turn. Local boys could be found at all hours striding the perimeter, and a few of them threw rocks or otherwise tormented the animals. To prevent these assaults, Major Babcock persuaded Captain Van Steendam to mount a regular guard duty, a decision little appreciated by the soldiers who pulled night watch, but much respected by the camel handlers. Hassan had never known people to have so little familiarity with camels. He was amazed at their lack of common sense.

The following day, Alex, Nate and Hassan counted themselves lucky, for they had drawn supply duty. They would spend the entire day in town while the supplies were gathered, tallied and recorded, before they had to assist with the packing. Loading the goods would require the careful attention of all three, as none of the soldiers had yet learned how to pack a camel properly. Alex, who stayed most nights out at Green Lake with the camels, grasped at the chance for a possible encounter with Elizabeth.

"I wonder who we'll see in town today," he murmured, half to himself. Hassan was quick to catch it.

"Maybe you wish to see Mrs. Eberly from the hotel."

"Stop it. You've been at me all morning. Let's just get these camels ready."

Nate joined in. "Naw, I'd guess it's Captain Van Steendam that he's longin' for sight of."

"No, no, it is the cousin of Major Babcock, Mrs. McDermott. That is the one he wants to see." Hassan kept the game going.

"Quit it, will ya?" Alex's fair skin had turned an odd shade of crimson, with brighter splotchy patches over his nose and cheekbones from a recent sunburn.

"I can not get used to this color of your face. I can never make such a color."

Nate doubled over laughing at the combination of Alex's blushes and Hassan's stilted English.

Alex was not to be outdone. "What about you, Nate? What about that perky blonde who couldn't keep her hands off you the day we unloaded the camels?"

"Enough already. She ain't my girl, I explained that to y'all before." No one much believed this, and Nate secretly hoped that Evangeline Blauvelt might cross his path. He was still trying to work out the meaning of that startling kiss. "Too bad Hassan's girl isn't here for us all to see."

Hassan let this remark go unanswered. They would never see Sula, and he was perfectly happy about that. But he smiled, and Alex saw it.

"Hey, Nate. Look at that moony face on Hassan. Wonder what he's thinking about?"

"Nothing. Let's get going."

Hassan was glad to leave camp for a while, especially with Alex. He had not yet decided about Nate, but Nate seemed eager to learn about the camels and willing to do anything associated with their care, even the dirtier tasks. Hassan would keep an open mind about Nate, as his grandfather would have counseled.

Abdullah, shaking his head at the wondrous exuberance of young men, helped to prepare Massanda, Adela and Tullah for the trip to town. Erdem fitted Massanda with a riding saddle and dressed Adela and Tullah with packsaddles. Each camel was adorned with red tassels and bells, the latter being useful not only for decoration but as a means of alerting citizens that the camels were coming.

A rider on horseback always rode ahead, lest horses be taken by surprise. Before the Camel Corps made it standard procedure to have a herald, several startled horses had wrested control from their riders and bolted in panic. Once a wagon had overturned. By announcing the camels, a crier gave prudent people time to dismount, tether their wagons, or vacate the road. Alex rode ahead cheerfully waving his hat and shouting. He enjoyed playing like Paul Revere on his famous ride.

"The camels are coming! Good morning, and make way! Hear ye! Hear ye! The camels are coming!" When he saw frowns or heard complaints, he smiled and called out, "Sorry for the inconvenience! Thank you for dismounting. Enjoy this historic occasion!" Sometimes he called a simple announcement, but he waxed more poetic if he happened to have a friendly audience. He imagined what lyrical flourishes he might use if Elizabeth McDermott happened to be in town today.

A respectable distance behind Alex, Hassan rode on Massanda. He drew stares and comments as he pitched forward and back in rolling motion, one leg crossed before him on the saddle. Sometimes he deliberately slowed down, allowing Alex to develop a bit of a lead, and then let Massanda trot to catch up, bouncing gently and smiling at the people along the road. Tethered behind him, Adela and Tullah seemed to like the exercise. Most onlookers admired the way the red and green leather bridles swung and the bells tinkled when the camels moved quickly. Not all were of one mind, however, and unfortunately for Hassan, his English was good enough for him to understand the abuse as well as the admiration.

Following the camel procession, Nate drove a supply wagon pulled by two mules. He had developed a fondness for the camels and jumped at any chance to travel with them. He wanted to be fully ready for the inland trek. As they neared the Depot, where they were to pick up hay for the camels and stores for the men, Nate scanned the thickening crowd for Evangeline Blauvelt, but instead set his eyes upon Drew Johnsville, grinning widely and making some disparaging remark. He nodded a curt greeting to Drew and then smiled at Amos Prudeau whom he spotted a few yards further on. The camels were already tying up behind the warehouse when Nate noticed his grandfather on the porch.

Jeremy Blackstone had for all practical purposes become a permanent fixture at the Government Depot, having left the lighthouse in the care of several off-duty pilots who rotated at the post. His mysterious behavior confounded Nate. At first he figured that his grandfather was just keeping tabs on him. For as long as Nate could remember, his grandfather had surveyed, monitored, reconnoitered, and observed his every movement. A perfect watchdog, that's what he was, always hovering at the edges of whatever Nate was doing. But, recently, his grandfather had also started asking questions. He inquired about camels, routes to San Antonio, and plans for quelling the Indian uprisings. He asked about how horses and mules stood up to the desert, how fast the camels could travel, and what weapons the Army issued to their frontier soldiers. He posed questions about all sorts of things in which he had never shown one speck of interest. For most of Nate's life, Jeremy's steely gray eyes had revealed nothing more than stoic composure. Lately his grandfather's gaze sparkled with curiosity.

Jeremy had taken to cooking for the men at the Government Depot on a regular basis. Nate was not sure whether this was an official assignment or a way that Jeremy paid for the right to bunk in town. He had heard the soldiers praise his grandfather's meals as far tastier than anything they could conjure themselves. He knew, too, that the camel handlers appreciated Jeremy's solicitous efforts to cook for them without pork. Maybe his grandfather liked the work. Or maybe Jeremy had taken the post because chow time provided a guaranteed occasion for him to check on Nate. Nate hadn't yet confessed that he planned to sign on with the camel train. He expected that his grandfather would be none too fond of that notion, so he delayed bringing it up. Besides, Major Babcock hadn't decided when they were leaving.

Nate dismounted at the Depot and greeted his grandfather casually, hoping to avoid further conversation. When Amos Prudeau and Drew Johnsville offered him a bite and a beer, he quickly accepted. As he scanned the crowd, Nate saw no sign of Evangeline Blauvelt, but sure enough, there stood Elizabeth McDermott across the street, carrying a lime green parasol and watching intently.

Delighted by her good fortune, Elizabeth thought how easily she could have missed out. She had been practicing her piano for two hours, enjoying her one distraction in this backwater town that otherwise pleased her little. These Indianolans were quite proud of their role as "Gateway to the West" and hoped to pull business away from Galveston, but somehow she couldn't picture it. The place was too rustic, and she was quite sure that her father and his friends would not allow this upstart town to displace Galveston. She sighed. Galveston! So sophisticated, so attractive, and how she longed to go back. She tried desperately not to think that her next steps would be further away from home.

She was supposed to have a lesson after her practice time, but today Frau Klug had cancelled because of headache. Happy for the change of schedule, Elizabeth decided to meander about town. Without conscious intention, she was drawn toward the Government Depot where she caught wind of the welcome cry: "The camels are coming!" Quickening her steps, she joined the gathering crowd in time to watch Alex Babcock waving his arm enthusiastically.

"Ladies and gentlemen, make way for the camels. Uncle Sam's camels are coming! Make way, if you please." He caught her eye, swept his hat in a dramatic arc, flashed her an ebullient smile, and leapt off his horse in front of the Depot.

Elizabeth watched how people reacted. Even those who objected to the camels relaxed in Alex's warmth. Everybody liked him. In a way, he reminded her of her father. Not in looks, but in temperament, that part of her father who laughed easily and enjoyed a good time. It was impossible not to have fun when Alex was around. When Alex looked back down the road, she followed his direction to see the camels appearing.

She gasped. It was Hassan, seated high on a beautiful golden camel bedecked with a fringed bridle hung with three bells. Elizabeth could not say what was most pleasing: the light reflecting off the tinkling bells, the smooth carefree motion of the promenading camel, or the way that Hassan's ebony hair and eyebrows framed his dark eyes and straight patrician nose. He looked masterful, and apart from being on a camel, not one bit exotic. Hassan was outfitted like a true American in breeches, boots, a cotton shirt, leather vest, and wide-brimmed hat. Except for the sharp contrast between blond and black hair flowing below their hats, he and Alex were dressed alike, a set of slightly mismatched twins.

She watched while Alex and Hassan and Nate Wilkers tended to the mules, Alex's horse, and the camels. The camels were very cooperative, and Elizabeth was impressed that each of the three young men seemed to know what to do. Alex stepped forward to answer questions from the onlookers that had congregated, while Nate and Hassan finished caring for the animals. Then, almost as if she had missed a scene, Nate wandered off with two of his friends, and Alex was coming straight toward her with Hassan at his side.

"Hello, Elizabeth." Alex smiled broadly.

"Hello, Alex. What a beautiful day! How was the ride in?" Elizabeth was dismayed that she could think of nothing more original to say. In truth, the most basic conversation escaped her as she was overcome by Hassan's proximity.

"Great, no problems. The camels are doing well, and Major Babcock is quite pleased. You would not believe how much they're eating now, and Ibrim in particular is getting really frisky."

Elizabeth smiled. She knew that Alex was about to hold forth on the state of one or another camel, and that once started, he might not be easily dissuaded from an excruciatingly detailed explanation. Although Alex had told her Hassan's name, she had never been properly introduced. Still smiling, she nodded at Hassan, raising a curious eyebrow to Alex.

"Excuse me. Elizabeth, I'd like you to meet Hassan ibn Yusuf, from Egypt."

"Pleased to meet you." She almost said something about having seen him in Galveston, but caught herself just in time. Memories of the jail would not offer an auspicious beginning to their acquaintance. "I hope you are enjoying your stay here."

"The pleasure is mine, Miss Eleezabet." Hassan replied with a phrase that he had verified with Alex as being a polite form of reply. He bowed slightly, but did not extend his hand.

Bewildered by Hassan's unexpectedly good English, Elizabeth lowered her eyes and curtsied. She had never heard her name pronounced that way, as Eleezabet, but found it charming.

Hassan was taken aback by her modesty, quite in contrast with the image he held of her brazenly slipping into the Galveston jail against her father's wishes.

Alex carried on. "Guess what, Elizabeth? We have a couple of hours until we need to be back. Mr. Blackstone and Captain Van Steendam have to cross check the inventory. In the meanwhile, would you care to go for a stroll?"

"What a lovely idea! And then how about a lemonade at the hotel?"

"Let's go."

Elizabeth couldn't believe she was spending the afternoon with Alex and Hassan instead of with her dull piano teacher. Alex acted the good host, telling camel tales, generating conversation and helping Hassan with his English. About halfway toward the hotel, they stopped along the waterfront. A patchwork of clouds provided respite from the sun. When she admired the gulls floating overhead, Hassan said that the birds were similar to those near his home. Elizabeth learned that Hassan was well educated and polite as well as being marvelous to look at. As they ambled toward the hotel, Elizabeth found Indianola far more agreeable than before.

The letter was written on crisp, high quality paper that reeked of formality and prosperity, with Quentin Mc-Dermott's initials embossed in gold. It now lay crumpled accordion-style in Sylvia McDermott's lap, where she sat motionless on the veranda at the hotel. Her hands tightened clawlike around the letter, as if to suffocate its potency, while the damp indentations of her fingers abused its polished surface. With effort she stifled the temptation to jump up and rip the letter to shreds. She wanted to jettison it like a scorpion, both disgusting and dangerous, that had somehow slithered onto her skirt. This struggle with the menacing text occurred silently and unobserved, a private battle.

A welcome breeze rustled the scarlet and white geraniums in brightly painted Mexican pots placed attractively on the raised veranda. The scent of pink tea roses at ground level lifted with the wind, bringing a soothing sensation. Sylvia raised her eyes to trace the flight of a heron and loosened her hold on the letter enough that it fluttered slightly. This nearly imperceptible attempt to escape her clutches angered her almost as much as the letter itself. Slapping the wrinkled text smooth, she folded it severely and repeatedly until it was a small rectangular packet squished between her two cupped hands. No matter how she analyzed it, the ridiculously brief note was completely wrong.

My dear Sylvia,

Business matters will take me to New York, unfortunately preventing me from joining you in San Antonio as soon as I had hoped. I do not wish to leave the house unattended, so I have rented it to the British Consul. As my return should coincide with the completion of his new residence, this arrangement suits us both well.

I am sorry for this unforeseen change in plans, but I am sure you will make good use of the extra time to set up house before I arrive. I count on your great capability to make the most of this situation. I look forward to providing you a longer explanation as soon as we are reunited. I miss you most sincerely and send you my deepest affections.

Your devoted husband,

Quentin

Something was seriously out of kilter. Sensing dissimulation, Sylvia was devastated. This letter held the clue to some deep calamity, either already occurred or yet to come and, if the latter, perhaps preventable. With absolute clarity, she also knew that whatever the reason for this letter, it was not because of another woman.

She knew this with certainty. Such knowledge is not defensible in any objective manner, but is absolutely real, as she felt any woman would understand. To an outsider, Quentin McDermott's flirtatious banter with beautiful women may have provoked skepticism. But Sylvia knew her husband to be fiercely loyal, though he loved to be the center of attention. He would maneuver in a crowded room, kissing a hand, barely touching a shoulder, admiring a gown, and exchanging repartee. His taste for women ran the gamut. A room full of perfumed and adorned women was as exciting to him as a buffet table loaded with an assortment of the richest foods. The more variety, the better. Surprisingly, Sylvia was never jealous at these occasions. The innocent fun nourished her husband's confidence, kept him cheerful, and made him a more ardent lover. He confined his risks to business. His thrills came from gambling on crops, imports, and politics rather than dangerous liaisons with other women.

Of course there were those females that a Southern lady carefully ignored with every fiber of her being. Quentin would travel to the plantations in unusually close intervals and stay over a night or two longer than necessary. A piece of newly purchased fabric or an item of children's clothing would be missing. She would find a bill of sale on his desk that read "woman and infant mulatto child, sold to T. Jones, Mississippi." On the rare occasions when she visited the Brazos farms, she sometimes scanned the slaves for a pale complexion. Although a light color could as easily have come from the overseer, she was unable to resist searching for telltale signs, such as build, gait, or tilt of head. When she caught herself doing this, she stopped immediately.

Still squeezing the remains of Quentin's letter in one hand, she ran the other over the inlaid mosaic squares that decorated a small wrought iron table. She took up her glass of tea, now tepid and diluted from ice long melted, and wondered how much time had passed. Her feet and ankles were heated by an orange sun angling lower to the horizon. She would have to move the chair back into the shade, and she would have to seek further understanding of Quentin's message. Why was Quentin going to New York? Why was he letting others into their home? How long would she have to wait for him?

The sound of laughter interrupted her reflections. Sylvia stuffed the letter into a pocket and prepared a face of maternal comfort to greet Elizabeth who walked jauntily down the street escorted by Alex and one of the camel handlers.

Spying her mother sitting on the porch alone, Elizabeth sighed. Her mother had been moody of late. The easy banter when they brushed each other's hair had become strained. Elizabeth feared bringing up a topic that would distress her mother, which ruled out mention of San Antonio, Galveston, her father's absence, their departure for the interior, or any other subject remotely related to their uncertain future. She hoped her mother would rally now for the sake of her companions.

"We're almost there. I'm ready for some lemonade. How about you?"

Alex smiled. "That sounds great, Elizabeth. Wait until you taste this, Hassan. Let's go."

Sylvia welcomed the young men and chatted with them easily. Elizabeth was delighted that her mother put up a good show, whether she felt it or not.

Alex loved the lemonade. "Isn't it wonderful, Hassan?

"Very good, yes."

"You don't sound that excited."

"Alex, it is delicious. I expected it to taste like home, that's all. We use honey. This tastes different, but I like it."

Elizabeth watched closely, impressed with Hassan's polite reply. He seemed to understand everything they said, although his spoken English had a most unusual lilt. Seeing the two boys together laughing and smiling at her, she felt like the belle of the ball even more than she had at the real May Day ball. If she could wish it, she would make this afternoon last forever.

In the shade of the live oak tree behind Mrs. Eberly's hotel, Esther and Agnes sat balanced on two wobbly three-legged stools, taking a break from preparing dinner. The children, Sally and Mabel, were playing a game of jacks at the far corner of the house.

"Whew, that Malvina sure is trouble. Can't never please her. I work as good as the next one, but even Miz Sylvia don't demand like that high yaller gal puttin' on airs."

Agnes had never heard Esther complain like she had these last few days. Agnes often felt that other people understood things long before she did. Usually Esther was the one who explained, translating the obvious so that Agnes knew what to do and how to act. These days Esther had no patience. It was easy to understand some of it. They didn't sleep well, two women and two girls crowded together on a simple raised platform in a shack that also served as a storeroom. The floor was bare earth, not well tamped, that sprouted rivulets during the least rain, while the scraps of split rails that passed for walls showed large gaps that let in wind and water. The mosquitoes were the worst that Agnes had ever known. In Galveston the slave quarters had thin cotton window covers that, though they stifled the air, kept out most insects, and they sometimes burned citronella oil in the evening. Never had she encountered mosquitoes so plentiful and so ravenous.

"I know, Esther. It ain't right. And them mosquitoes was buzzin' my head the whole night."

"Sure ain't Galveston. We ain't sleepin', and we workin', and we ain't even workin' for our own missus. Ain't nobody much talkin' to us."

Agnes didn't know what to say. She wanted Esther to feel better and start explaining again. She needed to know what was going to happen to them, and nobody seemed to be able to tell her. She had given up asking, for fear of Esther's sharp reprimand.

Esther appraised Agnes and softened a little. "We got to hold on. Miz Sylvia ain't quite right. You can see the worry on her. Watch her hands. If you see 'em workin' the sides of her skirt, that's a given sign she worryin' 'bout somethin'."

Agnes exhaled a sigh of deep relief. This was the Esther she knew. That kind of explaining helped Agnes no end.

She would watch for Miz Sylvia twisting the fabric of her skirt or pulling on her pockets, and she would be extra quiet in her work. She wanted Miz Sylvia to be happy, because when Miz Sylvia felt fine, everything went better.

Over in the stable, Antoine and Samuel sprawled across a cot, their backs against the wall and their feet dangling over the edge, killing time. They had fed and curried the horses, swept the barn and the yard, and trimmed the bushes. Malthus should have done those jobs, but for the sake of harmony, Samuel and Antoine helped out. The afternoon heat had disgorged a multitude of flies, intent on interfering with their rest. The men batted the pesky insects aside and contemplated their vulnerability. The anxiety was especially heavy on Samuel, who prayed daily that Precious had not been sent to the fields. Like the rest of the McDermott family, the slaves hoped that this excursion to San Antonio would last no more than the summer, but as they lingered here in Indianola with no stated time for moving on, despair was a constant hazard.

"Antoine, did you see Miz Sylvia after that letter came today? She ain't moved from her chair in hours. Seems every time she get a letter she feel bad."

Something was clearly amiss, but Antoine would not encourage this line of thought. Samuel was too close to an abyss of anguish. "She got a lot to think about. It can't be easy."

"I s'pose not, but still. I wish she'd tell us somethin'."

"She can't say nothin' if she don't know it herself. She's used to havin' Massa Quentin 'round to make decisions. I'm sure as daylight that she gotta be lonely."

"Yeah, you right." Samuel swished the flies away from his face. Antoine instantly regretted the comment about loneliness as he watched Samuel drift inward to a place of loss and longing that would only make him morose and crotchety. Their monotony was broken when Malvina stuck her nose out the back.

"Miz McDermott wants the carriage fitted out, and make it quick."

Samuel knew that the last part was Malvina's addition. She always accused him of laziness, which he took as a profound insult. He got the horses while Antoine ran the polishing rag once more over the brass fixtures as they brought the carriage forward. Antoine assisted the two ladies into the forward-facing seat, and the young men climbed in opposite them. Holding the reins, Samuel marveled at the young Egyptian's improved circumstance, comfortably ensconced in the McDermott carriage, a far cry from the Galveston jail.

Sylvia instructed, "Please take us to the Government Depot." She turned to Alex. "Thank you for suggesting this outing. I'd like to see how the camels are loaded." She kept the small talk flowing to help Alex, who was utterly at sixes and sevens in the company of her daughter.

Elizabeth peered out from under her sunbonnet and spoke to Hassan. "I forgot to ask earlier. Have you seen the Great Pyramids?"

"Yes, my grandfather took me to see them, but they are not close to our home. We live in Alexandria and they are near Cairo."

"Were they terrible to behold?"

Hassan cocked his head, thinking that "terrible" meant very bad. Alex intervened. "I believe she would like to know if they are big, and how you feel when you stand next to them." Alex smiled warmly at Hassan and beamed at Elizabeth.

"Ah, excuse me, now I understand. They will make you feel small like an ant or a grain of sand. There are thousands of blocks. Each one is bigger than a house."

"Thank you, Hassan, that's exactly what I wanted to know. Mama, someday perhaps we shall travel to Egypt. I would so love to see the pyramids."

Sylvia patted her daughter's hand. "Perhaps we shall. One never knows." This latter platitude struck her as the truest observation of the day as well as of the last few weeks.

"In that case, my grandfather will welcome you to our home. He is a highly respected scholar." Hassan had specifically learned the words to describe his grandfather's education and standing, in order to honor him in conversations whenever possible.

Alex laughed heartily. "What a great invitation! But for now, ladies, you'll have to settle for the bit of Egypt we brought to you."

As they neared the Government Depot, Alex spied Nate gesturing for them to hurry. "Looks like we're wanted. If you walk nearer to the Depot, you'll be able to see better."

"Excuse us, Mrs. McDermott, Miss Eleezabet." Hassan bounded out of the carriage and jogged with Alex toward Nate.

"Samuel, stay with the carriage. Antoine, follow us."

Antoine helped the ladies to alight, overjoyed to have this chance for a closer inspection of the camels. As before, he tried to notice everything in order to make a full report to Esther, Agnes, and the children. By the time he and the women had slipped into an open space along the street, Major Babcock could be seen with several gentlemen who were arguing with him rudely. The Major addressed his opponents.

"Gentlemen, perhaps the way to settle this is to offer a demonstration. I assure you that these animals are both obedient and strong. Observe, please, while we load this camel."

His voice tense, Nate greeted Hassan and Alex. "Where've y'all been? The Major's carryin' on, and I think he's talkin' himself into a heap of trouble. Sure am glad you're here in case we have to beat a hasty retreat."

"What's he up to? Can't be that serious, can it?"

"Could be. Keep listenin', Alex. Say, Hassan, Adela's been loaded with the oddest bunch of supplies. We've done our best to pack her, but stuff is kind of danglin'. To my mind, she looks like a peddler, with a table, pots, and a couple of kegs strapped to her. I'd feel a whole lot better if you looked her over." Hassan verified that Adela's straps held everything securely without chafing. He was pleased that Nate had done a first rate job of it, and Nate savored the praise.

Meanwhile Major Babcock asked Alex to bring Tullah to the front. Because of her mild disposition, she was always chosen to be the experiment. Alex hoped she would perform satisfactorily whatever task the Major had in mind. When Tullah was presented to the spectators, now growing both in number and in their loudly voiced opinions, she responded to Alex's gentle touch on her legs by kneeling calmly. She remained immobile, as if being surrounded by a host of curious onlookers was a common occurrence, and quietly began chewing her cud. Only the flicking motion of her tiny ears betrayed her alertness.

Major Babcock ordered the men to bring forth two large bales of hay. "Gentlemen, load the camel!"

Nate and Alex exchanged looks. Grappling with the heavy bales and straining under their weight, two soldiers wrestled first one and then another out into the street. Aided by Nate, they hefted one bale onto the camel and held it steady while Alex and Hassan secured the hay to Tullah's packsaddle. They then repeated the process on Tullah's other side. Hassan struggled to look confident as he made sure the lashings were placed correctly.

Speaking softly in Arabic, as if to the camel, Hassan asked Alex, "What is he doing? Why is he making a big show of this?"

"I don't know."

Amos Prudeau and Drew Johnsonville, agreeably relaxed from their afternoon of drinking beer and playing cards with Nate, worked their way to the front of the crowd, near the spot where Jeremy Blackstone stood shaking his head in bewilderment.

Amos asked, "What do you make of this?" Jeremy shrugged in reply.

Drew rolled a cigarette, leaned back against the porch post, and grinned. "Time for a show, looks like. Damn if that camel ain't ugly."

Major Babcock projected his voice so that his remarks reached far into the crowd, but concentrated his eyes on the small group of skeptics whose taunting had provoked him earlier.

"Good gentlemen, I wish you to note that this camel is loaded with 613 pounds of hay, sufficient to feed any number of your horses. Imagine yourself on the trail, assured that your horses will not starve because this kindly beast carries food not for itself, but for your animals."

A shouted retort came from his left side. "That only works if she gits her butt off the ground! I don't see her carryin' a dern thing, just sittin' as she is. She looks to me like she could sit there until kingdom come."

Another skeptic joined in. "She ain't goin' nowhere. I'll take bets she can't even git up!"

"You'll get no takers, 'cause none of us thinks she can do it!"

That assessment of the betting climate proved inaccurate, as anyone who knew Texans could easily have predicted. Shouting erupted. Wagers were exchanged in all directions, with a few foolhardy gamblers betting on the camel's strength. Amos and Drew wanted to bet against the camel, but they didn't want to push through the throng. They glanced hesitantly at Jeremy. They knew that he appreciated a game of chance, but doubted whether he would take their bet against the camels. "Well? You in?"

Jeremy weighed the risk, which was considerable. "What odds?"

Barely able to catch his words above the din, the two men laughed. "Jeremy, you always gotta have some angle. A straight bet won't do for you. It's gotta be temptin' odds or you ain't in it. All right, then, three to one."

Jeremy looked over the scene again and took his time. Amos and Drew, though edgy for an answer, knew that you could not rush Jeremy Blackstone. Finally, he decided that a bet on the camel was really a bet in favor of Nate, who believed in the beasts completely. "As I see it, you ain't got no comers. Make it five to one, and I'm in."

"Done."

The clamorous crowd focused on the spot where Major Babcock had been speaking quietly to Hassan, Nate, and Alex. Nate was beside himself, but held his tongue.

With all the pizzazz of a ringmaster, Major Babcock called, "Bring two more bales!"

Hoots rose from the crowd. Yelling arguments erupted, and the wagering became frantic as those who had bet in favor of the camel sought to retract their bets or negotiate better odds. Jeremy's odds with Amos and Drew rose to ten to one.

Hassan tried to reassure Nate and Alex. "She can do this. She is rested enough, and I think she is strong enough. But we must stay calm. She looks to us. She senses us. If we are upset, she may choose not to get up."

Panic hit Nate in the stomach. "Choose not to get up?"

"Yes, a camel can sometimes do what it wants instead of what you want. So you must make it happy to do what you want."

"All right, Hassan, you know best," added Alex as they wrangled a third hay bale on top of the first one. "Nate, I've seen camels carry amazing loads in Egypt. We have to believe that Tullah is ready for this."

"Yeah, and what if she's not? Then we'll be the laughingstock."

"That's for sure, but it's too late to do anything except get on with it. Major Babcock has confidence, so we should, too.

Hassan reasserted, "She will do this. I am sure she will do it."

Elizabeth clutched her mother's hand, her face flushed by so many thrills combined: Major Babcock's dramatic pronouncements, the intensity of emotion, and the crush of people. She admired the uncomplicated collaboration of Nate, Hassan, and Alex, whose motions ebbed and flowed as if they were one unit. Alex, as usual, was everywhere, guiding, talking, encouraging, lifting; in short, a pleasure to behold. She noticed a bit of disturbance in Nate, but Hassan appeared unruffled. Disproportionately her gaze fell on Hassan. She observed how his biceps flexed against his shirt as he attached the lashings, how his eyes grew tender when he nuzzled the camel, and how he stood respectfully while Major Babcock was speaking. As for Nate, this was her first time to watch him carefully. Though a bit shorter than the others, he was uncommonly strong and seemed to know without asking where an extra hand was needed. She could see that the other men, especially the soldiers, appreciated his presence. Alex, Nate, and Hassan were so unlike the boys she knew in Galveston. Those boys were caught up in finding their futures in Galveston society, inheriting their fathers' businesses, and selecting the proper wives to enhance their prospects. When she looked back on the May Day celebrations, the faces of the Galveston boys melded together, indistinct. By contrast, these three had unique, well-defined personalities, and she was thoroughly intrigued, examining first one and then another.

When the fourth bale of hay was securely attached on top of the second one, Hassan and Alex went around and around checking the fastenings, monitoring the load's balance, and speaking gently to Tullah. Satisfied, they nodded to Major Babcock, who made his own tour and rubbed Tullah's nose. Then he stood back and raised his hand in a signal for silence.

"As you can see, this camel is loaded with four bales of hay. She is here not for show, but to work. Her job is to carry much-needed provisions to our forts from Texas to California. Ladies and gentlemen, her name is Tullah, and she is but one member of the US Camel Corps. We must now let her do her work."

In spite of his confidence, Hassan could not quell the beating of his heart nor loosen the tightness in his throat as he stepped forward. He wondered what his family would think if they could see him reach out to give Tullah the signal to rise. At his touch, Tullah unbent her back legs, causing the load to incline awkwardly forward. Gasps and curses coursed through the assembled townsfolk. Hovering nearby, Nate and Alex were relieved to see that the hay bales held securely. Hassan continued to speak calmly to Tullah. She stretched her front legs and let out an enormous groan that terrified those standing nearby. Once again the hay bales tipped at a peculiar angle. With a final horrific moan, she stood up completely, prompting another set of shrieks and exclamations from the crowd. Before a flabbergasted populace, Tullah stood fully erect with over twelve hundred pounds strapped tidily onto her back. Thunderous applause broke out.

Amidst the ensuing cacophony of swearing, praise, and demand for payment, Jeremy permitted himself a satisfied smile and turned his open palm to Amos and Drew. Neither man had the cash on hand to settle a ten to one bet. "No matter. I know you're good for it."

Drew Johnsville was astounded. "Well, I never in all my days!"

Amos replied, "That critter got up like it warn't nothin' special."

"Yeah, 'cept for that hellish sound it made."

Jeremy remarked, "Seems I've heard you groan once or twice when you had to lift a heavy load out of the boat."

Amos was forced to agree. "I may have to change my opinion about camels after this. Can't say I thought much of 'em up to now, but, shit, if they can lift weights like that, maybe I'll have to give 'em the benefit of the doubt."

Drew wasn't going to roll over so easily. "Yeah, well she's standin', but she ain't movin'."

As if taking Drew's comment as a signal, Alex set off to warn that the camel caravan was en route back to Green Lake. "Make way for the camels, make way! Stand aside and see what they can carry! Make way for the Camel Corps!"

Hassan mounted Massanda gracefully, unable to contain his glee. As she rose gently, he smiled proudly at Tullah with her four large bales and Adela with her assortment of goods hanging. He waved to the crowd, hoping the McDermott ladies would see his gesture as a personal greeting. Elizabeth saw and blushed, but her mother was so astonished by Tullah that she did not notice.

To cheers and continuing applause, Tullah strolled by, placing one softly padded foot in front of the other without any appearance of effort, a picture of perfect contentment. Behind her in the wagon, Nate luxuriated in the congratulations and praise of cynics now transformed into believers.

INDIANOLA, TEXAS, THE NEXT DAY

M RS. EBERLY PUT DOWN the newspaper, thinking that Sylvia McDermott was in for a shock. The hotelkeeper had seen enough of her guest to know that Sylvia was stouthearted, but perhaps not sufficiently so for the news in today's paper. The headline read: *Run on Williams & McKinney Paper.* Mrs. Eberly signaled Malvina to set another place as more of her guests joined the table. She would allow Sylvia time to absorb the news before showing her the letter from her husband.

Sylvia was taking a late breakfast with Lt. Halter. He was not her preferred dining companion, but the children had left early with Alex Babcock for a day at the camel paddock, and she had luxuriated in a late rising. Winston Halter was a most vexing man, prone to peevish comments, or worse yet, scowling silences. She had struggled on numerous occasions to engage him in civil conversation, finding few topics that held his interest. Her Philadelphia childhood had provided them with some commonalities, but these were quickly exhausted. Fortunately, he had an active penchant for current events. When forced to dine with him, she could usually converse by posing questions about the newspaper, even if she then had to listen to his pontifications.

Winston Halter was not ignorant of the emotions of women. He had three sisters, as well as a wife whom he truly cared for, and he had devoted considerable intellectual energy to deciphering a woman's looks and gestures. Even a man less studied could see that Sylvia was upset. She had stopped speaking in the middle of a sentence. A rare thing it was for any woman to cease talking in mid-conversation, but especially for Sylvia, whom Winston found to have impeccable manners. A ruddy color climbed up either side of her neck from her collarbone toward her hairline and her breathing had gone shallow.

"Mrs. McDermott, is there something of particular interest in the news today?"

"Thank you for asking, Lt. Halter. There's a run on Williams and McKinney paper. Tom McKinney and Sam Williams are friends of ours. This must be terrible for them." She tried to keep her tone light, knowing that her husband was heavily invested in business ventures with both men.

"Williams paper. That's a form of currency in Texas isn't it?"

"Yes, it is."

"I have some understanding of banking and credit systems, but perhaps you could enlighten me about their specific organization in Texas."

"These two fine gentlemen received a banking charter while Texas was still part of Mexico. When Texas became independent in 1836, the charter was accepted in practice until legal authority was granted in 1841. I remember it well because my husband threw a huge party to celebrate. Elizabeth was a babe in arms, so I missed some of the festivities, but what an evening it was! Music, dancing, French champagne! But excuse me, I digress."

"Not at all, Mrs. McDermott, please continue."

"Five years later the new State of Texas wrote a constitution very restrictive to banking. It was annoying, I tell you. There would have been no Texas without McKinney and Williams. The anti-banking faction even went so far as to bring charges against Sam Williams. Can you feature being dragged to court as an illegal bank when it was your gold that kept Texas afloat all these years? Fortunately the judge refused to support the stupidity of the prosecution. Let's see, that was in 1849."

"I thought I heard something along the lines you describe, but more recently."

"Yes, that's because the case was appealed several times, and Mr. Williams was finally vindicated last year. You can imagine the stress on his family. The whole thing is ridiculous. We Texans depend on that money."

"It may surprise you to learn that even in New York, where my father-in-law has business interests, Williams paper is highly regarded."

"The newspaper says that a default up north has panicked the banks in New Orleans. That created a ripple effect and a run on Williams and McKinney paper. As if the court problems weren't enough, now this!"

Lt. Halter warmed to the conversation. "Mrs. McDermott, you are well informed."

"No, no. I know things only from conversations with our friends. I do hope everything will turn out well for them."

Mrs. Eberly motioned for Malvina to offer more coffee and biscuits as the conversation drifted toward the gentler subject of last night's rain. Sylvia was grateful for the change in topic, as her mind worked rapidly to assess the situation. Perhaps this catastrophe was looming when Quentin wrote his last letter. He must have been working with other Galveston businessmen to forestall this situation. Failing that, he must now be trying to solidify a response to these startling events.

A great calm swept over her. This had to be the explanation for Quentin's odd behavior. He was absorbed in his business dealings, enjoying the risk, even savoring a hint of danger. She had learned over the years not to react to frightening business news. Her husband thrived on getting out of a scrape, at his happiest when outfoxing his competitors. When confronted with dire circumstances in the past, he had devoted his full energy to the problem, and they had come out in a better position than before. Finding this explanation satisfying, she relaxed and chatted with Winston Halter about the reaction of different water birds to changes in the tides. Anyone watching her easy smile and bright eyes would have thought them the dearest of friends.

Mrs. Eberly was confused. Perhaps Sylvia had not fully comprehended the issue. If Williams paper failed, the economy of the coast could crash. Whole fortunes could evaporate, especially those based on commercial transactions, loans, credit, and promissory notes. She was not worried for herself, because she was invested in land. However, the losses could be enormous for the McDermott family if Quentin was holding much of his wealth in paper.

Quentin McDermott had long confided in Angelina Eberly regarding his financial dealings. They had met during one of her shopping trips to Galveston, and he had become her Galveston agent and banker. A paragon of good taste and discretion, she was also plucky and spoke her mind. Quentin valued her business acumen and thought of her as a wise aunt. For the past eighteen months he had been "depositing" a stash of wealth with Mrs. Eberly. At first, he asked her to retain the sums she owed him for items she purchased. Later he sent confidential letters, rolled in bolts of cloth or stitched into the lining of hatboxes, and he embedded gold and stacks of Williams paper in barrels of dried beans or rice. He notified Mrs. Eberly by underlining key items on the bill of sale. Mrs. Eberly collected the paper and gold from Mr. Wellbourne's warehouse to store in her personal safe.

Mrs. Eberly had been holding a sealed letter for Sylvia McDermott addressed, "*To Be Opened In The Event Of A Weakness In Williams & McKinney Paper.*" One glance at the newspaper this morning had sent Mrs. Eberly straight to her safe to recover the letter, which she now fingered in her pocket. As soon as Winston Halter departed for Green Lake, she took Sylvia aside.

"How was your breakfast, Mrs. McDermott?"

"Delicious as always, Mrs. Eberly. We have been so fortunate to be your guests."

"The pleasure is all mine. Excuse me, might I have a word with you in private, upstairs?"

Sylvia nodded at this most unusual request, wondering as she mounted the steps why Mrs. Eberly wished a meeting in her room. Any official business, whether about fees or arrangements for the trip to San Antonio, had always been conducted in the hotel office.

"Thank you, Sylvia." In private the two women had given up formalities and spoke to each other on a first-name basis. "It is most fortuitous that the children are away, as I wish to speak to you in complete confidence."

"But of course, Angelina, what is it?"

"I believe you noticed the article in today's paper about the run on Williams paper."

"Yes, and I confess to having some concerns about it."

"Well, on that topic, I have a letter from your husband. Actually, two letters, one addressed to me, which I read this morning, and a second addressed to you, which is still sealed."

Sylvia stared at the "To be opened" message. It was dated weeks earlier.

"Yes, Sylvia, I have been holding this letter, unopened, until this morning. I know this is surprising. Please read the letter."

Sylvia trembled, not sure whether her emotions were fear or anger or some diabolical combination of the two. Her husband had included Mrs. Eberly in his dealings, but he had not bothered to communicate an inkling of this to her, his own wife.

My dear Mrs. Eberly,

Because you have opened this letter, there must be an attack on Williams & McKinney paper. I have been concerned for some time that the forces of ignorance in Austin would prevail against us. I have also been wary of lax practices at a few banking houses that may put us all at risk. Whatever the case, I anticipate that the following may have relevance.

First, please be advised that I will personally honor all the paper that you are holding on my behalf. Next, rest assured that the Galveston banking houses have sufficient reserve to survive such an eventuality. Perhaps by the time you read this letter, a solution will already have been arranged.

My greatest concern is for my family. I would appreciate it if you would transfer to my wife sufficient gold for her needs, after you have retained enough specie to cover the paper mentioned above. Please also consign to her an amount of Williams paper. Remind her to use the paper first, if it is still accepted, and to hold the gold in reserve. Keep the rest of my accumulated deposits yourself until you hear from me again.

I ask you to allow Mrs. McDermott to read this letter and then please convey to her the private communication enclosed herein. As always, I am sincerely recognizant of your kind attention to my affairs in Indianola, especially as they contribute to the well being of my wife and children.

Respectfully yours,

Quentin McDermott

Mrs. Eberly sat with her hands folded in her lap, while Sylvia read the letter once, raised her eyes questioningly, and then read it twice more.

Sylvia's confidence disappeared like a puff of smoke in a magic show at the moment when the magician's solid object, be it bird or flower, vanishes into gaping emptiness. Her husband had foreseen a run on Williams paper, which meant that problems had been developing for some time, and yet he had not confided in her. Sylvia felt her face flush. A tightness settled upon her neck and shoulders, making it difficult for her to speak. She was furious. How could Quentin, with whom she had shared everything for so many years, treat her as if she were a simpleton or untrustworthy? She was beginning to feel faint.

"Sylvia, would you like me to leave you alone?"

"Oh no, Angelina, I'm sorry. This is all a bit of a surprise. Please stay here."

"As you wish, dear. Take your time."

Sylvia's hands quivered as she broke the seal on the second letter. Her anger welled as teardrops forming at the corner of her eyes, and she struggled to prevent them from tumbling onto the page.

My most darling Sylvia,

Please do not be annoyed. I am sure you must question the need for my secretive behaviors, but I assure you, every step that I have taken is intended to preserve our family against dangers known and unknown. As you have never heard such language from me, you may fear that I have developed a suspicious nature. I assure you that is not the case. I engage in these subterfuges to protect us from several individuals, including some with whom you have had social discourse, whose sole purpose is to undermine us.

Take comfort from Mrs. Eberly, whom I trust and hold in trust and high esteem. She is committed to your welfare. She may be of valuable assistance in the days ahead.

I beg for your patience and forbearance, and I promise that this will all make sense to you in the future. We shall then have long talks during which I shall tell you everything.

Your devoted husband,

Quentin

Before she could fold the letter, Sylvia's tears flowed, at first quietly and then in sobs. This was the Quentin that she knew, planning, guiding, protecting. Her sense of relief was palpable. Her anger dissolved with her tears and she forgave her husband on the spot. This was another one of Quentin's dealings, like so many she had observed before. She wondered about whom he had reservations, remembering moments when he had responded ever so correctly but without warmth to certain social invitations. She recalled similar hesitance at the mention of possible suitors for Elizabeth. She began to understand the pattern. Her anxiety lifted and she wept deeply.

Mrs. Eberly let her cry for a moment and then tried to console her. "Sylvia, please don't worry. The financial matters are well in hand and you will want for nothing."

Sylvia laughed out loud, shocking Mrs. Eberly, who began to fear an onset of hysteria.

"My dear Angelina, do not mistake my tears. These are happy tears. This is the first clear communication I have had from my husband in weeks, and I now grasp his intentions."

Mrs. Eberly was perplexed. Sylvia continued between sobs.

"It has been so hard for me, knowing that my husband has not included me in his decisions. With this letter I understand his peculiar behavior." Sylvia wiped her eyes. She laughed and cried simultaneously.

Mrs. Eberly was still a bit wary. "I see. There, there, let me get you a dry handkerchief."

Sylvia dabbed her eyes, blew her nose, and regained some measure of composure. "It may be difficult to understand, but as long as I have known my husband, he has been straightforward in his communications with me. These recent weeks were such an aberration that I feared for our marriage. Now I realize what he is doing. I don't know the details, but the fact that he is working on difficult business problems is evident. Quentin undoubtedly has sound reasons for keeping the family at some remove from it."

Mrs. Eberly considered this comment thoughtfully.

"Don't you see, Angelina? I can stop fretting. I can simply allow Quentin to do what he does and I can go forward. I would like to have a dinner party to celebrate!"

"A dinner party?" Mrs. Eberly found this whole scenario scarcely believable. "To celebrate?"

"We will celebrate the arrival of the camels, as we should have earlier. Had I been less worried, I would have seen to it at once. But it's not too late. I believe we still have at least a week before our departure. Shall we plan it for Tuesday?"

Mrs. Eberly decided that planning a party might be an excellent way to occupy her guest's time and attention. "By all means, Sylvia, if that's what you'd like. Why don't you compose yourself a bit? When you are rested, come downstairs and we can start to make arrangements."

"Thank you, Angelina, that would be lovely."

Mrs. Eberly had her hands on the doorknob, when Sylvia called her back into the room. A terrible thought sent chills of premonition through her. "I'd like to ask one more question. Angelina, are there other letters with enigmatic or prophetic addresses like this one?"

"Yes, Sylvia, there are."

Sylvia took a deep breath. "May I know their messages?"

Mrs. Eberly hesitated for a split second. "One is addressed *'To Be Opened On Your Departure For San Antonio.'* There is another, the contents of which I hope may never be revealed: *'To Be Opened In The Event Of War.'*"

Sylvia gasped. "I know that Quentin has worried about this possibility. Still I am surprised that he composed such a letter."

"Your husband has succeeded because he plans so thoroughly and because of his superb political intuition. I doubt that he sees war as an imminent threat, but rather as a possibility for which he hopes to be ready. As I understand it, your move to San Antonio is one of his many stratagems of preparation. Really Sylvia, you are fortunate to have such a far-sighted husband."

"Yes, indeed. Let us pray that we may never need to open that letter. For now, we shall organize an elegant soiree in honor of the camels."

"All right, Sylvia, I'll see you downstairs shortly." Mrs. Eberly closed the door behind her and stepped out into the hotel hallway. She felt only somewhat guilty about not disclosing the presence of a third letter.

When the McDermott carriage returned to the hotel in late afternoon, Zeke and Zach leapt out to tell their mother about their outing to Green Lake. Alex led his horse to the stable, but turned back when he saw that Elizabeth remained motionless.

"Elizabeth, what is it?"

"Oh, Alex. We had such a wonderful day today. I hate to see it end. What a nice surprise that you and Nate could join us for a picnic. And the camels! I loved everything."

"Me, too. So what's wrong?"

"I have no idea what temper my mother will be in when I go inside. She has been so dejected lately. I know she tries to hide it for our sake, but it spills over. Sometimes I feel like I'm going to drown in her sadness."

"You go on in. If she's out of sorts, I'll tell a story to cheer her up."

"Thank you, Alex! That could be just what's needed."

Stepping gingerly through the front door, Elizabeth was surprised when her mother hugged her heartily, with a huge smile on her face.

"There you are, daughter. I'm glad you're back, because we have a lot of planning to do. We're going to have a party!"

GALVESTON, TEXAS

PRECIOUS HAD STARTED SLEEPING on the floor in the kitchen because it was the only place she slept well. The slave quarters were vacant, and the emptiness filled her with a sense of foreboding. The walls echoed her pain at losing Samuel, and the rattling silence of the big house disturbed. But in the kitchen the scale of things was smaller. The space was familiar, and it spoke to her of Esther, whom she missed like a big sister. Although the kitchen sometimes made her sad, it did not scream of uncertainty.

Having taken over all of Esther's duties including both house maintenance and food preparation, her days were long and taxing. It helped if she visualized Esther telling her how Miz Sylvia liked things. She heard Esther reminding her to use a damp, not wet, mop on the wood floors, to move the furniture when she swept, to carefully replace the vases exactly after she dusted. She remembered Esther saying that Massa Quentin liked his eggs well cooked, not runny. She must be up very early to have coffee and biscuits ready. She struggled against her fear of making a mistake. She prayed that her recollections were accurate, that she was doing things the right way. It was hard without anyone to ask, but as long as the voice in her memory was Esther's, she felt reasonably confident.

Massa Quentin spoke to her seldom, usually only to inform her whether he would be dining at home or not. He gave no instruction regarding care of the house or tasks to be completed. He would move about, appearing to notice nothing, but then would suddenly criticize. Last week he had chastised her for not having fresh flowers on the table, and then for three straight days, when she took pains to cut the best flowers from the garden, he made no comment.

Doing the shopping helped, because she could converse with slaves of neighboring families as she walked to market. Everyone sympathized with her situation, especially Henry, the father of Esther's girls, who was devastated by the loss of his family. He and Precious scavenged for gossip, but rarely heard stories about the McDermotts. Sometimes Moses brought tidbits of news when he came to town from the McDermott plantations on the Brazos River, but often he knew less than they did. Yesterday Henry heard a rumor that the British Consul was planning to use the McDermott home while a new official residence was being built.

"Is that good or bad?"

"Cain't say. It ain't clear if'n the British Consul's comin' as a guest of Massa Quentin or takin' over the house."

"Takin' over the house? Well, where would Massa Quentin go? And what 'bout me?"

"Dunno."

They tried to work out every angle, but simply didn't have enough information. Tomorrow, when Moses came, she would ask if he had heard anything.

Tonight she was alone in the house, because Massa Quentin was across the road attending a grand dinner party at the Williams home. She made a simple supper of a leftover breakfast biscuit and a plate of beans. She walked the house from front to back to be sure that everything was neat and clean, and then lowered onto the top step of the rear porch.

She would have loved to be sitting with Samuel, laughing and talking now that her chores were done. Miz Sylvia had been easy with them, and they had managed plenty of chances to be alone together. Based on how well things had worked out for Esther and Henry, they hoped to request a similar arrangement. Miz Sylvia had almost said as much. But then the tumult had happened. Precious thought it was Antoine who had first called it that: The Tumult. She smiled as she remembered his fondness for big words. Then she sighed heavily, fearful of this disturbing rumor about the British Consul. The future felt like a dense Galveston fog, immeasurable and impenetrable, that she had entered without a path through to the other side.

Fighting off these melancholy thoughts, Precious decided to count her blessings. She was grateful that she had not been sent to the fields, and she knew Miz Sylvia had personally seen to that. The fields were dangerous, not only because of the backbreaking work, but because the overseers could do what they wanted with you, including selling you off for spite. Massa Quentin rarely questioned his overseers, and even if he didn't agree with a sale, it was too late. Once you were sold, it was impossible to come back and rare for friends and family even to find out where you had been sent. Tonight, she was still in Galveston, still in the house. Although lonely, she was safe and healthy, and for that she was thankful.

A dog barked. The wheels of a carriage crunched the shell pavement in front of the house, and a hummingbird fluttered over a multicolored lantana bush. The sky was lit a powder blue, randomly sprinkled with soft, puffy clouds. Precious sat for a while, until a deep fatigue came over her. With all the responsibilities she had been carrying, this was the first time since everyone had gone that she let herself rest. Rising stiffly, she stepped inside the kitchen, curled up in the alcove, and promptly dozed off.

Hours later, the soothing, profound sleep that enveloped her blocked the sounds of the partygoers leaving the Williams house across the street. She didn't hear the backslapping and well wishes, the mounting of horses, the departure of carriages, and the banter of those who lived close enough to walk home. Had she been sleeping fitfully as she had for days before, the pounding, uneven steps on the porch might have warned her of her master's return. The noise might have alerted her to the lateness of the hour and to his state of high inebriation. Instead, she awoke precipitously to an overwhelming stench of whiskey breath blasting her full in the face.

As her senses came to life, she felt the pinch of Quentin McDermott's large hand gripping her two wrists. She willed herself to focus. "What is it Massa? You all right, sah?"

Still pinning her wrists together, he grabbed her waist and lifted her to a standing position. "Get up, gal."

His voice had a hissing, raspy quality that she had never heard before. Terror gripped her hard in the pit of her stomach. She choked a gurgling sound. A flash of green shot before her eyes as the situation became excruciatingly clear. Even if she protested, no one would hear.

He didn't speak. There was no need for superficial niceties. Miz Sylvia wasn't there, and she was. He twisted her around until she was facing the table and pushed her down at the same instant as he raised her skirt. He had not touched her breasts, an oversight that Precious would find oddly satisfying in the weeks to come.

She watched what was happening as if suspended from the kitchen ceiling, spying the scene like a spider. Her senses cried out, but in her somnolence, her mind still could not accept what was happening. Like every female slave, she had heard stories, but not about Massa Quentin. She knew what was coming, in theory. But this harshness was unlike what she had known before. With Samuel there had been kissing, tender caresses, tickling, and an easy buildup of passion that left both of them sweaty, laughing, and spent. Now her cheek scraped against the table, her arms ached from being pinned against her back, and her thighs were cut by the rough edges of the wooden corners. So open and yielding to Samuel, her body closed down tight and dry, overcome by the same fear that took away her ability to scream.

His first thrust shot pain through her, and he swore. "Open up!"

He spread her legs wider and tried again. The searing pain felt like her privates being torn. Quentin grabbed a jar of cooking oil from the shelf and poured some on his hands. As he turned to set the jar down, he missed the edge of the table, and it fell shattering in a thousand shards. Sticky droplets splattered everywhere. The crashing pot reverberated, loud enough it seemed to Precious to wake the whole neighborhood. A dog's yelping complaint was the only response. He rubbed his oily hands on himself, rammed Precious again, and in a few jabs, it was over.

"Clean up this mess." He left her and went upstairs.

Precious lay half prone on the table, crying silently and surveying the kitchen. She studied the smudges and little pools of cooking oil all over the table and floor. The spilt oil offended her. Miz Sylvia prided herself on always having oil in the house, sometimes corn oil or sunflower oil. She refused to cook with the heavier animal fats, except of course a bit of lard for seasoning the beans or working into biscuits. But for frying chicken or potatoes, she preferred oil, which was carefully sieved after each meal and reused. Oil was a valued commodity to be treated with respect. There were standards in the house, and tonight these standards had been roughly violated. Precious shuddered in revulsion at the image of the prized cooking oil slathered on Massa Quentin. She staggered to the back door to vomit.

Upstairs, Quentin longed for Sylvia. He stared through a drunken haze at his wife's empty armoire. By sending her away with only trunks and valises, he had tried to convince her, and himself, that this was a temporary move, but tonight he was sure it would be permanent. He slammed the armoire door. Somewhat unsteadily, he poured water from the pitcher into the bowl, spilling a little on the wooden stand. Methodically he stripped naked and washed his hands, face, and groin before donning a navy blue silk robe. He felt the absence of his wife like a physical ache at the nape of his neck. He took up his pen.

My dear, dear Sylvia,

How I have longed to write you openly and honestly. Tonight I shall. Williams paper is strong. At my urging, most of the merchant bankers of Galveston have been stockpiling specie for some time. They were able to honor every scrap of paper with gold, thereby earning the gratitude of the entire populace.

I've just come from a celebration at Sam Williams' place. It was a feast of such extravagance that no one would believe, as I do, that the crisis is far from over. The dinner was a kind of show to the town, a demonstration: "See, the bankers are fine." Look in the Galveston

News. I am quite sure that Sebastian Smith will feature a story of the town's survival, crediting the excellent planning of its leading citizens. He will use it as an opportunity to attack the banking regulators in Austin and the upstarts in Houston.

But it is a farce, a falsehood. It saddens me to report that the reserves of every merchant banker have sunk to perilously low levels. Some of the gold that was used to honor our paper was borrowed from banks in New Orleans or New York, banks that themselves face runs. I think they will call for payment of their notes earlier than expected. We have survived the first salvo and preserved the confidence of the people, who will, if I judge correctly, continue to spend and keep the local economy going. But we will have to save much of our incoming revenue from the docks to replenish our base and we will be obliged to reduce our own lending. I fear a dampening effect on trade.

The Galveston merchants are becoming greedy. We rake in enormous profits from the wharves. We should be satisfied with this excellent situation. But we are tilting toward monopoly, and though profitable in the short run, monopoly pricing will certainly raise the ire of competing ports with disastrous long-term results. Houston and Indianola will not put up with gouging.

Tonight, while everyone was in a good mood, I raised some of these points, only to be publicly chastised. It was an appalling scene. Byron Hurlinger has more sense than the others. Not only did he agree with me, he also reminded us of Galveston's susceptibility to severe storms and said we should expand our business inland in cooperation with Houston merchants. The others mocked us.

Sylvia, my darling wife, how I wish you could be with me, but alas, it is far safer for you to be in San Antonio. I hope you understand now why this move is so important to us. I wish us to have options. I appreciate the sacrifice you have made in leaving Galveston. This seems unjust, as Galveston has in recent years become the place of refinement that you deserve. But please trust me. This is best, and I must work hard to secure the gains we have made so far.

Your devoted husband,

Quentin

Satisfied by this catharsis, Quentin McDermott collapsed across his bed without even turning down the sheets.

The following morning, with his head throbbing and a mouth full of cobwebs, he stared in shock at the letter on his writing table. It was smudged and sloppy. It was also dangerously frank. He crumpled it and set it ablaze.

Nevertheless, it had been useful to read the letter in the light of day. It confirmed and solidified his thoughts. Much as he hated to be disloyal to his friends in Galveston, he would diversify. He would look to opportunities in San Antonio, as he had been planning for some time. Then, if necessary, he would swallow hard and align himself with Houston.

He penned a short chatty note to Sylvia. Just as he finished, Moses arrived from the Brazos. He greeted his slave at the front door and instructed him to take Precious to the plantations. Without passing by the kitchen, Quentin McDermott set off to confirm his passage to New York.

INDIANOLA, TEXAS

DELIGHTED WITH HER MOTHER'S improved disposition, Elizabeth thought the dinner party a splendid idea. It would give them all something to do while waiting for the camels to depart. Her mother chatted amiably, sought her advice on the guest list, and asked her opinion of the menu choices. For the first time in her life, Elizabeth had a voice in planning a proper McDermott entertainment, and she relished the sense of having attained stature in her mother's world. After quick but intense planning, they were ready to distribute chores to the slaves.

Caught off guard, Esther and Antoine warned Agnes to be quiet. The last time Miz Sylvia had convened a meeting like this she had announced their exodus from home. Agnes could tell they were scared by the way they held their arms at their sides with heads downcast. They anxiously examined Miz Sylvia from head to toe, not staring directly but glancing sideways cautiously, trying to ascertain her state of mind. Even Agnes could tell that her mournful expression had given way to a pleasant composure. Looking carefully at Miz Sylvia's hands, Agnes was glad to see that she wasn't working them at all.

Flanked by Elizabeth and Miz Eberly on the back porch, Miz Sylvia came straight to the point. She declared that she would host a dinner in honor of the camels' arrival. Guests would be Major Babcock, Lt. Halter, Mrs. Eberly, Mr. Wellbourne, Captain and Mrs. Van Steendam, Mr. and Mrs. Blauvelt, and Alex Babcock. Frau Klug would be invited to play the piano. The table would be set for fourteen, as Miz Sylvia would allow Zeke and Zach to join the adults. Antoine, Samuel and Esther, overcome with relief, nodded their comprehension of her instructions by murmuring, "Yes'm" at appropriate intervals. Incapable of such restraint, Agnes let a great enthusiastic grin spread across her wide smooth face as a little giggle escaped her lips.

"Esther, you'll cook. Antoine and Samuel will drive us for today's errands. Tomorrow evening, Antoine will greet the guests before serving dinner. Samuel will also serve and may need to fetch Frau Klug. Agnes…"

Before she could finish, Agnes clapped her hands. "Yes'm, I know. I followin' Esther and doin' everythin' just so!"

Sylvia laughed the first genuine laugh that Elizabeth had heard from her mother in weeks. "That's right, Agnes. You do exactly that."

In the shabby room that passed for their quarters, Esther and Agnes contemplated the trunk that Samuel and Antoine had carried in moments before. As if its arrival were a matter of great mystery and serious import, they admired the heavy cedar valise, anxious to open it yet somehow hesitant. The initials QM were burned into its rectangular sides and curved top. It was a sturdy trunk, reinforced with leather lashings and fitted with brass latches. Esther had shined those fittings herself, and they were about due for another polish. Reverentially she unbuckled the leather straps, unhooked the clasps, and lifted the lid. Smells of home entered the dimly lit space, transporting the two women to brighter days they had known in Galveston.

The top tray contained an assortment of cloth table napkins, pressed and stiffened, along with a number of embroidered runners. Esther lifted the tray out and handed it to Agnes, who paused to inhale the yeasty smell of the starched linens before setting it carefully onto the raised plank that served as their bed. Below the tray rested tablecloths, their lace edges carefully preserved between thin layers of cotton batting. Esther thought how prudent it had been for Miz Sylvia to place a potpourri of dried herbs in the trunk. A flowery fresh scent enveloped the fabric to fight off any tendency toward the mustiness of travel. The two women removed the tablecloths carefully, stacking them in neat piles. Finally they reached the coveted items at the bottom. Here lay Esther's serving uniform, along with Antoine's butler jacket and Samuel's formal footman's breeches, exactly as she had placed them there more than four weeks ago.

Agnes couldn't stand the suspense. "Esther, is mine there, too?" Agnes had a simple maid's dress that she prized highly.

"Yes, it here. It all here."

Esther sighed ruefully. She remembered times when the McDermott household was ablaze with gaslights and enriched with the animated conversation of a dozen guests; evenings when Antoine clicked his highly polished black leather heels on the hardwood floors as he opened the heavy mahogany doors to greet each newcomer; and days when she and Miz Sylvia decorated the parlor with freshly cut garden flowers set in delicate porcelain and crystal vases. Despite the hard work of it, she loved to supervise the cooking, set out the table, and put the finishing touches on the room before donning her starched uniform to act as lead server. Running her hand over the pristine fabric of the carefully folded uniforms, she wondered when those days would return.

She had never expected to be going about like this, first as a passenger on a ship, then at a hotel in Indianola, and soon as part of a caravan to San Antonio. Her imagination had not led her anywhere other than Galveston where she expected to live and die in the McDermott household. Worries that kept other slaves in a continuous state of dread were unknown to Esther, who heretofore was confident of her role as an essential member of the family. Now she had been yanked from her complacency and forced to confront the same terrors that bedeviled other slaves.

Her most immediate distress was her disunion from Henry. Years ago, Massa Quentin had lectured them about the laws that prohibited slaves from marrying, an act that signaled his acceptance of their conjugal relationship. They were allowed to visit on Tuesday afternoons and in the evening if their work was completed. Massa Quentin explained that his indulgence toward them was given in memory of Esther's mother's lifelong service. He admonished Esther to exhibit the same loyalty, and she had so promised. Henry's owner, Mr. Williams, also agreed. After that, neither she nor Henry feared that they or their children would be sold. But now, with all this discombobulation in the household, she was deeply unsure. She told herself that even if Massa Quentin got into financial trouble, he would not sell her family, but for the first time in her life, she harbored doubts. She wriggled her shoulders and shook off these thoughts. She would not dwell on such questions today. Tomorrow would be a party, and she wanted it as close to the way things used to be as she could make it.

Agnes could see expressions moving across Esther's face, like rocks dropping into a pool of water. The ripples tangled in all directions and changed in an instant. Each time Esther waved her hand to shoo away a fly, the look in her eyes shifted, as if another pebble had been dropped into that confused pond. Agnes couldn't keep up.

She decided to risk a question. "Esther, how you feelin'?"

"Agnes, don't you worry none."

Agnes sighed with relief. Esther was for some reason in a good mood and would certainly explain. Yes, Agnes could feel an explanation coming. How grateful she was when Esther told her what things meant.

"Just thinkin' 'bout home. I be missin' Galveston." That was it. Agnes thought so. She missed their old life, too, but nobody spoke much about it, like it hurt them too much to talk of it. So she had kept quiet, but now she felt free to add her own thoughts.

"I miss it too. That Althea can't make a biscuit like you Esther, and she don't put enough salt in her stew!"

Esther smiled. Everything was so simple for Agnes. "No, Agnes, and nobody here seems to know how to fry bacon as good as you. Not too crispy, not too soft. I like yours best, Agnes."

Agnes beamed. Esther was herself. Ever since Miz Sylvia had told them to start packing, life had been hard for Agnes, who had trouble with new situations. She didn't much like it here, with everyone either tense or bored. The camels helped. Although she and Esther hadn't seen them yet, Samuel and Antoine told stories. Agnes especially liked the part about the baby camel. As the dust mites danced in the streaky light that slipped through the crude wallboards, the memory of Miz Sylvia's good hearty laugh almost made life feel predictable again. Esther even started humming! Agnes smiled. They would prepare today and cook all day tomorrow. Then she would change into her uniform and she would serve and everything would be almost like normal.

Samuel was content to be out and about in town, running errands and taking charge. Being busy kept his mind off Precious and made him feel useful again. Back from the post, he handed Miz Sylvia another letter from Massa Quentin. He hoped this one would not upset her as the last one had.

"Thank you, Samuel." Sylvia retired to her room to open the letter.

My Dear Sylvia,

By now you have heard of the run on Williams & McKinney paper. Be advised that these excellent men have backed every note with gold. However, this situation has reaffirmed the need for our businesses to be more diversified. I depart tomorrow for New York.

Thank you for your most recent letter. How unfortunate that Major Babcock is delayed. We need not have been so precipitous with your departure. I regret that you had to rush about. Be that as it may, I hope you have enjoyed Mrs. Eberly's companionship. If you have not yet departed, I pray for a safe and uneventful journey. Know that I will join you as soon as I return from the East Coast. Forbearance is required in the meantime.

I send my most heartfelt endearments to you and to the children. Sylvia, you are my life. Please take care in the weeks ahead.

Your most affectionate husband,

Quentin

Sylvia was satisfied with this letter. She noted Quentin's comments about diversification and forbearance, but a business crisis was like a tonic to him. He would be happy on his trip, he would succeed, and they would soon be reunited. She folded the letter gently, placed it in her jewelry box along with the others, and went downstairs to organize.

Elizabeth's primary responsibility today was to accompany Esther to buy vegetables from Mr. Paul Diefendorf. "Mama, what about Agnes?"

Clambering for attention, Zeke and Zach insisted, "And what about us, Mama?"

"All right. Everyone can go."

On their way across town, they passed buildings whose false fronts made a stair-step, multi-colored roofline along the main street. As she did every time they traveled this route, Elizabeth admired the long docks sticking out into the bay, like swamp reeds floating on the glistening surface. She had come to love the optical illusion that made grand ships at the ends of the wharves appear tiny while smaller craft looked larger as they came toward shore. Although less bustling than Galveston, the docks were noisy with stevedores hefting goods onto groaning wagons, many of which headed directly for Mr. Ashbeth's store, Mr. Blauvelt's lumberyard, or the German immigrant camps.

"All right, all right," Elizabeth said in response to her brothers' pestering. "First we'll get the vegetables, and then we'll see if there's time to stop at the camel camp on the way home."

Agnes smiled. That was why the boys had been so keen to come along. Esther hadn't had time to explain, but that had to be the reason. Agnes realized with some satisfaction that she had figured out this explanation all by herself. She became quite excited thinking she might see a camel.

Elizabeth chatted with Mr. Diefendorf while Esther and Agnes walked up and down the rows. Esther selected fresh ripe tomatoes, shiny red and green bell peppers, jalapeños, shallots, sugar snap peas, crispy spinach and bright yellow summer squash. From the herb garden she chose fresh cilantro and parsley, as well as basil and sage, filling the basket that Agnes carried. Mr. Diefendorf seemed to appreciate

Elizabeth's conversation, especially when she praised his vegetables. Then he chanced to turn his head away from the garden.

"What the hell?" He grabbed his bullwhip, run out the gate, then doubled back on the other side of the wood and cactus fence. Elizabeth gasped.

Agnes couldn't believe her good luck. A camel was coming right toward them, not too fast, but steadily. It loomed larger than she expected, bigger than the biggest horse, with a coat that was shaggy, not smooth. Most unbelievably, it had two humps. Why had no one told her that some camels had two humps?

Mr. Diefendorf ran toward the camel, shouting at it to go away. He flung his arms and yelled. Then he moved closer to the camel and attempted to whip it. When he aimed for its head, it twisted its long neck around and tried first to bite, then to kick him. It howled. Terrified, Agnes grabbed Esther's hand. In the nick of time, two foreign camel men ran toward the angry animal. Agnes was surprised to see that they looked pretty much like any white man, except the younger one was a bit darker than the other. Their dress was not unusual, none of the exotic clothing that Antoine and Samuel had described. The women held their breath as the older one approached the camel and tried to grab a tether that was hanging from its mouth. The younger one called to Mr. Diefendorf. His words sounded a little funny, but they were clear enough. However, they had no effect.

"Stop, please stop. Sir, you are hurting the camel."

Elizabeth stared in disbelief. Having recognized Hassan and Abdullah immediately, she quickly came around to stand outside the garden with her brothers.

Hassan moved closer to Mr. Diefendorf. "Sir, it is dangerous. Please stop."

Mr. Diefendorf was hopping mad and in no mood to listen. It looked like he might be crazy enough to aim the whip at Abdullah and Hassan. At the top of her lungs, Elizabeth cried out.

"Mr. Diefendorf! That's Hassan, a friend of our family. Please don't hurt him!"

Agnes couldn't work that out, hoping Esther would explain later. But Esther was equally confused as she thought again how frustrating it was to be relegated to the back of the hotel with little idea what was going on. In Galveston, she had been an integral part of the children's lives. She should have known whether this camel handler really was a friend of the family.

"What is that Miss McDermott? A friend of your family?" Mr. Diefendorf's voice dripped vinegar.

"Yes, sir. Please, be careful. I understand that camels can be quite dangerous when riled."

"I'll thank you to refrain from stating the obvious." Paul Diefendorf's anger, only a second before directed at the camel, now flew across the yard toward Elizabeth. "'Course them camels are dangerous, and this one here wants to eat my garden, startin' with the fence. I ain't about to let that happen. So," he added with a sneer, "if this 'friend of you family' gets in my way, he'll git a taste of my Whacker, just like the camel."

Taking umbrage at this tone toward their sister, Zeke and Zach stepped a bit closer. When they started to say something, Paul Diefendorf cracked his whip high in the air.

"Y'all best stay out of the way, boys." The brothers backed off promptly.

Abdullah and Hassan took advantage of this brief distraction to turn the large Bactrian away from Mr. Diefendorf's garden. Abdullah was furious. Pertag had let the camel escape, and now it had several deep gashes on its neck. Covered in camel blood, Abdullah managed to calm it.

Elizabeth's heart was pounding. It had been a close call, and she regretted being unable to exchange a single word with Hassan. As he walked away with Abdullah and the camel, Hassan unexpectedly turned back and tipped his hat to her. Completely surprised by his gesture, she lifted a modest fingertip to her bonnet in return, trying desperately to suppress a grin. How had he thought to do that? It was such a typical American gesture, so unconventional coming from him, yet very sweet.

That evening as her mother brushed her hair, Elizabeth relived the afternoon. Although unable to say what vegetables they had purchased, she recalled certain images in every particular. Hassan standing unyielding, face-to-face with Paul Diefendorf. Hassan with confidence in his eyes, a smoldering fire of anger below the surface, the sweat of exertion on his high cheekbones. Hassan's voice, the timbre, pitched to be assertive but not confrontational. Hassan's body, upright, tense, alert and ready to act. Hassan serious, unsmiling, businesslike, working smoothly with Abdullah. Hassan's hat, dusty yet somehow jaunty, tipped respectfully in her direction. Hassan's eyes twinkling at her as he turned away.

"Mama, what shall I wear tomorrow?" Elizabeth asked to keep from revealing these thoughts.

"Well, it is a special occasion. Would you like to wear your dress from the May Day ball?"

"Oh Mama, what a lovely idea! Just the other day at breakfast Cousin Babcock said he regretted leaving Galveston before our May Day festival."

"Indeed, and I believe Alex expressed similar regrets." Sylvia winked at her daughter's reflection in the mirror.

Elizabeth blushed but said nothing. Pulling the brush through her mother's long auburn tresses, she inhaled sharply.

"What is it, dear?"

"A gray hair! I mean, a hair that appears to be gray in this light."

"You've only now noticed? Never mind. We are having a party tomorrow, and we shall both wear our gowns from the May Day ball. We will celebrate the camels' arrival in our finery!"

The next day, Sylvia ordered her sons to the back porch for a wash while she and Elizabeth indulged in a bath in their room. The women usually limited themselves to what they could accomplish with a bowl and pitcher, but a sponge bath was inadequate today. Agnes brought up the heated water, bucketful by bucketful, until the ladies were content. They took turns luxuriating in the warm tub. After bathing and drying, they stayed in their underclothes for as long as possible in order to stay cool. Hair was brushed, swept up, pinned, taken down, brushed again, tried in a different form, tacked with a comb, and finally arranged into styles that satisfied. At last the corsets were pulled tight, layers of petticoats donned, and the gowns slipped on. The final step was a little rouge on the lips and cheeks and a twirl in front of the mirror.

"My gorgeous daughter!" The lemony dress was perfectly made. "You know, I can't get over how well that off-the-shoulder style suits you."

"You look quite wonderful yourself, Mama. That deep emerald color is so pretty. It makes your hair shimmer like polished copper."

"Tonight we are going to have a dinner that your father would be proud of. Let's go check on your brothers."

Alex came out of his downstairs room, freshly scrubbed and dressed in dark trousers, a starched white shirt, a burgundy vest with matching cravat, and a well-cut jacket. He glanced up to see Elizabeth descending, a shimmer of pale citrus alive with the sound of rustling petticoats. Her raven hair was captured in an elaborate swirl of upward spiraling curls, capped with a tortoise shell comb and a fresh yellow rose. Several wavy strands that draped along her neck softened the effect. Her azure eyes flickered against her pale skin, now turning pink as he watched her descend. He was utterly captivated.

Elizabeth couldn't believe how handsome Alex looked now that he was cleaned up. He had washed his hair, which was not quite dry. Unrestrained by any sort of hat, it hung loose and wavy to his shoulders. She smiled at him enthusiastically. Alex surprised her by stepping forward and offering his arm.

"Good evening, Miss McDermott. You look beautiful tonight. May I escort you into the drawing room?"

Elizabeth had never heard Alex speak in such a courtly manner. Taken aback, she giggled. "Why of course, Mr. Babcock. Since you present yourself so formally, it shall be my honor to accompany you to the next room."

Joining them at the bottom of the stairs, Sylvia laughed with them. "My goodness, Alex, you certainly look fine. I do believe your hair is exactly the same color as Elizabeth's dress."

"And you Madam, are startlingly lovely this evening, if I may be so bold."

Mrs. Eberly admired her charges. "You are all three a joy to behold, and I hope the rest of the evening proceeds as auspiciously as it has begun. Let us join Major Babcock and Lt. Halter while we wait for the others to arrive."

Although their guests had dined before at Mrs. Eberly's hotel, a different atmosphere was signaled by the presence of a tall, impeccably dressed servant awaiting them atop the stairs. His meticulously tailored scarlet butler's jacket, dark trousers, and white gloves gave a regal air to their reception. Such pomp was not usual in Indianola society. He bowed slightly, and most astonishingly, spoke to them in a straight-forward style with perfect diction.

"Good evening, Mr. and Mrs. Blauvelt. You are most welcome this evening. Mrs. McDermott is expecting you. Please follow me."

Before they had time to react, Sylvia appeared. "Thank you Antoine. Good evening, may we offer you something to drink?"

They joined Captain and Mrs. Van Steendam, who were also a bit wide-eyed, in the entry hall where another uniformed slave served mint juleps. With a silver spoon she lifted Mrs. Eberly's frozen ice shapes from a huge porcelain bowl and set them gently into each glass. She then poured a mixed whiskey punch from a cut crystal carafe over the ice and topped each serving with a fresh sprig of mint. Her movements were slow and deliberate, almost ritualistic, but she made no errors. She placed the four drinks on a silver tray, and then carefully offered them to the guests as an odd grin stretched across her entire face.

Crossing into Mrs. Eberly's dining room, the women guests were astonished to see it festooned with flowers. Vas-es of porcelain, crystal and silver stood on tables, on stands, even on the sideboard. Though they were many, they were artfully positioned to give an aura of natural beauty rather than excess.

"Look at all those vases."

"Can you imagine how far they had to go to find so many wildflowers?"

Standing at attention against the wall between two windows, Samuel knew the answer. He and Antoine had ridden several miles inland to find fields where fresh wildflowers grew in abundance. It had been hot work, and he had resented the task. Now, hearing the admiration in the guests' voices, he stood straighter. He was a slave, yes, but he was in the McDermott household, and that counted for something.

"Please take your seats everyone."

The menu included a magnificent array of dishes reflecting both northern cuisine and a mélange of southern tastes from New Orleans to Mexico. After a shrimp bisque came a seemingly endless supply of roast chicken, turkey with oyster sauce, gulf snapper in tomatillo sauce, pork cutlets with sauce piquante, sausage jambalaya and grilled beef steak. Side dishes brightened the table with an array of colors: fresh green sugar snap peas with serrano pepper, ratatouille of eggplant and summer squash, cabbage salad, sauté of red and green bell papers with onion, wilted spinach with bacon, fried okra, hush puppies, tomato rice, and baked sweet potatoes. Both red and white wines were offered. For dessert there was custard pudding with cinnamon, lemon pound cake, sweet tamales with raisins, peach pie, sugar cookies, and most luxuriously, freshly made vanilla ice cream. Though the guests had not seen its manufacture, Esther's children Sally and Mabel had taken turns grinding the ice cream maker while the guests ate. The ice cream was a perfect accompaniment to the other sweets.

"What a delicious dinner, my dear cousin Sylvia, and what a fitting tribute to the new camel cavalry!" Major Babcock swelled with pride at his cousin's graciousness.

Mrs. Eberly joined in, "Mrs. McDermott, thank you for a most splendid repast."

Feeling congenial, especially given the supply of fine drink, Winston Halter proposed a toast. "To Mrs. Sylvia McDermott, we extend our appreciation for offering us a refinement and culture of the highest order and for inviting us to this most delightful occasion."

"Hear, hear!"

"Thank you, gentlemen," she demurred, "but it is you who deserve our heartfelt appreciation, for bringing the camels to America and for working to advance the unification of our country."

Captain Van Steendam had been rather uncomfortable with the extravagance of the evening. Perhaps that explained his negative remark. "The arrival of the camels is indeed a momentous event. But I beg to differ on the subject of unification. I believe that the railroads will link our two coasts long before there are sufficient camels to make any difference."

Major Babcock retorted. "Yes, the railroads are important, but hardly a panacea. We don't yet know which route shall be selected. If the northern route is chosen, camels will be essential to support migration along a southern road. But I do agree about the insufficiency of numbers. That's why I am urging the War Department to start breeding camels before the second shipment arrives in January."

Pleased that coffee, port and brandy were being served, Winston Halter tried to calculate how many times he had listened to this tedious argument. He directed his attention to the light shimmering on his snifter of French cognac.

Mr. Blauvelt joined in. "Mustn't one first perform some experiments to test the animal's suitability for our terrain?"

Mr. Wellbourne added, "And mustn't one also address the complications of their day-to-day management? A man grows up with horses and knows how the animal behaves. These animals are such a mystery. Do you think Americans can ever acquire the same facility as your imported camel men?"

A bit ruffled, Major Babcock tried to regroup. "Sir, I will stand any American lad against any foreigner for his ability to learn quickly and develop a workable way of doing things. Look at Alex here. He's as good with a camel as any of the foreigners."

Elizabeth cast an appraising eye on Alex, as did the entire table. No one could say for certain whether it was Elizabeth's smile or the unexpected attention of all present that caused him to turn crimson.

Major Babcock nodded at Alex and continued. "No, the problem is not talent, but attitude. Whereas some of our men are eager to apply themselves on behalf of our nation, others are visibly contrary. It's actually quite vexing, because had they taken greater interest, more of the men would be well versed in camel management by now."

"Major, my men are soldiers, not gamekeepers. Perhaps when you have tested your animals and shown them to be military steeds, you will get a more positive regard from the cavalry."

Sylvia was not pleased with the direction of this conversation. "Shall we rearrange the room to enjoy the piano, if I may presume upon Frau Klug to entertain us? Perhaps you gentlemen would also like a cigar?"

The slaves jumped into action. They cleared the dishes, cutlery, and linens, before removing the table and lining the chairs along the wall. Finally, they rolled up the rug, thereby transforming the drawing room into a dance floor. Frau Klug warmed up with a gentle ballad, and then shifted to a waltz. Major Babcock invited Sylvia to open the floor, and the Van Steendams and Blauvelts soon followed. Lieutenant Halter surprised Mrs. Eberly by being light on his feet and waltzing her all around the other couples.

"Thank you, Lieutenant, but you must allow me to rest during the quadrille. A woman of my age, you know, doesn't have the stamina she used to." Mrs. Eberly reached for her fan.

"Nonsense, Madam, you are as spry as a young girl, but I shall respect your wishes and ask Miss McDermott to join the square."

Major Babcock in turn called for Alex to take his place. As the dance unfolded and the partners exchanged places, Elizabeth had a first electrifying touch of Alex's hand. When he next came around to her position, the step called for a two-handed swing. Elizabeth was amazed at her own reactions. Kindled with intense attraction, she couldn't keep her eyes off his flowing hair as they spun with arms extended, his hands holding her steady. After a do-si-do, each placed a right arm on the other's waist, left arms in the air for a pirouette that ended with them both facing forward for a circuit of the room. Not once during the dances at the May Day celebrations had she felt such invigoration from the touch of her dancing partner. As the dance ended, Alex kept his arm on her waist a fraction of a second longer than necessary.

"Frau Krug, if you please."

"Yes, Mrs. Blauvelt?"

"What about a polka?"

Everyone laughed. It was well known that, despite her rotund figure, Mrs. Blauvelt could dance all night to a lively polka. "We shall leave the floor to you," replied Captain Van Steendam.

The floor shook as the energetic Mrs. Blauvelt led her husband in step-step-step-hop, step-step-step-hop from one end of the room to the other. Zeke and Zach stood to the side clapping and stomping along with the adults. Alex looked quizzically at Elizabeth who nodded in the affirmative, and the two of them took off after the Blauvelts.

Antoine and Esther had become invisible to the revelers, standing along the wall near the kitchen door. Esther thought she might tip over, so tired was she from two days of non-stop work, but the lively rhythms revived her. The music and clapping were loud enough that she could whisper to Antoine unnoticed.

"Antoine, look at Missy 'Lizbeth. I been knowin' that chile since she was a baby. Saw her first steps, heard her first words, cooked her first real food. I'm here to tell you, I ain't never seen her lookin' like this before, not even at the May Day."

"She lookin' real beautiful, all right."

"I'm tellin' you! But more than that. I ain't really seen it before now. She all grown up."

Antoine tapped his foot to the music. "You tell it true, Esther."

Alex and Elizabeth swung by them, panting but jubilant. The twirling couple spun like a top of dazzled gold, like a single melded entity, so perfectly congruent were the daffodil colors of his hair and her dress.

A revelation struck Esther. "My word, Antoine, I do believe she gonna marry that boy."

THE CAMEL CORRAL, GREEN LAKE, TEXAS

T HE CAMEL PROJECT WAS doomed, of that Abdullah was certain. This camel importation would not provide a basis for diplomatic ties between Egypt and America nor strengthen Egypt's hand against the European powers. None of that would happen. He wished otherwise, because he did not relish the idea of reporting failure to the Viceroy's office. But failure would happen. The Americans rejected or ignored every suggestion for helping the camels to acclimatize. They refused to do their chores, slacked on the important task of rubbing the camels with calomel to prevent the itch, and talked back to their officers. Their lack of obedience appalled him.

Discipline had been maintained on the *Supply,* but here in Texas the situation was deteriorating rapidly. Major Babcock did not supervise as he had on board ship, and Captain Van Steendam's duties often kept him in town. That left Sgt. Stacy Bly in charge of soldiers whose utter disdain for the camels and for the camel handlers was on display every single minute. Abdullah grappled with the incomprehensible notion that many, if not most, of the men did not like the camels. Their insults, foul jokes, and incessant complaining about every aspect of normal camel behavior offended him. Although Alex and Nate had become quite capable, as had the four solders from the *Supply*, they were outnumbered by those who simply hated the camels.

Abdullah did not like most of the soldiers any more than they liked the camels. He found them crass and ignorant, with no refinement in their personal habits. They rarely bathed, seldom washed their clothes, spat tobacco anywhere without looking, and spoke a most uneducated English. Although they could be friendly, the Texans often reserved their generous acts for their own kind, ignoring the needs of Mexicans, slaves, and foreigners. They hardly ever prayed and were markedly uncivil to each other, demonstrably un-Christian. Moreover, instead of respecting piety, they derided the Muslims for praying. It alarmed him to remember that Hassan had been attacked in Galveston while at prayer.

Had he felt camaraderie with the Americans, perhaps he would have been less upset with the indignity of their living conditions. As it was, he objected mightily to sleeping in the tiny lean-to instead of in the bunkhouse. What kind of hospitality left a guest to fend for himself? Inadequate lodging was particularly uncomfortable in this horrid climate. Used to the parched air of his homeland, Abdullah drowned in the Texas humidity. He sometimes struggled for breath as if enveloped in a wet cloth. On foggy days, condensation formed on his face and trickled in runnels down his neck. When low-lying humidity formed spectral apparitions, he was repulsed by these soggy illusions and longed to see an ordinary dust devil. At home, the sun baked. Here, when the sun lifted its heat lamp full in the sky, he felt boiled alive. Hassan's Auntie Fatima had warned him that wet heat is more oppressive than dry heat. How she knew this, he had no idea, but she was absolutely correct. The heavy air reminded him that he was far from home.

An army of mosquitoes, organized into battalions, attacked every bit of exposed skin including eyes and ears. They were particularly vicious at dusk and in the early morning, making prayers a form of exquisite torment. He covered himself with blankets at night to keep them away, but was forced to throw off this protection by the stifling heat. Last night had been a trial and he had slept poorly.

"Good morning." Abdullah took his breakfast and went to sit away from the soldiers. In Egypt, his knowledge of camels was appreciated, his opinions carried weight, and he was in the habit of having people listen to him. That rarely happened now. He could not tolerate the disrespect. He and the other Egyptians had an implicit obligation to stay with the camel herd until a permanent encampment was established, but then Abdullah planned to be on the first ship back to Alexandria. He wished he knew when that would be.

"Abdullah, you have supply duty today."

"Yes, I know." He took another sip of coffee. The Americans never made their coffee strong enough for his tastes.

Abdullah was particularly grumpy because he was partnered with Pertag today. His dislike for Pertag, having begun on the *Supply* when Pertag took advantage of Abdullah's seasickness to act like an expert on camels, escalated with each passing day. Pertag had taken to calling himself Pete and spent most of his time smoking tobacco and joking with the Americans. He had even learned their card games. His disparaging remarks convinced the Americans that he, Pertag the Armenian, was the most knowledgeable about camels when in fact he knew even less than Ali the Interpreter. His chummy attitude toward the Americans and condescension toward everyone else infuriated Abdullah. Abdullah's mood worsened when he realized that Pertag's pal, Sgt. Bly, was leading the supply detail.

Abdullah started to select four camels for today's outing when Pertag called out the names of Ibrim, Ayesha, Perguida and Mahomet. Abdullah protested the selection of Mahomet and turned to Nate for support.

"Nate, I think we should leave Mahomet here. His behavior has not been so good lately."

Caught between Abdullah and Pertag, Nate considered his options. Alex, Hassan and Erdem, who might have weighed in on this debate, had taken ten camels out for an exercise caravan, so Nate would have to decide on his own. He had come to trust Abdullah's camel knowledge, and he had personally observed Mahomet's feisty attitude.

"Right, I'll go get Massanda."

"Nope, we'll go with Mahomet," countered Sgt. Bly, coming to Pertag's defense.

"I don't know, Mahomet's been kinda jumpy lately. Maybe he should stay here."

Sgt. Bly raised his voice. "You heard me, Nate, I said Mahomet."

For Sgt. Stacy Bly, the camel experiment had been a continuing series of slights and affronts. Taking orders from a bunch of foreigners galled him, and he was none too fond of the animals either. Worse yet was that young whippersnapper, Alex Babcock, who acted superior to everybody because his uncle was the Major in charge. It wasn't as if anybody respected the Major, either. He was a staff officer, not in their chain of command. They yielded to Major Babcock only because Captain Van Steendam did, and anyone could tell the Captain had mixed feelings about the situation. But what really stuck in Stacy's craw was the way Nate Wilkers acted like these camels were some kind of God-given solution to all the problems with the Indians, the desert, and the route to California. And Nate had taken to bunking with Alex and the foreigners. Stacy had come to think of Nate as a traitor. So it was with some degree of satisfaction that Stacy forced Nate and Abdullah to submit to his wishes.

Powerless to override the order, Abdullah and Nate prepared Mahomet for the trip. Abdullah decided that the safest course would be for him to ride first on Mahomet, followed by the two females and then Pertag on Ibrim. Nate would bring up the rear in the wagon. Nodding his consent, Nate helped Abdullah organize the departure, while Sgt. Bly pranced around issuing a stream of meaningless orders. Like a pompous warlord leading his band of followers, Sgt. Bly set off on his horse to announce the camel train.

Nate's mood improved on the way to town, as he overheard comments from people along the route, comments far more positive than they had been just a few days ago. His happiness soared when he noticed Evangeline Blauvelt.

"Hello, Nate! Camels are looking good today!" He returned her smile and waved. Yes, the camels did look good, and he felt sure that they would soon depart for San Antonio. Then he would be rid of Sgt. Bly.

When he reached the Government Depot, Nate was disappointed to see Lt. Halter on the porch. Ever since their first encounter in the rowboat leaving the *Supply* for Saluria, Nate had disliked Winston Halter. The man acted like he was a cut above the lowly residents of Indianola. He carried himself closed in, as if he feared contamination by the slightest touch. The sight of Lt. Halter, looking as officious as ever with a sheaf of papers in his hand, dampened Nate's spirits. He hoped that Sgt. Bly would have to deal with him.

Nate turned to scan the corral. Foreboding hit him the moment he saw Abdullah trying to get Mahomet into a resting position. Instead of kneeling calmly, Mahomet was twisting his neck towards Ibrim as if to challenge him. Ibrim, who had been quiet, was rising, and Pertag was helpless to restrain him. Leaping off a half-kneeling

Mahomet, Abdullah quickly stationed himself directly in front of the large camel to distract him from Ibrim's aggressive noises. When that approach failed, he yanked sharply on Mahomet's lead to take the camel outside the corral to the other side of the Depot.

Sgt. Bly barked an order at Abdullah. "Keep all the camels in the corral. We can't be having a side show here."

Speaking soothing words to Mahomet, Abdullah tightened his grip on the camel's tether and turned to Stacy. He kept his voice low. "We must separate the males. I will take Mahomet out and tie him on the other side."

A white flash crossed Stacy's eyes as his stomach clenched in anger. Abdullah was going to disobey him, and in public. The uppity Arab was leading Mahomet out of the corral in full view of the other soldiers. If Stacy didn't take charge now, he would be the butt of jokes at every mealtime from now for a month of Sundays.

Stacy bellowed, "Like hell! Bring that camel back right now. You ain't takin' it out there!"

Ibrim was making loud provocations toward Mahomet. Pertag danced in front of Ibrim and tugged pathetically at the camel's lead. None of the Americans came forward to help. Nate was quickly tying his mules, but it would take him a few seconds to reach Pertag, a few seconds too many by Abdullah's reckoning. If he would prevent a camel fight, Abdullah would have to act. Without a backward glance, he grabbed Mahomet firmly and walked him through the gate, past the crowd that had congregated on the street, and over to the far corner of the Depot. He attached Mahomet to a hitching post near the spot where Lt. Halter stood alone. Mahomet was half in the street, but at least one camel was out of the other's line of sight.

Abdullah breathed easier when Nate secured Ibrim at the far corner of the corral. Abdullah tried to control his thrashing heartbeat and to suppress his rage, reserved for Pertag and Stacy in equal measure. A near disaster, again. A potential catastrophe caused by the same two blundering idiots. A crisis narrowly averted by his own quick thinking. Would anyone appreciate how he had saved the day? Probably not. A thousand Arabic curses ran through his mind.

Sgt. Bly was in no mood to tolerate such blatant defiance. He strode toward Abdullah, irate, his cheeks purpled the color of an old wound. "Who the hell do you think you are? How dare you disobey a direct order?" His grating voice had become shrill.

Still patting Mahomet's side, Abdullah turned to face his accuser. He struggled to maintain an even tone. "If I did not separate the animals, there would be a fight. It was not safe to keep them together."

"I gave you a direct order!" Livid, Sgt. Bly scanned the crowd. To his dismay, he saw whispering and a few sniggers. He sensed that he was being unmanned in front of the rank-and-file soldiers.

Abdullah's voice quavered with indignation, but he replied steadily. "Your order was a wrong one. I took Mahomet away to stop the fight. You should thank me."

"Thank you? Thank you!?!! Are you crazy?"

Stacy Bly was beyond logic. He was like a steam engine that had been over stoked, hissing hot vapor and set to explode. Each of the many aggravations associated with the camel project was like another chunk of wood on an increasing flame. It had started with the chaotic unloading. Then the foreigners had refused to eat. Next came the humiliation of the camels chewing on his cactus fence. The Arabs bowed and chanted endlessly, disrupting chores even in the middle of the day. The camels were unruly and they stank and, as an added insult, Major Babcock treated each one like it was a prized Kentucky thoroughbred. Most galling was the utter lack of respect that the ignorant foreigners had toward the US Army. These newcomers lorded it over everybody, and Major Babcock deferred to anything they said. It was maddening. Only Pertag appeared to be a reasonable fellow who was trying to be a true American. The others held themselves apart, even though they spoke English and could have tried harder to fit in. The worst one in his opinion was Abdullah, standing before him this very minute in an act of direct disobedience. He had to be put in his place.

"What the hell do you think you're doin'? Y'all can't have a camel out here in the goddamn street. Git him back in the corral. And git your own ass over here. Now. That's an order!"

"Please calm down."

"Ain't no question of calmin' down. Y'all just do as you're told, and git that animal back inside. I've 'bout had all I'm gonna take of your backtalkin', so move it!"

Abdullah had had enough of Sgt. Bly and his stupidity. Everything about him was inadequate: his knowledge of camels, his ability to command, and his contorted grammar. Not only was he unschooled, he was also insecure and unable to think for himself. This was a dangerous combination in a man with authority. Checking his anger, Abdullah spoke firmly but did not shout.

"No, you must listen to me. Mahomet stays out here or we will have a very bad problem."

"Listen to *you*? *I* should listen to *you*? And who in tarnation are *you*? A camel boy what don't even speak English good! A sneaky, no 'count connivin' son of a gun, that's what you are! I don't give a good goddamn what *you* say. I gave an order. Obey me or there'll be hell to pay!"

Abdullah prided himself on having acquired some very pungent English swear words during his employment with the British, but refrained from using them now. Instead, the irony of Stacy accusing him of speaking English poorly made Abdullah smile.

Seeing that smirk, something in Stacy snapped. He grabbed his pistol, flipped the barrel into his hand as if holding a hammer, and reached out to strike Abdullah in the head. A split second before the blow would have landed, Abdullah ducked. But as he rose again, the wooden butt of Stacy's gun cracked hard against Abdullah's temple. In the instant that Abdullah sank to his knees in crashing agony, Stacy lost his grip on the barrel. The gun slipped in his sweaty palm and went off, shooting Stacy in the left shoulder.

Stacy tumbled backwards and let out a full-throated scream, stunned and bleeding as the sharp pain blinded him. Never had he known such a hurt. The shock of it knocked his breath away, and he gulped huge mouthfuls of air. What he felt was excruciating. While the action around him moved with unusual slowness and clarity, he remembered hearing soldiers brag about being shot and, to hear them tell it, they had all taken it like a man. He wondered whether he would tell similar lies when his turn came. With that thought, he passed out.

Pandemonium broke loose. Jeremy Blackstone, who had been inside assembling supplies, ran out the door. Completely unaware of what had happened, he saw at once that Sgt. Bly was wounded and promptly stepped out to determine the severity. Jeremy ordered two soldiers to lift Stacy to the porch and dispatched another for the doctor. He then applied pressure to the wound and was relieved to see that the shot had missed any major arteries. It appeared to be superficial.

Rounding the corner from the back of the lot where he had been settling Ibrim and scolding Pertag, Nate Wilkers arrived in time to see Jeremy take charge. Nate was surprised to see his grandfather be so authoritative. Apparently among his grandfather's secret talents was some very useful medical knowledge. Also impressive was his low-key style of directing people, all the more remarkable because his grandfather had no official standing whatsoever with these soldiers. Jeremy's mandate lasted barely a few minutes before Captain Van Steendam came running. In that brief span, Nate had seen his grandpa's masterly performance and was awed. Nate's contemplation was interrupted by shouts from the crowd.

"He shot him. That foreigner shot him!"

"No, he didn't. Stacy Bly shot himself."

"No way, that guy grabbed the gun. Can't let a man shoot a soldier like that."

"Yeah, them foreigners ain't got no respect for authority."

"They'll shoot you just as soon as look at you."

Nate realized with a sudden shock that the crowd blamed Abdullah for the shooting. Among them, he saw some roughs that loved a ruckus, no matter how it got started nor how it might end. That bunch was uncontrollable once they found an excuse to fight. To make matters worse, the soldiers at the Government Depot who had been ministering to Stacy were now paying menacing attention to Abdullah.

"Yeah, that Ay-rab's a tough one, all right. Stacy ain't never liked him."

"Y'all see how it happened?"

"Can't be sure, but it wouldn't surprise me none if he did it on purpose."

The noise and chaos agitated Mahomet, who strained at his tether, jerked his head and tried to move away from the din. The crowd pushed in closer, causing Mahomet to let out an annoyed screech, which sent everyone backwards a few paces. Abdullah was afraid the animal would break loose and cause even more problems in the street. Dabbing at the blood on his head with one hand, he tried to soothe the camel with the other. When he turned from Mahomet, Abdullah confronted a sea of angry faces and froze.

Nate became alarmed. Rapidly looking around, he picked out Drew Johnsville, avidly shouting at Abdullah along with the rest of the crowd, and rushed over to him.

"Did you see that, Nate? One of them camel boys shot Stacy Bly. Can't even believe it."

"Yeah," said Wiley Beem, the man standing next to him, "A goddamned mess."

On the verge of panic, Nate tried to sound assertive but was sure he sounded desperate. "Drew, that's Abdullah, and I swear to you he didn't shoot anybody. I'm gonna go stand by him. I'd be obliged if y'all would join me."

"What? You outta your mind?"

"I ain't goin' out there. That feller shot a soldier, for Chrissake," whined Wiley Beem.

"Come on, Drew. We can't be havin' a riot here. I'm goin' and I'm standin' with him." Nate saw people edging toward Abdullah and shouted, "It's gotta be now!"

Drew frowned. "I'll be damned if you ain't completely lost your head, but hell if I'm lettin' you do somethin' that stupid by yourself."

And thus, in that split second, Amos Prudeau's assertion that Drew Johnsonville would stand by his buddies in a scrape was proven true. A full head taller and at least forty pounds heavier than Nate, Drew mumbled a few more curses under his breath and turned to his friends.

"Let's go!" When Wiley Beem held back, Drew threw him a dirty look. "That's Jeremy Blackstone's boy. I'm goin'. You with me?"

"Shit, y'all gone crazy now." Shaking their heads in disbelief, Wiley and the man next to him stepped forward. Though still limping a little from his riding injury, Drew caught up with Nate and resolutely marched to Abdullah's side, followed closely by the two other men. They formed a small phalanx around Abdullah. Drew said nothing. There was no need. Everyone knew that Drew Johnsville would fight at the drop of a hat.

Nate called Pertag to keep an eye on Mahomet, then caught Drew's eye and pointed toward the Depot. The four Americans, each with his back to Abdullah and stern eyes on the loudmouths in the crowd, escorted Abdullah in that direction. As they nudged their way toward the porch, a path opened, albeit reluctantly. The verbal abuse continued, but they made progress.

Now it was Jeremy's turn to be surprised and impressed. With the arrival of the doctor, Jeremy had stood up in time to see his grandson lead the small group of Abdullah's defenders. He still didn't understand Nate's fascination with the camels nor his friendship with the Arabs, but none of that mattered now. Jeremy grabbed his rifle.

"Outta the way boys." He walked to meet the intrepid group and nodded to Nate. "Let's get y'all indoors."

Jeremy stared down a group of angry soldiers, cocked his rifle and positioned himself to defend his grandson if needed. To the astonishment of all concerned, Lt. Winston Halter stepped next to Jeremy between the soldiers and Abdullah's party. Looking straight at Captain Van Steendam, Lt. Halter spoke loudly and clearly in a rather stilted manner, as if reading from the scriptures.

"Captain, I believe your man has injured himself through an accidental and unfortunate series of missteps and misunderstandings. I have witnessed the entire exchange, which involved a disagreement between Sgt. Bly and this Arab over the proper management of a particular camel. The conversation became overheated. One might be forced to concede that Sgt. Bly acted in a provocative manner, though it must also be acknowledged that the Arab failed to accede to a direct order. During the first exchange, Sgt. Bly raised his hand to strike the Arab, who dodged away in an effort to avoid an altercation. Nevertheless Sgt. Bly hit the Arab in the head. Sgt. Bly's strenuous movement caused his gun to slip in his hand and discharge. Based on fact and observation, one must conclude that the Arab is not guilty of this misfortune that has befallen Sgt. Bly. I shall be happy to provide a written affidavit to that effect."

Mesmerized by Lt. Halter's unexpected intervention, the crowd quieted down. "That was some speechifyin'."

"Yeah, what the hell did he say?"

"He said it was an accident. The foreigner didn't shoot him. When Stacy hit the Arab, his gun slipped and fired."

"That what happened? Helluva thing."

The crowd's angry shouts reduced to speculative murmurings. The lull allowed Captain Van Steendam to reassess what had transpired. "Mr. Wilkers, take the camel keeper inside."

Not quite trusting the quiet that followed Lt. Halter's theatrics, Jeremy kept his rifle poised. Once Nate and Abdullah were in the building, Drew Johnsville's friends melded back into the crowd and Jeremy lowered his gun. He stood rock still, his back braced against the doorframe. Anyone would think that nothing was going on at all unless they noticed his eyes in continuous movement over the scene. Drew leaned nonchalantly against the nearest porch post, and Jeremy thanked him with a glance.

Lt. Halter once again addressed the crowd. "I shall take statements from any and all who wish to describe the events that we have just witnessed. Your contribution of factual evidence will be most appreciated by the magistrate who will certainly be called to review the case. Form a queue to the side here."

Someone in the crowd shouted out: "He means if y'all saw what happened, line up and he'll write it down for the judge."

As Winston Halter settled on the porch with a fresh piece of paper in hand, his invitation served better than any pleading to disperse the crowd. None of the residents of Indianola cottoned to the notion of testifying in court. Besides, the truth was widely acknowledged: Sgt. Bly had shot himself.

Inside the Government Depot, Abdullah sat on a chair, forlorn and furious, his head throbbing. Jeremy bandaged his wound while Nate went to check on the camels. Captain Van Steendam returned from the doctor with confirmation that Sgt. Bly was not seriously hurt.

"I'll send Nate back to Green Lake with Mahomet. I'm keepin' the other camels in town for the night. Jeremy, you be sure that this one stays indoors." He gestured towards Abdullah.

"Yes, Cap'n. I'll get him some grub and set up a cot."

Captain Van Steendam left without further commentary. Abdullah still couldn't believe what had happened. He had prevented a potentially disastrous fight between the two male camels, yet no one had given him even token appreciation. Instead he had been verbally abused, physically attacked, and accused of assault. Like Hassan in the Galveston jail, Abdullah was dumfounded.

INDIANOLA, TEXAS, JUNE 2, 1856

OUT AT GREEN LAKE, Nate rode hard into the camel paddock, slid off his horse, and hurried in search of Alex Babcock. "Alex, we're finally goin'! Day after tomorrow!"

"Hooray! It's about time!" After a month in Indianola, Alex was more than ready to go.

Hassan shouted, "Alhamdulillah! Nate, what do you shout when you get good news?"

These questions from Hassan always made Nate pause, as he was not in the habit of thinking about words. Then he laughed and shouted, "Yee haw!"

"Yee haw!" Hassan danced around in a circle.

Sgt. Bly scowled. Although happy that he would soon be rid of the camels and the camel keepers, it annoyed him that he hadn't been told first. He should have been the one to tell the men, not the other way around.

Nate turned to Alex and Hassan. "I guess y'all know I'm goin' along. Took a little while to work it out. Major Babcock hired me under his authority. Civilian assignment. Six months for starters, and then we'll see what happens. Depends a little on the camels, I guess."

Alex laughed out loud. "I figured you were up to something!"

"You did?"

"Hell, yes. Ever since I met you on Matagorda Island, I've been trying to work out what you've been planning. You've been scheming to go with the camels all along!"

"Yup. I wanna see what they can do, and I wanna go west."

"Well, I'm mighty glad to have you with us."

"Yes, it is good," added Hassan. "You know the camels better than any of the soldiers."

"Listen boys, if you can handle things for awhile, I'd like to ride to town to tell the McDermotts." Without waiting for their assent, Alex mounted a horse and galloped off. As he passed the Government Depot, he waved to Jeremy Blackstone on the porch.

Anticipating the trek, Jeremy felt the weight of inevitability. He had convinced Captain Van Steendam to engage him as cook for the camel expedition as far as San Antonio. Even before the *Supply* had arrived in the Gulf, he suspected that Nate would follow the camels. Weeks had passed since he had resolved to accompany his grandson. Nevertheless, his decision had been difficult, especially because Nate had still not said a word.

The two men were at an awkward impasse, both preparing to depart with the camels but neither revealing his plans. Jeremy wanted to tell Nate personally. He hoped to give him an understanding of a grandfather's reluctance to part with his grandson, but he didn't quite know what to say. The truth was, whenever he tried to imagine life without Nate, he simply couldn't feature it. The gaping hole would be like a terrifying break in the road over which there was no bridge. He feared that his need for Nate might stifle his grandson or hold him back, and he was certain he must not do that. He wanted to move parallel without hindering, to be a comforting presence that still gave Nate space for a man's action and self-determination.

He looked up to see Stacy Bly dismounting. Stacy nodded, but didn't speak as he walked past Jeremy into Captain Van Steendam's office.

"Mornin', sir." Stacy was wary, unsure why he had been summoned.

"Good mornin', Sgt. Bly. I'll come straight to it. You've been reassigned to San Antonio. Transfer effective immediately."

"What? Why sir?"

"The Army needs a Sergeant there. I thought you'd like to get away from Indianola." Never a strong leader, Stacy's authority had been considerably eroded since he accidentally shot himself.

Sgt. Bly was stunned. "How long sir?"

"Permanent transfer."

"But, Captain…"

"No use talkin' about it. I know it's a surprise, but this is the Army and an order's an order. You'll leave day after tomorrow with the camels. I know you're none too fond of them, but you won't have them around much longer. Mind that you have no further problems on the road. Do you understand me?"

"Yes sir." Sgt. Bly saluted and turned, lowering his head to hide the wave of fury that had to show on his face.

Captain Van Steendam was pleased to see Sgt. Bly transferred, and he wouldn't regret the camels either. Although a Camel Cavalry was historic, he found it frivolous. Without the camels he would have more time to provision the outlying forts with the horses, mules, and wagons that they really needed.

Stacy felt his frustration as a stabbing pain in his sore shoulder. Although things hadn't been that great around Indianola lately, he was content enough. He enjoyed the kind of Army life that came without any serious soldiering. No dangers, no Indians, no camping on the trail with only hardtack to chew on. He had it sweet. The little German tart who worked from her tent in the immigrant camps let him have a poke for cheap and sometimes even gave him a meal. In San Antonio, there was no predicting where he might be sent, and he still had to deal with the godforsaken camels. He stomped across the porch without even looking at Jeremy Blackstone, who had heard the entire exchange through the open window.

Thinking he might have to keep an eye on Stacy, Jeremy reviewed his preparations. As always, he leaned toward the practical. Even though full summer was coming, he packed for winter: extra blankets, his wool long johns, a heavy outer coat, and a hat that Hilde had made him in a German style that pulled down over his ears. He dried herbs, ground spices, and prepared a stash of jerky. He took writing paper and ink and the family Bible that Melissa had brought from Alabama. He had little else remaining from Melissa, only a small crocheted rug that she had made soon after they moved to Texas. Wherever he was, he liked to set it beside his bed, so that rug had already moved with him to Indianola.

Yesterday, on his last visit to the lighthouse, he had transplanted a selection of live herbs from the garden into a small traveling box that he planned to attach to the outside of the supply wagon. It was a personal tribute to Hilde, who had taught him to enliven his cooking with something besides salt and pepper. Among his clothes he carefully laid a tintype of Hilde, wrapped in a bandana. He set his bags on the porch, inhaled deeply, and pondered again the chain of events that had led him to this lighthouse, first to the building of it and now to the leaving. He would miss the peacefulness of the island. Lowering himself onto the rocking chair that he had whittled from driftwood, he looked out upon the gulf's blazing turquoise. When he could delay the moment no longer, he reached for the bags that held his mementos and stepped off the lighthouse porch for the final time, his chair still rocking.

Today, all that remained was to check the wagon at the Government Depot before driving to the camel pen at Green Lake. He had two Dutch ovens, an oversized stew cauldron, cast iron skillets in several sizes, two coffee pots, and various iron rods that assembled into rotisseries or tripod supports to hold pots over the fire. Stacked against one wall were sacks of coffee, pinto beans, flour, and cornmeal, a jar of bacon fat, smaller jars of salt and pepper, and a precious cone of sugar. He had several cages of live chickens for eggs and a crate of freshly purchased carrots, potatoes, and onions. He had rigged the backside of the wagon to pull down as a table, supported by a wood strut that braced against the wagon when the workspace was open. Once more he made sure that it was sturdy and would not wiggle loose along a bumpy trail. Crawling around inside the wagon, he was startled to hear the voices of Amos Prudeau and Drew Johnsville.

Amos was talking loudly. "In all my days I ain't never seen a pair so close but so quiet. One of 'em'll never tell the other what he's up to. One's gotta guess, and then the other one's gotta guess back."

Drew started laughing. "Yeah, I figure the whole town knows what's goin' on with them two."

Amos called. "Come on outta there, Jeremy. We got Nate with us. Found him lolling about near the Blauvelt place." Drew chuckled.

Jeremy backed out of the wagon, jumped down and blinked in the bright light. "Howdy, Nate. Looks like it's fixin' to be quite a trip."

"Yeah Grandpa, that's for sure." Nate grinned sheepishly.

Amos burst out laughing. "I swear you two are somethin' else. Seein' as how y'all are both gonna leave us and there's no tellin' when you'll be back, me and Drew got somethin' for you."

He handed Nate an object wrapped in a leather cloth. Nate knew immediately it was a firearm, but he was stunned when he unwrapped a brand new Colt revolver. Nate had never owned a gun and to be given one of this extravagance left him speechless.

Amos broke the silence. "Yeah, it's a new Colt, but don't get too excited. I can assure you we didn't spend any twenty-four dollars for it." Nate was relieved to hear that. A Colt was the best, but a new one was expensive. "Naw, Drew got us into a poker game the other night and we won it off a guy stayin' over at the Alhambra. Turns out that fella is a representative of the Colt Company. He had samples to show Captain Van Steendam. Oh, he told us great stories."

"Yeah, and while he was tellin' stories, we kept winnin' at cards!" Drew smiled proudly.

"That's right. This here is the newest model. You shoulda heard him callin' it the Navy model. We had to tell him that out here it's called the Ranger."

Drew laughed. "Turns out the 'representative' can't hold his liquor too well, and he can't play poker for shit. So we took this Colt right off him. Left him sputterin' mad, but he had more with him. It's not like we took his last gun. Seems to us you'll have more use for it than anyone."

Nate was awestruck. "Thanks Amos, Drew. I don't rightly know what to say."

"Just make sure you don't get yourself killed by any Indians or rattlesnakes. Not to mention thieves and roughnecks." Then Amos turned his attention to Jeremy. "And we brought somethin' for you, too."

Jeremy noticed that they were pulling a small wagon, with a blanket covering the cargo. Drew walked over and in one quick jerk unveiled Jeremy's rocking chair.

"Well, I'll be..."

"Now, don't you start in tellin' us how you can't take it with you. The plain fact is that you can't leave it. Seein' Jeremy Blackstone without his rockin' chair is like seein' a man naked. You ain't been quite right ever since you started sleepin' over here at the Depot while your chair was still on the island. So we figured you needed to have it."

"Well, I suppose you've got a point there." Jeremy was flabbergasted. Nate laughed out loud to see his grandfather so completely surprised.

"No fussin', Jeremy. We even worked out a way to lash it onto your wagon, so it won't take up space on the inside." With that Amos and Drew took out precut lengths of rope and handily suspended the rocking chair.

"I guess it's my turn to thank you boys. Let me buy y'all a drink."

"Now you're talkin'!"

PERMANENT HOME

U P AT FIRST LIGHT, Elizabeth found her mother downstairs with Esther, checking a packing list.

"All ready, Esther?"

"I hope so, Miz Sylvia. Just worryin' we have what we need for cookin'."

"Check the list again then. Good morning, Elizabeth. What a beautiful day to make history! Tell your brothers to get down here with their trunk. We need it right now."

In their room upstairs, Zeke and Zach tumbled over themselves, their awkward teenage limbs flying in all directions. Hearing the arrival of Alex Babcock, they scrambled downstairs to find out what was happening.

"Good morning, everyone. Major Babcock sent me to tell you that things aren't going so well. We probably won't leave until at least ten o'clock. You can start as late as noon and still catch us before nightfall. In spite of all the drills we did packing the camels and lining them up, they're still not right. I'm sorry, but I can't stay. I'll see you tonight." As he left, Elizabeth's smile added a spring to his step.

Sylvia was glad for the extra time. Although the boys were impatient, she insisted that they take a proper breakfast, complete with a prayer for their safe passage.

"Now children, I want to read your father's letter. He wrote it weeks ago for us to open today.

My dear Sylvia, Elizabeth, Ezekiel, and Zachary,

As you leave for San Antonio, know that I have envisioned your journey many times. You will certainly suffer some inconvenience, but I hope that you may also enjoy the beautiful Texas countryside that unfolds between Indianola and your destination. It is a wonder to behold. I wish you a safe trip. Children, obey your mother, and Sylvia, you have my abiding gratitude and my deepest affection.

Your devoted husband and father,

Quentin

With the warmth of her husband's blessing, Sylvia and her family prepared to depart. Mr. Blauvelt had arranged for two covered wagons, one designed for the comfort and personal affairs of the family and the other to carry goods and foodstuffs. One or two slaves would have space to rest in the second wagon along with the kitchen supplies and large trunks. Elizabeth climbed up beside her mother and Antoine in the lead wagon. They had rolled back the canvas cover so that Zeke and Zach could have a view of the new country. Samuel took the second wagon, with Esther and Agnes at his side. Esther's daughters rode inside along with the supplies. Two horses, also hired from Mr. Blauvelt, were attached to the second wagon, but her mother had forbidden the boys to ride until they were in open country and used to the rhythm of the journey. Mrs. Eberly escorted them as far as the outskirts of town, and Elizabeth felt a sudden sadness at leaving the older woman.

At the junction with the main road to San Antonio, they observed ample evidence of the camels having already passed. The footprints, wagon tracks, camel dung, and general stirring up of the track offered dramatic proof that they were commencing a grand adventure. Elizabeth's feelings were the opposite of what she had expected. Leaving Galveston had been traumatic, unplanned, and fraught. Distressed by her father's peculiar refusal to explain anything, she had neither wished the move nor comprehended the reasons for it. She had been petulant, a response that she now regretted since coming to a fuller understanding of her mother's worries. By contrast, this trip felt like fresh air after the confines of a stuffy room. She felt light and worry-free, surrounded by potential. She wanted to catch up to the camels as soon as possible, to hear what stories Alex would tell, and at last to ride a camel.

En route to San Antonio, June 6, 1856

My dearest Annabelle,

You may imagine my enormous vexation with what I confirm herein. No orders arrived from Washington, and I have been obliged to follow the camel caravan to find what Major Babcock curiously refers to as a "permanent home" for the creatures. We have been fitted out with Conestoga wagons, much like the ones you have seen in newspaper accounts of westward-migrating trains. The Major and I share one that also carries our personal valises, a small writing desk and the official documents of the mission. Our quarters are cramped, but serviceable.

Major Babcock describes the camels on our first day as "frisky" or "a bit unruly." What prevarication! They leapt about, hectored each other, bunched up along the route, dallied at will, and left the main road. Several saddles slipped off and had to be repacked. We made a scant twelve miles to Chocolate Bayou. If the camels continue to advance in such a disorganized fashion, I fear we will be further delayed by the Texas rainy season, which is known for deluges and inundations. We pause frequently at Major Babcock's insistence that the camels require time to acclimate. My disagreement with his view is of no consequence to him.

Apparently, a camel has a persistent memory for any affront from a handler and will refuse direction from said handler again. Some of our soldiers have made errors and have been subjected to kicking, biting and spitting. I will not trouble you with a description of a camel's spit, which is actually a vomit of the contents of its first stomach. Suffice it to say, it is disgusting. The Arabs insist that it is a simple matter to learn to guide a camel and blame our soldiers for improper handling. These foreign camel men are generally useless, but one, who has adopted the moniker of Pete, is beginning to have the confidence of our soldiers. In my view, the problems derive not from mismanagement but from the absolute foreignness of the beasts. The natural incompatibility that obtains between everything American and these bizarre creatures is too great to be overcome.

One of the Arabs got into an altercation that led to a soldier being shot. Because I was a witness, I shall have to return to Indianola in a few weeks to participate in a tribunal. Let us pray that orders to return to Washington await me then.

Your devoted husband,

Winston

En Route to San Antonio

T HE FIRST SIGHT OF the prairie stunned. Elizabeth came over a slight rise onto a vast expanse of waving grasses, an ocean of fresh green interspersed with small hillocks, some of which sprouted trees. Never had she seen a terrain so verdant, in so many shades of aliveness. Each little breeze caused the individual blades of grass to blow in different directions, making patterns and circles and back-and-forth motions like children chasing each other in a game of tag. When they moved, the grasses shifted from pale yellow to bright green as the sunlight reflected on their supple stems. At first she thought that some small animals were disturbing the grasses, causing so many ripples and gyrations. It had taken a moment for her to understand that these subtle hues of perpetual motion were caused by the wind. The delicate stalks seemed eager to be caressed, bent, and reinstated upright by the shifting puffs of air. Elizabeth felt blessed to see such beauty.

By the second day, her mother became pleasant company again. Sylvia smiled often, chatted easily, and excitedly pointed out a hawk in the sky or an unusual wildflower in the grass. She told stories of her childhood in Philadelphia and recounted how she had met Elizabeth's father. Her description of their harrowing journey to Galveston, first overland to Cincinnati then down the Ohio and Mississippi rivers to New Orleans, left Elizabeth breathless. She could scarcely credit her mother's depiction of Galveston in the days before the merchants made real money and constructed their stately homes. Elizabeth loved the stories of her mother as a young wife, not much older than she was now, learning how to manage a home from Esther's mother. In the evening around Major Babcock's campfire, her mother laughed and joked with her cousin, a radiance spreading across her face. Sylvia's transformation lifted a weight off everyone, and Elizabeth cherished their intimate moments.

Elizabeth did not miss Galveston, so amusing was it to travel with the camels. She never tired of their gangly gait as they steadfastly followed along in a line. Sometimes she was permitted to ride, always under the watchful eye of one of the Arabs. She developed a healthy diffidence toward the male camels, which she preferred to observe from a comfortable distance, but became fond of the females, especially Tullah and Adela. The young Uncle Sam entertained everyone when he played among the females. She pondered what it would be like to see herds of camels wandering the plains or running at top speed to fight the Indians. Major Babcock had told them that the British loaded their camels with Gatling guns. Truly, this camel trek was a historic event, and not just because Alex Babcock said so at least once a day.

The serendipity of the camels made Elizabeth reconsider everything. Her life in Galveston had been structured, timed, and planned. She studied her languages, practiced her piano, learned difficult stitches, and read her Bible along with as many books as possible from her mother's collection. Because her mother required it, she became conversant with the principles of arithmetic and money management. She gossiped with her friends, attended chaperoned soirees, and picnicked at the beach with her family. In church, she was pious and demure. Praise from her father's friends was her highest reward. That had all disappeared with their wrenching move, to be replaced only with endless waiting and uncertainty.

With the forward movement of the camel caravan, Elizabeth felt unencumbered, physically as well as mentally. Surprised when her mother suggested that corsets were inappropriate for wagon travel, she reveled in the freedom of her body, a feeling full of promise that reminded her of her childhood. She began to think that her destiny might involve something other than being matron of a prominent Galveston family, a radical idea. Although her mother still spoke of returning to Galveston, Elizabeth nurtured a profound inkling that her future might unfold elsewhere.

Last night Major Babcock told them that they would camp at this gorgeous spot for three days to let the camels rest. Lying in the wagon with her mother, Elizabeth awoke with a start. "I know what we must do!"

Bleary-eyed, Sylvia gazed indulgently at her daughter who was now sitting bolt upright. "Yes, dear, what must we do? About what?"

"We must find a way for the President to know about the camels. We can't leave this to the military alone or even to Congress."

"My goodness, where have you been getting these lofty ideas?"

"Mama, don't tease me, please. Cousin Babcock has been telling us his fears about the project ever since we met him in Galveston. I think we can do something to change the image of the camels."

"Whatever do you mean, child?"

"Well, most people think of the camel as a circus oddity, an exotic creature, don't they? The camel is nothing more to them than something to gape at. Definitely not part of the new America. For all we know, people laugh when they hear about the Camel Corps."

Sylvia barely suppressed a smile. "Yes, I'm sure they do."

"If we could get the attention of the President in a way that shows the camel to good purpose, maybe he'll have a better attitude toward Cousin Babcock's proposals. My idea is to knit him a pair of socks from the camel's wool."

"Socks? From the camel's wool?"

"Yes, for the President. And when he's wearing the socks or even if he just keeps them as a memento, he can be thinking about the camels. It will keep them in his mind."

Sylvia struggled for the correct reply. Though proud of her daughter's creativity, she thought the proposal hare-brained and unlikely to make the desired impression. Still, it would give Elizabeth something to occupy her time.

"Well, then, why not? I think I can find my knitting needles in our crates, but you'll have to get Cousin Babcock's permission to get the wool. Then the wool must be washed and carded and spun, but you may ask Esther and Agnes to help you. You'd best start before we move again."

Energized by her plan, Elizabeth demonstrated a spirit that Sylvia had seldom seen. Over breakfast, Elizabeth recounted her plan to her brothers, who scoffed loudly.

"Socks! What an idea. Just what you'd expect from a girl." Zeke sneered.

"These are supposed to be military camels." Zach joined the taunting.

"For battle or transport, for saving the frontier."

"They're not supposed to be growing wool like a bunch of sheep!"

Hassan approached the McDermott wagons to ask if Zeke and Zach wished to accompany the camels on an exercise. He continued to be astonished at the comforts they had brought along. Each morning Antoine set up a folding wooden table with a tablecloth and four folding chairs. Agnes set the table with the everyday service, but each place setting was complete with china, glassware, and cutlery, along with a vase with wildflowers. Today's breakfast was coffee and griddlecakes with sugar syrup. Hearing the tone of the animated discussion around the table, he hesitated.

"Hassan, good morning." Sylvia called him over.

"Good morning, ma'am."

Elizabeth smiled at the way Hassan still pronounced his consonants distinctly, like Alex, but had started to admit a few contractions to his speech, saying "ma'am" exactly the way Nate did.

"Would you like some coffee?" Sylvia had long since given up trying to figure out how to treat Hassan. While an enlisted soldier would not have been offered coffee at her table, Nate and Alex were welcome, so she treated Hassan the same as those boys.

Elizabeth blurted, "Hassan, you can tell us. What do people do with camel's wool in Egypt?"

Fearing that he had stumbled into an argument, Hassan replied gingerly, "It is used for blankets and clothes."

"And is this true even if the camel is a *military* camel?" Elizabeth glanced at her brothers.

"Yes, but the wool is collected only sometimes." Hassan could say quite a bit more about camel hair, but he wasn't sure of his English, and he still didn't know what was going on.

"Hassan, my daughter is asking this question because she wants to knit a pair of socks from the camel hair to send to the President of the United States. Her brothers are skeptical."

Hassan felt a tightness in his throat as he looked at Elizabeth tilted forward with eagerness. He had never seen her eyes so bright with enthusiasm, and he felt as if he might fall right into them. He suddenly realized that everyone was looking at him for an answer. "I am not sure how to explain."

Elizabeth suspected she had spoken too fast and restated her question slowly. This time Hassan forced himself to listen. "What is the best way to get the camel hair? Do we cut it?"

"Ah, sorry Eleezabet. I understand now." Hassan sighed with relief. "The best hair is the soft one underneath, but it is easy to get the outside hair. The camels are losing it now."

Sylvia was intrigued. "You mean shedding?"

"Yes, ma'am."

Elizabeth clapped her hands. "Then we can start right now. Hassan, thank you so much. Can you show me how to collect it?"

Avoiding the intensity of Elizabeth's gaze, Hassan turned to speak directly to Sylvia. "Ma'am, I will collect it. I will ask Ali and Abdullah to help. We will bring it to you, but please, it will not be soft."

"Thank you, Hassan, that is very kind."

Esther and Agnes had no inkling that they had been committed to an arduous enterprise. When Ali brought them piles of camel wool, they thought its stink the worst they had ever smelled. Miz Sylvia instructed them to put it in the sun, wash it, rinse it and then wash it again. Finding it coarse and difficult to work, they carded it and combed it again and again. The results of their first spinning had to be undone and respun. Ali had told them that this was not the best wool that a camel could produce, but what could they do? Missy 'Lizbeth had her heart set on sending a pair of socks to the President of the United States. What a notion!

Esther observed that the rhythm of the camel's welfare dictated her own, but in an opposite direction. While the camels trekked, she was able to ride in the wagon. Although she sometimes strolled alongside, mostly she preferred to ride. She had no responsibilities once the caravan was moving. When the camels, mules, and horses trudged on, she rested, and though it was a rolling, bouncing rest, it was more time with nothing required of her than Esther had ever known.

Once the caravan's forward momentum ceased, Esther's work began. She had to prepare food under conditions that she found taxing and alien. Her greatest anxiety was cooking on the trail without a proper kitchen. She missed having a hearth and disliked the open fire. Different woods produced uneven heat that was subject to the vagaries of wind and weather. Water was also uncertain. They carried drinking water with them, but hauling water for washing dishes and general cleanup was a new and unwelcome task. Moreover, with the bulk of the kitchen utensils crated for the trip, she had to make due with the bare minimum. Missing the ability to get fresh food everyday at the market, Esther had to limit her menu to what she could concoct with salt pork, flour, beans, and corn meal.

Her first night's meal on the trail had been improperly cooked, but Jeremy Blackstone ambled to her fire with suggestions. She found it a mystery how a man, and a white man at that, had such ability with a skillet and Dutch oven. He made stews and eggs and biscuits both savory and delicious. She knew this, not because she ever tasted so much as a morsel of his cooking, but because Alex Babcock did and Hassan did and Nate Wilkers did. Those three hovered around Missy 'Lizbeth like bees to honey. Praise for Mr. Blackstone's food was a reliable topic of conversation among them.

Tonight, after all the work with the camel hair, she still had to cook. Antoine had gone hunting with Zeke and Zach and had brought back a brace of rabbits from which Esther simmered a stew that drew smiles of satisfaction all around.

Finally Esther hung the iron pot on the side of the wagon, inhaled deeply, and pulled her rolled-up sleeves back down, a series of gestures that Agnes took as proof that they had finished with the chores. Agnes looked forward to this time of day. Already seated on the log, she scooted over to make space for Esther to plunk down wearily in front of the fire that Samuel kept going at a high blaze. He fanned the dazzling flames not so much for warmth, which was superfluous on the sultry night, but in a vain attempt to dissipate the mosquitoes that came out at dusk. Apart from the carnivorous insects, the place was beautiful.

Esther was grateful for company when the sun set. She wasn't comfortable out in the open at night. Agnes, Antoine, Samuel, and the children, preferring fresh air to the stuffy wagon, slept outdoors next to the fire or under the wagon, but Esther chose to be inside. The compact space of the wagon wrapped her in a cocoon of safety and let her sleep. Too much of a city person, Esther was bereft without the sounds of urban life. She missed the noisy carriages on the shell-paved roads of Galveston, the sounds of hawkers, the bark of dogs, and especially the morning calls of roosters and doves. Here on the prairie the sounds were fewer and somehow windy, making them hard to interpret. This wide-open expanse could hold any number of dangers, and Esther imagined all of them: Indians, wild animals, storms, losing her way. She feared that Sally and Mabel might become ill or injured. Her dreams were haunted by a premonition that she would never see Henry again. From these scenes she often awakened with a terrified jerk that shook the wagon. Tonight she simply longed for clean clothes and a bath.

Agnes on the other hand could not have been more content with their new life. Though the first day's walking had made her limbs ache, she soon reveled in the strength of her muscles. She loved the rhythm, placing each foot forward in turn, sometimes counting one-two-three-four, one-two-three-four over and over. The boundlessness of the landscape before her drew her onward and lifted her cares. She did worry a bit about Esther, who seemed to carry a load on her shoulders. When they stopped, Agnes worked hard to help make the biscuit dough or stir the stew. She was especially good at fetching water and washing up, and she knew that was a big help to Esther. But while they moved, Agnes felt a lightness of being that she had never known. The sky was so huge, the spaces so vast, and the colors so intense that she could scarcely take it all in.

Most of all, she loved the camels. Had she been allowed, she would have walked right next to them. She envied those who knew how to talk to them and how to make them stand and kneel. The first time she saw one get up from its resting position, tilting on its spindly legs, she shouted, "Whoopee!" Even though the soldiers laughed at her, she didn't care. A camel rising was a wonderful thing to behold. She found the baby camel especially adorable. She often saw Nate riding next to it or playing with it in the evening. Maybe if she asked Nate very nicely, he would let her touch the baby. She so wondered what its nose felt like.

The slaves sat at their own fire. The McDermott family was settled some yards away around a fire with Major Babcock and Lt. Halter. A third fire was the gathering point for the enlisted men, who lounged about playing cards, whittling, cleaning their weapons, and retelling the day's events. The camel men often felt unwelcome to join them, to the point where they sometimes built their own fire and sat apart. Tonight, Hassan and Abdullah strolled over to sit with Antoine and Samuel. They understood that consorting with the slaves might diminish their status in the eyes of the soldiers, but also knew that they didn't have much status to lose. By the time Esther joined them, with one of her girls leaning against her on each side, the men were engrossed in a complex dissection of the English language. Hassan and Abdullah had long sought to find a polite way to inquire about the differences in language between the slaves and the whites.

"It's easy to understand. We talk how white folk want us to," Antoine opined.

Samuel gawked at him. He had never considered this. "Antoine, sometimes you make too much of a thing. How you gonna talk any other way?"

"We talk the way we talk. But other folks talk different. The way of talkin' says somethin' 'bout you. That's all."

"That's too much for me to figure. I just hope my talkin' says what I wanna say."

Antoine laughed, as Abdullah and Hassan followed closely to get the gist of the argument. Esther by now was fully engaged.

"Of course you gonna say what you wanna say. But *how* you says it. That tells a person somethin' 'bout you. Can't you tell if white folk come from Texas or someplace else?"

"Why sure, I can tell a Yankee from a Georgia man the minute he open his mouth."

"That's right. So when we talk, it tells of us. My pa told me that some of our words are African, brought over in the ships and stayin' with us to remind us where we come from. Words like goober, for peanuts. On the plantation there was folks from different parts of Africa, and they had different names for things. They had to get by with mixed-up words until everybody understood. 'Course most of that mixed up talk be gone now, but African words like gumbo and okra, they still around."

Samuel reflected. "I remember somethin'. Maybe okra ain't English, like you say. An old lady in the Galveston market once started talkin' to me funny. She had a big bright head tie and somethin' voodoo 'round her neck. She was lookin' at me with faraway eyes, like she was seein' somethin' from the past. Told me she saw my elders eatin' yam with okra. She pronounced 'em both funny, too. Like een-yam and oh-kroh."

Antoine nodded.

"She jus' kept lookin' at me, then she said I was a strong African and I was supposed to do somethin'. She sayin' agin and agin like it was real important. Made me feel strange. But just when I was gonna ask her what I was s'posed to do, she looked at me hard, kind of scared. Then she snapped out of it and blinked her eyes some. She looked at me with those blinky eyes like it ain't never happened and tried to get me to buy her okra."

"Could be she was seein' your future. Or maybe rememberin' her own past. Hard to say. But okra and yam, yup, African words."

Esther was embarrassed by this talk of Africa. Her family had been with the McDermotts for at least four generations. Africans in her view were superstitious and savage. Every so-called African she had seen was raw. Her image of Africa did not correspond with her view of herself and the other McDermott slaves. She was offended by any hint of connection, even as little as language.

"Why you speakin' of Africa? We ain't like Africans, no way. White folks'll be happy to think poorly of us if we start callin' things by African names."

Antoine gawked at her. His father was African, stolen from Africa years after the slave trade had been outlawed. Although his father carried a deep anger for what had befallen him, in no way was he ashamed of where he came from. On the contrary, he was proud. Antoine's acquaintance with his father had ended abruptly at age twelve, when a nearby farmer needed a field hand. He had suffered mightily, both from the loss of his family and from the sheer physical exhaustion that came with field work. Eventually his second owner recognized the wits behind Antoine's brawn and elevated him to a house servant, a position from which he had been sold to Quentin McDermott a few years ago. He never saw his parents again. But before being wrenched from his father's knee, he had spent hours listening to stories, absorbing strange words and concepts, and most of all, promising his father than he would remember.

Hassan, too, was shocked by Esther's comments. Esther obviously came from African roots. How could she dishonor her ancestors? Although he wished to say something, the fresh lessons of the Galveston jail precluded any mention of his own ancestry. Uncertain, he kept silent.

Agnes was hopelessly lost in the intricacies of this conversation, but wanted desperately to contribute. "The Bible got beautiful English. Y'all ever hear the girls recite the Bible?"

Completely oblivious to the fact that Abdullah and Hassan might not appreciate a Biblical text, Sally and Mabel suddenly felt all eyes on them, sat straighter, and said, "Mama, which one? How 'bout your favorite? Psalm 23?"

Esther nodded, and the girls stood up in front of the fire, the light flickering on their ebony skin. They recited in unison with perfect enunciation:

The Lord is my shepherd; I shall not want.
He maketh me to lie down in green pastures: he leadeth me
  beside the still waters.
He restoreth my soul: he leadeth me in the paths of righteous-
  ness for his name's sake.
Yea, though I walk through the valley of the shadow of
  death, I will fear no evil: for thou art with me; thy rod
  and thy staff they comfort me.
Thou preparest a table before me in the presence of mine
  enemies: thou anointest my head with oil; my cup run-
  neth over.
Surely goodness and mercy shall follow me all the days of
  my life: and I will dwell in the house of the Lord forever.

A rapt attention descended on the listeners. Agnes closed her eyes, Esther smiled, and the men sat motionless. The girls looked around expectantly when they had finished.

Hassan spoke first. "Thank you, that was beautiful. Your words have touched me."

Sally and Mabel made little curtsies and sat down next to their mother, who congratulated them with hugs.

Abdullah added, "Very, very beautiful. What you have said reminds me of the Qur'an, Chapter 93. Please allow me to try, although it is more beautiful in Arabic." Before beginning, he leaned over and drew something in the sand with a stick.

By the glorious morning light,
And by the night when it is still,
Thy guardian-Lord hath not forsaken thee, nor is he displeased.
And verily the hereafter will be better for thee than the present.
And soon will thy guardian-Lord give thee that with which
  thou shalt be well-pleased.

Did he not find thee an orphan and give thee shelter?
And he found thee wandering, and he gave thee guidance.
And he found thee in need, and made thee independent.
Therefore, treat not the orphan with harshness,
Nor repulse the beggar.
But the bounty of the Lord rehearse and proclaim!

Silence encircled the campfire. Antoine stared at Abdullah, confused. "That sounds like the Bible, but I don't know it."

"Our Qur'an is like your Bible."

Antoine pressed. "Excuse me, Abdullah, but y'all don't usually talk like that."

Abdullah lowered his head, "I like to translate the Qur'an into English. I change the words many times. Then I memorize them. I can speak those few passages better than I can speak everyday. I believe it is because they are holy words."

Hassan, too, was astonished by Abdullah's performance. "Abdullah, my grandfather would be pleased."

Antoine was curious. "Why?"

"His grandfather is a religious scholar, very respected. Hassan honors me by saying that his grandfather would be pleased."

"And what is that picture that you drew on the ground?"

"That is Arabic for Inshallah. It means, 'If God wills.'"

Antoine trembled. Although he didn't believe in coincidence, he sometimes felt confluences of events. When Abdullah and Hassan spoke, he felt he was hearing his father's voice echoing. Abdullah's gesture in the sand had most disturbed him. In a crisp image, he saw himself as a child squatting on his heels next to his father, as his father drew similar lines in the dirt and taught Antoine words in Arabic. He had long since forgotten everything. His second owners had been adamant that all their slaves go to Christian church. It was a special service designed only for slaves, with emphasis on "render unto Caesar that which is Caesar's." Rewards would come in the afterlife. He had forgotten his father's lessons. Now he was quite sure that "Inshallah" had been one of his father's words. He resolved to speak to Hassan, but he would not do this in the group, especially after Esther's criticism of Africans. No, he would wait until the time was right to show Hassan his most prized possession.

Samuel rose to throw another log on the fire. "Agnes, how 'bout a song? Sing that new one we learned before we left Galveston."

Agnes rose and sang "What a Friend We Have in Jesus," her contralto voice carrying throughout the camp. Esther and Samuel were content; Abdullah and Hassan respectful, but Antoine wondered who he was and what he believed.

En Route to San Antonio, two days later

THE AFTERNOON SUN HAD already stolen all speech from the small group of travelers. Antoine held the reins listlessly, relying on the mules to follow the well-established track while his mind wandered. He imagined his father's African home and was filled with odd nostalgia for a place he'd never seen. Next to him, Sylvia McDermott fought a losing battle with lethargy. Her eyes refused to confront the brightness of the day and closed of their own will. To keep from fading, she occasionally glanced inside to check on Elizabeth, who was napping. As she pondered what would become of her daughter, the weight of her eyelids overpowered her again. Riding alongside them, Alex Babcock slouched on his horse, occasionally falling behind to check on the second wagon, where Zeke and Zach leaned against each other and Samuel struggled to keep from nodding off. Esther slept inside the second wagon, curled up with her two daughters on the small space where she made her bed. The only person walking was Agnes. Once she had established a pace, Agnes seemed to have a limitless capacity to continue, never speeding up or slowing down, like a perfect trekking machine destined to march on forever.

The McDermott wagons were some distance behind the camel caravan, but they would soon catch up. A comfortable routine had been established that suited everyone. The soldiers rose before dawn to depart with the camels after first light. The McDermott household usually stirred as the camels left, enjoyed a relaxed breakfast, stopped briefly for lunch, and met the camel train at evening camp. Sylvia was particularly satisfied with this arrangement, as she felt it inappropriate to be taking every step with the soldiers. She was acutely conscious that it was a special dispensation to be traveling with her cousin, and she wished not to abuse the privilege. Nevertheless Major Babcock had insisted that someone accompany them at all times. It was a coveted task, because the designated man was able to sleep in and had no responsibilities for the camels. Today it was Alex's turn, and he was especially content to be so close to Elizabeth.

The unrelenting heat invaded the covered wagon where Elizabeth dozed fitfully. Peculiar people flitted in and out of her dreamlike consciousness, connected in wholly unlikely patterns. A classmate from Galveston chatted with Mr. Wellbourne of Indianola about lemonade. Her brothers engaged in a lively conversation with a dolphin whose capacity to communicate was known only to them. Between scenes, Elizabeth sank into a deep sleep that felt safe and soothing. She was happy when her father appeared next. She had been having problems conjuring a clear picture of his face, a distressing concern that she revealed to no one. She loved her father deeply and missed him sorely. She saw her father speaking with the slave Moses in front of their house in Galveston, a perfectly common occurrence that made her slightly homesick. Then, abruptly, the two men burst into song and began dancing arm-in-arm. The incongruent image so unsettled her that she sat straight up and let out a little whimper. She was drenched in sweat.

"Elizabeth?"

"I'm fine, Mama. Just a strange dream."

Riding next to her wagon, Alex startled to hear her speak. He looked about and spied another vehicle coming from the right to join their road. He was annoyed. Had he been more alert, he would have noticed it as a speck on the horizon in that flat prairie. He should have been more vigilant. It was a simple uncovered wagon pulled by a mule team with two men seated up front and cargo that he couldn't quite make out.

"Mrs. McDermott, someone's coming. May I have the spyglass?"

"Of course, Alex."

Alex focused on the wagon. "Oh no! Shit! Excuse me, Ma'am, but we may have a problem. The men in that wagon are the same two that accosted Hassan in Galveston. The slavers. One called Slim and the other Josiah. It looks like they're about to cross paths with us."

Antoine had slowed the wagon, but Alex urged him onward. "Keep going. We don't want to meet up with those two any sooner than we have to." Antoine snapped the reins, as the remnants of his sleepiness evaporated instantly.

"Perhaps we can stay ahead of them." Sylvia was concerned, but not half so worried as Elizabeth who stuck her head forward.

"Mama, we must warn Hassan. What if he is away from the main camel caravan? What if they try to capture him again? We must do something!"

"Alex, do you think these two have ill intent toward Hassan?"

"Well, Ma'am, it's safe to say that they were humiliated when Hassan escaped their clutches in Galveston. I reckon if they were to find him again, they'd be more than happy to get revenge."

"In that case, Alex, I agree with Elizabeth. You must ride ahead and warn Hassan. I would send one of the boys, but you are a faster rider and a more credible witness to the level of danger."

"Yes, ma'am, that's true, but I don't like the idea of leaving you alone."

"What could these men want from us? Are they robbers, too?"

"It's hard to say. They are a rough pair, but they have a wagon full. Let me look again." He saw heads sticking up from the wagon's sidewalls. "They're carrying slaves. It's an unsavory sight, Mrs. McDermott, and you may not want your children to see it."

Sylvia shuddered. Always a somewhat reluctant slave-holder, she harbored guilt about the whole system and hated to be exposed to its seamy side. "Let's hope those vile men want nothing from us. I think it more prudent for you to warn Hassan. I have a rifle here under the seat, and Zeke can handle the one in the second wagon. He's a fair shot, so I'm sure we'll be fine."

"I don't like it much, but I can see the sense in your idea. I'll ride hard and be back as soon as I can. The camels can't be much further ahead of us now."

"Go quickly, Alex."

"Yes'm, and please be careful." With those words, he looked directly at Elizabeth and dashed ahead.

Antoine slowed the wagon to allow Samuel to pull alongside. Sylvia explained the situation, asked Zachary to mount one of the horses, and told Zeke to lay the rifle visibly across his knees as he sat next to Samuel. Elizabeth came out to join her mother on the seat.

"We will avoid conversation with these people if at all possible. In no circumstances are you to let on that you know anything about them. We're just travelers on our way toward San Antonio. Is that clear?"

The afternoon's lassitude vanished as the members of the McDermott caravan went to their assigned posts. They quickly caught up with Agnes, who had not stopped when the wagons did. She was on the left side of the wagons, while the strangers approached from the right. Sylvia decided not to confuse her and let her keep walking.

"Mama, what if they recognize me from the courthouse?"

"I would prefer that they not know who we are."

"All right, I'll go back inside the wagon." Elizabeth crawled in and peeked out the back. Inexplicably, sermons came to her, lessons about good and evil and admonitions to do the will of God through kindness and charity. When she used to sit serenely in church in Galveston, well-dressed and satiated after a full breakfast, it had been easy to hold such aspirations. Evil seemed a remote concept. Here on the open road, she felt exposed, vulnerable. Embodied in

Slim and Josiah, evil approached with every turn of the wheel. She said a little prayer for the triumph of good.

The tracks across the prairie were multiple. Rather than follow in another's ruts, especially if it were rainy or muddy, many travelers simply began another track parallel to the main route. In boggy areas, the ruts could be as much as a quarter mile apart. Because the slave wagon traveled a few tracks to the right of the one occupied by the McDermott wagon, it looked as if no conversation would occur.

As the slave wagon came closer, its contents became visible. Esther grabbed Samuel's arm. Never had she seen such misery. Six slaves in filthy rags sat chained hand and foot to a large metal strip that ran down the middle of the wagon bed. Their manacles forced them to lean forward or slouch sideways. Sitting straight was impossible. The brutal sun assaulted them. They were covered with dust, and their lips and hands were cracked and dry. Esther had never before come face to face with a load of slaves. Tears ran down her face and she started to recite the twenty-third Psalm softly.

Samuel, who had once been carted in such a fashion, felt the despair of those slaves. It dawned on him how utterly pampered Esther was and how naïve about white people. The occupants of the wagon could now be clearly seen: four men near the front where the drivers could keep an eye on them, an elderly woman and a young woman shackled at the back. In a single motion, Samuel yelled out, broke free of Esther's grip, and jumped down from the wagon screaming.

"Precious! It's Precious!"

He ran across the ruts toward Slim and Josiah's wagon, struggling to keep his balance on the uneven terrain. Without asking permission, Antoine leapt down from the front wagon and rushed to restrain him.

Astounded by this assault on his cargo, Slim jumped to the ground. He uncoiled an enormous bullwhip which let loose a sharp, biting crack that brought Samuel and Antoine to a standstill.

"You two niggers git away from my property. Git back on your wagons."

"Drop your whip, sir. Do not threaten us." The rifle that Sylvia pointed firmly at Slim emphasized her resolve.

When Josiah reached under the seat, Zeke raised his rifle and shouted, "You there in the wagon. Sit still. Or I'll blow your head off." The latter he added for good measure, not quite sure whether he could do it if needed.

Sylvia called out. "You had better explain yourselves. That woman belongs to us."

Slim and Josiah burst out laughing. "Ma'am, you must be joking. That worthless piece of nigger ass is the property of Mr. Kleinhart of San Antonio, and we're takin' her to him."

Samuel was still calling, "Precious, Precious, it's me Samuel. Can you hear me? Look at me!" Antoine, who was taller and stronger, held him firmly.

Sylvia spoke sternly. "As far as I can see, you are thieves. That slave is mine, and you will turn her over to me right now."

Slim turned his bulk and his bullwhip to face Sylvia directly. "I don't know who you think you are, but we are in the *le-git-im-ate* business of transporting property." Josiah snickered at the exaggerated pronunciation.

Sylvia was aware that the rifle was becoming heavy, but she dared not waver. "And I suppose you have a bill of sale for her?"

"Sure enough."

Zach called out from the horse. "Move slowly and bring only the paper." He had a pistol trained directly on Slim, whose girth would be an easy target.

Zeke added, "And you in the wagon, keep your hands up where I can see 'em."

Though her sons were city boys, Quentin had schooled them in the manly arts. They could ride, shoot, and handle a sword better than most adults. From the time they were toddlers, the boys had been taught how to fight. Quentin had also insisted when they were first married that Sylvia learn to handle a rifle and a pistol. The only one who had not been thoroughly trained was Elizabeth. Sylvia made a mental note to remedy that once they reached San Antonio.

Precious watched the scene unfold from the bottom of a dark pit. Everyone moved with a slow lumbering action. Samuel. She heard the name, but it didn't register. Samuel was a name from another life, one so long gone that she could scarcely recall its forms. That life was before Quentin

McDermott had overwhelmed her on the kitchen table, before her sense of who she was had been shattered with the broken bottle of cooking oil.

She had neither seen nor spoken to Massa Quentin. She had a vague, misty recollection of traveling to the plantation with Moses. Although she had done nothing wrong, she had been tossed from the house to the fields like so much rubbish. Consumed by disbelief and rage, she began plotting how she would get back to the house, back to Samuel. Moses had warned her there would be more trouble coming, but she couldn't conceive anything worse.

When they reached the plantation, it was worse. The work was relentless. Muscles ached that she didn't know she had. There was not as much food as she was used to, and what there was tasted coarse. They rose before dawn and went to the fields before eating. A breakfast of gruel was brought to them at mid morning, and then they worked again until late afternoon supper. They didn't get back to the cabins until after nightfall.

"How can y'all live crowded together in these shacks? Ain't no fit quarters. No way no how."

"It bad, but it ain't so bad. People share. We all tries to help."

"This how it always is?"

"Yup. We work from see 'til can't. Every day the same."

When her bleeding time didn't come, Precious confessed to Rebecca. "I got Massa Quentin's baby."

"He won't take you back to the house. Don't even think 'bout it. But if you lucky, he'll make the overseer treat you good and he'll care for the child. Best you can hope for."

But that hope proved false. She had been sold and handed over to those two stinking white men. The first day in the wagon, when she had complained to the other slaves that the irons hurt her ankles and wrists, they told her to be grateful she wasn't walking. When she thought things were as bad as could be, her captors started arguing over who would have her first. She had been slow to grasp their meaning.

"I'll take the first poke."

"No, you ain't gonna. I hate the sloppy seconds. You'll go after me."

In the end it hadn't mattered, as each one took her more than once. They yanked her from the wagon, bent her head down to the ground, and entered her from the back. This had gone on for three days now. She learned to take her mind away. One time she watched an ant crawling along the dirt in front of her, focusing on its labors instead of the violent thrusts ripping her body. For Precious the only thing to do was to retreat into a place where everything that happened was happening to someone else. She cut herself off from the devastation that confronted her each morning. She strived for numbness.

When Precious heard Samuel's voice calling her, that numbness prevented her from believing her ears. She would never see Samuel again. Better he should not know what had become of her. Better he could hold in his heart a picture of her face, the smell of her clean body, the memory of their touches. Samuel existed only as a remembrance. But she heard Samuel shouting her name. She must be going crazy. Had she lost her mind so completely? Slowly ever so slowly, she raised her head and saw not only Samuel, but also the whole McDermott family, everyone except Massa Quentin.

Agnes had stopped when the wagons did, thinking it time for a drink. She cut an odd figure these days. She had taken a length of rope and tied it around her simple skirt as a kind of belt from which she hung all manner of interesting items. She had a hawk's feather, a possum tail, and a squirrel's skull. She had flowers and grasses from the day's trek that she tossed away each morning to collect anew. She was especially proud of her tin cup, tied to the rope waistband with a red bandana looped through the handle. Loosening it now, she walked around to the other side of the second wagon and lifted the lid on the water barrel. She was happy that she had learned things on this trip. Like Miz Sylvia had taught her, she scooped water with the ladle rather than dipping her cup straight into the barrel. She carefully poured the water into her tin cup. Then she turned and saw Precious.

She shrieked. It was a piercing sound, somewhere between a scream and a wail. She kept up the strange keening as she marched passed Antoine and Samuel, crossed in front of Zach on the horse, and went straight to Precious. She dunked her bandana in her water cup and then carefully and tenderly wiped the grit from Precious's face, still screeching an ethereal high-pitched sound that mesmerized everyone. Nobody moved. She howled. She gave Precious a taste of the water, cleaned her neck and held her hands, all the while whining like a wounded animal. Finally, she reached up and hugged Precious as best she could. Precious, now believing, sobbed soundlessly.

Samuel fell to his knees, wracked with grief and helplessness. He pounded the ground. Antoine held him tight, afraid that the situation could go very wrong. With tears streaming down her cheeks, Esther sat paralyzed on the wagon seat, riveted to the scene.

Josiah was the first to snap out of the spell cast by Agnes. "What the hell? Git that woman away from our wagon!"

"Yeah, and make her quit that hollerin'!" added Slim.

"That one is slow." Sylvia explained quickly. "She doesn't know what she's doing. We will take her away. Zeke, Zach, you keep your guns right where you've got 'em."

"Yes, Mama."

"Esther!"

"Yes'm!"

"Go get Agnes. Take her to the other side of the wagon."

The last thing Esther wanted was to go closer to that slave wagon, but she had to. Agnes passed some water to the old woman and wiped her face as well. She still wailed. The pitch went high and low in a kind of ululation before settling back into a screeching sound. When she headed back to the water barrel to refill her tin cup, Esther was able to intercept her, steer her to the far side of the McDermott wagon, and get her quiet.

Sylvia demanded, "Now let's see that bill of sale."

Josiah took a box out from under the seat and rummaged around in it for the bill of sale. Suspecting he had a pistol in the box, Zeke sat in a state of high readiness while he searched. When Josiah passed the paper to Slim, Sylvia slowly put down her rifle. Taking care that Slim would not be able to grab the rifle out of her hands, she leaned down to accept the paper. The Bill of Sale was written on McDermott stationery: "One Negro woman, about 20, known as

Precious" to a Mr. Hendrick Kleinhart. Dated a week ago, it was signed by the overseer, J.B. Beaulieu. The sale price was $500. Sylvia was stunned. A conscientious house slave, young and healthy, Precious was worth $800-$1,000. Why would her husband sell her? And at such a ridiculous price?

"Where did you pick up this slave?"

"We got her at the McDermott plantation on the Brazos along with that old crone. We showed y'all the bill of sale, so give it back and let's get outta here."

Sylvia sighed audibly. It was time to use her husband's name. "I am Mrs. Quentin McDermott and that is my slave."

"Whooo-eee! You don't say!"

Josiah grinned snidely. "Pleased to meet you, Miz McDermott, but it don't matter who you are. We've got rights to every nigger in that wagon and we gonna make our delivery."

"This bill of sale gives Mr. Kleinhart's address as San Antonio. Where are you taking her?"

"To his place out of town."

Josiah flashed Slim a frustrated look. "That ain't none of her business. Give us back the paper, and we'll be goin'. You don't wanna mess with us."

Sylvia thought quickly. Samuel had collapsed on the ground, but his eyes never left Precious and he was in a state of extreme agitation. She spoke as firmly as she could.

"I will keep the Bill of Sale and the woman Precious. I will write an IOU for $500 that you can deliver to Mr. Kleinhart, and I will settle with him when we reach San Antonio."

"That ain't right and you know it. Slaves is scarce over there, and he paid plenty for the transportation. He's gonna want at least a thousand dollars for her, maybe more. We ain't gonna make deals for him."

Sylvia had no illusions about the ruthless nature of her opponents. At any moment they might choose to overpower her or take a shot at her sons. She was not about to put the family in jeopardy. "All right, you may go. But I will keep the Bill of Sale. Tell Mr. Kleinhart that I will sort this out as soon as we reach San Antonio."

With that she stuffed the document into her skirt pocket and took up her rifle. "Move out, and make it snappy."

Elizabeth had been listening to all this from inside the wagon. Once her mother used their name, she felt no compunction about looking outside. She was amazed at her mother's strength of will, but shocked that she would let Precious stay with the slavers.

As the wagon pulled away, Samuel clamored to his feet, thrusting himself forward. "NO! No! Precious. Don't give up. You gotta live. Be strong. Precious!"

Antoine had braced for this. He stepped in front of Samuel and caught him in a vise grip before he took two steps. Zach maneuvered his horse between Samuel and the wagon.

"Samuel, you gotta calm down. My mama won't leave her like that. We'll get her back."

Samuel had seen the way the men leered at Precious. He knew what they had done to her, what they would do again this very evening. He became as strong as two men. Still, Antoine was stronger. Precious stared at him the whole time, never smiling, never calling his name. The vacant look in her eye terrified him.

Only when the slave wagon was out of range did Sylvia, Zeke and Zach lower their weapons. Elizabeth climbed onto the front seat. Her mother was flushed, sweaty, and very angry. Antoine still had an arm around Samuel's shoulders.

"We will get her back, Samuel, I promise you. I will find Mr. Kleinhart and buy her back. Antoine, take Samuel to the second wagon. Esther, you and your girls walk with Agnes. Let Samuel alone for a bit. Zeke can take the reins here, and Zachary, I want you to stay on the horse. My sons, you were a sight to be proud of. I wish your father could have seen you."

As they rode on, Elizabeth trembled, unable to say a word to her mother. She kept seeing Precious, kept imagining the torture she was enduring. Why hadn't they forced the slavers to release Precious? She felt the power of evil like a cold draft, chagrined that she and her family were complicit.

Inside the second wagon, Samuel brooded. Unable to sit still, he rocked, wiggled, and threw punches at Esther's bedding. He wanted to shout, to have his words free Precious from her bonds. But he was powerless, and his inevitable powerlessness created fury. He moaned and cried. He bit his arm to keep from screaming. Antoine let the second wagon fall behind a little to allow some privacy to Samuel's grief.

Samuel knew he would never be the same. He would never be able to drive the carriage, curry the horses, or repair the harnesses. He would never be able to laugh with the children or listen to Esther singing hymns. He was consumed by thoughts of Precious. What if Miz Sylvia couldn't get her back? What if they got her back only after she had suffered weeks of torment? He was her man. He should do something. Yet he was a slave who could do nothing to protect his woman. What was the point of living if you couldn't live as a man should? He had seen too much of this, too many slave men forced to let their women be used by whites. He wouldn't be one of them. He crawled to the back of the wagon where the second horse was tethered. In an instant, he was on the horse, releasing it from the wagon. He had no plan, but he had to do something.

A few miles ahead, Alex arrived breathless and rode straight to Major Babcock, relating his tale as he dismounted.

Major Babcock was appalled. "You left the family unattended to come and tell me this? Those slavers wouldn't dare approach the US Army, but did it occur to you what they might do to a group of women and children? Get back to those wagons as fast as you can. I'll send four soldiers along behind you."

Stung by this unexpected criticism, Alex didn't even try to defend himself. Nate walked over to Alex in time to hear Major Babcock's reprimand.

Nate had no idea what danger Hassan might be in because no one had ever repeated what happened to Hassan in Galveston. But if there was risk to the McDermott family, the urgency was obvious. "Sir, with your permission. Ibrim is still saddled, and I can ride with Alex right now while the others mount up."

"Good. You're looking for a wagon with a load of slaves. Avoid them. Find the family and bring them back to camp."

"Yes, sir!"

Nate could feel his blood racing as he leapt onto Ibrim and charged out of camp. Ibrim was one of their finest dromedaries, a courser trained for speed. Nate had developed a special relationship with Ibrim after lots of help from Abdullah. He had acquired the knack of sitting on the camel saddle, adapting to the camel's motion at different speeds, riding with his hands free, and shooting accurately. Now he was on a rescue mission of sorts, and he let Ibrim have his head.

The camel seemed to love the speed as much as Nate. They passed Alex almost immediately. Alex thought them quite spectacular: Nate, the lone rider on the vast green prairie with the wind sweeping his hair and Ibrim, a majestic camel conquering the countryside. He only wished he had thought to take a camel. He urged his tired horse onward, but there was no chance to catch up. Nate soon spied the slave wagon. Following his instructions to avoid contact, he took Ibrim off the road. He knew the camel was sure-footed on cross-country outings, and he wished to give the slavers a wide berth.

Elizabeth was the first to catch sight of the camel. "Look Mama! It's Hassan! What is he doing?" The fluidity of motion, the perfect harmony of camel and rider had deceived her.

"Look again, my dear, I don't think it's Hassan."

"Oh my goodness, Mama, you're right. Who is it? Could it be Nate? He's coming so fast. I wonder what's the matter."

"He'll be here in a moment and we can find out. You know, seeing him riding like that, I can actually imagine a camel cavalry."

"That's what Cousin Babcock has been saying!" Their laughter broke the tension that still clung to them after their encounter with Slim and Josiah. Together they indulged in the pleasure of watching Nate and the camel.

Behind the second wagon, Samuel rode the horse, hanging close so no one would notice. He chose his moment as the track took a wide left turn. Far ahead on the horizon he could see the slave wagon and calculated that he could reach it if he cut straight across the prairie. Like a shot he took off, angling away from the McDermott wagons. By the time he was even with the front wagon, the curving road had left a wide space between them.

"Samuel! What are you doing? Stop, Samuel, come back!"

Nate saw a slave on horseback headed more or less in his direction. The McDermotts were standing on their wagons, gesticulating wildly and calling out. He couldn't quite catch their words, but he gathered the slave was a runaway. He thought it odd that a slave would make such an attempt in broad daylight, but stranger things had happened. Nate shifted direction to intercept, and he pulled out his Colt. In spite of his target practice from camelback, he would have to get closer and then slow Ibrim a little to have a good shot. The McDermotts kept waving and shouting. He heard, "Stop!"

The slave wasn't stopping. Nate debated whether or not to shoot. He didn't really know the slaves, who usually kept to themselves in the camel camp. The McDermotts seemed quite familiar with their slaves and treated them amiably. This one had no reason to be running off, as far as Nate could tell. A healthy slave was far more expensive than even the best horse, so the logical thing would be to shoot the horse. But this was Mr. Blauvelt's horse, and somehow that complicated things for Nate. Besides, a horse was an innocent. The horse didn't choose to run off, but only obeyed its rider. Nate decided to fire a warning shot, hoping to shoot neither man nor horse. He raised his pistol and prepared to pull the trigger.

The horse reared. Perhaps it had caught the scent of the camel, although it should have been familiar with camel odors. Perhaps it feared the apparition of the lone camel and rider moving at top speed, so different from the strolling camels in caravan. For whatever reason, the horse was terrified. The slave, obviously a skilled horseman, reined the horse in. But as Nate kept advancing, the horse reared again, and threw the slave to the ground. Nate's gun went off. Elizabeth screamed.

The slave's horse raced off at right angles to the wagons, with Zachary in pursuit. Mrs. McDermott, Elizabeth, and two female slaves ran toward the fallen slave. Elizabeth hoisted her skirt well above her knees and sped ahead of her mother, who, seeing the wisdom in this, abandoned all decorum and did the same. Elizabeth's bonnet fell off, dangling around her neck while her hair flew in all directions. Zeke and a tall male slave abandoned the wagons and hurried to catch up. Zeke carried two rifles.

What had he done?

By the time Nate dismounted, got Ibrim into a kneeling position, and reached the slave, Mrs. McDermott was crouching over the crumpled body.

"Oh my Lord, Samuel." She cradled his head in her hands and spoke to him gently. Nate had never seen anything like that, a white woman so solicitous with a male slave. "God in Heaven, help us. He won't even open his eyes. Esther, run and get the medical box. Let's see if smelling salts will revive him. Hurry!"

Agnes cried out. "He dead! Samuel dead!"

"Shush, Agnes, Mama doesn't think he's dead." Seeing Nate approach, Elizabeth turned on him harshly. "How could you? How could you shoot Samuel?"

Nate was dumbstruck.

"Quiet everyone," Sylvia commanded. "Samuel has not been shot."

"But I heard a gun go off!"

"Yes, but there's no gunshot wound. Samuel is hurt from falling off his horse. I can feel a pulse, but he's stunned."

Nate stood with his hat in his hand, shifting from one foot to the other. No one spoke to him. Everyone gave him angry sidelong glances.

"Antoine, help me to straighten his legs. I want to see if they're broken."

Samuel made no sound as Antoine unfolded first one leg and then the other. Antoine carefully felt each limb. "Nothin' broken, Ma'am."

Esther came sprinting with the medical box. Sylvia opened the smelling salts and passed the bottle twice under Samuel's nose. He snorted a rapid intake of breath and opened his eyes.

"Samuel, Samuel, can you hear me?" No response. "Samuel, say something please or make a sound if you understand." Again, nothing. "Samuel, blink twice if you hear me."

He blinked twice, and Agnes shouted, "Hallelujah! He hear Miz Sylvia. He hear her!"

Sylvia spoke directly to Samuel. "You've had a bad fall. I think you have a concussion, but you don't seem to have any broken bones. I hope this will wear off and you'll be able to speak soon." Then she leaned over and took his head in her hands again. "Samuel, I will get Precious away from those slavers and Mr. Kleinhart, no matter what it costs. I give you my word of honor."

She looked up. "Mr. Wilkers."

Nate flinched. Sylvia had never been so formal with him. Her tone was icy.

"I believe your camel is the fastest steed here. Ride back to camp and inform Major Babcock that we have a grievous injury in our party and that we will arrive as soon as possible."

He wanted to tell her it was not his fault, but all he said was, "Yes, Ma'am. At your service."

As he walked rapidly to Ibrim, Elizabeth followed. "I just want to know one thing. What was the matter? Why were you coming at us so fast?"

He answered in a melancholy voice, his eyes pleading for forgiveness. "I was sent to protect you from those two slavers. I was meant to escort you back to camp."

Elizabeth burst into hysterical laughter and turned her back to him as tears streamed down her dusty face.

Alex and the four soldiers were astonished to see Nate on Ibrim driving toward camp at top speed, alone. He refused to answer their hails.

Moments before, from far ahead on the slave wagon, Precious had looked up in time to see a rider breaking away from the McDermott wagons. It had to be Samuel. He headed straight toward her. She took in every movement of his body as he rode confidently, one with the galloping horse. She permitted herself the memory of his lips on her cheek, his hand on her thigh. Keeping her gaze firmly on Samuel, she spoke to the old lady chained opposite her.

"That my man. You seen him? You seen my man?"

"I seen him, chile, I seen your man."

Precious clamped her lips tight to keep from calling his name while she tracked him fiercely with her eyes.

She watched, drinking in what might well be her last sight of her beloved. This could not end well, she knew. A bad ending had been coming long before Samuel lit out on the horse, long before she encountered the McDermotts today, long before she had been sold to these slavers. Bad had gone to worse ever since that night in Galveston. Nothing about this, not one single part of it would turn out good.

She should have been devastated, but she wasn't. Instead she reveled in Samuel with his bravery on full display. This was her man and he was telling the whole world that she was his, that she had been wronged, and that he would do his best to protect her, no matter the outcome. Even though he was a slave, he was someone to reckon with. He had taken this huge risk for her. She was proud that he would do such a thing. She gained strength from the notion that, in spite of everything he guessed had happened, he still found her worthy. She witnessed his love for her soaring silently, flowing toward her in ever-widening circles until the edge of it touched her where she sat shackled on the slave wagon. A tangible comfort enveloped her. She breathed deeply and her skin tingled with the thrill of his touch.

She saw the camel and heard the shot. When Samuel fell from the horse, her hands flew up as high as the chains permitted in a kind of last salute, but she did not scream. She stared at the shrinking figures of the McDermott family around the fallen Samuel. Her gaze held, unwavering, even when she saw that Samuel did not get up. Her eyes strained until the tiny specks blurred into the retreating horizon. Then she turned her face back to the wagon, weeping silently, but with her head held high.

"You seen my man?"

"I seen him, chile. I seen him."

Back in camp, Jeremy set up the cook fire after a march during which the camels had traveled at a good clip, pleasing Major Babcock. Not two hours earlier they had flushed a covey of prairie chickens. After much shooing and hollering, they had managed to bag a dozen of them. The soldiers who had drawn kitchen duty were at work plucking feathers with less grumbling than usual in anticipation of dining on roast quail. Everything else was unfolding according to a routine that Jeremy had devised, one that he found efficient and satisfying.

"Y'all can bring me them soakin' beans from the wagon."

One of the soldiers lugged the kettle over while Jeremy started the fire. Each evening after supper, he set a portion of dry beans to soak overnight and all the next day. When they made camp, he lit the kindling, rinsed the beans and set them to boiling before he whipped up a batch of cornbread to bake in the Dutch ovens.

"Mind if I ask, sir, but what do you put in them beans? Not to say ill of me Ma or nothin', but yours sure are the best."

"Thank you, soldier. After the beans are boiled good and soft, add salt pork, pepper, and some dried cilantro."

His mate teased, "What you askin' for? You plan on bein' a cook one day?"

"It ain't so bad, is it Mr. Blackstone? Beats some other jobs in the Army, like goin' on patrol or chasin' Indians!"

His buddy retorted. "I hate cookin'."

"But you love eatin', don't ya?"

"Mr. Blackstone, will we have enough birds for everyone?"

"Plenty." Jeremy tended the fire. The large blaze would create a good bed of coals for roasting the birds while the cornbread baked. From his collection of iron rods he built a rotisserie on which he would skewer the birds as soon as they had been rubbed with salt, garlic and sage. He began to salivate as he thought of grilled game. Tomorrow's breakfast of leftover beans and fresh biscuits would be spruced up by livers and gizzards fried with onions for the officers, and he'd keep aside a taste for himself.

Glancing up, he saw Nate ride hard into camp on Ibrim and immediately recognized disaster on his grandson's grime-streaked face. Not since Hilde had died had he seen such anguish on Nate. With a tremor of foreboding, Jeremy mindlessly stirred the beans while tracking Nate's path straight to Major Babcock and Lt. Halter. The three spoke briefly before Nate led Ibrim to the other camels. Some observers might have taken Nate's stomping as an effort to dislodge the dust that clung to him, but Jeremy saw in that stride a combination of regret and anger. Before Jeremy could think what to do next, Major Babcock beckoned.

"Mr. Blackstone, please come here and bring your medical kit."

"Yes sir." Jeremy instructed his kitchen staff. "You boys keep those birds rotating and see the beans don't boil over."

Jeremy was more than a little uncomfortable in the role of medical fix-it-man. Somehow he had ended up the one who bandaged scrapes, made poultices, and treated insect bites. True, he had learned a few things from his first wife, Melissa. But this summons had an air of urgency that he didn't much like, and he had no idea what it might have to do with Nate.

"Mr. Blackstone, your grandson tells me that one of the McDermott slaves has been badly hurt falling from his horse. Alex and four soldiers are with them. They should be here soon."

Lt. Halter broke in, "It is an awkward situation. The family is not under official protection, and their property even less so. We do wish to act humanely, but we can't command one of the soldiers to tend a wounded slave. We're asking whether you would do it."

Northerners never ceased to amaze Jeremy. They professed to be anti-slavery and yet were embarrassed to care for a slave. "I'll see to it. Set the McDermott wagons up over yonder." He deposited his carpetbag full of medicines. Not knowing the extent of the injuries, he boiled water, prepared clean bandages, and got a bottle of whisky ready.

In the meantime, Hassan went directly to Nate. "What happened?"

"Nuthin'. One of the slaves fell off his horse."

"Oh no! Is he hurt?"

"Hurt pretty bad, I guess."

"Who is it?"

"Not the tall one; the other one."

"Samuel?"

"How the hell should I know? I don't hang about with slaves like you do."

Hassan blanched, stung by the hostility in Nate's tone.

"Goddammit, Hassan, what are you lookin' at?"

"What's the matter, Nate?"

"Mind your own business. To hell with you and all the stinking camels." Nate abruptly walked away.

When the wagons rattled into camp, Jeremy saw with one glance that his preparations had been unnecessary. Samuel's breathing was shallow and, though conscious, he was unable to move or speak. Jeremy felt carefully around the slave's head and shoulders and discovered that his neck was broken. He suspected that the paralysis was severe and that the internal organs would soon shut down.

Off to the side, Hassan and the other Arabs watched as the four women, two white and two black, took turns wiping Samuel's brow, holding his hand, trying to get him to take a sip of water, and speaking to him in gentle, low tones. As soon as one stepped away, often overcome by tears, another took her place. Hassan especially noticed Elizabeth's tenderness toward Samuel and the way she sobbed when she left his side. Antoine stood at the foot of the makeshift bed, immobile like a guardian statue. Cautiously, Hassan approached and heard a quick but complete summary of the day's events.

"Antoine, I'm so sorry. This is a very bad story! Samuel, his woman, everything. What can we do?"

"Ain't nothin' to do. Pray, I guess."

"Of course Antoine, we will pray for Samuel."

"Thanks, and pray for Precious, too." Antoine hesitated, fidgeting with something in his hand. "Hassan, I been meanin' to ask you somethin' ever since that night around the campfire."

"The night you talked about your father?"

"That's right. My father used to draw that same picture in the sand that Ali drew."

"You mean the Arabic script? Inshallah?"

"I think so."

"This means you come from a family of Believers, a Muslim family."

"Maybe, so, but I'm a Christian."

"Antoine, I believe there is only one God. He has revealed Himself to Jews, Christians, and Muslims, and I don't know how many other peoples. He reveals Himself to each of us in different ways at different times."

"Maybe, I dunno. Hassan, my father gave me this. Do you know what it is?"

He opened his hand to reveal a small square leather amulet, firmly sealed on all sides. It had a long leather string affixed on two corners to allow it to be worn like a pendant. Two decorative black lines outlined each edge of the square. Its raised center was tinted an auburn brown that once might have been red. Hassan had seen similar amulets that his grandfather Alhaji Mustafa had brought back from his travels. The workmanship looked Hausa or Fulani. To see such a thing in America was extraordinary.

"It is to protect you. Inside the leather there must be a sacred text from the Qur'an, a blessing from your father."

"My father said his own father gave it to him."

"It is a special thing. Was it not difficult for your father to keep it? And for you, too?"

"My father told me the whites tried to take it away from him more than once. He hid it somehow, and he also made 'em understand that if they touched it, there would be a mighty big curse on 'em. They left it alone. I guess he was lucky."

"Or it protected him."

"So it must contain a powerful charm or somethin'?"

"I don't think so. But the word of God is very strong, and that is what you carry in this."

"Do you think I should cut it open to read the words?"

"No, your grandfather probably arranged for special prayers to be said over it when it was made. Do not cut it. Keep it with you."

"What I want to know, Hassan, is should I give it to Samuel? Do you think it would help?"

Hassan sighed. "I think it is for you, not for Samuel. All we can do for Samuel is pray for his recovery, Inshallah."

"Amen to that." Carefully Antoine placed the amulet around his neck under his shirt and resumed his vigil over Samuel.

Ali recommended a prayer. "O Allah, remove this hardship. O Lord of mankind, grant Samuel a cure, grant Precious peace, for You are the Healer. There is no cure but from You."

They repeated this and other prayers throughout the night. They also wondered what this tragedy might mean for the camel experiment. If Ibrim were blamed for Samuel's death, would there be retribution? Would the incident be used to further assert the incompatibility of camels and horses?

Erdem was adamant. "That they cannot do. The horses and camels get along well now. The soldiers say this only because they do not like the camels."

"I know, but I worry. And Pertag always tells the men to be careful. It spreads fear."

"Ssshh, I am praying." Ali silenced them.

During the long night while Jeremy sat with the dying slave, he listened to the McDermott boys recounting the day's events. Patiently, he pieced together Nate's unintentional yet pivotal role in the tragedy. As he did so, his apprehension for Nate grew.

Nate had not yet come to check on Samuel's condition. Major Babcock had made an appearance every hour, and Lt. Halter had graced them with two brief visits. Alex hovered continuously, though Jeremy suspected it was more to offer solicitous attentions to Elizabeth than out of concern for the slave. None of the soldiers had come anywhere near the McDermotts that night, and maybe Nate thought it prudent to behave like the others. Still, Jeremy was troubled. He had raised his grandson to take responsibility for his actions, to right a thing if it was wrong, and to straighten out misunderstandings before they grew big. In the midst of his reflections, he looked up to find Sylvia coming towards him.

"Mr. Blackstone, may I have a word?"

"Why, yes Ma'am," he said, rising.

"First, I want to thank you for caring for our Samuel. I can see that my worst fears will soon be realized, but I wish to thank you for remaining with us this evening."

"It's nothing."

"Perhaps not; perhaps so. But it is a comfort to us, and we appreciate it."

Jeremy was a bit embarrassed. He didn't feel that gratitude was in order when he had done so little. "You're welcome, Ma'am."

"I want you to know that we do not blame your grandson for what happened. You must not fear that we will seek compensation in any way. It was simply an accident."

Silently, Jeremy gasped. He had not even considered that Nate might be asked to pay for the lost slave. He should have thought of it. Maybe Nate already had. He would have to reassure his grandson as soon as he could.

"Please tell Nate that we forgive him. We don't quite understand why he had his gun raised, but we are completely sure that he acted out of genuine care for us. If only the camel had not spooked Samuel's horse." She paused to glance at the slave and wipe her eyes.

Jeremy began to grasp what was keeping Nate away. Nate could not stand feeling foolish or reckless. He would be upset at being blamed, and he would regret providing another excuse for the soldiers to denounce the camel experiment. The talk in camp would be harsh. Most of all, he would feel remorse for Samuel's injury. Jeremy reckoned that Nate must be in turmoil, trying to figure out where he stood, both with himself and with the others.

Jeremy's ruminations had let the silence go on a bit too long. "Well, ma'am, it's a shame. I'm truly sorry for Samuel, and I'm sure Nate is, too."

"Yes, of course. Such a shock." She paused again and involuntarily shook her head. "Perhaps you could convey to Nate that in spite of everything he is always welcome at our campfire."

"Thank you. I'll do that." Another brief silence hung between them. "Mrs. McDermott?"

"Yes, Mr. Blackstone?"

"These hard things in life, they hold important lessons for the children. But the learnin' can be mighty rough on 'em. And that can make it mighty rough on you. You let me know if you need anything."

Sylvia's eyes widened slightly. That was the longest speech she had ever heard from Jeremy Blackstone, and she was astonished by its insight and by the gentleness of it. She sensed that she might have to revise her appraisal of the man she knew only as the camp cook and former lighthouse keeper.

"Thank you, Mr. Blackstone. That is a most kind offer."

"And a sincere one, Ma'am. You let me know." He went to put more wood on the fire.

The stars twinkled in full glory on the moonless night. On any other night, the beauty would have captivated, soothed and revitalized, but not tonight. Fear assailed Hassan: fear that Samuel would die, that Nate would remain hostile, that the Americans would somehow punish the camel herders. He felt alone with his fear, unable to ask his grandfather for advice. At that moment he wished he had never left Alexandria.

Elizabeth felt that nothing in her life had prepared her for this. She had no idea what to do or how to react. She found herself shaking, sobbing, pacing, and feeling helpless. She was grateful for any assignment that her mother gave, anything to distract her from the waiting that left her drained.

Only Esther noticed the magnificent sky and felt a little of its healing power. To her, the stars resembled granules of corn scattered by a celestial housewife to feed the souls of her charges below. She imagined picking one up, its illumination nourishing her, sustaining her in her grief. She, too, had been praying while tending Samuel.

"Oh Lord, I been talkin' to You all night. Thank You for lettin' me see this beautiful sky. Dear God, please let Samuel live, but as the Bible says 'Not my will but Thine be done'. If he gotta go now, thank You for lettin' him look on this sky before goin' home to You."

As the pitch-colored horizon brightened with the bluish hint of a new day, Samuel's breathing ceased. The shadowy wagons and trees, limned by the pale first light, gave the whole scene an eerie aspect. Elizabeth stood beside Samuel's cot, crying softly, and meditated on her first experience of seeing someone die. She was unable to move, glued to this spot on earth. Alex stepped closer, near enough that she could have reached out to take his hand. Comforted by his presence, she glanced at him briefly and then watched as her mother and Esther lifted Samuel's arms, crossed them over his chest, and closed his eyes. When they gently pulled the blanket over Samuel's head, Agnes let loose a piercing shriek.

The ethereal sound stabbed the sleeping soldiers, rousing them from their escapist dreams and forcing them to acknowledge that death trod in their camp. The wail had a physical quality that entered their brains and created pains and dizziness, as if the voice of the Grim Reaper were gloating. Some feared that Death was hunting another victim. The unnatural sound was as mournful as anything they had ever heard, worse than a lone coyote howling at the moon.

Antoine started digging the grave, every thrust of the shovel showing the anger that he must not express. He was no stranger to anger. He had lived through the wrath that came from being sold away from his parents, forced to work the fields, and later, separated from a sweetheart. He had tried to practice patience and gratitude in order to ease his pain. Now his fury rose again, fueled by Samuel's brave but unnecessary death. His feelings rippled through his muscles to overflow in the sweat pouring off his body. At the precise instant when he thought his ire would burst forth, the thud of Hassan's shovel breaking ground next to him brought him back to himself. Soon, Ali, Abdullah, and Erdem were helping, having foregone breakfast in order to dig Samuel's grave.

The rest of the camp sprang into action, not from the joy of the day, but to escape the bad luck of the night. The men sucked in their coffee, chomped their biscuits while standing, and crammed in a few spoonfuls of beans. No one had much appetite. The slave's death cast a pall over everyone. The soldiers moved about without making eye contact, skittish and short-tempered. They kept the horses farther away from the camels than usual and hesitated before reining in too close. Nate, with an unmistakable increase in the empty space around him, moved among the camels as if his affinity with the animals would soothe the rough edges of human interaction.

Jeremy sighed. He had not yet spoken to Nate. His grandson had still not visited the McDermotts, who stood with Lt. Halter, Alex, and the Arabs, while Major Babcock said a few words over the grave. He could see no way to get to the boy without disturbing the flow of the camp's exodus. He didn't want to be obvious, and he hadn't quite worked out what to say. He watched the men, horses, and camels depart before packing his wagon. After the last camel passed him by, Jeremy scooted his rocking chair close to the fire, scrambled an egg into the remaining livers and onions, put a big scoop of beans on his plate, and sat back with a cup of hot coffee. He would catch up to the camels later, but now he had to think.

En route to San Antonio

E LIZABETH'S SENSE OF ISOLATION began the day after Samuel's death. Gloom settled on her as the sweeping prairies metamorphosed into scrubby chaparral, a conglomeration of low bushes, thorns, and disagreeable plants that clogged together. The dancing prairie gave way to grama grass growing in patches beneath the increasingly common mesquite bushes. Prickly pear, yucca, and other plants that favor drier climes intruded at random. The wide, multi-tracked road narrowed, pinched in by the impenetrable tangles. She felt confined to a future that she could no longer see in front of her like the happy expanse of wavy grass that had encouraged her during the first part of their journey.

They encountered fewer travelers on their route. Most of the Germans had turned north toward New Braunfels and Fredericksburg. She missed these starry-eyed immigrants, who told tales in quaintly rudimentary English of a paradise they had never seen. She needed something to take her mind away from her mother's incomprehensible decision to let Precious remain with the slavers. She didn't want to blame her mother, but she believed fervently that Samuel would be alive today if they had only been able to free Precious. Zeke and Zach morosely took turns driving the second wagon in Samuel's place, a tension visible between them. On the rare occasions when they sat together, an argument broke out, usually about slavery. Zachary was strident in his opposition. Antoine did his duty in rigid silence, while Esther spent most of her time hugging her children, whispering, and weeping softly. Agnes, who found it increasingly difficult to walk alongside the wagons without being scratched by one or another aggressive bush, became irritable. Elizabeth had never felt so alone.

Only the camels were content, stopping willfully to graze on whatever cactus or mesquite bush attracted their attention, much to the consternation of the soldiers who tried to keep them moving. Elizabeth spotted Alex with Tullah and the baby camel, Uncle Sam.

"Hello, Alex!" She waved enthusiastically, with the first spark of life that she had shown in days.

Alex blushed to his ears. "Morning Elizabeth, Mrs. Mc-Dermott."

"Hey Alex," shouted Zeke, "what's going on? Can we help?"

"No boys, I wish you could. We've been having one heck of a time with the camels. They like these spiny plants better than even the sweetest fresh grass. Can't figure it out, myself. They've become as stubborn as mules."

"Tullah looks like she could stay there all day."

"Yup, she's stuck to the spot. I'm kind of worried about the way the camels have taken to this stuff. It's good they're adapting, but there's a lot of talk about how much trouble they've become. The camels are dawdling, and the men are acting like they don't want to be bothered."

"Goodness," cried Elizabeth. "You'll never get to San Antonio if they're all behaving like this. I can see why the men would get frustrated."

"It's not that bad. Most of the camels follow along just fine, and Major Babcock is stopping more often to keep them from getting strung out along the road." He paused slightly. "'Course most of the men don't like the frequent stops either. We're close enough to San Antonio that they're starting to get itchy." He turned to see that Tullah had wandered off the trail. "Drat! Excuse me a moment. Tullah! Come back here, Tullah! There's a good girl."

Alex made a somewhat comical appearance, hopping through the bush and dodging brambles while trying to persuade Tullah to turn around. Elizabeth admired the way he moved, sure-footed and athletic. She shivered at the tactile memory of his arm around her waist when they had danced the quadrille. Then, out of the corner of her eye, she saw Agnes marching forward.

"Oh no, Agnes!" Elizabeth's call fell on deaf ears. Agnes was headed directly toward the baby camel with her hand outstretched, cooing in some undefined language. Still trying to retrieve Tullah, Alex was too far away to intervene. Elizabeth held her breath. Much to everyone's relief, the young Uncle Sam came gently toward Agnes, who patted his nose as her face lit up with excitement. Then the camel nuzzled her and wrapped his ungainly neck around her entire upper body. Laughter and applause erupted from the wagons. "Good girl Agnes! The baby likes you!"

Soon after this moment of levity, they caught up to the camel train as the road narrowed even further for the last two miles into San Antonio. They were ushered into a kind of collapsing corridor that squeezed them toward the city. Somewhat abruptly, they came upon two lines of one-story stone houses capped with thatched roofs. Although the buildings looked sturdy enough, the windows were small or nonexistent. The houses sat directly on the road with no gardens or green spaces, presenting an unwelcoming façade.

They had the misfortune to arrive at San Antonio in the middle of a downpour. Elizabeth's initial views of the city were marred by flinty skies that rendered the whole atmosphere drab and inhospitable. The so-called camel corral was far less acceptable than at Indianola. The space lacked fences or enclosure, and there appeared to be no decent housing for the men. Moreover, word of the camels' arrival had already spread to town, and, in spite of the intermittent rain, people were descending on the place. Major Babcock's full attention would be required to sort things out. Elizabeth could see that her mother had not anticipated being left to her own devices.

Fortunately, one of the local soldiers volunteered to accompany them to town. They soon stalled in front of the Alamo, trapped behind a long mule train. Undeterred by the rain, Zeke and Zach begged to explore. They leapt down and splashed their way to the buildings, exclaiming all the while about Jim Bowie, Davy Crocket and William Travis. Soldiers with dripping hats pulled low slogged through the mud hoisting barrels and bags of goods. Huddled under trees and in doorways, a colorful assortment of merchants and workers slipped through the main gate each time the rain slackened. Twenty years had passed since the famous battle, and the more serviceable buildings had been rebuilt and converted into an expanding Army barracks and depot. Half-repaired walls, makeshift scaffolding, and stacks of unlaid bricks waited for the next round of construction. This was the Alamo, spoken of in reverential tones, yet everything was utterly mundane and smaller than Elizabeth had expected. She was vaguely disappointed.

Sylvia asked their guide about a newer house across the road. "Yes, Ma'am. Belongs to Mr. Samuel Maverick. He missed the fight at the Alamo, 'cause he was over at Washington-on-the-Brazos declarin' independence. Lost a lot of friends. He's built his house so he can see where they fell and remember 'em. He owns plenty of land 'round here."

While they waited, Elizabeth asked her mother about San Antonio. "Mama, didn't Mrs. Eberly tell you what we should expect? You've said almost nothing up to now."

"She said that San Antonio has ten thousand people, about one third each Americans, Mexicans, and Germans. The city used to be larger and more prosperous, but half the Mexicans fled in the days of the Republic. It's been reviving in recent years, with help from the Germans and from Mexicans coming back."

"Where do people live? Apart from Mr. Maverick's new place, I don't see houses around here."

"Mexicans live in the older section of town. We should recognize it by the Spanish architecture, probably built today the same way as when the town was founded. Then there's La Villita, formerly inhabited by families of Mexican soldiers, but now lived in by German, Swiss, and French immigrants."

"And the Americans?"

"The Americans can be found everywhere, building new wooden homes, as we've seen.

"And where shall we go?"

"Your father has arranged a house in the established part of town, built in the adobe style."

Elizabeth's eyes widened. "Adobe? Isn't that mud and straw?"

Sylvia sighed audibly. "I can't imagine him sending us to live in a mud house, but Mrs. Eberly said that adobe actually insulates well, especially against the summer heat. She assured me that the house was comfortable and what she called 'well situated' for us. We'll see what that means. We'll go first to Señor Jose Antonio Navarro, to whom we have introductions."

"Who is he?"

"A prominent businessman, an acquaintance of your father. He's descended from the first settlers of San Antonio, purcblood Spanish of the Canary Islands. He signed the Texas Declaration of Independence, helped to write the constitution for the Republic, and later worked on the State Constitution. I believe he is the only person who has signed all three documents."

"My goodness."

"Mrs. Eberly says he has a large family and that they are all gracious."

When they finally found a way to circumnavigate the congestion at the Alamo, Zeke and Zach scrambled back to their posts. They were muddy to the knees but more agreeable with each other. The McDermott wagons advanced slowly around the seemingly endless train of mules, oxen, cattle and carts. They learned that this particular train, possibly a hundred wagons in total, had been dispatched by Captain Van Steendam from Indianola a week before their own departure, laden with supplies for the Western forts. Elizabeth was astonished at its length. She couldn't help wondering how camels would fit into such a practiced way of doing things.

Eventually they crossed the river and rolled past La Villita. The architecture was charming, if diminutive. Houses built of local white limestone and wooden lintels were set in neat rows. Some of their entrances were at street level, but others were raised a few steps in a style that reminded one of the coast, although without the grandeur of Galveston. There was even an adorable little church.

As they entered the main square, the rain mercifully ceased, allowing them to pause in front of the dilapidated cathedral. Their escort explained. "It's over a hundred years old, and I know what you're thinkin'. It's a mess, Ma'am."

"Yes, I expected better."

"Santa Ana used it as a lookout. There were cannons on the roof. Didn't fare too well durin' the battle. But folks are workin' on some big plans to fix it up."

The oozing mudpit of a square gradually came back to life as its citizens resumed their activities. The diversity of people was striking. They saw Germans and Mexicans as expected, but also French, Irish, and blacks. An Indian on horseback with a huge feather in his hair was selling blankets. They heard accents of Tennessee and Kentucky, drovers and ne'er-do-wells by all appearances. As they moved sloppily down the sticky street, Elizabeth had an intense longing for the shell-paved roads of Galveston. Her spirits lifted slightly when the guide pointed out their destination. Though mired, Laredo Street was wide and straight, and the two-story clapboard house at the corner shimmered in the damp light.

"That's Sr. Navarro's place. Built it last year or two years ago, somethin' like that."

"And the other building?"

"His family's dry goods store. Upstairs is the office. He's a lawyer. Ma'am, maybe I shouldn't be speakin' out of turn, but you know he ain't your typical Meskin."

"You are not fond of the Mexican Texans?"

"We dunno for sure if some of 'em really came over to our side, that's all. But Sr. Navarro, him and his family, they're different, on our side from the beginning. He's a true patriot."

"I see. Thank you soldier."

"Yes'm. Let me go and call someone for you." He bounded from his horse, landing splat in the mud. He carefully ran his boots over a cast iron boot scraper before stepping onto the covered porch and ringing a small bell that was suspended next to the open door.

Sylvia took a deep breath, straightened her bonnet, brushed her skirt, and prepared to begin the next phase of her life. By her side, Elizabeth copied her motions, aware that her hands were trembling.

Washington, DC, Office of the Secretary of War, July 1856

J EFFERSON DAVIS HAD JUST left the briefing room. Tension lurked in the darkened corners, hovering in the lining of the heavy draperies and under the oak conference table.

"Of course, he's riled. Why can't a bunch of educated men make a simple choice, especially when he laid it all out for them?" Major Greeson defended the Secretary's abrupt departure.

Congress had failed once again to agree on a route for the transcontinental railroad. Three years ago they had authorized $150,000 to investigate the best possible route, and five separate expeditions had been dispatched. Now, the twelve-volume report was written and Jefferson Davis had made his official recommendation.

"I understand," replied Colonel Cole, "but he's got no call to be rude. Decisions have to be made regardless."

"He made the decision, didn't he? He chose the southern route! Congress is dithering. Why can't they come to an agreement?" Major Greeson was as ruffled as the Secretary.

"Congress has its own prerogatives. The Secretary can only advise them."

"Their inability to decide can only hurt the country. The Secretary has every reason to be annoyed. My advice at the moment is for us to leave him alone."

"Well, he's the one who's gone and left *us* alone." Colonel Cole was upset that the report advocated the southern route. Divisions were shaping up along starkly regional lines. With his allies in Congress, he would work hard for the northern route, not only because it made more sense to him, but also because he stood to become wealthy if the northern route was selected.

"Maybe there are other items we could address during the Secretary's absence, in a preliminary fashion of course." Clerk Habberford Smith wanted to distract the senior officers from the Secretary's outburst. "Let me review some other correspondence."

A lively discussion ensued regarding yet another letter from Mr. Gail Borden touting the benefits of his meat biscuits as a nutritious form of army rations. Visions of soldiers eating the artificially prepared food generated laughter and a return to better spirits.

"The letter also mentions Mr. Borden's success with manufacturing a condensed milk. Perhaps I should clarify. Mr. Borden regards it as a success."

Another officer had actually tasted it. "I can attest that the meat biscuits are an abomination, but the milk is not bad, kind of sweet. Mr. Borden says it's energizing, and I'd agree."

It was decided that Mr. Borden should be politely but firmly dissuaded from any further correspondence about the meat biscuits, but he might nevertheless bring condensed milk samples to the Quartermaster for testing.

The subject of camels came up next. "Gentlemen, as you may recall from his last correspondence, Major Babcock arrived at Indianola on May 14 with the camels. He reached San Antonio on June 19, camping about two miles outside of town. In this letter, dated a few days later, he says, 'Finding that this proximity to town was not beneficial to my men or animals I moved them out to Medina, about twelve miles.' He is seeking a permanent base where he proposes to set up a breeding farm."

Major Greeson laughed out loud. "A breeding farm! What in blazes could the good Major be thinkin'? Are they cows? I thought they were supposed to be the latest military weapon. Maybe the Texas sun has addled his brain." The other two southerners at the table chortled.

"If you'll excuse me, Major, I must take exception. Major Babcock is an intelligent and loyal servant of his country who does not merit your disparaging tone. Mr. Smith, does Major Babcock elaborate his reasons?"

"Yes sir, Colonel Cole. He believes that the camels thus far imported are too few in number to form the base of a military unit, even with the expected arrival of a similar number in January of next year. He urges that a herd be established in Texas, that the animals be tested and developed, and that every effort be taken to increase their numbers. He also emphasizes the need for more soldiers to be trained to manage the beasts."

"Read between the lines, man!" Major Greeson was worked up. "Can't y'all see what he's tellin' us? The men don't want the camels. I said as much right here in this room several months ago."

"Nonsense, Major. In the military, the men want what their officers tell them they must want. They have to follow orders. It's as simple as that."

"Colonel, you are obviously not a cavalryman. A man and his animal must understand each other, and a red-blooded American boy will have no way to understand a gawky camel. It's as simple as *that*."

"No sir, it's a question of leadership and authority. If Major Babcock and the other officers exercise their full authority, the men will fall in line."

"Perhaps that's the problem. Maybe Major Babcock can't relate to those Texas boys, tryin' to foist somethin' on them that's contrary to their natures."

Clerk Smith was inclined to agree with Major Greeson that the camels were too foreign, but it was not his place to have opinions, especially when his boss, Jefferson Davis, was so strongly in favor of the Camel Corps. Clerk Smith glanced up as the Secretary entered the room.

"Mr. Secretary."

Jefferson Davis returned to his chair, still discouraged about the lack of resolution to the railroad issue and further dismayed to see his staff officers arguing. When he grasped the subject of their disagreement, he weighed in. "If I understand correctly, Major Babcock is requesting permission to concentrate his efforts on breeding the camels?"

"Yes, sir."

"That's not what Congress authorized. Colonel Jessup, as Quartermaster, this issue falls in your sphere of responsibility. Draft a reply stressing the military objective of the camel project and denying his request for a breeding farm."

"Sir, you don't want to reply from this office?"

"No, you go ahead. We have other issues to consider."

Both Major Greeson and Colonel Cole were well pleased with this outcome. Colonel Cole's son-in-law Lt.

Winston Halter predicted that the camel experiment would fail, so it was easy to speak in favor of it. By feigning support for the camels, he built influence with the Secretary. Colonel Cole believed the camel project would be nothing more than an amusing anecdote to history, while the railroads would tell the grand epic of uniting a country.

Major Greeson, although he usually supported Jefferson Davis, was glad to see attention diverted from the camel project. His greatest interest was in selling horses to the Army. The stage was set for expanding the cavalry with vast numbers of steeds for the western forts, and he had no desire to be competing with camels. Yesterday he had concluded a deal to ship horses through Indianola to San Antonio. His business partner claimed that the future of the South would lie with Texas, a slave state that was also part of the new West. Although amused by this arrogant attitude that commonly prevailed among Texans, Major Greeson nonetheless planned to invest. After yesterday's meeting, his financing and shipping were secured. With opportunities for profit abounding, he looked forward to his lucrative arrangement with Mr. Quentin McDermott.

San Antonio, Texas, July, 15, 1856

My dear Annabelle,

Will this ordeal never cease? I miss you most intensely and long for a pleasant conversation, a dinner with friends, and a quiet evening at home in your most enjoyable company.

I am stationed about 12 miles outside of San Antonio at a temporary encampment where I sit at a small writing desk acquired in Indianola. In misguided frugality, Major Babcock refused my request that the government purchase it, so I was required to do so with my own funds. Ironically, the Major now employs it more frequently than I do. Yesterday he somewhat sheepishly proposed that the Army should reimburse my costs, in order that the desk might be considered official government property. I declined but graciously offered him the use of it at his convenience. I rather like having him in my debt, and this situation gives me occasion to see his correspondence with Secretary Davis.

You may imagine my disappointment at no longer being lodged in town, but I concur with Major Babcock in one regard: our displacement was completely necessary. Compared with the good people of Indianola, the residents of San Antonio are far more exuberant and unwilling to be restrained. You cannot imagine with what ease the citizens here engage in street affrays, often resulting in murder. Two men meeting each other at random may dredge up some real or imagined grievance and quickly take to arms. As they are frequently in a state of high inebriation, their aim is likely to go astray. Last week an old Negro woman crossing the Plaza caught a ball in her arm, and more grievously, a young German man was shot in the head by an errant bullet and died on the spot. This sort of encounter can occur at any hour of the day, but dusk appears to be the most dangerous time when assorted rowdy types, especially the Mexicans with their effusive Latin temperaments, wander about in groups. It can be amusing, however, to watch what happens when the combatants have used up their lead and powder. Rather than reverting to swords or fists, they tend to call upon their fellows to separate them before any serious damage is done. The next day one might see the very same men drinking together in jovial company.

You can certainly deduce the difficulties of maintaining order at the camel camp when such types could stroll over for a casual look, bringing with them a propensity to create mayhem. One is forced to conclude that, though inconvenient, it was the right decision to install the camels further from town.

Winston Halter sighed. He had enjoyed staying in San Antonio at the boarding house and brewery of William Menger and his wife. He had especially appreciated his conversations with Mr. Menger, although perhaps the felicity of their chats was partially due to the quantity of beer consumed. San Antonio was recovering financially and held numerous commercial prospects. Lt. Halter would recommend the city as a vital terminus if the railroad took a Southern route. He was even considering investing in Menger's plan to build a 40-room hotel near the Alamo. He decided not to mention this to his wife.

> *Major Babcock has identified a small military outpost at Camp Verde that could be adapted to the camel project. He waxes eloquent about the abundant grass, running stream, and rolling hills. Let us pray he does not exaggerate yet again.*
>
> *You may recall my mention of a soldier who shot himself in a rather embarrassing display of incompetence during an altercation with a camel herder. The accused Arab must attend a tribunal in Indianola, and as I am a primary witness, I will accompany him. The soldier has dictated a statement in which he begrudgingly acknowledges that the accident was his own fault. It shall pain me to utter such bad English, which I had to transcribe exactly as he spoke it. Nevertheless, I shall escape the camels for the time being.*
>
> *I pray my orders to return to Washington will await me in Indianola.*
>
> *Your devoted husband,*
> *Winston*

San Antonio, August 1856

E LIZABETH CLIMBED OUT OF the water and joined the other women on the riverbank. She scattered droplets from her damp hair on her friends. They reciprocated in kind, and soon all the young girls were back in the river, splashing and giggling. When the thermometer that her mother had hung carefully in the courtyard registered a hundred degrees, Elizabeth could usually be found at the swimming area, often accompanied by two of Sr. Navarro's granddaughters. A dip in the shallow water was nothing like bathing in the Gulf, but the river was spring fed, clear, and delightfully cool.

After six weeks in San Antonio, Elizabeth was relatively pleased with her new life. The city intrigued her. Its inhabitants were all tossed together in a mishmash of architecture, food, and language that provided countless new experiences. She enjoyed the puzzle of it, especially since the Navarro girls had begun teaching her to speak Spanish. On Sundays, she and her family traversed cultures from the Protestant church in La Villita, where they worshipped with as many Germans as Americans, to dinner with Sr. Navarro and his family, where Elizabeth enjoyed the taste of new foods such as cabrito and menudo. Among her new experiences was target practice every few days. Elizabeth had not expected to enjoy these shooting lessons, especially because her brothers teased her for lack of skill, but her recent improvements stopped their remarks and gave her a sense of mastery. The shooting lessons also provided a break from the less exciting routines that her mother imposed. She and her brothers already had tutors in history, grammar, and mathematics. After her mother purchased a piano for the salon, daily practice and weekly lessons were scheduled. Her brothers even had a fencing instructor. With all this activity, Elizabeth thought the summer would pass quickly.

However, Elizabeth had one major grievance: her mother's search for Precious had stalled. As yet they had failed to locate anyone called Mr. Kleinhart. Her other complaint was the absence of Major Babcock, Alex, Hassan, Nate and the camels, all relocated to Camp Verde. She especially missed Alex whose storytelling could enliven an entire evening. Thinking of him often and wondering what he would do with his life, she began to discern feelings for Alex that might be more than casual. She also missed her easygoing conversations with Hassan and Nate. She even missed Ali the Interpreter who loved to practice his English with her. Major Babcock had promised that he and Alex would visit San Antonio from time to time, but so far they had been to town only once.

When Elizabeth returned from the river, she found the salon empty. She suspected that her mother might be resting in her room. Fresh from the laughter of her newfound friends, she dreaded her mother's glum moods. In

Elizabeth's view, her mother should be more adaptable. She understood that her mother wasn't fond of the house, but there was no need to point out every defect. They were only living here temporarily, and even though it was vastly different from their home in Galveston, Elizabeth rather liked it. She particularly enjoyed the seclusion of its courtyard. She stepped through to the back, and when she glimpsed her mother sitting outside staring into space, Elizabeth retreated to her own room.

The next morning, Sylvia sent her children off to their activities and returned to the veranda carrying a pile of books. She hoped to keep her mind busy. If only Quentin would arrive soon!

Esther brought her some tea, then joined Agnes and Antoine in the stable. They sat on his bunk, with Esther's children playing nearby. When Miz Sylvia was outside, they tried to stay out of sight. They sensed it unwise to crowd her in any way. Although she seldom spoke harshly to them, they felt acutely vulnerable as they tried to get used to their new world. They had plenty of their own frustrations. Antoine managed their recently acquired horses and carriage, and he tended to any chores requiring a man's physique, but the compact adobe house required little maintenance. Esther and Agnes tripped over themselves in the kitchen, and Esther's children were constantly underfoot. The house was not properly equipped for slaves, so Esther, Agnes, and the girls slept in a newly constructed outbuilding next to the kitchen, while Antoine made due in a partitioned area of the stable. They all felt cramped and confined and out of their element.

"I hate these tile floors. Gotta mop 'em all the time. Can't just sweep 'em like a wood floor."

"Better get used to it, Esther. Looks like they gonna settle in here."

"Lordy, I wish we knew what was gonna happen. I can't stop thinkin' 'bout Henry."

"I know Esther, but you lucky. Massa Williams let y'all live like husband and wife. And he sent word from Henry."

"Yes, those were good years. And that note was a blessing. I sure am glad to know Henry's all right. But I miss him. So do the girls. I wish Massa Williams would send another letter."

"Don't you go gettin' greedy. What if Massa Williams knew you could read that by yourself?

"Whooee! I'd probably never hear from Henry again."

Agnes didn't like the sadness that hovered around Esther. She tried to change the subject. "There's one thing I like 'bout this new house. I like the bell!"

Antoine laughed in agreement. He also liked the bells at the entrance to many homes in San Antonio. Each had its own shape and tone that he discovered when he drove Miz Sylvia on her visits. Some were musical and others bland, but he enjoyed solving the little mystery of how each one would sound. He was fond of the tinkling of their own bell. Although he missed standing in full uniform at the top step of the Galveston house, he enjoyed the frequent look of surprise on the faces of Miz Sylvia's callers when he opened the door.

"Why you think they so surprised, Antoine?" Esther asked him.

"Dunno. Maybe Miz Sylvia's bringin' a higher way of life. Maybe folks here ain't used to this much finery."

"Maybe they surprised to see a black face. Ain't many of us 'round here."

"Yeah, but I seen some free black folk."

"I been meanin' to ask you 'bout that, Antoine. I heard Massa Quentin say it ain't legal to be free if only one of your great-grandparents was a slave and all the rest of 'em white."

"It's true. But hereabouts, some of 'em got special permission, 'cause they fought for Texas independence or 'cause they been in Texas a long time."

"I met a man rented out full-time in town. Seems almost as good as free."

"Esther, ain't nothin's good as free. Think about Precious. Even Massa Quentin couldn't help her. Who knows? Maybe he done sold her off."

"Hush! Don't you say nothin' like that!" A deep sigh escaped Esther. "That poor chile. What you think, Antoine? Miz Sylvia gonna find her?"

"She say so. She can't find any German called Kleinhart."

"I know what she sayin', but do you think she really tryin'?"

"I heard her askin' the last time we was out. She tryin', but I can't say she tryin' night and day. "

"I wish Massa Quentin would get here."

"Listen, Esther, I ain't tryin' to upset you none, but you gotta think. He been mighty strange lately, sendin' us away from Galveston, sendin' the others to the fields. After what happened to Precious and Samuel, seems to me we can't be sure of nuthin' no more."

Esther hated it when Antoine said anything against the McDermott family, but she had to agree.

"Nope, nuthin' sure anymore. Nuthin' at all."

The gentle peal of the front bell startled them. It was too early for guests and Antoine wasn't dressed properly. But he pulled himself up tall and rose to answer the door. With shock, he recognized the petite silhouette against the portal. Bowing deeply to cover his surprise and sudden fear, he greeted their guest.

"Miz Eberly. Please come in and take your ease. I'll call Miz Sylvia right away."

SAN ANTONIO, THE SAME DAY

JEREMY FRETTED ABOUT NATE. This morning, like every morning, his first waking feeling was a frisson of anxiety. He rolled into a sitting position, swung his feet onto the small rag rug, and imagined Melissa crocheting it for him so many years ago. He resisted the urge to talk out loud, but stared at the rug, musing, "Our grandson's in a rough patch, and I don't know how to help him." He scratched under his arms, thinking it might be time for a bath, and sighed again to the rug. "What do you reckon, Melissa? Maybe I'm not supposed to help him. Maybe it's time he has to figure things out on his own. We got this far together. Maybe I have to let him be."

The tiny space was barely big enough for a narrow cot. He squeezed his rocking chair next to the bed at night, but it had to be stacked on his cot during the day in order for Jeremy to move around. Attached to the kitchen of Mr. Menger's boarding house, the infinitesimal room was constructed of properly planed, tightly fitted boards rather than loose lumber hammered up any old way. In spite of its size, the solidity of the place pleased him. It was plain dumb luck that he was here.

Major Babcock had sent him to carry a message to Lt. Halter, who was lodging with Mr. Menger at the time. The camels were decamping to a new location, a move that coincided with the end of Jeremy's employment with the Army. Not ready to abandon Nate and return to Indianola, he had been debating his options with some apprehension. Then he overheard Lt. Halter's conversation with the proprietress.

"Ja, Herr Halter, it is very bad for me. Dat cook go to California. No telling me. Just going."

"I'm so sorry. It must put a strain on you to do so many tasks that would naturally fall to the chef."

"Dat one was not chef, almost not cook. He could only fry pork and mix corn pone. I can not explain." She shook her head in frustration. "Please excuse my poor English."

"Madam, let me assure you that your English is excellent, and I understand fully your predicament." Lt. Halter could not explain why Mrs. Menger's lilting tones added to her charm whereas the similar accent of the plump innkeeper's wife in Saluria, whose name he could no longer recall, had so offended him. "You will need to find someone right away."

"Ja, I should take care for guests, not cook. But it is very hard to find someone to cook German food. I want fresh and good food. Sorry, but some Texas cooks don't know potatoes and vegetables."

"Yes, Ma'am, I've heard it said. But I have been fortunate to eat well at Mrs. Eberly's hotel in Indianola and also at the Alhambra."

"In Indianola, ja, there are good hotels. Also many Germans. But the young families go to Fredericksburg or New Braunfels. Any woman who can cook has a husband. It is not easy."

Jeremy Blackstone seized this opportunity. After delivering his message to Lt. Halter, he followed Mrs. Menger to the front desk and offered to be her new cook. He talked up his knowledge of sauerbraten, sausages, Weiner schnitzel, noodles and dumplings based on what he had learned from his second wife Hilde, bless her soul. Mrs. Menger was interested, but not yet convinced. To Jeremy's great discomfort, she marched him back into the dining room where Lt. Halter, over another glass of whisky, provided a character reference that included a discourse on his ability to make even camp food palatable. Jeremy said not a word while the two dissected his story as if he weren't standing right there in front of them.

"Thank you, Herr Halter."

"My pleasure, Madam. He's a reliable fellow, Mrs. Menger, but he is prone to silences."

That remark, delivered in Winston Halter's obsequious tone, was enough to make Jeremy want to shout insults. Instead he followed Mrs. Menger to the kitchen where she engaged him for room and board and $20 a month. So here he was, several weeks later, frying bacon and eggs for the guests. A mug of hot coffee burned away his worries about Nate, and the rapid rhythm of the kitchen left him little time for thought until he paused for his own breakfast after the first rush had died down.

It irked him to be in such torment about Nate. It bothered him that the crisis was so unexpected, precisely because he had expected many problems. None of the possibilities of disease, injury, or Indians that he prepared for had come to pass. None of the tensions, slights, and social complications that he watched for had erupted. He had harbored many fears, knowing full well how easily a young man can be disappointed in love or disillusioned in his dreams. He had feared that Nate might regret leaving Evangeline Blauvelt behind, but her absence seemed completely irrelevant. He had been afraid that Nate would be disappointed with the camels, but his grandson continued in his affection for the animals. He had worried that Nate's sensitive nature would get him into scrapes, especially when the soldiers tauntingly accused Nate of turning into an Ay-rab. Surprisingly, Nate had learned to laugh it off, taking care to get on well with the soldiers. Jeremy had especially feared open conflict between Nate and Sgt. Bly, who became more insufferable with each passing day. But Nate had learned to control his temper, to deflect Stacy's sarcasm, to hold his peace and move away.

Jeremy was more than pleased. He was down right proud to see how Nate had learned to handle himself.

He had relaxed as one after another of his fears had proven unfounded, even his greatest dread: losing Nate. Jeremy knew that keeping distance was a young man's way to show himself capable without his elders. Although he understood this, he had no wish to experience it. He simply wilted without Nate's regard. Although his grandson must certainly pull away, Jeremy could not conceive how he would survive the loss. Luckily, his pivotal role as cook had drawn Nate naturally to his side. Not that they spoke much, but Jeremy was grateful when Nate let slip short fragments that revealed his ideas, even though some were a bit fanciful to Jeremy's way of thinking. Nate imagined a camel cavalry, a postal service, and a transport scheme. About the camels, Jeremy still harbored doubts, but he conceded that his hesitation could be an old man's inability to take on new things. Nate saw his future with these foreign creatures, and the more Jeremy listened to his grandson, the more he came to believe.

Then the trouble came. Out of the blue and bad for Nate, the accident with the McDermott slave had upset everything. Nate's suffering was profound. Jeremy pictured a gargoyle seated on each shoulder pecking away at Nate's soul, but he could not find the weapon to use against them. He had already tried food, drink, conversation, and leaving the boy alone. Nothing worked. Jeremy knew that time would heal, but he wished he could do something to hasten the cure. Now Nate and the camels were out at Major Babcock's so-called "permanent home" while he languished here in San Antonio, seeing Nate only sporadically. He surely hoped that something would set Nate right again.

Holding his Bowie knife loosely in his hand, Jeremy gazed upon a mound of onions. He mused that chopping vegetables is the most boring job on earth, the part of cooking that kills the cook. He might have to ask Mrs. Menger for an assistant. The young boy who did the washing up could probably be trained. He raised the knife, split an onion in two, and commenced slicing first one half and then the other in neat semicircles. What should he do about Nate? Maybe Jeremy could entice him to leave the camels

and come to San Antonio. Perhaps he could contrive a way
for both of them to go back to Indianola. He slammed his
knife into another onion, tormented by the unlikely options,
as the minced pile grew higher. Tears ran down his cheeks,
whether released by the onions or by his emotions, he had
no idea. He chopped as if hacking demons.

"What the hell? Look at that! What do ya think he's
doin'?" said an oddly familiar voice in the doorway.

"He's stabbin' so rough, looks like he's tryin' to defend
the Alamo!" retorted a larger shadow filling the space.

"Imagine that, will ya? Jeremy Blackstone protectin' the
Alamo from a pile of onions!"

Hoots and howls filled the room as Jeremy turned to see
Amos Prudeau and Drew Johnsville.

"I'll be damned."

"And howdy to you too, Jeremy."

Jeremy looked them up and down and could figure no
reason on earth why these shorebirds would be so far inland. "Howdy, boys. Want somethin' to eat?"

"Breakfast would be good, and are you servin' whisky
with that?"

"Yup, and Mr. Menger's finest brew for a chaser."

"Thanks, Jeremy. We been eatin' a lot of dust. A bite
and a beer would help a lot, hey Drew?"

"They would indeed. And then I'll be wantin' a poke.
You know a place, Jeremy?"

"Yup."

"Good." Drew shook his head. "I know he's dyin' to find
out what brung us here, but do you think he's gonna ask?"

Jeremy smiled as he tossed a few of the freshly chopped
onions into a skillet with some bacon fat, peppers, potatoes,
and eggs, and scrambled them all together.

"Where's Nate, Jeremy?"

"With the camels out at a place called Camp Verde."

"Camp Verde?"

"Yeah, 'bout sixty miles northwest."

Amos whistled, knowing that Jeremy had never been so
far away from his grandson.

"He's all right. Comes into town once in awhile for
supplies."

Drew grumbled, "I'll be damned, Jeremy, if you ain't the worst one for storytellin'. You travel all the way here with a troop of camels. Then they go off with Nate, leavin' you in this kitchen, and you ain't got one thing to say about it."

Amos had his eye on breakfast. "Hold on Drew, we got time."

"We ain't got that much time if we're headin' back tomorrow."

This time it was Jeremy with the questioning look, but Amos wasn't ready to talk. "How about we taste some of Jeremy's grub first?"

"Eat up, boys, and when you get 'round to it, maybe you can tell me why y'all are here."

With the tinkling of the bell, Sylvia left the veranda to set her book indoors on the nightstand. Even the furniture here was different, the design heavier and darker, unlike the lighter English style bed on which she had made her life and conceived her children in Galveston. Yet somehow she didn't mind this bed with its smooth round pedestals supporting the four corners of a maroon brocade canopy. She had come to appreciate its substance. She paused to run her hand over one of the bedposts, thinking that someone had taken care in the workmanship. At the sound of Antoine's steps on the Saltillo tile, she turned to receive her visitor. She expected a workman to check on the pump and the cistern.

Antoine called her. "Miz Sylvia. Please come out."

Detecting an odd inflection in Antoine's voice, she stepped out onto the veranda. "Where's the workman?"

"Miz Sylvia. It's Miz Eberly from Indianola."

"Here?" Her heart sank. Angelina Eberly, adventurous though she was, at her age had long since given up treks to Austin and San Antonio.

"Yes'm. In the salon."

Sylvia brushed past Antoine and walked briskly into the room. Before she could speak, Mrs. Eberly grabbed her two hands and escorted her to the settee. "Sylvia, are you home alone? Where are the children?"

"Elizabeth is with friends and the boys are with their fencing master. Angelina, you are frightening me."

"My dear Sylvia, I bear bad news. I wish there were an easy way to convey it. Your husband has died. I'm so sorry."

Sylvia felt the words as a physical blow to her solar plexus that took her breath away. She was not the type of woman to swoon, but fainting would have been preferable to her next sensation, a wave of intense nausea. Mrs. Eberly took her shoulders and bent her head down between her knees until her stomach settled. When Sylvia raised her head, her tears cascaded. "How?"

"Fever. After he returned from the East."

"He was always afraid the fever would take the children." Sylvia spoke with exaggerated calm, each word floating out perfectly formed and separate from the words that preceded and followed.

"Sylvia, I'm so sorry."

"My husband dead of fever? He planned for everything. He protected us. It's impossible."

"I know it's hard."

Sylvia stood up suddenly, flung her arms in the air and screamed. "No! Not Quentin, no!"

In all her years in the McDermott household, Esther had never heard Sylvia scream. Sensing disaster, she rushed into the salon to find Sylvia shouting her litany, as if repeating it might undo the misery. "No, no it cannot be. My dear Quentin, dead! No!"

Esther was stricken. "Lord have mercy!" She fell at Sylvia's feet and clutched her skirt.

"Oh, Esther, he's gone." She hugged Esther tightly. Both women sobbed.

An instant later, Agnes entered the room and started to moan. When she understood what had happened, she let loose a blood-curdling shriek that startled everyone in the house and a good many people on the street. Esther's children tried to run to their mother, but Antoine held them back and stared, shivering.

Mrs. Eberly stood up and raised her voice above the din. "That's enough! I said, that's enough, y'all hear!" She walked over and slapped Agnes hard across the face. "Stop this carryin' on. Stop it right now." Agnes quieted, and slowly all eyes turned to Mrs. Eberly. "Think for a minute. Someone needs to fetch the children."

Sylvia began to focus. "Antoine."

"Yes, ma'am, I'll go right now."

Mrs. Eberly instructed. "Say only that their mother has visitors and wants them home." She turned to Esther and Agnes. "The men outside need to unload goods that I brought from Indianola. See to it that everything is stacked neatly in your storeroom and locked up. Then start cooking."

Esther nodded. Miz Eberly was right. There would be a crowd of people once this news got out. Numbly, she rose, squeezed Sylvia's hand and spoke to Agnes. "Clear out a corner of the storeroom. I'll check on outside."

"That's better." Mrs. Eberly softened her tone for Sally and Mabel. "You girls, bring a basin of water to Miz Sylvia's bedroom. Then help your mother and see that no one disturbs us."

In the relative privacy of her room, Sylvia wiped her face and struggled to contain her tears. Mrs. Eberly handed her two sealed letters, one from Byron Hurlinger and one in Quentin's hand labeled: *To be opened in the event of my death.* "Sylvia, I know it will be painful, but you must read these letters."

Sylvia chose her husband's note first. Breaking the seal carefully, she unfolded the letter in her lap and ran her fingers around the edge of the fine paper. She moved slowly. Both anxious and reluctant to know the contents, she gazed on the handwriting she knew so well. She gasped at the date: *Galveston, May 1, 1856.* Sylvia looked up, a hint of anger in her voice.

Angelina? This letter was written before we left Galveston?"

"Yes, dear."

"But you didn't mention it when I asked if there were other letters."

"I confess I did not. I assumed it would never be opened. I'm so sorry."

Sylvia wiped away new tears and forced herself to read.

My dearest Sylvia,

If you are reading this letter, then I am no longer of this world and our dream of growing old together has been rudely destroyed. Words cannot convey the depth of my disappointment at leaving you. It is nearly im-

possible for me to write this letter, so overcome am I with emotion. But I must care for you as best I can, and so I write out of duty and with my deepest affection. I pray that this letter will not be opened, but will be burned by my own hand after we are reunited in San Antonio.

I cannot imagine what would kill me, whether it would be some dramatic altercation, an untimely accident, or a dull yet deadly illness. All I know is that it should not have happened, but if this letter is necessary, then it has happened. I am so very sorry.

Byron Hurlinger will act as Executor of my estate. This choice may surprise you, but I trust no one better to care for you and the family. He is both more prudent and more worthy of confidence than others whom you may suppose to be closer friends. I am grateful that you and I shared so many conversations about my affairs. You have a good head for business, my dear, and you will manage.

You are the best thing in my life. You have been a superb wife and mother, a valued confidante, and a calming influence. I treasure our moments of intimacy. The sound of your laughter has always cheered me, even in the direst of circumstances. You helped me build our life in Galveston, and it has been most enjoyable. The depth of my gratitude and my love for you cannot be measured.

You can and must carry on for the sake of the children. I have done what I can to protect you financially. Trust Mrs. Eberly completely. Listen to Mr. Hurlinger's advice. Then make your own decisions and live without looking back. I wish you joy and long life. Think of me when you hold our grandchildren on your knee. And know that with my dying breath, I love you. With my deepest enduring affections,

Your devoted husband,

Quentin

While Sylvia shuddered with deep sobs, Angelina Eberly wiped her own tears. She had been twice widowed herself and knew in her bones the devastation of a husband's death. Regrettably, Sylvia would have little time to grieve in peace.

Sylvia opened the letter from Byron Hurlinger.

Dear Mrs. McDermott,

It is with deepest regret that I must inform you of the death of your husband, Quentin McDermott, in Galveston, this day August 8, 1856. He was but lately returned from the East Coast and was most anxious to depart for San Antonio. Unfortunately, during the scant week that he was here, he fell ill with fever. In spite of every possible medical attention, he succumbed. Please accept my profound condolences.

Your husband left a precisely written will, and I am named as Executor. You are listed as the sole inheritor, and though there may be some claims against the estate for payment of debt, you and your children should have ample means when the proceedings are completed. Please do not trouble yourself with worry. I will devote myself to your protection according to the wishes of your husband, whom I also considered my dear friend.

With deepest sympathy,

Byron Hurlinger

She passed this letter to Mrs. Eberly and rocked back and forth on the bed holding Quentin's letter. "Byron Hurlinger is such a dear friend. He has always been kind to us. Quentin's letter urges me to listen to his advice. I wonder what Byron means by claims against the estate."

The shift to practical matters gave Mrs. Eberly the opening she had been seeking. "Sylvia, with my deepest apologies, we must speak briefly about this. There are those, even among your friends, who may lay claim to your husband's estate, whether justifiably or not. If those claims should prevail, you may be left with little."

"Come now, Angelina, you cannot be serious. My husband manages his affairs very tightly."

"Yes, but he does make investments, and he is willing to take risks. He details some of these in several letters to me, including recent ones that you may read at your leisure." Mrs. Eberly realized she was still speaking of Quentin McDermott in the present tense. She tried to choose her words more carefully. "When there is a death, those who have assisted in financing certain ventures may claim repayment. If they all do so at once, there may be insufficient funds to satisfy all those requests simultaneously."

Something in Mrs. Eberly's demeanor had changed. Her inflections were tinged with urgency. Sylvia wiped her eyes again and tried to concentrate. "I see. Rather like a run on the bank?"

"Yes."

"But surely my husband would not be so overextended." When Mrs. Eberly did not reply, Sylvia pressed on. "Angelina, what do you know about my husband's affairs?"

"What I know is that you must return with me to Galveston, and we must go tomorrow."

"My God, Angelina!"

"Sylvia, I will have more than sufficient time to explain everything on our way to Galveston. Byron Hurlinger will do his best, but he will be under pressure from certain people to decide in their favor. The presence of the grieving widow, who knows them and their families, who has welcomed them into her home...well, you see what I'm getting at. You could temper them."

Sylvia burst into tears again. "This cannot be happening. It simply cannot be." Sylvia heard the front bell and knew that the children were home. She vaguely registered that Antoine had rung it deliberately to give her warning, and she thought she must remember to thank him for his thoughtfulness.

Mrs. Eberly got up. "I will leave you alone with your children." She exited the room by the veranda door and crossed the courtyard to check on the supplies that she had brought from Indianola. Abruptly, the children's wails rent the air.

Jeremy Blackstone pondered the story he had just heard from Amos Prudeau and Drew Johnsville while his two friends devoured second helpings and downed their third mugs of beer. Drew was talking between bites. "Still can't quite figure why Miz Eberly wanted us to come along."

"Hell, Drew, that ain't for us to figure. She told me she wanted someone who would be good in a scrape. She came with two whole wagons of goods and a couple of Mr. Wellbourne's men for drivers. Guess she wanted us for guards."

"Yeah, what you figure she's carryin'?"

"Dammit, Drew, I said that ain't for us to figure. The wagon we left at the McDermotts must be theirs, and the other one Sr. Navarro is probably gonna sell for her. Wouldn't want to make a trip all this way for nothin', would she?"

"Hell, you're right. It ain't our business. She's payin' us good enough."

Amos nodded. "She's somethin' else, when she sets her mind to a thing. Older than you, ain't she, Jeremy?"

"Hard to reckon, maybe a couple years."

"She's strong. Seems like she don't need no rest. Can't believe she wants to go back tomorrow."

"Well, Amos, she does. In the meantime, Jeremy, where can I get that poke?"

"Down the road. Tell Miss Amelia y'all are friends of mine and she'll take good care of you."

"Regular customer, eh, Jeremy?"

"Now and again."

Jeremy directed his friends to the bawdy house, finished preparing lunch for the guests, and set off to visit Sylvia McDermott. Several carriages were parked in front of the house, and a steady stream of women flowed back and forth from the Navarro house down the block. Antoine met him at the door, dressed in a splendid outfit the likes of which Jeremy had never seen on a slave: a perfectly fitted red jacket, brass buttons, and highly polished shoes.

"Mr. Blackstone, so good of you to come."

"Mornin', Antoine."

"Please wait here, sir."

In the small entry hall, Jeremy's eyes slowly adjusted from the bright sunlight to the dim interior. This was his first occasion to be inside one of the San Antonio adobe houses. The rust red floor tiles, the heavily beamed ceilings, the white walls with painted designs around the roofline, and the little alcoves in each room were all new to him. It was grander than he expected. To one side of the hall stood a large room crammed with people, many of them speaking Spanish and German. He spied several of Sr. Navarro's sons and recognized Samuel and Mary Maverick.

To his surprise, Antoine ushered him away from the crowd into an equally large room on the opposite side of the hall, where Sylvia waited alone in a high-backed Mexican style chair, her slumped shoulders revealing her grief and exhaustion. Jeremy stood, hat in hand.

"Thank you for coming, Mr. Blackstone."

"Miz McDermott, I came as soon as I heard. I'm so sorry."

"Thank you. It's such a shock."

"That's the way of it, Ma'am."

"Mr. Blackstone, I'm sorry. Please sit down. Forgive my manners. This thing has hit us all so very hard."

"Yes, Ma'am." Jeremy sat in a matching chair and laid his hat on the small table between them. He took in the room, furnished with an assortment of Spanish and English pieces.

Sylvia followed his gaze. "Yes, some of this is ours from Galveston and some belongs to Sr. Navarro. A bit of an odd mixture, I suppose." When Jeremy did not reply, Sylvia continued. "I was hoping you might grant me a favor. I leave for Galveston the day after tomorrow."

"Yes'm." Jeremy was sure Amos and Drew had said tomorrow, not the day after.

"Mrs. Eberly wishes to leave at dawn, but I have decided for the following day."

"Mmm hmm."

"The children will remain behind. I haven't told them yet. One of Sr. Navarro's daughters has offered to help. Our Esther is usually quite capable, but she is very upset and may want assistance. Sr. Navarro has promised to visit my children daily. I cannot express my appreciation for so much kindness. The family is generous to us beyond all expectation."

She paused, dabbed at her eyes, and looked up uncertainly.

"How dare I say this, Mr. Blackstone? The Navarro family has been wonderful, but they are of such recent acquaintance. I sorely wish that we had family or close friends nearby. Major Babcock won't even know about my husband until after I'm on the way to Galveston. Mr. Blackstone, although my family's association with you has been brief, I have come to trust you as a man of propriety and good judgment. You once told me that if I needed anything...." Sylvia was clearly embarrassed.

"Miz McDermott, please ask your favor."

She took a deep breath and spoke rapidly. "I was wondering if you would be willing to move into this house while I'm away. I would not presume to disturb your employment with Mr. Menger. But if you would spend your nights here, I would feel so much better knowing there is an adult in the house."

"Yes, ma'am. I get your drift." Jeremy hesitated.

"Mr. Blackstone, I only ask that you sleep here. The accommodation will be suitable. Of course, I would pay you for your inconvenience." Her rising anxiety was visible in a slight quiver in her hands.

"I'll stay in the house and keep an eye on things. There will be no question of payment. I'm honored to help."

"Thank you, Mr. Blackstone!" Sylvia reached over and fleetingly touched Jeremy's arm, then burst into sobs. "You have no idea what a relief it is knowing that you and your good sense will watch over my children."

Jeremy had lived long enough to know what to do when a woman was crying, but embracing Sylvia was out of the question. Instead, he produced a clean kerchief from his pocket and offered it to her in silence. After an appropriate interval, he prepared to take his leave.

"Don't you worry. I'll see to it."

"Thank you, Mr. Blackstone. Thank you very much."

"I'll be back tomorrow after you've told the children."

An appropriate time to tell the children did not come until nearly noon the next day. They railed against their mother's decision. Expecting that their father's death marked the end of their exile, all three had pictured returning home to Galveston. They did not anticipate that their mother would abandon them and were appalled that she planned to leave so soon.

"Quiet, my children. Listen, please, and try to understand. According to Texas law, the rights of a widow to her separate property as well as to her inherited property are clearly protected, but Mrs. Eberly and I feel that certain individuals may wish to take advantage of our circumstances. We suspect they will be less able to do so if I am present. I am determined to go."

Elizabeth sat rock still while her mother continued.

"I assumed we would all go to Galveston until Mrs. Eberly reminded me of a few things. Because your father has rented our home in Galveston to the English Consul, it is quite likely that we would not be able to stay in our old house."

"Whoa, I didn't think of that," Zach exclaimed.

"For all practical purposes, this house here is our only home. I was under the impression that your father had rented it from Sr. Navarro, but I have learned that he purchased it. Mrs. Eberly has brought me the deed, fully paid."

Elizabeth was shocked. Her mother had not known this most basic fact about their situation.

"Now, because it is your father's property, it becomes part of the estate and open to dispute."

Zeke interrupted, "That makes no sense if Papa's will leaves everything to you."

"It does. But business associates may make claims against an estate in order to recover debts. We have reason to believe that some individuals may press claims unnecessarily."

"Mama, who would do that?" Zeke spoke up firmly. "That is ungentlemanly to say the least."

"Perhaps, but business is business, and we must be prepared for whatever comes."

"Mama, I have a good head for figures, and maybe you didn't know, but Papa has told me quite a bit about his business. I think I should go with you."

Sylvia examined her eldest son, who had turned fifteen and was nearly six feet tall with a precocious beard that no longer resembled peach fuzz. He had something of his father's presence, an easy sociability.

"Hmm. Actually, you make a very good point." The children scarcely breathed while her mother considered this. "All right then, Ezekiel, you will come with me to Galveston. A man's presence, even though you are a young man, may be useful, and your familiarity with your father's affairs may come in handy. But you two must remain here."

Elizabeth and Zachary, at first cheered to think they would all go, were stunned. Elizabeth burst into tears again. "Why, Mama, why? Zach and I will be like orphans if you leave us, especially if Zeke goes too."

"As I said, this house could become a point of contention. However, there are certain rights that come to us because this property is our homestead."

"But isn't the Galveston house our homestead?"

"We won't know until we get copies of your father's arrangements with the English Consul. But this house definitely qualifies as a homestead, because we own it and we are living in it. Widows and unmarried daughters have the right to live on their homestead for as long as they wish. Sr. Navarro says Elizabeth must stay here to preserve our property rights to this home."

Elizabeth tried to take this all in as her mother continued.

"Zachary, I want you to stay with your sister. Your skills with a rifle and pistol are excellent, and you must be her protector."

Sylvia appraised her younger son, who would turn thirteen next month. He had not hit his growth spurt yet and barely stood as tall as his brother's shoulder. Sylvia suspected he had inherited her stature and would never be as tall as Zeke. Nevertheless, he had a firm resolve and strong opinions. He sat straighter when she spoke to him and seemed willing to take on this responsibility.

"Mama, what about the funeral?"

"One cannot delay such things. I'm sure that your father is already at rest in the cemetery behind the church. Zachary, go and help your brother pack. Elizabeth, I will speak to you again later, but for now, please leave me with Mrs. Eberly."

The moment her children were gone from the room, Sylvia broke down. "That was the worst conversation I have ever had with my children. I wanted to cry, to hug them, to tell them how much I love them, how much their father loved them. Why didn't I do that? I kept thinking how Quentin would handle it, and I was far too straightforward."

"You did very well Sylvia. It's cruel when children must grow up quickly. I assume you will tell Elizabeth about the gold that I brought you, stored among the rice and beans?"

"Yes, thanks for reminding me. This is so hard. I just want to hold her and comfort her, comfort all of them."

"You comforted them last evening, and you will do so again before we leave."

"I suppose so," she said, wiping her eyes and blowing her nose. "Thank you, Angelina. I don't know what I'd do without you." She paused and tried to regain the tiniest semblance of confidence. She felt completely adrift, struggling to navigate through a maze of difficult decisions. Even the smallest chores felt too taxing.

"Sylvia, do you want to go lie down for a little while?"

"No, thanks. If it's too quiet, my thoughts...."

"I understand." She took Sylvia's hand.

"Angelina, it's good to have you here." She took a deep breath, as the bell tinkled again. "I suppose I should see to my guests, but perhaps I'll sit a moment longer."

CAMP VERDE, THAT SAME WEEK

H ASSAN ROSE FROM HIS morning prayers, rolled his silk prayer mat, and tried to immerse himself in the beauty of his surroundings. His gaze traced the undulating hills sprinkled with widely spaced trees that clustered more densely along the banks of the meandering creek. Mockingbirds competed for attention, creating wildly original songs that danced upon the intermittent breeze. The grass, long since faded to the buff color of summer's desiccation, contrasted with the deep green of the oaks. The refreshingly cool air offered a morning respite before the coming day's relentless heat. Animating the landscape, the camel herd grazed contentedly in their new home.

Hassan fought a creeping pessimism that clashed with the morning calm. This defeatist view had come upon him only recently. He had departed San Antonio in high spirits, happy to embark on the real beginning of the camel experiment, his cheerfulness fueled by the enchanting landscape. The level countryside steepened into true hills, with long ascents cresting on ridges that framed attractive valleys. Because he had grown up where the Nile spread its life-giving water in a flat delta, this was his first occasion to discover the pleasure of coming over a rise to confront an unexpected rock formation or to catch a glimpse of a deer before it bounded away. Time passed quickly as each new vista brought different plays of color and shadow. This part of Texas pleased him.

Traveling with the usual assortment of wagons, mules, soldiers, and camels, they had taken a leisurely five days to make the trip, during which time Hassan relaxed. Relative harmony pervaded the camel crew, most of whom were glad to be on the move again. Even Pertag had been more helpful than usual, and Sgt. Bly kept his acerbic remarks to a minimum. Hassan and Alex, often riding together, renewed the camaraderie that they had enjoyed on the *Supply*. Alex revived his habit of practicing Arabic, uttering misstatements so hilarious that Erdem once nearly fell off his horse laughing. Ali, who unbeknownst to anyone sang a resonant baritone, was equally amusing as he tried to learn Texas folksongs. Apart from the loss of Jeremy Blackstone's cooking, Hassan found the trip a welcome escape from the ugly, mosquito-infested corral outside San Antonio.

The only person who didn't fully benefit from the change of scene was Nate. Ever since Samuel's death, Nate had been short-tempered and sour. Alex, ever optimistic, counseled that time would take care of things, but even he avoided Nate's scowls. Hassan still smarted from Nate's harsh words the day that Samuel died, words for which Nate had not once tried to make amends. Unwilling to let Nate's grumpy attitude cast a pall over them, Hassan and the others left him alone with his demons.

Everyone's spirits had fallen when the eagerly anticipated Camp Verde proved a huge disappointment. Although situated in a lovely spot, the Army outpost was completely unready for the camels. Corrals needed to be built, as did accommodations. Once again, the camel keepers were not invited to join the soldiers in the bunkhouse, but were relegated to a lean-to of their own construction. With his heightened sense of protocol, Ali was especially offended by this blatant lack of hospitality. His temper rose when forced to scrounge scrap lumber for the walls while a pile of neatly cut pine boards was declared off limits. He demonstrated his prodigious ability to curse in several languages while tamping

the dirt floor. Some of his choicest phrases were reserved for
Pertag, who, back to his old ways, shirked his duties and left
the others to do the building in addition to tending the camels.

Care for the camels had degraded with each movement
inland. At Indianola, despite the rough start, a reasonable
system had eventually been established, and even on the trek,
after several arguments, a consistent schedule for grooming
and feeding had evolved. But San Antonio had been chaotic,
and the temporary encampment outside of town not much
better. Here at Camp Verde the order of things was deteriorating further. Captain Chisholm, the commanding officer,
seemed more interested in the construction projects than in
the camels. Major Babcock's attempts to set up a structured
duty roster were circumvented. As a ranking officer, he
should have had sufficient command authority, but the men
resisted. To make matters worse, Sgt. Bly was poisoning the
atmosphere and undermining the Major.

As Hassan saw it, the biggest problem was the inexperienced soldiers. The best men had been shed along their
route, like the hair of a molting camel. Two of the four
stalwarts from the *Supply* had been reassigned to San Antonio and several from Captain Van Steendam's command
in Indianola had gone back to the coast. A number in this
new set were rigidly antagonistic to the camels, while
those who had an open mind risked being swayed by Stacy
Bly and his cronies.

They were also a man short. Hassan didn't understand
why Abdullah had to return to Indianola while Stacy remained in camp, but he sorely missed Abdullah's superior
knowledge of camels. It was Abdullah whose guidance on
an autopsy determined that a camel had died of liver disease; Abdullah who managed the females that came into
heat; Abdullah who knew how to approach an intractable
camel. A few camels that had been mishandled had become
quite testy, responding best to Abdullah's commands. Without him, Hassan and the other camel keepers had to work
harder. He prayed for a positive outcome of the tribunal
and Abdullah's rapid return.

Then came the raid. Hassan shuddered to remember
the camp being roused in the middle of the night by a bu-

gler's call to arms and shouts of "Indians! They're stealin'
horses!" Neither he nor the other foreigners had given much
credence to the soldiers' dramatic tales of wild Indians until
the sounds of gunfire, neighing horses, and shouting soldiers
filled the darkness. Major Babcock raced to the paddock
from the officer's quarters, half dressed but carrying a rifle.
"You men, see to the camels!" Ali, Erdem, and Hassan, at
first frozen, quickly realized that the Major was right and
rushed to reassure the animals, who were in complete disarray. When lanterns were lit and a count taken, four horses
and two camels were missing.

Captain Chisholm paced among his ragtag soldiers,
roundly chastised the guard for negligence, and dispatched a
search party. At Major Babcock's suggestion, Massanda was
loaded with hay and water in case the chase led to dry terrain. Deputized as leader, Sgt. Bly called for his pal "Pete"
to go along. Several days later, when the detail returned
empty-handed, Hassan had overheard the men grumbling.

"Hell, that goddamn camel was a curse, wasn't it? Take
one to chase one, they said. It'll carry your supplies, they
said. What did it get us? Nothin' but trouble."

"Yeah, and that dirty camel boy kept stoppin' to fix the
pack. He always had some excuse. I figure he was scared."

"Maybe, but he sure as hell didn't know how to pack
that camel neither."

"Because of him we lost the trail, and the Captain's fit
to be tied."

Once again, Pertag's incompetence had made them all
look bad. The soldiers passed off the mission's failure to
"the Arabs" without mentioning that the party's scout was
a remarkably inept tracker. Hassan thought this incident
doubly discouraging: a camel was blamed for hampering
the pursuit of the Indians, and the Camel Corps had lost
two camels.

Shaking off these disquieting memories, Hassan took
another deep breath of the morning air. After breakfast
with Alex, the two strolled over to the temporary officers'
quarters, where they found Major Babcock under an oak
tree, perfecting his correspondence. His desk, rigged up using a slab of wood balanced on two empty barrels, was the

object of much derision behind the Major's back. Mocking its makeshift quality, the soldiers guessed that Lt. Halter had left his fine writing table in San Antonio as a deliberate provocation. Although they were none too fond of Lt. Halter, the soldiers enjoyed a laugh at the Major's expense. Alex had heard the sniping, but had sufficient discretion not to report it. Major Babcock was hunched in concentration. His quill hung over the page, indecisive.

"Hello, Uncle."

"Ah, Alex, you've come at the right time. I'm debating what to write to Washington. And good morning to you, too, Hassan."

"Good morning, sir."

"Two letters came at once, the first dated July 5 from Secretary Davis. Listen."

I have received your letter announcing your arrival with the camels in good order at San Antonio. It appears to me that, after so long a sea voyage, the animals should be allowed a considerable time to recuperate before being put to work. Horses, under the same circumstances, would require many months to regain their full efficiency, and animals of a larger size would require a still longer period of rest.

"Encouraging, would you not agree?"

"Yes, sir."

"Then this one on July 14 from Quartermaster General Jessup:

The Secretary forwarded your letter to this office. The establishment of a breeding farm did not enter into the plans of the department. The object at present is to ascertain whether the animal is adapted to the military service and can be economically and usefully employed therein. When this is satisfactorily established, arrangements can be made for importing or breeding camels to any extent that may be deemed desirable."

"That sure is different."

"I fear that something of a political nature may have occurred in Washington. The upcoming election promises to be raucous. Perhaps the Secretary is already embroiled."

"Didn't President Pierce appoint him?"

"Yes, but the slogan among Democrats is 'Anybody but Pierce', so my bet is they'll nominate James Buchanan. Whichever party wins, they'll appoint their own Secretary of War. Jefferson Davis may already be planning his next move."

"Wasn't the Camel Corps his pet project?"

"Yes, but if he's distracted…"

Unsure how to respond, Hassan and Alex looked at each other. Major Babcock stood up abruptly.

"Well, if Washington wants a military experiment, I guess we'll give them one, starting with tomorrow's supply detail. Call the men scheduled to go to San Antonio."

"Yes, sir." When Alex returned with the soldiers, Major Babcock laid out his requirements.

"It will be a test. You two men take the usual six-mule team, while Alex and Private Munoz take a wagon pulled by the two Bactrians. I want Nate and Hassan to go with camels, riding two and taking two as pack animals. All three details will set out together at first light. You are to go directly to the Army Depot at the Alamo and log your arrival times. When all three teams reach San Antonio, load the supplies on this list and record the weight. Depart together and I shall mark your arrival here."

"Sir, is this a race?"

"No, merely an experiment. Each of the three teams will go at normal speed, neither racing nor holding back for the other. I want a true comparison: same road, same departure times."

They left in the cool dawn as the sun kissed the top of the hill to their east. Shading their eyes, they headed straight for the intrusive stiletto of light before turning slightly to the south. Hassan and Nate glided along on Ibrim and Adela, with Tullah and Massanda tethered behind, and soon settled into a steady rhythm. The wagons dawdled at the rear. Though lighter than the heavy Mexican oxcarts and supposedly speedier, the Army wagons did not tolerate being bounced along uneven roads without risking damage. Rough patches in the trail would dictate the wagons' languid pace.

Hassan took a last look back. "We will arrive first, then Alex with the Bactrians, then the mules."

"Yup. Looks like it." Nate was taciturn.

Atop the next rise, the camels fell naturally into single file for the descent into an arroyo. With the wagons far behind, Nate and Hassan rode alone in complete silence. Contentedly, Hassan scanned the countryside, appreciating its dips and bends, its meadows and limestone outcroppings. He admired a red-tailed hawk circling for prey, marveled at the speed with which a small snake crossed the trail, and applauded a pair of monarch butterflies as they performed a flitting duet. He smiled at the way Massanda, at the back of the line, would hesitate just long enough to grab a bite of thorny bush before catching up with the others.

Finally Nate spoke. "Stop for lunch under them trees yonder?"

"Yeah, it's a good spot." Hassan's English was near perfect now, although Ali complained that Hassan had acquired a Texas accent and persistently tried to correct his pronunciation.

After lunch the road widened, and it was easier to ride side by side. Hassan had not relished an outing with Nate, who remained distant and morose. Ali advised him to avoid provoking Nate but also asserted that it was possible for Nate's mood to improve, Inshallah. Hassan ventured a question.

"Nate, what do you think will happen with the camels?"

"Dunno. Gotta wait and see, I guess."

"Yes, but the soldiers do not like them."

"Not much. I figure it's Major Babcock they don't like either."

"Why?"

"Loves camels more than he loves his own horse. It shows. And that don't set right."

"He has to take care of the camels, if they are the future for the Army."

"Yeah, but that's just it. He sees the possibilities. Most of the soldiers don't."

"But Nate, you see the possibilities. You have talked to me about many ideas for the camels."

Nate sighed. "I used to figure all kinds of things, like a postal service takin' letters right across to California, a lot faster and safer than with horses or mules. But now I ain't so sure."

"I think it's a good idea. Also your idea for a transport service."

"Yeah, but what am I gonna do if every horse I meet rears up and throws its rider?"

Hassan replied carefully. "The Army horses are not scared of the camels. If riders know we are coming, they can control their horses. It's the surprise that makes horses afraid."

Nate considered this. There would be ways to organize a camel transport without terrifying horses. The residents of Indianola had become quite comfortable with the camels over time. This thought gave him new hope.

"Maybe so, Hassan, maybe so." Yet, if surprise was the culprit, then he was at fault for what had happened with the McDermott slave. If he had approached more slowly, perhaps the slave would still be alive.

Reading Nate's frown, Hassan guessed that he was thinking about Samuel and said nothing more. Miles went by while the sun hammered them. Their copious sweat evaporated instantly and left them drained. Hassan had little energy to force a conversation. His own thoughts drifted to Sula, and he imagined sitting with her in a verdant spot, perhaps his grandfather's inner courtyard, escaping the midday heat. He tried to guess what she might be doing this minute, a world away, and pictured her looking after her younger brothers and sisters. In his imagination, the youngsters metamorphosed into his children, their children. Hassan grinned.

When they took a break, Hassan tried again. "Nate, how would you get your camels? For the transport service?"

"That's been troublin' me, Hassan. I figure the Army might bring in one or two shiploads a year, maybe even more. They might not want all of them. Seein' as how they'd want the coursers for fightin' and the Bactrians for pullin' wagons, there might be some that wouldn't suit that I could buy. I've been savin' my wages. But I ain't got no idea what a camel should cost."

"Probably Alex can tell you the price in Smyrna."

"Yeah, might cost more here. Guess I'll need more dough."

"That could be difficult." Hassan sensed that Nate was opening up.

"I been thinkin' 'bout that, too. I'm gonna take some of my saved wages when we get to San Antonio and buy tobacco, sugar, tea, and a few necessities. I heard Private Orson complain that he needed a new bandana. A couple of the other boys mentioned a razor. I'm gonna bring back an assortment, nothin' that I can't carry with me on Ibrim, but enough to do a little tradin'. I figure to make a tidy sum, and if I get supply duty very often, it could work out real good."

"Great idea! I have saved my pay, too, and I have a little of it with me. We could use some of that and both make money."

They rode until nightfall, camped by a creek, and conversed at length about their new venture. They discussed what goods to buy, where in San Antonio to find them, what prices to charge the soldiers at Camp Verde, and how to do their transactions discreetly to avoid a reprimand from Major Babcock. If this deal were to turn out as lucrative as it sounded, they hoped it would go on for some time.

"Say, Hassan, one more thing."

"Yes?"

"I shouldn't have talked to you that way. On the road to San Antonio."

"It's all right."

"Really. I had no call to treat you like that."

"Thanks, Nate. It's all right."

By the time they reached San Antonio the next evening, having easily covered nearly sixty miles in two days, the tension between them had eased. Nate's gloom had receded, replaced by a new enthusiasm for everything to do with camels. After recording their arrival time at the Alamo, they led the four camels in the corral. Both men noted that the Army horses, although jittery around the camels at first, quickly quieted.

"Say, Hassan, my grandpa's workin' as a cook at the Menger place. It's close by. We might get some grub there."

Hassan smiled broadly at the thought of Jeremy's food. "Let's go see your grandfather."

"I figure we've got at least a full day until the wagons arrive, maybe two. We should have plenty of time to buy our goods and still have time for fun."

"Maybe we can go see the McDermotts."

Nate jerked his head to look at Hassan askance. Even though Sylvia McDermott had sought him out to express the family's continuing friendship, Nate was unsure of his reception at their home. Hassan saw the hesitation but was determined to go, with or without Nate. He wanted to see Elizabeth.

"Yeah, maybe. Let's hear my grandpa's news first."

Nate realized that he very much wanted to see his grandfather, especially now that he felt more encouraged about the commercial possibilities for the camels. They walked around back to the kitchen, and Nate slipped through the open door. Nothing could have prepared him to find Amos Prudeau and Drew Johnsville, one sitting on his grandfather's rocking chair and the other sprawled on his bed, drinking beer and smoking cigarettes. Drew held a compress over one eye.

"Hey, look at you!" Amos said as he rose to shake Nate's hand and slap him on the back. "In town from the western wilderness, I see. How is it out there with your furry friends?"

Nate burst out laughing. "I never expected to see you here. What are y'all doin' here anyway? And where's my grandfather?"

"Who's your friend?" Nate looked at Hassan, his breeches dusty, his vest open over his cotton shirt, his unruly black hair stuffed under his hat, and saw an ordinary cowhand. He gathered that his friends didn't recognize Hassan as the camel keeper they had seen in Indianola.

"Sorry, forgot the introductions. Amos Prudeau, Drew Johnsville, Hassan..." Nate stammered, realizing that he couldn't remember Hassan's full name.

"Hassan ibn Yusuf, but Hassan will do. Pleased to meet you."

"Say, ain't you one of the camel men?"

"That's right."

Not one to miss an opportunity to pester, Drew chided, "So Nate, how y'all doin' with the camels? Y'all ready to start the circus yet?"

"Yeah, and we'll need a juggler, too. You juggle somethin' that landed in your eye, Drew?"

Amos guffawed. "Drew happened upon an argument in the middle of the Plaza and couldn't resist contributin' to the debate himself, ain't that right?"

"Hell, some overdressed, swaggerin' dandy outta New Orleans was pickin' on a local boy, best as I could tell. Figured he needed a hand."

"Yeah, and then someone else needed a hand." Amos motioned toward Drew.

While the three traded barbs, Hassan wondered at this style of greeting. He could tell that the men were happy to see each other, but their conversation seemed unduly coarse. In Hassan's view, Amos and Drew, because they were older than Nate, should be addressed respectfully. He longed for the formal greetings that would be used at home. He missed the predictable exchanges and polite comments that made a guest feel welcome. He had to admit that he was still having trouble understanding American ways.

"Nate, your grandfather's fine, but he's over at the McDermott place right now. Asked us to wait here in case you came to town. We pulled in yesterday with Miz Eberly."

"Miz Eberly?"

"Yeah, she brought word to Miz McDermott that her husband's died."

Hassan's heart sank. Thinking of Elizabeth, he murmured a prayer under his breath. Nate's thoughts, too, went straight to Elizabeth. He wondered what he could say to her.

"Bad news."

"Yeah, helluva thing. Fever. Took him quick. Miz Eberly asked us to escort her here. She wanted to go back to Indianola today, but Miz McDermott said to wait a day. So we're goin' tomorrow. Plain good timing that you got to town so we could see you."

"The family's going back to Indianola?"

"Naw, just Miz Eberly, Miz McDermott and the older boy. The girl and the younger boy are stayin' here. Can't quite figure that, but that's the plan. We leave at dawn."

"I guess we better get on over there. Where is the McDermott place anyway? Can you point us in the right direction?"

"Sure, we'll walk part way with you. Me and Drew want one more visit with the ladies. Tell your grandfather we'll see him later."

Elizabeth's mind ran toward architecture, a subject that had never held any interest for her whatsoever. That utter lack of appeal was precisely the point. Rooflines and paving stones were exactly what were required to dispel her ruminations about her father's death and her family's unfathomable future. She began in the center of the courtyard, examining a bucket suspended above the well. Her eyes traced its round wooden bottom, then the larger circumference of the well. Resisting the temptation to sink into the depths of the water, she shifted her gaze to the raised bench on which she sat, outlining the way it surrounded the well. The concentric circles held her in a kind of fixation for many minutes before she scanned the series of rectangles that constituted the courtyard.

Her eyes were drawn to the right angles formed by the inner grounds. She traced the long dining room until it abutted a corner room at the front of the house. Used as a chapel by the Spanish, that small room was now an office. With a right turn came the salon, overflowing with people who had come to pay their respects. The salon connected to a small entry hall that ran straight through the center of the house to the courtyard. From her position at the well, Elizabeth could see the door on Laredo Street opening and closing. On the other side, the hall opened to a mirror image of the salon, where guests filed in and out to mourn privately with her mother. Next came the corner guest room, where Mrs. Eberly now stayed. Another right turn led to her brothers' room. Zeke and Zach were both inside with the door closed. Then came her own room, and last, her mother's bedroom, with doors opening to the veranda on two sides. An eight-foot high adobe wall extended to the kitchen and stables along the rear, parallel to the main part of the house. A gate opened onto an alley, and the wall continued back to the house, leaving no gaps. The outer perimeter was a solid rectangle, enclosing her family and their agony.

Smaller rectangles were formed by stacks of adobe bricks intended to finish an addition to the kitchen. She studied an errant adobe brick at her feet, one that had somehow eluded the worker who had neatly stacked the others. It was an agglomeration of mud and straw, rude and unattractive. But when dry, laid well, and painted, it would be transformed. She had grown used to adobe structures and found their appearance could be appealing.

Elizabeth had been crying intermittently ever since Mrs. Eberly's arrival yesterday. She could not conceive of herself as a fatherless child nor of her mother as a widow. She could not envision what would become of her. As the sun traversed the day she left the fountain to seek shade in a different part of the courtyard. Sometimes she paced in an effort to quell her anger and disbelief. Sounds from the house assaulted her from all sides, intruding on her reflections. Esther and Agnes rushed back and forth between the kitchen and the dining room carrying bowls, receiving gifts of food, serving their guests, and washing up. The daughters of Sr. Jose Antonio Navarro brought pots of chile verde and baskets of spicy pork tamales. Her piano teacher came with a crock of German pot roast. Even though she had no appetite, her mother foisted upon her a taste of every new dish that arrived. She knew they were delicious but found no pleasure in them.

She conjured memories of her father, as many as possible, beginning from childhood right through to the recent May Day celebrations. She tried to sear into her mind his look of pride as he had walked her into the hall that spring day. She wished to implant a permanent remembrance of his face beaming when her name had been announced. She had often imagined seeing that same look when he would walk her down the aisle to be married. Knowing that would never happen, she sobbed.

Only once did she manage the wherewithal to walk into the dining room to express appreciation for the staggering quantity of dishes piled on the sturdy wooden table. She accompanied her mother through the salon accepting expressions of sympathy from their guests, but she broke down so often that her mother excused her from that chore. She sensed that something was expected of her, but felt totally incapable.

She longed for her childhood friends. Surely the girls with whom she had grown up in Galveston would know what to say, would sit with her day and night, would render this ordeal less arduous. A granddaughter of Sr. Navarro, with whom Elizabeth had become friendly, visited several times, accompanied by other young women her own age. Although their kindness touched her, she craved familiar faces, and lacking that, preferred to sit alone. She ignored the continuously ringing bell in favor of her analysis of the geometry of the courtyard.

Antoine, opening the door for what seemed the hundredth time that day, was surprised to find Nate with Hassan at his side. The two looked like trail riders fresh from the road. Hassan spoke first. "Antoine, we are sorry to hear the bad news."

Nate added, "Yeah, really sorry. How's the family doin'?"

Nate felt somewhat intimidated by the way Antoine in uniform presided over the comings and goings with more authority than usually accorded to a slave butler. Nate's awkwardness was exacerbated by his uncertainty about seeing the McDermott family, especially Elizabeth. Cautiously, he stepped into the house. He was further discomfited to find the entry hall more elegant than he supposed and the salon replete with people who were very well dressed. Suddenly he was conscious that he carried the odor of camels and dust.

"They're doin' well enough, but it's hard. Your grandfather is with Miz Sylvia. I'll show you in." He motioned Hassan to wait.

Although the idea of mixing with the fashionable crowd in the salon was overwhelming, Nate was even more reluctant to receive a private audience with Sylvia McDermott. Yanking off his hat, he crossed the threshold of the sitting room, not quite sure what to do next. Fortunately, his grandfather made it easy by rising quickly and enveloping him in a hearty bear hug.

"Good to see you, Nate. Really good."

"Howdy, Grandpa." Nate turned awkwardly toward Sylvia.

She stood and extended her hand. "So good of you to come, Nate."

Nate shook it briefly, noticing her emerald ring and the light touch of her dainty fingers. He couldn't remember when, if ever, he had greeted a woman like this, formal and yet somehow intimate. Again, he was uncertain what to do.

"So sorry about your husband, Ma'am."

"Thank you Nate, please have a seat. Are you in from Camp Verde?"

"Yes'm. Just arrived. Went to find my grandpa at the Menger place and was told he was here. Sorry, but I came straight." Nate apologized, looking down at his gritty buckskins.

"It was very kind of you to come so quickly. Oh dear, you probably haven't eaten. Antoine! Ask Esther to bring food and a glass of water for Mr. Wilkers."

"Yes, Miz Sylvia."

Hassan was still standing in the hall. Antoine wanted to talk to him, but now was not the time. "Why don't you wait outside? Esther can bring a plate for you there." They exited the hall's back door into the courtyard, and Antoine went to find Esther.

Hassan paused to get his bearings, taken aback by the remarkable resemblance of this inner courtyard to the one at Auntie Fatima's house. He leaned against a support post on the wide veranda, admiring how the shaded area framed the house, how its proportions extended the size of the rooms. He breathed deeply. The air held the fragrance of a host of wandering vines, succulents, and flowering plants. Hibiscus splashed a palette of red and pink. Adding a deeper purple accent, fuchsia sprouted in earthenware jars and climbed over trellises to create a natural alcove for a wooden bench. For an instant he thought he heard Auntie Fatima's voice. He smiled to imagine what delicacies she might offer him and with what admonitions she would serve them. He indulged in one more image: Sula slipping out from behind one of the bushes. He closed his eyes and let his mind wander, appreciating the quiet seclusion from the street noise. He felt more at home than anywhere he had been in Texas. Enthralled by the lush tranquility, it took him a moment to notice Elizabeth.

Elizabeth perceived the shifting shadows of yet more visitors and turned away. But for some reason, it occurred to her that the visitor might be Nate. She raised her eyes to find Hassan standing directly in front of her. Without hesitation, she flung herself toward him, sobbing, "Oh Hassan, you've come."

Completely unprepared for this, Hassan nearly tipped over backwards, but steadied himself quickly as Elizabeth wrapped her arms around him, and rested her head on his shoulder. She gripped him tightly, giving no indication that she intended to let go. His neck and shirt were soon damp with her tears.

"Eleezabet, I am so sorry."

"Hassan, Hassan, thank you for coming."

She looked up into his face, her eyes dazzling. For Hassan, every sound except her voice faded away. Instinctively, he hugged her close, stroking her hair and speaking softly. He had never held a woman this way, her body fully pressed against his. The comfort of it, and the thrill, caught him off guard. A soothing sensation contrasted with exhilaration. Her vulnerability excited him. Enraptured by these divergent perceptions, he allowed himself to drink them in undisturbed, as if taking water after days of drought. With determination, he ignored a hazy suspicion that this much pleasure was somehow indecent.

For Elizabeth, Hassan was the familiarity that she had been craving. She let her emotions go, crying uncontrollably and mumbling uncensored whatever thought came to mind. She clung to him, afraid that she would crumble if she loosened her grip. She noted with relief that he held her firmly. Enfolded in his arms, she felt secure and protected.

He was sanctuary.

Gently, her tears diminished and a sense of safety relaxed her. With this repose, she became aware of Hassan's body, the contraction of his biceps supporting her, the taught strength of his legs keeping them balanced, the firmness of his chest against her cheek. Tingles ran from the nape of her neck to the small of her back. Unconsciously, she leaned in closer and luxuriated in his refuge. All at once she comprehended a steely pressure against her groin and backed away slowly.

Hassan felt the inches between them as a chasm, an unnatural divide, but one bridged by the intensity of those deep blue eyes. He held her gaze. Taking his hand, Elizabeth led him to the bench by the well, where the two of them sat in stupefied silence, both breathing hard.

Esther stepped out of the dining room in time to see the last of their embrace. Shocked, she nearly dropped a plate piled high with dishes carefully chosen, according to Antoine's instructions, to avoid anything cooked with pork. "Lord have mercy!" she muttered under her breath as she crossed the courtyard to deliver the food to Hassan.

Inside the house, Nate bent over his plate, gratefully attacking a chunk of barbecued ribs and an ear of fresh corn. With his back to the veranda, he had not observed Hassan with Elizabeth, but Sylvia had seen them.

Jeremy had also noticed. "An emotional time, when someone dies."

Distressed by her daughter's behavior, Sylvia did not quite follow his train of thought. "Of course, Mr. Blackstone."

"People seek comfort. Gotta find ways to get the sadness out. Don't mean much in the long run."

Again, Sylvia was impressed by the timeliness and profundity of Jeremy's observations. She took a slow breath. "Why yes, thank you, Mr. Blackstone." She inhaled again. "Nate, how are Alex and Hassan?"

"Miz McDermott, I'm sorry. I got so wrapped up with eatin'. Hassan's here. He's out in the hall with Antoine."

"Ah, no, I see that he's in the courtyard, and by the looks of it, Esther's already given him something to eat. Let me call him in, along with Elizabeth."

Nate set down his food and awkwardly wiped his mouth. Elizabeth accepted his sympathies while she watched Hassan greet Jeremy. When Hassan greeted her mother, he made an obvious effort to find vocabulary for the proper condolences. Everyone chatted while the two young men enjoyed their second servings. An appearance of normalcy prevailed.

"Elizabeth, I've learned from Nate that Alex will arrive with a wagon, maybe tomorrow. I wish we could push back our departure, but we really must leave at daybreak. It will be a shame to miss him." Sylvia glanced pointedly at her daughter, who rallied in response.

"I'm sure he'll come to see us, and I'll give him your greetings." Her stomach tightened as she studiously avoided looking at Hassan. Her conflicting feelings threatened to overcome her carefully fabricated poise.

"Nate, which of you is going back first? I want to send a letter to my cousin."

"We're all leaving together in a couple days. Hassan and I are on camels, so we'll get back first. We'll take your letter straight to the Major."

After awhile, when the young men moved to leave, Jeremy held back. "Don't you worry none, Miz McDermott. I'll keep a close eye on things."

"Thank you, Mr. Blackstone. And thank you for your sage comments. I shall have a talk with my daughter."

"Yes, ma'am. But then you go on and do what has to be done in Galveston. And Miz McDermott, if I may...."

"Yes, of course."

"You gotta give yourself time. Grief is sneaky. Comes on you when you're not lookin', usually when you think everything is fine again. Sometimes jumps out right in front of you, fixin' to knock you where you stand. Can't keep it from comin'. Can't fight it neither. When it comes, don't let it get you down. Take time to live that grief, and you'll pass through."

SAN ANTONIO, TWO MONTHS LATER, OCTOBER 1856

S EATED ON A BENCH in the courtyard, Esther dumped the shelled peas into the basin balanced on her lap. Leaning over to retrieve one that rolled away, she felt like that lonely pea, ripped out of its protective shell and thrust upon a great unknown. She picked it up and replaced it in the basin. "There. Back where you belong. Wish we knew where we belong."

On a chair opposite, Antoine was repairing a bridle. Their conversation was hushed. "This is somethin' else, ain't it? This waitin'. Always waitin'."

"I'm so worried 'bout Missy 'Lizbeth. She the most mixed up I ever seen her."

"Esther, you ain't her mother."

"No, but I gotta look out for her. I been brushin' her hair at night. She don't really wanna talk, but she talkin' some anyway. She lettin' out little things, like 'Alex this' and 'Hassan that' and 'Nate said'."

"You worryin' too much. They around, so she naturally gonna talk about 'em."

The McDermott household resembled a boarding house. Esther didn't mind Mr. Blackstone, who kept to himself, but that had been just the beginning. Major Babcock came to San Antonio more often, bringing Alex with him whenever possible. On those occasions, Major Babcock used Miz Sylvia's room and Alex bunked with Zachary. When Nate was along, he shared the guest room with his grandfather. If Hassan traveled with Major Babcock, he lodged at the Alamo, but when he came with Alex or Nate, Elizabeth insisted they all stay at the house.

"It perks her up when they around, but it makes me nervous, watchin' her halfway in a tizzy over 'em. Besides, it sure do make more work. More cookin', more washin'. No sooner'n one leaves the next one's here!"

"Esther, y'all are gettin' hard to please. You used to say you was bored sittin' 'round here. Now you complainin' 'bout too much to do." Antoine's laughter lightened her mood. "And you know, Esther, she likes 'em."

"Yeah, you right. No better way for a girl to fight the blues than a boy payin' attention."

"Nuthin' better."

"But one day she gonna have to choose."

"I think she got eyes for two o' them boys for sure, maybe all three."

"Antoine, it ain't only Missy 'Lizbeth what's tied me in knots. What's gonna happen to us with Massa Quentin dead? We dunno nuthin' 'bout his money. We dunno nuthin' 'bout what Miz Sylvia doin' in Galveston. We dunno if she fixin' to sell us or take us back to Galveston or keep us here. Or even send us to the fields. Don't get me wrong. I like Miz Sylvia, but she ain't family like Massa Quentin. She married into it. We can't be sure what she thinkin'."

"Esther, for pity sake!" Antoine's patience had worn thin. "I know your family been with Massa Quentin's family a long time, but...."

"A long time. Hmpf. More like always. Back to my great-grandma in Tennessee. Him and me, we growed up together. He like a big brother to me, even if he was our massa. My mama helped to raise him and taught Miz Sylvia when she didn't know nuthin'."

"I know Esther, but we got no say in what's gonna happen to us. None. And when it come down to it, I trust Miz Sylvia better'n Massa Quentin. She gonna do her best."

"But what that gonna be? Am I ever gonna see Henry again?"

"Esther, you gonna make yourself sick thinkin' 'bout it." Seeing Elizabeth stroll out onto the veranda, they continued their work in silence.

Although she suffered occasional bouts of melancholy, Elizabeth was thriving in her new circumstances. She enjoyed testing herself as head of the household and believed she had done a good job giving directions to the slaves, setting menus, managing the finances, and receiving guests. Her Spanish was improving, as was her piano playing. Once a week, she and Zach went to the edge of town for her pistol practice. She particularly liked playing hostess to Major Babcock, Alex, Hassan, and Nate. She felt as if she had become an adult woman overnight, not artificially as she had at her May Day debut, but in reality, a status that she had earned.

Mr. Blackstone's unobtrusive ways fit in well with the household's new routines. Elizabeth often sat with him on the veranda in the evening and consulted him about the many little chores that were now her responsibility. He always responded, but never asserted himself into her realm. Often he just listened to her, providing a safe outlet for her still intense emotions, while she watched him whittle on elongated pieces of wood. Zach sometimes sat with them, learning to carve with Jeremy's oversight. One evening she concluded that Jeremy's pieces were purposeful creations.

"Mr. Blackstone, are you making something in particular?"

"Yup. Makin' a chair."

"A chair? Goodness, that must be complicated?"

"Not too bad. Should be done before your Mama gets back."

"If that's your timetable, you may have weeks to finish it. I wish these legal problems didn't take so long to work out. I hope she'll be able to leave it with the lawyers soon."

"Yup, and come on back."

"Or perhaps send for us?"

Jeremy had had a brief but highly illuminating conversation with Mrs. Eberly before the women had departed. Mrs. Eberly felt sure that Sylvia would reside permanently in San Antonio. She intimated that Sylvia might have to fight for her husband's estate, and if so, that she would probably not care to remain in Galveston.

"Hmmm, maybe. Wouldn't plan one way or the other for now. Your mama will let you know."

"Yes, of course. She must make many decisions on our behalf, and without our father's help."

"She'll do fine."

In spite of her comfort with Mr. Blackstone's presence, Elizabeth found his conversation frustratingly sparse. By contrast, Major Babcock was a fountain of ideas and specific suggestions. His first visit, within a week after her mother's departure, brought the solace that only comes from family. He advised her on financial matters and counseled patience. He recounted numerous stories about her father that she had never heard. She learned more about how her parents had met, their first years in Galveston, and even details about her own birth. Major Babcock and her mother had corresponded throughout their lives, and he knew much about her family's major events. He clearly held deep affection for her mother. That warmth flowed into Elizabeth like a balm, his avuncular manner soothing her unlike anything else.

However, she learned from Alex, Nate, and Hassan that the Camel Corps was in a critical phase, so she did everything she could to avoid exacerbating Major Babcock's worries by distressing him with her own. She so wanted the camel experiment to succeed. One afternoon, Major Babcock arrived with a stack of letters and a package under his arm.

"Do I have a surprise for you, Elizabeth! Come see. It's a package from the President of the United States addressed to you."

"What? Something from President Pierce for me?"

"Actually, it's addressed to your mother and you. Have a look."

She removed the paper to find a sturdy wooden box with a metal clasp. Inside was a soft royal blue velvet cloth wrapped around a silver urn, engraved:

To Mrs. Sylvia McDermott and Miss Elizabeth McDermott
In appreciation for socks produced from the wool of the
United States Camel Corps
PRESIDENT FRANKLIN PIERCE

"What a wonderful thing! I can't believe it. A gift from the President of the United States, and such a fine one, too. I do hope this indicates his positive regard for the camels!"

"I hope so, too, Elizabeth, I hope so too."

She set the urn in one of the little alcoves dotting the house that had been used by the Spanish to display statues of saints. Everyday when she walked past it, she smiled and remembered the socks that she and her mother had knit for the President. Unbeknownst to her, Esther, Agnes and Antoine also paused regularly to admire the presidential gift.

"Shoulda had your names on there. You's the ones did all the cardin' and cleanin' and washin' and rinsin' and spinnin', all the work that had to be done before the knittin' could start."

"Hush, Antoine, we know what we did. Don't need no name. That's ours as much as anyone's. I'm proud as a peacock. Agnes, too."

Major Babcock repeatedly connived some assignment in San Antonio that required Alex, Hassan, or Nate, singly or in combination, a thoughtfulness that Elizabeth much appreciated. Although still aching from her father's death, she regained a certain carefree spirit in the company of the young men. Seeing them one by one or sometimes two together, observing their interactions with each other or Mr. Blackstone or Major Babcock, enjoying their conversation in the evening and again at breakfast, she came to know them with a familiarity that would otherwise have been impossible. Without question, she had never had better friends. In spite of the fact that they were male, they seemed to understand her more than any of her old Galveston girlfriends or her new acquaintances in San Antonio.

She paid close attention to tales of their lives before she met them. From Alex she learned about his family in Philadelphia and was touched by his tenderheartedness toward his sisters. However, she was dismayed to learn that he favored the abolition of slavery, even if such a change would be enforced against the will of Southerners. She had never followed politics much, although she had heard about the Missouri Compromise and the proposed transcontinental railroad. She had been taught that slavery was necessary for southern cotton and that northern objections amounted to nothing more than economic rivalry. Never had she encountered the abolitionist argument laid out in such precision as the night that Alex launched a soliloquy, both logical and passionate, that kept her awake for hours afterward. Zachary had been profoundly affected by Alex's postulations, and henceforth spoke openly about his own objections to slavery, often citing the example of Precious, who had still not been located.

No one could make her laugh like Alex. He told hilarious stories about the camels and life at Camp Verde. He often arrived with a flourish, swept into the room with a bouquet of wildflowers or a small gift, and brought an irresistible cheeriness into the house. Once when all three friends had been in town together, Alex proposed having their picture made. Laughing heartily, she had perched on a kneeling Adela, with Alex, Hassan, and Nate poised around her. It was all the four of them could do to adopt a sober demeanor and keep still for the photographer. She had set the daguerreotype on the nightstand by her bed, and now smiled at it often.

At first she had been annoyed with Nate's presence, never having quite forgiven him for Samuel's death. An enigma, Nate was neither as voluble as Alex nor as withdrawn as his grandfather. Sometimes he was subdued, as if ill at ease or outclassed by his surroundings. Perhaps his reserve was merely a watchfulness inherited from his grand-father. He didn't speak until he had assessed the situation, but then, once he found his stride, his conversation was interesting, his opinions well articulated. Through Nate she learned that Mr. Blackstone had been twice widowed, and that fact led to the remarkable story of Nate's having survived the massacre at Linville when he was a toddler. Elizabeth was amazed that such poignant tales of loss and survival were the foundation of Nate's experience.

When she heard about Nate and Hassan's budding merchant enterprise, Elizabeth was determined to help. Because her mother had relationships with several quality merchants, she introduced Nate and Hassan all over town. On one occasion, after they had secured a quantity of sugar and salt at very agreeable terms, the three were so pleased that they skipped down the street arm-in-arm, laughing and exultant. In Galveston, such a public display would have been reported to her parents, who would have reprimanded her. In San Antonio, she didn't care and reveled in the good fellowship of her friends.

One evening, when a chill that presaged autumn had driven everyone indoors, she found Nate and his grand-father in the salon reading. Mr. Blackstone was random-ly thumbing through James Audubon's *Birds of America*, whereas Nate was so deep in concentration that he didn't even glance at her when she entered the room.

"Good evening Mr. Blackstone, Nate."

Jeremy replied. "Evenin' Elizabeth." Nate looked up, a bit flustered.

"May I ask what you gentlemen are reading?"

Seeing his grandson at a loss for words, Jeremy found his. "I'm not much for readin' really. Just lookin' at this pic-ture book. That man Audubon had a fine eye and a good hand for drawin'."

"He certainly did. Every time I gaze upon one of his birds I see some new detail. My mother especially cherishes that book."

"Yup, mighty fine. I learned to read late in life, so it ain't easy for me. But Nate here, he'll read for the pure pleasure in it. I envy that. Not somethin' I've ever known."

Nate was surprised by his grandfather's personal revelation to Elizabeth and thrilled by the note of praise in it.

"Well, then Nate, what is it that has you so engrossed?"

Nate flipped the book closed to show Elizabeth the front cover. "Oh Nate, my ancient history book! It's one of my favorites, though it's a bit serious for some tastes."

"No, I like it. When you read this, you can imagine life thousands of years ago. You can believe that you're far away, seein' new things. Besides, with Hassan, Abdullah and Ali always talkin' about Egypt, I figured I'd better get some idea about the place."

Adjusting the light on the hurricane lamp, she turned pages with Nate until Esther came to ask if they'd like a cup of tea before retiring. The next morning they went shopping, as had become their habit when he was in town. This time she escorted him into Dupuy's Emporium to look at bolts of fine cloth, buttons, ribbons, ladies' shoes, hats, gloves, and bonnets. She practically had to drag him through the door, so complete was his aversion.

"Elizabeth, what are we doin' here?"

"Didn't you tell me that Mrs. Chisholm accompanied her husband to Camp Verde?"

"Yes, but..."

"And didn't you also mention a few settler families in the region?"

"All right, yes, on both counts."

"Did it occur to you that these women might be exceedingly grateful for a bit of finery in their lives? That they might appreciate a piece of lace or a few buttons or some yards of fabric from New Orleans?"

Standing open-mouthed, he quickly calculated the possibilities. Without warning, he hugged her. "Elizabeth, you're a genius!" In a split second, he backed off and became all businesslike. "Will you help me choose?" She and the store clerk giggled as they advised Nate about the potential wishes of his female customers.

With Hassan, she noticed in herself an odd push-pull. She was disappointed when he didn't come with one of the others. Elated when he happened to be along, she nevertheless became tongue-tied and embarrassed. She initiated conversations with Alex or Mr. Blackstone or Nate or her brother Zachary, in short anyone but Hassan. Then she hung eagerly on his every word. When their eyes met, it was like pulsating fire from a hot poker. How could such a feeling happen from just a look? She pieced together information about his learned grandfather Alhaji Mustafa who, she concluded, must possess true wisdom, and his Auntie Fatima, a stubborn character. Sometimes they talked of their faiths, Islam and Christianity, finding remarkable similarities in the values of their two religions and innumerable differences in specific beliefs.

Recently Alex had become edgy, even sarcastic, when Hassan was around. He developed a competitive way of interrupting, trying to tell a better story or making deprecatory remarks. Elizabeth considered it immature and began to question Alex's character. She wondered what could have caused these two to have a falling out, and could find no plausible explanation. She had not the slightest idea what to do.

CAMP VERDE, TEXAS, OCTOBER 1856

TIGHT-LIPPED AND DISTANT, ABDULLAH rode into camp encircled by a bubble of shimmering anger that rendered everyone who approached him tentative. His mood did not improve when confronted with the shack that passed for his living quarters, even though the others had neatened the lean-to and offered him the most desirable sleeping spot. Hassan questioned him, only to be met with a stolid refusal to describe the trip to Indianola. Erdem tried to engage him with humorous narrations of their life at Camp Verde during his absence. Erdem made light of Major Babcock's rickety desk, noting that the Major had settled anew at Lt. Halter's writing table. His mocking imitation of Lt. Halter's self-satisfied smirk left everyone except Abdullah laughing out loud.

"Come on, Abdullah, what was it like to travel with the stuffy Lieutenant?

Abdullah scrunched his face into a grimace. "It is time for us to go home."

Not one to be put off so easily, Ali eavesdropped on the two new soldiers who had arrived with Abdullah, prompted Alex to share information, and even contrived to have a conversation with Lt. Halter. After each investigative foray, he sidled up to Abdullah, posing new questions. His meticulous research enabled Ali to deduce that Abdullah had been confined by Captain Van Steendam "for his own protection" at the Army Depot, not for a single night as before, but for the duration of his visit. Confronted with his secret, Abdullah's silent humiliation mutated into a lengthy rant. He detailed every indignity that he had suffered at the hands of Lt. Halter and angrily recounted the boring and offensive circumstances of his confinement, which had been prolonged from day to day without any intimation of when he might be released.

"You mean they kept you in the Depot and didn't tell you when the tribunal would take place?"

"That's right. Every morning the same. Every day no news."

"Was there no explanation?"

"Apparently the tribunal required the presence of a military judge who rides circuit in Texas. I was held captive, waiting for this judge." Abdullah had languished in detention, subjected to stares, taunts, and unkind remarks. He retold each affront with unbearable precision, punctuating his story with invectives against the barbaric rudeness of Americans. Distressed at the high color darkening Abdullah's neck and ears, Ali tried to change the tone.

"Did no one treat you well?"

Abdullah resisted Ali's attempt to make him admit that anything good had transpired. "Almost no one."

"Perhaps someone then?"

Reluctantly he acceded. "Captain Van Steendam's wife personally oversaw my food preparation. It was tasty and correctly cooked."

Ali breathed a sigh of relief and pursued the conversation. "Yes, she was always kind."

"She is a good woman. Sometimes she asked after the camels. She even remembered the names of Tullah, Ibrim, and Uncle Sam. She seemed to be truly interested, more so than her husband."

Seeing that the mention of Captain Van Steendam drew a frown across Abdullah's brow, Ali quickly asked, "Was anyone else kind to you?"

"The presiding officer of the tribunal, when he finally arrived, was polite and well-bred. He listened patiently to Lt. Halter's pompous recitations and dismissed the charges. I memorized his name: Robert E. Lee."

"Ah, good, so there is some understanding of the law in this country."

"Minimal, I would say. Their law is slow and disrespectfully administered.

"Yes, but in the end, the result was just."

"I suppose so. In the end."

Erdem tried for a jocular tone. "Come on, Abdullah, something amusing must have happened. One funny thing at least?"

Abdullah actually smiled. "You'll never believe it, but that wild man, the friend of Nate, came into the Depot one day with a basket of fried fish, hot and delicious."

"Drew? He brought you food?"

"Yes, Drew Johnson. He brought good food, but he insulted me from the moment he crossed the doorway, shouting at the top of his lungs." Abdullah launched into an imitation, exaggerating an accent that came out a ridiculous cross between Arabic and pure Texan. Hassan laughed so hard he nearly cried. This was exactly the same blustery Drew Johnson he had seen a couple months ago in San Antonio. The hilarity did everyone good, especially Abdullah. "It was very strange. He never said one kind word, never asked after my health, never offered any condolence. But he brought that excellent fish with a food called hush puppies, a fried corn ball a little bit like falafel, very nice."

"Yes, remember? Mr. Blackstone cooked those along the trail. I liked them." Hassan's mouth watered thinking about the hush puppies.

"Anyway, Drew's friend came in later. He brought playing cards and a bottle of whiskey. The two maligned each other constantly while they tried to teach me to play poker. I took no whiskey, but they drank most of the bottle, becoming louder as the night wore on." His audience was fascinated, trying to picture such unlikely visitors. "They started betting and wanted me to gamble with them, but I had no money. They started betting with matchsticks. I lost badly and soon had none left. The two of them continued playing, though neither really gained anything."

"How long did this go on?"

"All night. Until the whiskey was finished, another bottle sent for, and half of it gone, too. When they left, they slapped me on the back, which I took as a friendly gesture. It was very strange, yet somehow satisfying. I never saw them after that night."

With Abdullah's silence finally broken, all the camel herders except Pertag talked late into the night. As Hassan crawled into bed that evening, he realized that they were all homesick.

Early the next day a soldier jogged up to the clearing adjacent to their lean-to to find the men finishing their morning prayers. "Hey, guys, you're wanted right away. Come quick."

Abdullah, not about to go trotting off at the behest of Sgt. Bly or Pertag, replied somewhat peevishly. "Who wants us?"

"Capt. Chisholm, Major Babcock, Lt. Halter, all of 'em. Hurry up. A camel's dead. Out in the field near the creek."

Quickly putting away their prayer mats, the four dashed across the dew-laden fields to join a mass of soldiers clustered around a camel carcass. Detached from the group, Alex was pacing. As they approached, Stacy Bly called out. "Which one of you is responsible for this? Was it you, Abdullah?"

Captain Chisholm snapped. "Quiet, Sergeant. I'll do the questioning."

The soldiers parted to reveal Major Babcock crouching next to Tullah, his hand resting on her neck.

"No, not Tullah!" Abdullah fell to his knees next to Major Babcock and began examining Tullah, feeling her limbs, probing her midsection. When he reached her neck, he turned pointedly to Major Babcock, speaking loudly and clearly in English. "Her neck is broken. There are no scrapes or marks on her legs. She did not fall. Someone hit her."

Abdullah had never before known blind rage, but found the experience aptly named. Brilliant light streaked before his eyes, his breath stopped, and an intense energy rushed through him. His frenzied heart pounded like metal on an anvil as he gasped for air. In a single swift motion, he jumped to his feet and let loose a furious howl. When his eyes could focus again, he scanned the soldiers in all directions, shouting the single word "Who?" again and again as his stare blazed at each man. When he took a step toward Sgt. Bly, Ali rushed to restrain him.

Captain Chisholm was not happy. "I see that your temper is as violent as they say. Are you sure you had nothing to do with this?"

"Me? Why do you ask me? Why don't you ask that son of a worm Sergeant Bly? Or Pertag? They were on guard duty last night."

Ali whispered in Arabic. "Let me talk to him." He stood straight and formally addressed the Captain. "Sir, this camel was a favorite of Abdullah, of all of us. Ask your own men. Many of them loved her too. This is a cruel act. Only a bad person could do such a thing. We could not."

"I said, I'll ask the questions. You'll speak when spoken to." As if physically slapped, Ali retreated to the little group, his own anger sparking. Captain Chisholm continued. "I'm going to ask each one of you again. Did you harm this camel?"

Abdullah spat his answer. "I should not even answer such a stupid question. No I did not."

Abdullah was treading dangerously close to Captain Chisholm's abhorrence of insubordination, but Major Babcock's presence constrained. Had it been up to the Captain, Abdullah would have gone straight to the brig. At that point Pertag showed up, sauntering over next to Sgt. Bly.

Annoyed, Captain Chisholm called, "You, Pete, get over here with your countrymen. Do you know what happened to this camel?"

Abdullah was glad to see Pertag included in the suspicions cast on all the camel herders. Each man present was subjected to further questioning before Major Babcock insisted that the cause of death be officially determined. Kneeling by Tullah, Abdullah refused to leave her. Hassan, Ali and Erdem squatted on the ground off to the side, downcast and miserable. Alex stopped pacing and joined them, blowing his nose. Ali spoke in Arabic simple enough for Alex to follow.

"Will they find out who did this?"

"I don't know. I don't know."

"It was the one we guess, don't you think? I am so angry, I could kill him with my own hands."

Ali was careful not to say Sgt. Bly's name. Everyone knew that Stacy had irritated several of the camels with his rough handling. A few would not let him near them. Recently, even Tullah had shown a stubborn side when he was around. They figured that Tullah had wandered off in the night and that Sgt. Bly, unable to control her, had lost his temper.

Because the soldiers regarded them suspiciously, Hassan switched to English. "It's very wrong. Tullah was so easy."

Alex replied angrily. "You're damn right. Tullah put up with everything, did everything she was asked. She was always so friendly."

Hassan spoke as if delivering a eulogy. "Do you remember? She was one of the best ones offered to us by my grandfather's friend, Alhaji Ibrahim Muhammad, from his own personal stock. She was with us from the beginning, all the way to Smyrna, then in those terrible storms to Jamaica and on to Indianola."

"I remember. She was the first one swung over the side of the *Supply* when we tried to lighter the camels onto the *Fashion*."

A couple of soldiers gathered around, adding their remembrances. "Whoa, she howled over that one!"

"Sure did, but took it in her stride anyway."

"Yup, she was one of the first to touch Texas soil."

"And the first one to give rides to the children in Indianola. Every Sunday while we were there. The children loved to ride Tullah."

"Remember when she lifted the four bales of hay? Never thought she could do it, but she did, as smooth as anything. Poor Tullah." Alex clenched his fists.

At last, Major Babcock rose and addressed the gathering. "Captain Chisholm, the cause of death is confirmed.

Brute force snapped this camel's neck. This was not an accident." Visibly shaken, he turned to the clutch of mourners. "I'm so sorry. You may bury her."

Nate heard the news when he returned from San Antonio later in the day. Shouting blasphemies against the murderer, he stomped back and forth in front of the spot where Tullah was buried. He plunked down and proceeded to nurse his sadness with a bottle of whiskey, becoming drunk and raving. Had Alex and Hassan not pinioned him, he would have initiated a fistfight with Sgt. Bly.

The men were hopeful when Major Babcock assigned Lt. Halter to lead the investigation, because he had demonstrated a penchant for truth-seeking in Abdullah's case. However, they soon began to doubt the outcome. The interviews, conducted with pretentious language and Lt. Halter's haughty style of questioning, guaranteed that even the men who knew about Tullah's death would not cooperate. The official report implicated the "Arabs" by default, and the actual perpetrator was never brought to justice.

Rifts between the camel herders and Sgt. Bly's cohort deepened into permanent fissures. Taunts flew. The care of the camels deteriorated, infuriating Nate, Alex, and the camel men further. Major Babcock's protestations went unheeded, and Capt. Chisholm was so preoccupied with the construction that he neglected the animals.

On his next trip to San Antonio, Nate brought back a leather belt with a brass buckle, embossed with the lone star of Texas. Sgt. Bly had ordered it some weeks before. Now, with glee, Nate offered the belt to Abdullah instead.

"Thank you, Nate, but I do not have money for this."

"Abdullah, it's my gift to you. Something good-lookin' to remember us by, to chase away the bad memories once you get home. Besides, I'd rather you have it than Stacy."

"Ah, I see." Abdullah fingered the belt buckle, which was of exceptionally fine workmanship. "It is beautiful, and I am honored. Still, I must pay something." After a token payment, Abdullah wore the belt proudly, tickling his friends and annoying the heck out of Sgt. Bly.

"That slimy Ay-rab got no call to be wearin' a symbol of Texas. That's as wrong as it gets."

"Yeah, we'll have to do somethin' 'bout that."

A few days later three soldiers ganged up on Abdullah, intending to rip his belt off. Fortunately, Major Babcock happened by, but it had been a close call, and the camel keepers were shaken. Later that evening, under a wondrous wide sky festooned with delicately flickering galaxies and a myriad of stars, their mood remained somber.

"Abdullah is right. It is time for us to go home."

Camp Verde, Texas, October 22, 1856

My dear Annabelle,

Regrettably, no orders awaited me in Indianola, and I am now in the hinterlands. Luckily, Camp Verde's environs are not as abject as I supposed. The commanding officer has taken to heart the objective of constructing proper build-ings whether or not the camels remain at this locale. The officers' quarters shall be a substantial structure, 124 by 25 feet, with rooms for the local commander as well as for guest officers. In the meanwhile, we share a house with Capt. Chisholm and his charming wife who oversees preparation of wholesome and tasty meals.

A Frenchman, Monsieur Poinsard, has been engaged as architect and supervisor of the pisé work. A singularly well-informed individual, he enlivens a conversation with quotations from the French philosophers, appreciates a good cigar and occasionally manages to procure a bit of cognac. I hope to be in Washington long before I shall have occasion to inhabit the new quarters, but it pleases me to observe their meticulous construction.

Even more surprisingly, a thriving intellectual community exists a mere ten miles away in a village poetically named Comfort, established quite recently by German freethink-ers. These men came with their families, their libraries, and their enlightened curiosity. One enters the simplest of homes to find first class paintings on the walls, exquisite Limoges china upon the table, and beautiful wool rugs upon well-constructed wooden floors, instead of the pounded earth one finds so often. Abstract ideas carry great weight with them. My only reservation is that they favor reason above all else and give little appreciation to scripture. Atheist may be too strong a characterization, but they have no church.

The weather has improved mightily after the scorching summer. An effusion of pleasant warmth greets us most days, invigorating everyone, including Major Babcock, who has taken up the idea of mounting a major expedition to explore the wilder territories west of here. His intent is to compare horses, mules and camels in the rough desert terrain. The anticipated difficulties may result in a prolonged voyage, and the Major is intent on leading it himself. He plans to take his nephew and several of the camel herders. This exodus shall leave us with a rather more relaxed atmosphere in camp, and I confess that I look forward to evenings sans Babcock, elder and junior. Perhaps my orders shall arrive before the Major returns.

Wishing ever more fervently to be by your side, I remain,

Your devoted husband,

Winston

Camp Verde, Texas, early November 1856

W HEN THE EXPEDITION'S DEPLOYMENT was announced, those most skilled with the camels were evenly divided. Alex, Abdullah, Erdem and Private Munoz would accompany the expedition while Hassan, Ali, Pertag, and Nate would stay behind. Nate was devastated.

"Major Babcock."

"Yes, Mr. Wilkers." Nate was firmly planted with legs apart, like a bulldog. Slightly behind him, Private Munoz stood more sheepishly, his hat in hand.

"With all due respect, sir, Private Munoz and I would like to switch places. It would be better for the mission because

I'm more experienced with the camels. Also, Private Munoz's mother in San Antonio is sick. It would be a kindness if he could stay."

Impressed by Nate's unexpected assertiveness, Major Babcock agreed. When Hassan and Erdem approached two hours later to request a similar swap, he refused. Hassan was disappointed, but at least he would have Ali for company while the others were gone.

Alex could not contain his excitement about this first real outing with the camels. He envisioned an odyssey, a grand exploration into the impenetrable rough country of west Texas. The camels would be tested, would prove their inestimable value, and soon, shiploads of camels would be arriving every month. It was the chance of a lifetime.

But he dreaded being apart from Elizabeth, especially since she had been acting so strangely. Sometimes she was open, responsive, even overtly affectionate with him, but at other times hesitant, reserved or withdrawn. She seemed less composed when he and Hassan visited together, and once he caught her stealing glances at Hassan. Astonished, he became acutely aware of the way she acted in Hassan's presence, how she held her hands and the tilt of her head. He began to wonder if Elizabeth was developing feelings for Hassan, an unlikely but worrisome possibility. He was particularly upset that Hassan would remain at Camp Verde while he was away on a trip that could take weeks or months. Determined to see Elizabeth before he left, he pleaded with his uncle for one last visit to town.

When he reached San Antonio at dusk, he headed straight for the McDermott home, where he was warmly welcomed. After dinner, Elizabeth suggested that they relax in the courtyard. Somewhat awkwardly, they settled side by side on a bench and spread a light blanket across their knees against the evening chill.

"I'm really going to miss you, Alex."

"I'll miss you, too."

"It will be lonely around here with Cousin Babcock, you, and Nate away. Everyone except Hassan is going."

Alex twitched slightly at this. His mood changed subtly, and his voice took on a brittle quality. "Hassan and the other

Arabs will probably go home after we get back from the expedition. Or maybe when the next load of camels arrives."

This remark took Elizabeth unaware but she tried not to show surprise. "I suppose they must all be homesick by now."

"Yes, especially Hassan. He got engaged before he left Egypt, and he's chomping at the bit to go home and get married."

Feeling her stomach tighten at this unexpected news, she observed Alex closely. He was monitoring her reaction. What was he hoping to see? She resented this provocation and suspected a jealous motive.

"Well, congratulations to him. I guess it's been a long wait."

"He and Sula have known each other their whole lives. She's his third cousin or something like that. His family sounds fairly complicated."

Elizabeth tossed off a few lighthearted comments, but was angry that Alex had made such a point of telling her this and that Hassan had not mentioned it. Feigning fatigue, she proposed an early night. As she rose, Alex grabbed her hand.

"Elizabeth, I don't know how long we'll be gone, maybe a month or more. It depends on how the camels do. It would be great if you would tell me that you'll wait for me."

"Wait for you?"

"Yes, I mean, not let someone steal your affections while I'm gone."

"My affections are mine to give. They cannot be stolen."

"Of course. That's not what I meant. It's just that… well, since your father's death, I mean, there may be some pressure on you to marry, and who knows what your mother might say when she gets back, and, well…." Alex foundered, his usual flair with words completely absent. This was not going as he had planned.

"I will marry whom and when I wish, Alex Babcock, and I will wait for whomever I wish or for no one. I do not like your implication."

"Oh, Elizabeth, don't be cross with me. You know, you must know, of my feelings for you, and I would hope for a chance at your hand."

"Is that a marriage proposal? Right here on the veranda?"

"No, I mean, yes, I mean, I only want you to promise to wait for me until after the expedition."

"Perhaps, as you suggest, that is a matter to take up with me after you return. Good night, Alex."

By the time she arose the next morning, Elizabeth had softened. She realized how much she cared for Alex and wished she had not been so harsh with him. Unfortunately, he had already left for Camp Verde. Now agitated, she felt more confused than ever about Hassan and Alex. Assuming that Hassan would make Texas his home, she had never considered that he might have someone waiting for him. What had she been thinking? What, if anything, should she say to him when she next saw him? As for Alex, she had grown close to him, attached even. He cheered her, made her laugh and was solicitous of her needs, but did she love him like a husband or like a brother?

That Sunday at church, all her silent prayers were for guidance. After the service, when the family was dining at Sr. Jose Antonio Navarro's home, Antoine appeared breathless at the door. Elizabeth jumped up from her seat in anticipation. The look of consternation on his face made plain that he had not come to announce her mother's return from Galveston. Crestfallen, she asked, "Antoine, what is it?"

"Excuse me, Missy 'Lizbeth, there's a Mr. Kleinhart come to call."

"What? Is it the Mr. Kleinhart we've been looking for?"

"I dunno. I asked him to wait in the salon and came right over to tell you."

"You did well, Antoine. Let me make our excuses to Sr. Navarro, and then Zach and I will be right along. Have Esther offer him tea or a cool drink."

It had been all Antoine could do to be civil to Mr. Kleinhart. He doubted whether Esther would be able to serve him without throwing the drink in his face.

"Antoine, we have serious business with this man. There is nothing like hospitality to ease a discussion that might otherwise be fraught. Serve him well if you want us to have a chance to get Precious back."

Antoine nodded and turned smartly, thinking that Elizabeth had a good bit of her mother in her.

Mr. Kleinhart so little resembled Elizabeth's mental picture of him that she stumbled over the introductions. He was in his mid-twenties, simply dressed, and clean. Of medium height, his silhouette was rather like Nate's, with a sturdy build of muscle and strong hands. His blond hair reminded her of Alex and his straight Roman nose and sparkling brown eyes were the image of Hassan. In a brief insight she realized that she now compared any man she met to her three friends.

"Welcome to our home. I am Elizabeth McDermott, and this is my brother Zachary." Standing on the veranda out of sight, Esther and Antoine strained to hear every word.

"Ja, I am Hendrick Kleinhart. Very sorry about your father."

"Thank you, sir." Elizabeth was not about to show any vulnerability when delicate negotiations were in the offing. "You are well informed. You must also know that we are seeking the whereabouts of a slave called Precious."

"Ja, that is why I come. It is a sad story, and maybe you can help." His modest demeanor caught her off guard.

"We are at your disposal, Mr. Kleinhart. Please do tell us what you know of Precious."

"It is a long story."

"Please take your time."

In a rambling conversation, Elizabeth learned that Mr. Kleinhart was a German furniture maker who had emigrated to Indianola with his pregnant wife and young daughter. He had fallen in with the founders of Comfort, a tiny community established only two years earlier, where he had rented a room. Ambitious to buy his own land, he had traveled as an itinerant artisan, living frugally and saving as much as possible. While working in San Antonio, he had received the crushing word that his wife had died of a respiratory ailment. His customer, a Louisiana businessman, had commiserated. Monsieur Augustin found it untenable that a man should bear the responsibility of children without female help. Nevertheless, despite his

professed concern, Mr. Augustin absconded with the finished furniture without paying Mr. Kleinhart. Devastated,
angry, and broke, Mr. Kleinhart had returned to his children in Comfort.

"Ja, some time later two ugly men came to me with the
woman Precious. They claimed that Monsieur Augustin
sent her to me." Mr. Kleinhart squirmed. "I think she was
payment for the furniture."

"You did not purchase her?"

"No, definitely not, Miss McDermott. We at Comfort
are a cooperative. We are abolitionist. We would never
own a slave. Miss Precious was dirty and thin, and she
refused to speak. Ja, very sad. I convened a community
meeting. We decided that we must help her. It took us a
long time even to know her name. We have been caring for
her the best we can."

"Oh dear. How is she now, Mr. Kleinhart?"

"Better, but not strong. She gets up from her bed with
weakness. Ja, how to say, when she has fever she talks
nonsense. I understood the name McDermott and asked
everyone until I found you." He hesitated. "Miss McDermott, she is pregnant."

"Pregnant? Gracious! I suspect those awful men had
their way with her, if you'll excuse my frank speech. Hmm,
but I suppose it could be Samuel's baby."

"Samuel? She sometimes repeats that name."

"Another of our slaves, now deceased. He was especially close to Precious." Elizabeth sniffled and fought
back tears while she related their chance encounter with
the slavers, Samuel's attempt to rescue Precious, and his
fall from the horse.

"Miss McDermott. I am very sorry to hear this sad story.
It is even worse than we thought."

When Elizabeth produced the bill of sale that her mother had taken from Slim and Josiah, Mr. Kleinhart noticed
a small footnote: *as per G.A.* "The initials of the Louisiana
gentleman, Monsieur Augustin."

"It seems we've solved the mystery of how Precious was
delivered to you. But we still have no idea why she was on
our Brazos plantations. Perhaps she was sent to the fields

when our father rented out our home. Unfortunately, he will never be able to tell us." Thinking of her father, Elizabeth teared up again.

"I am sorry about your father. But please, what must we do? Precious was given to me and you have a bill of sale to prove it. I want to grant her freedom. As I said, we do not believe in slavery."

"But Miss McDermott, I do not know if she would be happy in our community. And at the moment, she is too ill."

Elizabeth reflected, but only for a moment. She knew exactly what she must do. "Mr. Kleinhart, I will come to Comfort. I must see Precious with my own eyes and determine her condition."

Zachary had been dutifully silent up to this point. "Sir, how far is Comfort?"

"About fifty miles."

Zach took seriously his assignment to watch over Elizabeth and spoke with great determination.

"Elizabeth, you shouldn't travel so far alone. I will come too, and we should bring Esther to care for Precious."

Elizabeth gave her brother an appraising look. "You're right Zach, you must come, but we'll take Agnes so that Esther can stay here with her girls. What about Antoine for the wagon?"

"No need. I can handle the wagon."

"All right. Mr. Kleinhart, my mother gave her word that we would retrieve Precious from the desolation in which we last saw her. Thanks to you, her circumstances are greatly improved. If I may say so, your character belies your name: you do not have a small heart at all."

"Thank you for your kindness, Miss. I plan to return the day after tomorrow."

"We shall make preparations. Mr. Kleinhart, we can't decide anything until we speak with her."

Jeremy Blackstone, though none too pleased with Elizabeth's plans, withheld his views and immediately commenced fussing. He checked every bolt and lashing on the wagon, felt every inch of the riggings for the horses, and inspected the wheels for cracks. He instructed Antoine on precisely the amount of fodder to pack for the horses in case the route lacked sufficient grazing and insisted that they carry double the amount of water they could possibly need. He offered detailed opinions on the food to be cooked on the road and how it should be packed to avoid spoilage. As if reading from a prescribed list, he asked Elizabeth repeatedly whether she had warm clothing against the chill nights and waterproof gear for the autumn rains. Had it not been so annoying to think he found her incapable of managing by herself, she would have found his behavior quaintly amusing.

"Elizabeth, do you and Zachary have your pistols? And Zachary a rifle?"

"Mr. Blackstone, that is thrice you have posed this question, and each time I have answered in the affirmative."

A smile crinkled his eyes. "All right, then, I guess y'all are ready. Make it as quick as you can. If your mama comes back, I'd prefer for you to do the explainin' yourself."

"Haha, yes, Mr. Blackstone, you have made your point."

Elizabeth reveled in her liberation. This trip was dictated neither by her family nor by the exigencies of the camel caravan but was wholly of her own volition. The first glorious day held a perfect temperature, fresh breezes, and a gigantic open sky with wisps of high clouds. When the temperature dipped that evening, she was grateful for the extra blankets, thinking she would have to express her appreciation to Mr. Blackstone and hoping that he wouldn't gloat. The following morning, when she poked her head out of the wagon, a blast of frigid air sent her ducking back under the covers. Agnes, although incapable of complex tasks, nevertheless could build a fire, boil water, and crack eggs, so Elizabeth was able to relax inside until breakfast was ready. Zachary, who was up and exploring in spite of the cold, called to her.

"You won't believe the color of this."

"The color of what?"

"The day! Come and look!"

Arranging her hair under a bonnet and draping herself in a woolen shawl, another item she might not have brought without Jeremy Blackstone's pestering, she crawled outside. The sky was split in half, as if sliced with a knife. Directly overhead and to the south, a sunny day beckoned, appealing and delightful, but to the north a dark, threatening charcoal roiled. A cloudbank, the color of gunmetal with midnight blue twinges, stretched from one end of the horizon to the other. Mesmerized, she turned her head first to one side, then the other. It was like standing on a precipice.

Mr. Kleinhart was nervous. "You are from the coast? This is your first time to see a blue norther, ja?"

"Yes, sir and no, sir." Zach's contradiction made Elizabeth laugh. "I mean, in Galveston, we get cold snaps, gray like this, and we can see 'em comin'. But I've never seen one this size, claimin' the whole landscape, like a curse marchin' towards us."

"It will bring heavy rain. When we feel the cold, the rain will be close behind. We must try to get to Boerne before it reaches us."

Elizabeth experienced the celestial turmoil as a blessing rather than a blasphemy. The untamed power of the storm invigorated her. The contrasting colors entranced. She thought that no painting could capture the play of light, that no music could recreate the wanton dominion, that only God could create such majesty and might, and she thanked Him for the spectacle. Luckily Mr. Kleinhart's estimations of the storm's progress proved too dire, and they proceeded without rain for the rest of the morning. Elizabeth celebrated the day.

By early afternoon, however, the wind picked up, determined and powerful. Billowing within itself, the lowering mass moved toward them, stalking, and at speed. Soon, the darkening overhead was complete, and the blue sky had retreated behind them into a thin line. The scene exploded dramatic and noisy, as great streaks of lightning leapt from the sky to the earth in a multidirectional dance. Some of the bolts even moved horizontally to create unique patterns. When the lightning was close, thunder clapped over them. This is when Elizabeth discovered that Agnes was afraid of thunder. Each boom from the sky received an echoing scream from Agnes, a single one, as if she were retaliating with her own threats.

Two miles outside Boerne the full force of the storm broke upon them, drowning the remnants of Elizabeth's joy. Frigid and relentless, the rain pounded hard. Zachary desperately wanted to retreat into the wagon with his sister, but he and Mr. Kleinhart were obliged to drive. Agnes trudged onward in her determined stroll, oblivious to the drenching. Conversation ceased as the two wagons struggled to advance in the downpour.

Their pace slowed to a crawl when the rocky parts of the road slicked over and the clay-based sections turned into a quagmire. More than once, they bogged down. Elizabeth had to climb out to help place planks under the wheels. These short, stubby boards had been another of Mr. Blackstone's requirements. Tempted to join Zachary in cursing the weather, Elizabeth fervently wished to be someplace warm and dry. Time dragged. Every foot of forward motion required strenuous effort, cajoling the horses, adjusting the boards, and pushing the wagons from behind. At last, soaked through to the skin and shivering, they rolled into Boerne, a hamlet almost invisible in the gray sheets of rain, where Mr. Kleinhart's friends welcomed them.

The next day, to Elizabeth's amazement, the norther was now to their south, and they were treated to a chill but sparkling day. It was as if the whole world had been cleansed and born fresh. She prayed it was an omen for the coming reunion with Precious.

San Antonio, that same day

S YLVIA McDERMOTT ABHORRED TRITE phrases, but could think of no other way to describe her transformation: she was a new woman. Whereas she had left San Antonio slouched and downtrodden, she returned perched straight and sure on the wagon seat. A refreshingly cool breeze enveloped her second arrival in the city, and the whitewashed adobe buildings sparkled. Knowing that this would be her home, she found the city utterly appealing.

She had paid dearly for her new resolve. She had cried enough tears to fill basin after basin. As if Quentin's death was not enough of a shock, her family's closest friends had betrayed her, seeking to pinch every penny and scoop up any shred of business that she might overlook. If Mr. Hurlinger had not helped to unravel the legal maneuvering, she would certainly have been taken advantage of. If Mrs. Eberly had not sustained her, she might have fallen into incurable despondency. Mrs. Eberly counseled perseverance. She urged practicality. Always, she insisted that Sylvia had the strength and wit to weather this storm, a conviction that buoyed.

Out of necessity, Sylvia discovered dormant skills acquired through years of observing her husband. She made hard decisions. She smiled and charmed her way out of some exceedingly complex business deals and into others. She analyzed numbers, estimated profit and loss, dissected contracts, and disentangled currency transactions. Zeke displayed a remarkable talent for sorting out what was really going on and what her husband had intended, but she was the one who faced down her opponents instead of playing the helpless widow. Her grief, temporarily driven out by the demands of her daytime activities, swooped in at night to deprive her of rest. Her complexion, once an irresistible peaches and cream, turned wan. When the weight of her responsibilities felt like a bale of wet cotton, she was tempted to yield. One day when she was particularly downtrodden and uncertain of every choice, she chanced to overhear two of her husband's business associates.

"I swear, she's exactly what you get with a red-headed woman."

"Yup, stubborn as can be. You can't pull anything over on her, either."

This comment revived her, supplying her with sufficient proof of success to face the good old boys of Galveston yet another day. She decided to sell the land on the Brazos River, surprising both Mrs. Eberly and Mr. Hurlinger.

"Sylvia," Byron Hurlinger was repeating himself. "The Brazos plantations provide your surest source of revenue.

You have some of the most desirable cotton land in the state."

"Then it should be easy to sell for a handsome profit."

"Mama, excuse me for speaking up."

"Go ahead, son. I've included you in these meetings for the express purpose of hearing what you have to say."

"I think Mr. Hurlinger is right. People say 'Cotton is king' for a reason. Everybody needs cotton and always will. Prices are rising. It's a sure thing."

"Cotton breeds a cruel form of slavery. It's hateful, and I do not care to own a part of it."

"But Mama, someone will own those plantations, and they will certainly treat the slaves worse than we do."

"We really don't know how our slaves are treated, do we? We are never there." Forced to admit the accuracy of that statement, Zeke had no reply. "Your father chose San Antonio. His last half dozen decisions took his business away from Galveston. He was moving inland to diversify beyond shipping, and so shall we."

"Mama, don't you want to come back here?"

"Back to this hornet's nest of intrigue and deceit? No. This place was our home, and we had many wonderful years here. But it's gone now. We shall cut as many ties as possible."

Sylvia felt wholeheartedly that her past life was over, and she wanted nothing that could draw her to Galveston. She believed without reservation in her husband's political acumen, and he had foreseen a war coming. A blockade of Galveston would certainly be attempted. If it came to that, cotton could plummet in value. If you couldn't ship it, you couldn't sell it.

"I want the plantation sold. We'll hold our New Orleans connections, and Byron, you may quietly explore alliances in Houston. Otherwise, our attention will be to Indianola and San Antonio."

Byron Hurlinger was used to dealing with the opinionated pronouncements of Quentin McDermott, but had not expected such feistiness from his wife. "All right, Sylvia, but it may be difficult to get a good price. People will see a distraught widow and try to secure a bargain."

"I want to hold out for top dollar. Let's sell to someone who is not from Galveston, someone whose entry into
the cotton market will cause consternation to our so-called
friends. What about that man, Major Greeson, that my husband recently met in Washington?"

"I'll draft a letter today."

The genuine sympathy in his regard caused Sylvia's tears
to flow again. "One last thing. Our house slaves shall not be
sold. I'll take them to San Antonio. Rebecca is the only one
remaining. Also Moses. He can take over Samuel's duties."

The final half dozen shipments were sold, profits realized, and all debts paid. The house was signed over to the
British Consul, a true gentleman with whom it had been
easy to negotiate a fair price. On a cloudy morning, she
departed Galveston without looking back. Six wagons carried her armoires, dining room table and sixteen chairs,
the four-poster bed that she had shared with Quentin, his
writing desk, her bookcases and library, along with a huge
assortment of lamps, linens, end tables, and salon chairs.
She also brought deeds to land, bills of sale for horses and
cattle, stacks of paper money, and, concealed among her
other possessions, gold in the form of both bullion and specie. The wagons and their drivers, rented from Mr. Wellbourne, would return to him laden with goods imported
from Mexico.

At Alamo Square, when they became mired behind
cattle being herded into the government holding pens, she
waved to Mary Maverick who came down from the porch
to welcome her. Sylvia waited without a hint of impatience
for the bottleneck to clear. Rather than being annoyed at the
cattle's smell and dusty disturbance, she inspected every aspect of the process. When sold to the Army, this herd would
bring a sizeable profit. She smiled, knowing that half the
cattle belonged to her. When at last they pulled into Laredo
Street, Zeke leapt from his horse, clanged the bell, and burst
in before Antoine could open.

"Young Massa Zeke! Miz Sylvia! Welcome home!"

Sylvia glanced around quickly. Everything appeared to
be in good order, but the house was too quiet. "Antoine,
where is everyone?"

"Esther took the girls to market, and Mr. Blackstone is workin' over at the Menger place."

"Where are Elizabeth and Zachary?"

Antoine took a deep breath. "They've gone off to a place called Comfort. Gone to see Precious. So sorry, Ma'am."

She took a deep breath. She was profoundly disappointed. Her apprehension about Elizabeth and Zachary trekking across country vied with her curiosity to know what had happened to Precious. "I can see that there's a lot to tell. Antoine, fetch Esther from the market and send one of the girls to tell Mr. Blackstone that we've returned."

Stepping out front to go for Esther, Antoine was taken aback by the wagon train. He was even more astonished to see Rebecca and Moses, who appeared dazed. "Y'all escape the plantation?"

"Thank God, yes." Rebecca smiled. "Y'all can't imagine. Plenty work and poor food. We was pulled outta there durin' harvest. I swear, pickin' cotton's like to kill a body. It sure is a blessin' to be gone from there."

Moses sulked. "Antoine, I left my Marybelle and three chillun, and we hear Miz Sylvia gonna sell the plantation."

"Sell the plantation?"

"No tellin' what that means. Grieves me somethin' terrible."

Antoine could see the ravages of worry. "Y'all get settled first."

"This the house? Don't look like much."

"It's better on the inside. Go round the corner and come in at the back. Esther'll be home soon."

When no one responded to the McDermott's bell, Jeremy Blackstone opened the door and went in. The house was a swarming beehive. Every spare corner was filled with a jumble of furniture, glassware, linens, and lamps. Bookcases chock full of costly leather volumes lined every wall, making hallways narrow and rooms crowded. He walked through to the courtyard where he found enormous piles of boxes, cartons, valises, and furniture. A large Army-style canvas tent was set up at the back corner, and two men were installing a raised wooden floor. The storeroom overflowed with barrels of corn, wheat, rice, and beans. He was amazed at the sheer quantity of goods being carted about and rearranged. Wondering how he had got mixed up with this family, he calculated that they were even wealthier than he thought.

Jeremy whistled under his breath. This was quite an operation, and Sylvia acted like the general in charge, a far cry from the grief-stricken and incapacitated woman he had last seen. He appraised her, as if for the first time. Not much taller than the tiny Mrs. Eberly, she was thinner than she had been and looked a bit more worn. Her fiery hair was unbonneted, and her upsweep threatened to come undone on one side. The sunlight revealed several strands of silver. Her eyes, mottled grey-green like a pond reflecting an oak's leaves, flashed here and there as her attention ranged over the scene. Although the toll of her grief was written in wrinkles around her eyes, she seemed somehow sturdy.

"Mr. Blackstone!" A warm smile spreading across her face, Sylvia walked briskly toward him with her hands extended. She took both of his and held them. "Mr. Blackstone, how kind of you to come. And what a pleasure to see you again!"

Surprised by her gesture and warm tone, he relaxed, unable to suppress a tiny smile in response. However, he replied in his usual quiet voice. "Miz McDermott, sure is good to see y'all safely back. I hope everythin' went well."

"Well enough, Mr. Blackstone, well enough." He noticed her eyes drifting sideways as a slight furrow appeared between her eyebrows. "What's done is done. San Antonio is our home now."

"That's good news, Miz McDermott."

"Mr. Blackstone, could I offer you some tea? And would you be able to sit with me to tell me what's happened with my children while I was away?

"Of course, Ma'am."

They remained outside on the veranda, where Sylvia could monitor the unloading while Zeke ran back and forth with questions and instructions, looking every bit a full grown man. By the time Jeremy had recounted all that he could remember about Elizabeth, Zachary, Major

Babcock, Alex, Nate, Hassan, the camels, and the bizarre story of Precious, the sun had already sunk below the courtyard walls. He noted with some surprise that this excessive amount of conversation had not displeased him. He had scarcely noticed the time passing.

"Mr. Blackstone, I'm so sorry. You must be late for your evening work with Mr. Menger."

"No, Ma'am. I have an assistant now, and I made arrangements before comin' over here. Cooked up some extra vittles, left instructions, and took the day off. I'm at your service."

"Well then, I insist that you join us for dinner."

"I'd be honored Ma'am, and then I'll pack my bags and move on back to the Menger place."

Sylvia let loose with a spontaneous, "Oh no!" Jeremy looked at her quizzically. "The house is so empty without Elizabeth and Zachary. I would be grateful if you would remain with us at least until my children return."

"Yes, Ma'am. I can do that."

The next morning, Jeremy was up and gone to work before breakfast. By the time Sylvia roused from a deep and refreshing sleep, the edge of a cloud formation could be seen to the north.

"Esther, look at that. I fear a storm's coming. And two of my children are out in it."

"Yes'm. But don't you worry none. Mr. Blackstone made 'em pack everythin' 'gainst the rain. Warm clothes, extra food and water, all kinds of things. They'll be fine."

Sylvia, once again impressed with Jeremy Blackstone, thanked him profusely when she saw him at dinner that evening, but was disappointed to learn that the rain might slow her children's progress. She would have to devise some way to cope with the fact that they could easily be gone for a week.

Camp Verde, the same day

N ATE WAS READY, BUT it seemed no one else was. He stood leaning against Ibrim, watching as the soldiers lined up the mule teams, tightened harnesses, lashed bedrolls, and tossed forgotten items into saddlebags. The cook bellowed a complaint about a missing pot and cursed loudly to dispatch one of the privates on a quest to find it. Lt. Halter, clutching a checklist, responded to inquiries from Major Babcock while doing his best to hold himself above the fray. Sgt. Bly, although he would remain behind, nevertheless found ways to prance about with an air of importance. At the center of the commotion, Captain Chisholm barked orders on all sides, trying to organize the chaos before him. At least his commands, unlike those of Major Babcock, were heeded. To think the Major had hoped for an early morning departure!

Nate took a deep breath. Pertag, as usual, was nowhere to be seen, while Abdullah, Ali and Erdem were busy adjusting the camel saddles. They checked that the loads of grain, water, and supplies were carefully balanced, testing and retesting each item's placement. In a minute he would lend them a hand, but first he took a moment to assess his own preparations for the umpteenth time. He regretted that Hassan, who had been sent on some frivolous errand, was not in camp to witness the expedition's send-off. In the last two weeks, he and Hassan had made a round of deliveries to their customers in the surrounding countryside to assure them of continuity while Nate was away. Elizabeth had agreed to maintain relations with their suppliers and to keep her eyes open for new goods to sell. They had pooled their money, and Nate looked forward to a share of the profits upon his return.

During his last trip to San Antonio, he had taken leave of his grandfather, who had been uncharacteristically voluble. Nate had never received so much unsolicited advice in such a short period of time. After reciting an interminable list of recommended provisions, Jeremy pulled out several pouches of dried herbs and set forth to explain each one. He then launched into a detailed review of the basic principles of first aid before presenting Nate with a satchel containing bandages, liniments, alcohol, tweezers, a scalpel, and assorted medical implements. The instructions were going on so long that Nate began to take offense. Would his grandfather never see him as a grown man, but always treat him like a child? When Nate was about to say something to that effect, Jeremy cut him off.

"One more thing Nate. I understand that you're in your prime and you can handle most anything that comes at you. But it's a heck of a lot easier if a man has the right tools. You've got your Colt and your gear, but you also need knowledge. That's why I'm tellin' you this stuff that I know full well you already know."

Disarmed, Nate laughed. "Thanks, Grandpa. I was just thinkin' somethin' like that."

Jeremy smiled for an instant and then became serious again. Nate could feel Jeremy's cautious nature threatening to descend on him.

"Son, the hardest part, the unpredictable part, is how other people will behave out there in the wilds. Some folks can't abide deprivations. Some get scared and others get bossy. You gotta watch 'em all close. Help folks out when you can, and avoid lettin' your temper rise, even when the other fella deserves it."

"Yes, yes, Grandpa. I will."

"One more thing."

"Grandpa, I swear you said 'one more thing' already a few 'things' ago!"

"This is the last thing." Jeremy let out a big sigh and looked directly into Nate's eyes. "You're a man, and a fine one at that. I couldn't be more proud."

Taken aback by this unexpected approval, Nate hugged his grandfather close. "I'll tell you a hundred stories when I get back."

"You do that, son. You do that."

As he smiled at the recollection, Nate concluded that he really was ready, but chaos still reigned at Camp Verde. If they would ever depart, he'd better do something. He walked over to help Abdullah.

Abdullah was thoroughly pleased that the caravan would soon be in motion, especially in a direction that would take him away from Sgt. Bly. The past few weeks had been a torment. Sgt. Bly, Pertag, and their cohorts had stepped up their bullying of the camel keepers and their allies. The two groups ate separately and lounged around different campfires. They had even rearranged the bunkhouse with an unofficial dividing line between the factions, although this development had no effect on those who slept in the lean-to. Most vexing, Major Babcock, Lt. Halter, and Capt. Chisholm were either completely oblivious or simply unwilling to take charge.

Feeling almost as imprisoned as he had in Indianola while waiting for his tribunal, Abdullah longed for the moment of exodus from camp. For days, he, Alex, Nate, and Erdem had spent each morning with Major Babcock selecting the camels that would accompany the expedition, drawing up lists of provisions, and modifying their plans repeatedly. Too often, a decision made in the evening would be altered the following morning. Abdullah could not determine whether this was due to Major Babcock's indecisiveness or to subterfuge orchestrated by Sgt. Bly. Regardless of the reason, the waffling drove him crazy.

There were endless debates about what the camels should carry and what goods should be relegated to the mules. Major Babcock worried about how the camels might respond to the unknown terrain and was reluctant to overload them. The soldiers mostly preferred the mules. As a result, the mules carried excess weight and within a day or two, some of it would probably have to be transferred to the camels. Abdullah counseled Nate and Alex to leave room on each camel for added items.

"Abdullah!"

"Yes, Major Babcock?"

"We must take two more camels, but don't load them. I want these animals in reserve."

"Yes, sir." Abdullah exhaled slowly. A few days ago his recommendation to take extra camels had been roundly rejected. Now at the last minute, Major Babcock changed his mind. It was so typical. Erdem and Nate finished adjusting the packsaddles and Alex lashed his gear. The camels were ready. It only remained for the riders and mules to be set.

The sun approached high noon before the caravan was poised to depart. Major Babcock, savoring his moment of glory, sat regally at the front of a long train consisting of some fifteen camels, thirty-five mules, and twenty riders. Alex couldn't have been more thrilled. This was the moment he had been waiting for, ever since he had stepped foot in his first dusty camel kraal in Alexandria. For Nate, the moment was more complicated, filled with excitement but also trepidation. The camels offered a promise, a hint of possibility. This expedition could hold the key to his life's direction. Or it might become little more than a memorable adventure.

Major Babcock raised his hand, signaling the bugler to call the group to order. "All hail! The United States Camel Cavalry hereby commences its first extended expedition. We embark on a historic mission to test the camels in vital service to our country. Hearken to this momentous occasion!" He pointed ahead. "Forward ho!"

Nate, Alex, and Erdem whooped and waved their hats in the air, while Abdullah limited his response to a modest grin. As the camels stepped out, Alex tossed his hat high, barely catching it as it floated back down. The cheering continued, and those who were to remain behind clapped enthusiastically. Abdullah suspected that many of these soldiers were happy to see half the camels leaving Camp Verde.

The procession snaked out of the valley alongside the creek that meandered toward the west. Alex waved one last time, then turned his attention forward. What a sight they were! He wished that he could draw a picture to capture the unusual procession. Then he remembered that the American they had left in Smyrna was a gifted sketch artist. Due to arrive with the second camel shipment, Gwynne Heap would surely make many drawings to capture the camels for posterity. But for now, Alex tried to memorize every detail, aided by the clear light that etched the scene with crystalline precision.

Major Babcock and two of his officers on horseback trotted ahead, followed by the camels padding calm and orderly. The camels had been positioned at the front of the caravan on the theory that the majority of the horses and mules would be more relaxed seeing the camels before them rather than picking up their scent from the rear. Also, the camels tended to cover ground more quickly. The experienced handlers were spread out among the camels, each riding one with an additional two or three in train. Nate on Ibrim was first. Then came Erdem on Adela, Alex riding Perguida, and at the back, Abdullah astride Ayesha with one leg crossed in front, sitting straight, his face at last beaming with satisfaction. Alex laughed out loud. He hadn't seen anything but a scowl from Abdullah for so long he had come to doubt whether Abdullah could still smile.

Less than a mile from camp, the expedition turned north toward Kerrville, stopping for the night after only thirteen miles. According to Major Babcock, the short distance allowed time to test the camel saddles and repack them if necessary. Although Kerrville had seen an occasional camel before, the size of this caravan attracted considerable attention. The assembled citizens pointed, laughed, and shouted as the camels traversed the town to make camp on the other side. Abdullah was relieved that, for once, Major Babcock did not organize camel rides.

The women of Kerrville could not be restrained from offering gifts of food. Loaves of hearty rye bread were delivered along with samplings of jam, butter, and fragrant sausages. One industrious soul enlisted her two sons to drag into camp a cart loaded with an immense cauldron of steaming potato soup. After serving the officers, she ladled out generous portions to the soldiers. The men were especially charmed by three pretty young women who presented them with small German cookies made of pecans and sugar. They guessed, quite correctly, that this would be their last sweet treat for many days to come.

Major Babcock intended to follow known routes for the most part, wishing to test the camels in the terrain rather than to forge new paths. He planned a loop. After Rock Springs, he would push westward to Beaver Lake, then on to Howard Springs before heading northwest to Fort Lancaster. They would continue to Comanche Springs, their furthest point, before turning back southwest toward the Rio Grande. At Ciudad Acuna, they would proceed east through Uvalde and Hammer's Station to the new cavalry camp, Sabinal.

Before reaching Castroville, they would turn back north through Bandera Pass toward Camp Verde. In total, the trip was estimated at 600-700 miles. If they made twenty miles a day, Major Babcock counted about a month for the journey. Allowing for unexpected delays, he figured six to eight weeks and hoped they might be back in time for Christmas.

The next day the caravan faced away from the sunrise to pursue the Guadalupe River toward their first destination, a natural watering place called Rock Springs, about eighty miles west. With the citizens of Kerrville watching and waving, they once again formed up and moved out with pomp. Alex Babcock was ecstatic.

"Yee haw! Let's go make history!"

COMFORT, TEXAS, THE NEXT DAY

THE SETTLEMENT WAS BARELY a crossroads, a tiny hamlet that nevertheless presented a neat and orderly appearance. The few dwellings were fronted with short picket fences framing well-tended gardens. Flowerbeds, mostly dormant, ran parallel to flourishing vegetable patches. A cornucopia of winter squashes, cabbages, and Brussels sprouts hinted at warm soups. The overall effect was inviting, but the town was miniscule and too far out in the wilderness for Elizabeth's taste. After hearing Mr. Kleinhart's tale of Indians in the environs, she kept her pistol close.

They pulled up in front of a small limestone building that looked sturdy, if a bit airless. There was no porch or veranda as with coastal houses, nor a courtyard in the center as with San Antonio adobe homes. Neither did the architecture follow the typical Texas "dog trot" style of two living areas connected by a covered breezeway. The house was a square box. Although it would certainly prevent the entry of chill autumn air, Elizabeth suspected it could become an oven in summer. Still, she admired the details that bespoke good workmanship, like the capstone over the front entrance and hand-carved wooden shutters to protect real glass windows.

Mr. Kleinhart called out, and in an instant, two cherubic children tumbled from the house squealing, "Papa! Papa!" They babbled mostly in German with a few English words thrown in. An older woman appeared in the doorway. She smiled and wiped her hands on her colorfully embroidered apron before stepping out to greet them.

"Willkomen, willkomen, Herr Kleinhart." After a brief exchange in which the woman was no doubt inquiring about the unexpected guests, she turned to Elizabeth and Zachary. "Willkomen, kommen Sie bitte herein."

"This is Frau Graubunden. She and her family have been caring for my children and for Precious while I was away in San Antonio. She understands English, but she is shy to speak it."

"Thank you, Mrs. Graubunden. We appreciate your hospitality to us and to our slave, Precious."

Mr. Kleinhart flinched at the continuing reference to Precious as a McDermott slave.

"I found her!" Agnes had slipped into the house unnoticed and located Precious. Mr. Kleinhart rushed in, followed closely by Elizabeth and Zachary. In the back room they discovered Agnes cradling Precious in her arms while making tuneless humming sounds. Elizabeth was relieved to see Precious in a much-improved state, lying in bed wearing a spotless blue cotton nightgown under a warm floral coverlet. She was clean, her hair washed and braided. A pitcher of water stood on a nightstand, and there were slippers on the floor. On the opposite side of the room was another bed that Elizabeth surmised belonged to the children. Precious still looked undernourished, but the warm chestnut color of her skin had returned. All in all, she seemed comparatively healthy given what she had been through.

Feeling a bit like an intruder, Elizabeth waited in the doorway while Agnes murmured to Precious, who sighed occasionally as if not fully aware of her surroundings. Finally Precious cracked open her eyes.

"Agnes, Agnes. Is it you?"

"It's me."

She gasped. "I can't believe it. Agnes, Agnes, tell me. Samuel?"

Agnes shook her head, and Precious started to cry. "I knew it. I seen him. My man. Comin' for me. I seen him."

She sobbed for a moment, her head buried. Then she leaned back, looking Agnes full in the face for the first time. "Agnes, how you find me? How you get here?"

"Missy 'Lizbeth bring me." Still a bit confused, Precious noticed Zachary and Elizabeth. She pushed into a more upright position, which Elizabeth took as a sign to enter the room.

"Precious, we've been looking for you high and low ever since that horrible day when we saw you on the wagon. We're sorry it took so long to find you. How are you keeping?"

"Good, Missy. These folks been kind to me." Precious was instantly alert and cautious.

"My mother will be very sorry that she couldn't come here herself. She's been so worried about you. But she had to go back to Galveston for a while. You see, our father has died."

"Massa Quentin dead?"

"Yes, of the fever."

"Too bad, Missy. I can't believe it. How your mama doin'?"

"It's been hard for all of us. But we're here to take care of you. Mr. Kleinhart says that you are, um, expecting, and that it has been difficult for you. We can bring you back to San Antonio with us to have the baby where Esther can care for you, or if you feel too poorly, we can leave Agnes here."

Precious tried to think, but the suddenness was too much for her. She had assumed she would never see the McDermotts again and had come to accept that Samuel must have died. She spent what little mental energy she had trying to understand Mr. Kleinhart and the peculiar town she was living in. Now she was being presented with a choice, the gravity of which was obvious but the consequences obscure. She was completely out of the habit of choosing. The last time she had made any decision about her own life was when she had decided to watch the sunset from the back porch of the Galveston house, before Quentin McDermott had come home drunk, before everything solid in her life had disintegrated.

"Missy, I dunno."

"I understand. It's all too unexpected, and you are not well. Take your time and rest now. We'll talk about it later."

Mr. Kleinhart interjected, "Ja, Precious. Our guests have come far to find you. Let me give them something to eat. Then we come back."

As they went outside for the canned peaches and a slab of bacon that Elizabeth had brought as gifts for their host, Zachary pulled Elizabeth aside. He swore that Precious had smirked when hearing of their father's death. The nasty expression had been fleeting and almost indiscernible, but nonetheless contemptuous.

"Come now, Zach. You couldn't have seen that. Why would Precious harbor hostile sentiments toward any of us?"

"She probably blames Father for sending her to the fields."

"Of course. Why didn't I think of that? Maybe we can ask if she knows why she was sent, but for now we'll have to let it go. She's too weak for that kind of talk."

"You're right. Say, did you see the way Mr. Kleinhart smiled at Precious? Enough to warm the whole room."

"Zachary, you have a powerful imagination today!"

"No, I don't. I'm watchin' while you're talkin'. There's somethin' between them. You wait and see."

"That would be quite extraordinary. Unthinkable, really. But I'll pay closer attention. Let's go inside before we appear rude."

Refreshed by Mrs. Graubunden's bounteous lunch of warm vegetable soup, slices of cold ham, boiled cabbage, fresh bread and hot tea, Elizabeth brought up the subject that had been weighing on her since they left San Antonio. "Mr. Kleinhart, I had occasion to speak with Sr. Navarro about Texas law regarding slaves and free blacks. Did you hear about the law passed this year?"

"No, Miss, until Precious came here I had no reason to know anything about slaves."

"Well, it's illegal for free black folks to come to Texas, and manumitted slaves are required to leave. This worries me. If you grant Precious her freedom, she may be forced to leave the state."

Zachary inhaled, shocked. "That can't be right. If people are free, they should be able to live where they choose."

"That's what I was told. And worse, there's a proposal to require every free black to sign on with a white protector. Anyone who fails to do so would be arrested and sold into slavery."

"Impossible! If a man is free, how can he suddenly be a slave? Because of skin color?" Mr. Kleinhart was outraged.

"It's not a law yet, but..."

"But I can see the intention. The sentiments of the people here..." He shook his head angrily. "Our people fought for freedom in Germany. For us, this is unbelievable."

Fortunately for Elizabeth, who had no idea how to respond, the Kleinhart children rushed into the room. "A camel, Papa! At Frau Altgelt's house!" They dashed back out again.

"Camel?"

"Ja, Zachary, the camp is only ten miles away. The captain's wife often buys vegetables from us. Do you wish to see?"

Zach had already leapt from his chair, and when Elizabeth nodded, he was gone in a flash. She followed him, doing her best to appear dispassionate when in fact her heart was pounding.

A single camel knelt patiently in front of the Altgelt home. Elizabeth wasn't sure which one it was, but it was definitely not Ibrim, so the rider was unlikely to be Nate. At the side garden, Mrs. Altgelt was energetically pulling vegetables and carefully laying them in a large basket while chatting to the rider, whose back was turned. With one glimpse of that silhouette—the long legs, the confident stance, and the curly black hair—she knew it was Hassan. She stopped in her tracks to catch her breath. Mr. Kleinhart spoke in rapid German to Mrs. Altgelt, who rotated to greet Elizabeth, causing Hassan also to turn.

"Eleezabet!"

Mr. Kleinhart and Mrs. Altgelt looked at Hassan sharply, whereupon he covered his awkwardness by removing his hat.

"Hassan, what a surprise. How nice to see you." Elizabeth mustered her manners. "Mrs. Altgelt, pleased to make your acquaintance. As I've told Mr. Kleinhart, our family traveled with the camel caravan."

Zachary burst around back shouting, "It's Massanda! She's my favorite camel." Everyone laughed. While Zachary and the Kleinhart children stayed outside with Massanda, Mrs. Altgelt invited the others, including Hassan, for tea.

Mr. Kleinhart explained, "Mr. Altgelt is one of the founders of our community. Perhaps he can offer advice."

Hassan was glad to learn that Precious was safe and hoped to tell her of Samuel's deep affection for her. When the talk moved to Texas law regarding slaves, he devoted considerable attention to the extraordinary conversation. He gradually comprehended that these laws would deem him a quadroon, possibly subject to enslavement. His efforts to concentrate on this appalling revelation were hampered by Elizabeth's presence. His gaze drifted to her slender ankle, revealed when she tapped her foot to emphasize a point. He stole furtive glances at her wrists and admired the dainty pink patches on her cheeks. Her sparkling blue eyes, ignited by a fire of righteous indignation when she spoke of Precious, were irresistible. So engrossed was he that he almost missed her change of subject.

"Thank you so much, Mr. Altgelt. I think you're right. Precious should stay here until her child is delivered, presuming that is her wish."

"I believe it is, but we will ask her."

"Agnes can stay here to help."

"That is most kind. I am sure her presence will reassure Precious. You are also welcome to stay as long as you like."

"Thank you. I am so grateful for your advice, but I wish I knew what my parents would say. I miss them so much."

"Yes, it is a shame."

"Oh, my goodness!" She said this as if the thought had suddenly occurred to her, when in fact the idea had been germinating for more than an hour. "Our cousin, Major Babcock! I would feel so relieved to hear his views. He's likely to know what my mother would recommend."

"Camp Verde is only ten miles away, but the road is rough. If you and Zachary take your wagon tomorrow morning, you could arrive by evening."

"Hassan, do you know when Major Babcock's expedition to the west will depart?"

"I am sorry, no. I took a message to Fort Mason, and I have been away from Camp Verde for several days. Maybe today or tomorrow. Perhaps they have left already."

"I so wish to speak with him. Is the road really bad?"

Hassan replied. "Very slow for a wagon, but a camel is much faster."

"A camel! Oh! I have an idea. Maybe Hassan could take me to Major Babcock today. Zach could come on the wagon tomorrow to fetch me back. What do you think?" She directed her question to Mr. Altgelt.

"You could reach the camp today on a horse. I don't know about the camel."

Hassan rallied. "I can take her on the camel. We will be there before dark. I think Major Babcock will send someone back with her tomorrow. Zach does not have to bring the wagon."

Mr. Altgelt was unsure. "Yes, that might work. But aren't you afraid to ride the camel?"

Elizabeth smiled. "Not at all. On the trip to San Antonio I rode them several times."

"Perhaps it is better for you to go now, on the camel." With Mr. Altgelt's pronouncement, the decision was made.

Elizabeth prepared a few things for overnight, imagining as she made her selections what Mr. Blackstone would advise. When Zachary argued with a pout that he should accompany her on a horse, she explained that the horse could not keep up with the camel. She tried not to say too much. She feared Zach's newfound ability to draw conclusions from small details.

She needn't have worried. Zachary acted the jealous younger brother but hoped she would not observe the false note in his complaint. He wished desperately to be left in Comfort. He wanted to have frank conversations with these people, to learn what abolitionists were really like. He was fascinated by their ideas on co-operative living. Although young, he thought deeply, and could not justify the institution of slavery in his own mind. However, he never felt able to articulate his minority views in the face of adult reasoning. Apart from once hearing Alex Babcock expound the abolitionist rationale, he had never talked with anyone opposed to slavery. He wanted Elizabeth to be gone for more than one night.

Hassan lashed the vegetable basket on one side of the camel and added Elizabeth's bag to his own things on the other. After helping her up, he climbed on behind and gave Massanda the signal to rise. He set Massanda to a trot until they were out of sight of Comfort, then let her slow to a walk.

"Elizabeth, are you comfortable? Was it too much bouncing? Going too fast?" He spoke to the back of her head. She had been leaning forward, clinging to the saddle, and he got the impression she was trying not to touch him.

She twisted her head in response. "I'm fine, but I'm more comfortable at this pace. Will we reach the camp in time?"

"Yes, yes. We'll be there before dark."

Elizabeth was in turmoil. She wanted to ask Hassan whether he really planned to go home to Egypt, whether he was truly engaged to be married. So accustomed had she become to his regular visits, to her shopping trips with him and Nate and Alex, and to their long talks about the meaning of life and faith that she could not imagine how incomplete she would feel without him. And yet, he had failed to tell her his critically important plans. Strictly speaking, he had not been dishonest, but he had certainly held back the whole truth. How could she bring up such difficult subjects?

How indeed, on a magnificent day when she was happily ensconced with Hassan on a camel? As Massanda settled into a smooth gait, Elizabeth rocked gently to and fro, gradually relaxing until she leaned back against Hassan. He inclined toward her, although he did not put his arm around her. He kept one hand on the camel's reins while the other rested on his knee. Their bodies melded together, swaying in harmony to the cadence of the camel. A flood of well-being came over Elizabeth, a warmth that spoke to her of hearth and home. She was utterly certain that she belonged with this man on this camel at this moment, regardless of what the future might hold. She had no desire to fracture this exquisite experience by talking about how it would all end.

Instead she pointed wordlessly at a great blue heron on the wing and traced its languid movement with her fingers. Hassan gestured at a late-blooming stand of summer wildflowers, riotously red against a scraggy rock face. Elizabeth identified them as Indian paintbrushes, and they speculated about the origin of this name. They surprised a lizard sunbathing in the middle of the track. It revived from its somnolence in a skittering escape that set them laughing. Elizabeth was entranced by the view of the countryside from the seven-foot height of a camel. Her visual perspective expanded and allowed her to feel a sense of possibility. From time to time she sighed with contentment, enjoying the rhythm of the camel's steps and of Hassan's heartbeat.

"Hassan, excuse me, but could we stop for a moment? I would like to, hmm, refresh myself."

"Of course." Massanda knelt within nibbling distance of a mesquite bush, as pleased as a kitten with a saucer of milk. Elizabeth descended with Hassan's help. She welcomed his reach for her waist and marveled at the elation that coursed through her when he lifted her off the camel.

"I'll go over here behind a rock." She stepped a few feet into the bush, and unhappy that Hassan could still see her, walked further in.

Hassan watched her movement, still feeling the heft of her as she slid off the camel, still sensing the curve in her waist. She carefully stepped around the brambles and over rocks, balanced and sure on her feet. He had visions of the form of her legs and buttocks underneath her flowing skirt. Aware that he was staring, he turned his back to her and forced his thoughts to less exciting subjects. He emptied his own bladder toward the opposite side of the trail and waited patiently for some sound to indicate that Elizabeth had finished. He couldn't help thinking how much easier it was to be a man. Female anatomy seemed so complicated when it came to basic bodily functions. He waited and waited until, feeling foolish like a lost traveler, he decided to turn around. He saw no trace of Elizabeth. She had apparently found the privacy she required.

A shot rang out. Elizabeth's head popped up from behind a boulder, and she screamed, "Hassan!"

With long strides he raced to her side, whereupon she turned toward him and fell into his arms. Almost immediately she pulled away and pointed with a gun in her hand.

"Look, look. I got him. A rattler. A big one."

Hassan had heard stories about the poisonous snakes of Texas but had yet to see one. Fearing the worst, he pulled her toward him in a tight embrace. "Are you all right? Did it bite?"

"No, no I'm fine. But I'm so stupid. I should have looked. I was trying so hard to find a secluded spot, that I didn't screen the area properly. Then I heard the rattling. Fortunately, I've kept my pistol in my waistband ever since we reached Comfort. I had to move so slowly not to startle the snake. I aimed and shot. And I hit it! All those practice sessions were worth it. My brothers will be so proud of me."

She was talking rapidly. When she started shaking, Hassan held her at arms length, looking her over. "Are you sure it didn't bite you?"

"Yes, yes." She was shivering and crying softly. "But I admit it was scary. I guess it's just now hitting me. I feel a little weak."

He hugged her close again. "All right, let's stay here for awhile. You will soon feel stronger. Over there is an open place. Let me walk with you there. I can bring a blanket for us to sit on."

"Good idea, and I have some jerky and biscuits. Can you bring those too?"

"Yes, and I'll get water."

When she tried to walk, Elizabeth realized that her undergarments were still down about her ankles. They both burst into laughter, though Hassan worried that Elizabeth sounded unnaturally giddy.

"You go ahead," she said. "I can walk over there on my own."

Hassan brought Massanda to the clearing, had her kneel, and spread a blanket next to her. Before he could retrieve the food and water, Elizabeth sat on the blanket, leaned against the camel, and fell fast asleep. Hassan stepped to the side, took a little water, and continued to watch her closely.

In about ten minutes, she opened her eyes. "Hassan, I'm so sorry. I don't know what came over me. I guess I was more shaken by that snake than I thought."

"Here, take a drink of water."

"Thank you." She swallowed big gulps.

As she started to rise, Hassan took her hand. "Come. I want to show you something."

"Oh my! What a spectacular view!" The clearing proved to be the flat top of an outcropping that plunged down for fifty feet. They sat with their legs dangling over the side, admiring the valley spread out before them and nibbling on their snacks.

"It's amazing. We're as high as the treetops. Where I grew up in Galveston, it's so flat. I could never imagine a view like this."

"My home is the same. Flat. To get up high, we must go near Cairo and climb the Pyramids."

The mention of Hassan's home gave her an opening, but still, she was unwilling to bring up her fears. She took a swig of water and swallowed hard. "Hassan, is it true that you will go home soon?"

"We are supposed to go after the next camels arrive."

"Oh dear! My uncle said that could be January or February. It's already November. Don't you want to stay here?"

Hassan stared at the horizon, torn. At any other time, he counted the days until he could go home to his family, to familiar food, and to his Sula. But when he was with Elizabeth, all that faded, and he imagined he could live here with her in great contentment. "My home calls me, it is true. I miss my parents and grandparents, my Auntie Fatima, so many people. I sometimes feel very alone without them. But I am also happy here with you."

"I see."

"Eleezabet, can you imagine living far from your family?"

"No, I guess I can't. I haven't really thought about it that way. I've been thinking only that I don't want you to go back."

"My family expects me to return. I do not wish to disappoint them. Do you think you could make your home in Egypt with me?"

Elizabeth jumped up, agitated. "My goodness, what a question! How could that possibly work?"

"I'm not sure. We could be married, but it might be hard for you. Everything is different: our language, what we eat, how we dress."

She stood with her back to him, fighting back tears, moved by his feelings for her. Had she heard him correctly? Had he suggested she go to Egypt as his wife? What an utterly unrealistic notion. Its improbability sobered her.

"What was I thinking, wishing for us to be together? There's no way for that to happen. You will not stay here, and I cannot go there."

Hassan moved to stand beside her, but she did not turn to look at him. He spoke softly. "When my grandfather traveled as a young man, he brought back a foreign wife. It can be done. She is happy in Egypt, and the whole family loves her deeply." He carefully avoided saying anything about his Grandma Ara's origins or skin color.

"Really?"

"Yes, but she is a Muslim, so that made it easier."

"Are you implying that I would have to convert? That's impossible."

"I know. I would not ask you. There are many Christians in Alexandria, so you could worship freely. But it would be easier for my family if we were both Believers."

"Or you could convert. How does that sound? It would be easier if we both accepted Jesus Christ. You don't like that idea too much, do you?"

"No. But you would not ask me, would you? No more than I would ask you."

"I suppose not. I guess we're stuck. Doomed, like star-crossed lovers in some ancient tale. We must live separated by oceans and continents."

Her voice was tremulous, bordering on shrill, and her eyes were damp. Hassan moved closer, embraced her gently, and led her by the hand over to Massanda. He motioned to the blanket.

"Let's rest here awhile. It is a beautiful day, and who can predict the future?" They settled with their backs against the camel, the afternoon's rays on their faces. "Perhaps we will find a way, Inshallah."

"I can't see how. But you are right, the day is lovely, and I am happy to be with you now. Perhaps we will find a way, God willing."

Another wave of exhaustion came over Elizabeth. As she leaned against Massanda, her eyes fell shut. Hassan held her hand, while the two dozed. Surrounded by low bushes, the napping picnickers were completely invisible to anyone who might have passed on the road. Had they been spotted, they would have made a most astonishing sight: a man and a woman, huddled against a camel, cozy and relaxed.

A sharp cry of a hawk overhead jerked them both to consciousness. Suddenly awake, each was acutely aware of the other. They turned and kissed long and passionately. Neither could say who had initiated it. It seemed a form of spontaneous combustion. The tinder of their repressed desires caught, and that one kiss was completely insufficient. They held each other tight and kissed again. Hassan ran his finger along the edge of her cheek and down her neck. Elizabeth had never felt such a rush of sensation, from her toes to her fingertips and everywhere in between including a most startling tingle in her groin.

Hassan slid down on his back and pulled her on top of him. She lay floating, conscious of each precise point where his body touched hers. Feeling his arousal, her own magnified. She planted tiny kisses all over his face, while his arms enveloped her. When he slid his hands down her back to her buttocks, she gasped.

The rain cloud caught them unawares, even though the northern sky had been darkening for some time. The first few drops, large and cold, smacked Elizabeth hard on the back, but she barely noticed. When a rat-tat-tat of wet pelted Hassan in the face, he forced himself to look away from Elizabeth.

"Oh no! Rain! Looks like a big one coming."

"No, no. It's a beautiful day," she replied dreamily.

"It *was* beautiful. Now it's a storm. We must go." Hassan lifted her aside, kissed the top of her head, and urged her onto Massanda while he stowed their gear.

Elizabeth shuddered. "What blasted timing. I wish I could swear like a man."

Hassan laughed and kissed her again. "I am very happy for you to do nothing like a man!"

Elizabeth grabbed her woolen shawl from her bag, wrapping it closely against the persistent wind. In a few minutes a frigid rain descended in torrents. Hassan mounted Massanda.

"I must sit in front to see the road. Drape the blanket over my shoulders. If you sit close to me under it, you will stay dry."

The last few miles to Camp Verde were desolate. Elizabeth's only joy was that she had her arms around Hassan's waist and her head against his back. She shivered from the cold. In a way, the rain had been a blessing, God's weather protecting them. It was best that they had been interrupted, because in truth there was no future for them. She would have to get used to the idea. Even as she determined to be grateful for God's mysteries, her tears sprang forth, mixing with the rain that trickled in though every gap in her makeshift tent. Clinging to Hassan, she vowed to give up her illusions about him and to marry Alex. She would speak with Alex at Camp Verde and try to make up for her harshness when she had last seen him in San Antonio.

By the time they reached the camel camp, the blustery part of the storm had ceded to a quiet, steady rain. Hassan commanded Massanda to kneel in front of the officers' quarters. Mrs. Chisholm, expecting her vegetables, rushed out to find a sopping Elizabeth McDermott.

"My goodness! Come in, dear. Let's get you dry." The light from the house beckoned with the promise of warmth, but Hassan was not invited in. "Thank you for the vegetables, Hassan."

"Yes, Ma'am."

Elizabeth glanced in Hassan's direction but did not meet his gaze. "Good night, Hassan. Thank you for the ride."

The flat tone in her voice unnerved him. "Good night, Eleezabet." In spite of the continuing rain, he tipped his hat. He caught a glimpse of her rueful smile as she turned away.

During dinner with Captain and Mrs. Chisholm and Lt. Halter, Elizabeth learned to her great disappointment that the expedition had left the day before, taking Major Babcock, Alex and Nate. She picked at her food. Unwilling to satisfy anyone's curiosity, she said merely that she had a family matter to discuss with Major Babcock. She retired early only to sleep fitfully, her head full of slaves and rattle-snakes, Alex and Hassan, and camels.

A nameless soldier escorted her back to Comfort at first light.

San Antonio, later that week

E VER WORRIED ABOUT HER absent children, Sylvia McDermott launched into a whirlwind of activity. She bought a large tract of land, about a dozen lots, in a newly developing area south of the river. Having sent letters from Galveston to put the purchase in motion, she closed the deal in two days. By the end of the week the foundation for a new house was staked out according to architectural plans that she had also commissioned while in Galveston. Though reminiscent of their old house, this one would be even grander: three stories constructed of white limestone from the Texas hill country and on the first two floors, wraparound porches adorned with the finest wrought iron railings from New Orleans. She paid for everything with Williams paper. After the bank crisis of a few months ago, she planned her land acquisition and home construction to convert her wealth into tangible assets. She thought Quentin would be proud.

Esther was grateful for the sense of purpose restored to the house by Miz Sylvia's return, but the prospect of never seeing Henry again tore at her insides. She lost her appetite. She had no idea what to tell her daughters. Rebecca and Moses contributed to her sense of unease with their hard tales of life on the Brazos in tiny, drafty cabins. Esther felt intense anguish for those slaves and their daily toils, guilt for her own fortunate position, and fear that something could further upset her security. Anxiety sapped her strength.

"Esther, I want to speak to you, please."

"Yes, Miz Sylvia." Hearing Sylvia's serious tone, Esther dropped what she was doing. She stood before the desk where Sylvia sat in front of a stack of papers.

"Esther, please sit down."

Esther lowered herself gingerly onto the straight-backed chair facing the desk, her muscles tense. Something was coming, that was for sure, whenever Miz Sylvia acted so formal.

"As you know, the relationship of your family to my husband's family goes back several generations. In appreciation of your service, my husband's will contains a manumission."

Esther held her breath. She had been praying to hear those words ever since her mother had died. Her mother had always believed that one day Massa Quentin would free someone in her family.

"Your children, Sally and Mabel, shall be freed when each one reaches the age of eighteen."

Esther clapped her hands. "Praise Jesus! Thank you Massa Quentin! Thank you Miz Sylvia!" Tears started streaming down her cheeks.

"You are most welcome, Esther. Before your daughters come of age, we must look to their future and how they may make their way in the world. It is not so easy for free blacks and not likely to get easier in the years ahead."

"Yes'm. Thank you." Esther could not conceive what Miz Sylvia might be thinking, worrying about the future. Her children would be free. If they had to struggle, it would be their own struggles. Her children would be able to make their own decisions, something she could never do. She twitched with joy, dying to run out and tell her daughters that they would be free.

"There is also some bad news. I tried to buy Henry, but Mr. Williams declined my offer."

"Did I hear you right? You tried to buy Henry?"

"Yes. I did not want you to be separated from Henry permanently. Mr. Williams refused to sell, even when I increased the price. I am very sorry, Esther."

Esther felt that she had fallen off a mountaintop. She gulped back her thoughts, not sure if she could speak without breaking down.

"I know, Esther. It's very difficult. You and I are both without our men, but at least Henry is still alive. Perhaps one day Mr. Williams will relent. I have arranged for Mr. Hurlinger to receive your letters to Henry and to see that they are delivered directly into his hand. That's the best I could do."

"Thank you, Miz Sylvia." Esther went straightaway to find her daughters, so excited that she nearly bumped into Jeremy Blackstone coming in through the back.

Jeremy puzzled over Sylvia, who spun like a top in a frenzy. Maybe she was keeping busy to avoid worrying about Elizabeth and Zachary. Maybe this was her way to navigate through her grief. But it seemed bigger than that, or perhaps more lasting. She looked to be rearranging every aspect of her life. It was something to see, Sylvia giving orders, shifting furniture, supervising construction of the new house, and making social calls to the American, Mexican, and German communities to announce her permanent residence in San Antonio. He began to feel awkward about the chair he had carved for her. Touched by her grief before she left for Galveston, he recalled spending many hours in his rocker after the death of his wives, letting the mindless rhythm soothe his pain. Because the McDermott household, inexplicably, lacked a single rocking chair, he had resolved to make one for Sylvia. Now he was uncertain whether to give it to her. He decided to wait.

One afternoon, he chanced upon Sylvia in the courtyard seeking warmth in a spot of sunlight. Seated on an uncomfortably hard chair, she held her head in her hands, weeping softly. Without a word, he went to fetch the rocker. When he returned, she was in the same spot, staring into space, her face puffy and her eyes red. He carefully placed the chair next to her.

"Why not give this a try?"

"Oh, Mr. Blackstone. A rocking chair! How thoughtful of you." She accepted his extended hand to help her rise. "My goodness, it's such a finely made chair!"

Unlike many rocking chairs, this one had not one right angle. Each of the lines was slightly bent, giving it a soft curved look. The back angled gently into the seat, cradling the sitter, and the smooth arms rounded down to connect with the rocking base. The back and seat were covered with cowhide cushions, stuffed with horsehair and bolted to the frame. Sylvia slid into the chair and involuntarily sighed.

"I have never sat in such a comfortable piece of furniture. How did you find it? It's as if it were made for me!"

"'Twas made for you, Miz McDermott."

"You made this, Mr. Blackstone?" She leapt from the chair and inspected it from all sides, noting the appealing proportions, the fitted joints, the fine sanding, and the metal studs that fixed the cushions.

"Yup. Thought it might help. I've lost two wives in my time. My old rocker was the best piece of solace."

Sylvia was overcome, her eyes glistening again. "Mr. Blackstone, you are a true friend. I do not know how to repay your kindness." Unable to contain her emotions, Sylvia sank into the rocker and cried.

"Now, now, it's all right. I'll leave you for a bit, but I'll be back for dinner."

"Thank you." She sniffled. "Thank you. This means more than you can know."

WITH THE EXPEDITION

THE CAMEL CARAVAN FOLLOWED well-established tracks for the first sunny and cheerful days. The nights were cold enough to dust everything with a thin frost, but by mid-morning a soothing warmth enveloped the troops as they pursued their way without hindrance. Abdullah was amazed at how agreeable the excursion was without Stacy Bly and his crew. Although he missed Ali and Hassan, he found the company of Nate, Alex, and Erdem enjoyable. Most of all, the camels pleased him, carrying their weight, moving faster than expected, managing the rough terrain without difficulty, and rendering Major Babcock positively ebullient. For the first time in months, Abdullah envisioned a true camel cavalry crossing the American desert.

Then came a solid week of icy winds, leaden skies, and freezing rain. The clay-based soil turned into slippery slopes, endangering the camels whose soft feet couldn't dig in but slid upon the surface. Deep ravines sliced the countryside. Although the caravan tried to follow paths atop the hills, sometimes the only recourse was to go down one side and up another. Water crossing became more frequent, as rain runoff filled the gullies between steep ravines. These arroyos were subject to flash floods, one of which carried off and drowned two of their mules.

When the rain finally stopped, they were camped high on a mesa, exposed to winds that howled like a child's temper tantrum. The area was rocky and muddy. Grumbling, the men struggled to find spaces to sit or sleep that weren't in a puddle or strewn with spiky rocks. Their clothes were soaked. Although the fire provided light, all its heating capacity seemed sucked out by the ferocious gusts.

"Alex, did you think it would be like this?" Nate asked.

"Like what?"

"This shitty weather."

"I didn't know what to expect."

Shivering, Abdullah inched toward the fire. "Why do you think the Major took the camels out in winter?"

"I was wondering the same thing," Nate added. "On the face of it, coming out now doesn't make much sense."

Although he felt a similar gnawing anxiety, Alex tried to mollify his friends. "It seemed like a good idea last week when the sun was shining. We're just wet and cold. It'll get better."

"Very observant, Alex. We're wet and cold, that's for damn sure." Nate was short-tempered.

Alex felt obliged to defend his uncle. "I reckon the Major had pressure from Washington. He believes in the camels with his whole heart, but he needs to prove their worth. He wants to have something to show before the next batch gets here."

"I hope he doesn't have to show 'em any corpses. Camel or human. I'm like to freeze to death." Nate rose to throw more damp wood on the fire, which sputtered and hissed before igniting in a feeble flame.

"I think no camel corpses." Abdullah was not worried. "When the desert at home is cold at night, their fur keeps them warm. They can even take the wet during our rainy season. And the Bactrians! They are bred in cold places. Have you noticed? They like this weather."

Nate, always interested in understanding the camels, hadn't thought about that. "Yeah, it's funny. The Bactrians do seem stronger than ever."

"But I hope the weather warms up soon, because I have never been this cold in my life."

"I'm with you. Abdullah. I ain't never, ever been this cold. We sure as hell don't have weather like this in Indianola."

"Look on the bright side," said Alex, "at least we haven't seen any Indians. They're probably holed up somewhere themselves."

"Some consolation." Nate groaned and attempted to settle his bedroll on a less soggy spot. Dog tired, he slept the moment his eyes closed.

Hours later, when Nate came slowly to consciousness, his face felt oddly stiff. Something frigid landed in his blinking eyes. There was no sun, only a slightly paler shade to the charcoal sky. Sitting bolt upright, he laughed out loud. It was snowing. An inch of white covered every animal and object in sight. Off to the side, Abdullah and Erdem said their morning prayers while standing in order to avoid soiling their prayer mats on the snowy, muddy ground. The camels, their humps resembling snow-capped mountains, were completely untroubled.

A few days later the bad weather abruptly ceased, like someone closing a window. A cloudless cerulean sky and a round full sun brightened everyone's spirits. For days the dry air freshened the atmosphere. The wet arroyos returned to a powder state, and before long the caravan needed to locate the next water source. Abdullah, Nate, and a soldier called Private Garcia scouted for a spring. Each rode a camel with another in tow that carried empty water barrels.

Coming over a rise with the sun in their eyes, they confronted an apparition. Silhouetted against the light, a tiny Indian woman, hunched and weather worn, stood as still as the boulders around her. Nate eased his Colt out of the holster and laid it across his lap.

"Buenos dias." She spoke softly.

"Buenos dias, Abuela," replied Pvt. Garcia politely.

Private Garcia's widening eyes and repeated questioning of the old woman set Nate to full attention. The woman moved toward the boulder, making a hand gesture. Nate cocked and raised his pistol, only to lower it immediately.

A young girl, scarcely fourteen years old, appeared with delicate, mincing steps. Her jet-black hair hung straight to her waist. She moved beside the old lady and clutched her hand.

"Pvt. Garcia, you'd best be translatin' some of this."

"Sorry, Nate. This woman is not from here. She ain't Comanche or Apache. She's Yaqui."

"Yaqui?"

"I have heard of them. They're supposed to be powerful healers, and they live in the deep desert between here and California. I'm trying to work out what she's doin' so far from home."

More conversation ensued while the woman's gaze fixed on Abdullah, who commenced to squirm beneath the visual interrogation.

"It seems the old lady has had a vision. Her granddaughter will marry a foreigner who comes with strange animals."

"What?"

"Si, si. It's hard to believe. She says they came looking for us, for the camels. They've been walking for days."

Abdullah was distinctly uncomfortable. He was not one to scoff at unexplained visions, especially from an elderly person.

"She says that Abdullah is not the one. She asks if there are others with us."

"You're joking? She wants to meet all the camel keepers to recruit a husband for her granddaughter?"

As if on cue, Erdem rode up with a message from Major Babcock asking the scouting party to return to the caravan. Nate, his eyes twinkling like a prankster, beckoned him. "Hey, Erdem, we've found a young beauty that wants to meet you. Maybe you'd like to settle down with her and start a family out here in the prickly pears!"

In Arabic, Abdullah quickly explained what was going on while the old woman stared at Erdem.

"Ese no es el uno."

Private Garcia translated. "She says he is not the one, either."

"What are we supposed to do, go back two hundred miles to let her interview Ali and Hassan?"

Nate couldn't help laughing, but Abdullah and Erdem regarded her with something between humility and fear. The old woman started speaking to Private Garcia again.

"She says that they have come too early, but she is not disappointed. She thinks her granddaughter is too young to marry now, but her vision was so intense that she had to be sure. She claims that because the camels are here, the man who will be this child's husband will come. They will go home now and will look for the camels again in the summer."

"Wait a minute. Garcia, did you tell her we had a second shipment of camels coming?"

"No, I didn't say a word."

"Hmm, maybe she really does have visions. Hey, ask her if she knows where to find water."

The old woman pointed and explained how to locate the water source. As she turned to leave, she paused. Gesturing toward Abdullah and looking him straight in the eye, she said a few words. She then nodded to Nate, speaking a bit longer. Private Garcia's tone became very respectful.

"Si, Abuela, si. Yo los diré. Gracias, Abuela, muchas gracias."

Followed by her granddaughter, the woman stepped behind a rock and disappeared.

"She gave a prophecy."

"Well, what did she say?"

"Abdullah, she said you will go home, in fact, you *must* go home. Nothing bad, but your future is there."

Abdullah muttered. "I've been saying it's time to go home for weeks. I hope she's right."

"Nate, about you she said, 'You are not born to this beast, but you are one with it. Do not despair. The camels bring you life.'"

Nate shuddered. "What do you make of that?"

"I don't know."

"Did she say anything about me?" Erdem asked.

"Nope, not a word. And nothing about me. She only thanked me for translating."

That night around the campfire, Nate listened to Alex. It was the only thing to do once Alex started talking. Not that the stories Alex told were boring; on the contrary, Alex knew how to spin a good yarn, and Nate especially enjoyed when Alex recounted how the camels had been acquired. But tonight, sitting around a campfire west of Howard Springs, Nate was annoyed by the simple sound of Alex's voice. Growing up in Jeremy Blackstone's household, Nate was used to peace and quiet. Something about Alex's incessant chatter seemed like a disturbance to the natural order.

He especially wished for quiet so that he could think about what the old woman had said. Why had she said he must not despair? What had she foreseen? He tried to dismiss her mumbo jumbo, but the words kept haunting him. The droning sounds of Alex's stories passed over him as he watched the sky. This west Texas night opened more expansive and imminent than any he had experienced at Indianola or even at Camp Verde. He was trying to locate the belt of Orion when Alex announced that he wanted to marry Elizabeth. Nate was not surprised, but he felt something else, an emotion he couldn't quite define, a bit like resentment.

"You asked her before we left?"

"No, not really."

"Seems to me you either ask a girl or you don't. Which was it?"

"Well, I kinda did."

"Kinda?"

"Yeah, I asked her to wait for me, until we get back from the expedition."

"Is that as plain as you made it?"

"Hell, Nate. It didn't go like I wanted. She got a little cross."

"Cross?"

"Yeah, I said it didn't go well. Anyway, she knows how I feel, I think."

Nate stared at the fire.

"Listen, Nate, I only know that I've got to have Elizabeth. I can't picture life without her."

Nate tried to picture his own life. He saw camels prominently. Then, Nate realized that he, too, wanted Elizabeth in his life. He couldn't envision visiting San Antonio without seeing her, any more than he could imagine not seeing his grandfather. He was at a loss to guess how it would be between them after she was married to Alex. The fact that Elizabeth was "cross" with Alex gave him an odd sense of satisfaction.

"So what's your next move?"

"Hell if I know, Nate. Wish I could've seen her once more before we left. Say, Nate, can I ask you something?"

"Sure, what?"

"You ever notice anything between Elizabeth and Hassan?"

"Hassan? No, why?"

"Nothing. Just asking."

As he lay by the fire, unable to sleep, Nate tried to make sense of what Alex had said, tried to discern what it might mean for him. Before dozing off, he gazed upward at the huge expanse of night and saw Elizabeth's face before him floating in the stars.

The following morning rose gray and bleak. A strange disquiet accompanied Nate while he rolled his bedroll, packed his saddlebags, and checked on Ibrim. The cook, nowhere near as capable as Nate's grandfather, never seemed to have the coffee ready. When he finally filled his tin cup, he let the scalding liquid refocus his mind on the task at hand. There was a camel expedition to bring in. Everything else would have to wait.

Camp Verde, Texas, December 1856

My dearest Annabelle,

Today a packet of your letters reached me. I picture you every Monday, starting your day in faithful devotion to your poor husband, who is stranded far from civilization and from your tender mercies. My gratitude to you is profound.

I apologize for not having reciprocated with the same level of constancy. There is so little to report that I fear being tedious. With half the camels and men away, lethargy has settled upon those of us who remain. The new officers' quarters are nearly complete, so even that distraction is about to disappear. My days are a mind-numbing cycle of waiting. Much as I found his leadership wanting, Major Babcock's conversation was far more interesting than present company. I grow weary of these Texans and their defense of slavery. Even a topic of national import, such as the expansion of the railroad, interests them only insofar as to whether or not the tracks shall pass near one of their cities. I die of boredom.

The camp is plagued by a marked decrease in discipline and increase in conflict among the troops. Sgt. Bly, whom I mentioned in an earlier letter, is sowing ill will. The hostility has fallen particularly hard on the Arabs. Although you may remember my disappointment in their general capacities, I do nevertheless feel they should be treated humanely. When I learned that the foreigners had not been paid, I did look into the matter. Apparently only Major Babcock can authorize dispersal of funds, and having forgotten to transfer that authority to me, the men cannot be paid. Another example of incompetence.

I hope the expedition may return before Christmas, along with my orders to come home. I shall endeavor to be more optimistic in a future correspondence.

Your devoted husband,

Winston

Washington, DC, Office of the Secretary of War, December 1856

"**I**'ve reviewed the files on all the Western forts, sir, and they seem to be in order. Everything is in these boxes here." His melancholy tone revealed Clerk Habberford Smith's distaste for his current assignment helping Jefferson Davis pack his office to make way for his replacement.

"Well done, Mr. Smith. Have all the requisitions been sent over to the Quartermaster's office?"

"Yes, sir." He sighed. "Even though we've known it for months, it's still hard to believe. James Buchanan will be President."

"It's because President Pierce took the blame for the violence in Kansas."

"What a mess. Sir, some say Kansas is a prelude to a larger conflict."

"Time will tell. If all goes well, I'll be back in the Senate in a few months. There are some sensible men in that august chamber who will work for compromise."

"I've heard that John Floyd will be the next Secretary of War, and if I may speak frankly, he is reputed to be inept. I've heard rumors about malfeasances, funds unaccounted for and that sort of thing. Sir, would you be needing a clerk in your Senate offices?"

"Probably, but let's get this office cleared out first. What's next?

"The camel experiment."

Jefferson Davis exhaled loudly. "So much potential, and I won't be able to see it through. I doubt if Floyd will give it much support. Nevertheless, put it on top of one of these piles in a prominent place."

"Yes, sir."

"And what about Major Babcock? We called him back didn't we? I don't want him stuck out there in Texas forgotten."

"Yes sir. We dispatched those orders not long after the Democratic convention, when we knew that Pierce was finished. But you may recall that he was taking the camels on an expedition to the Texas desert."

"Nevertheless, he should be on his way back here in due course?"

"Yes, sir.

"Good. He's a fine man, a valuable officer. He may be needed in the coming years."

"Sir? His were the only orders we sent. Do you want me to send similar orders regarding Lt. Halter?"

"Who?"

"Lt. Winston Halter. He's been with the Camel Corps since they first left for the Levant."

"Ah, Colonel Cole's son-in-law. No, we'll let the next Secretary decide what should become of him."

San Antonio, December 23, 1856

W ITH THE DARKLY OVERCAST day matching her disposition, Elizabeth wrapped her shawl tightly and stepped
out into the whipping wind. She had not planned a sortie
into the frigid winter, but when Pvt. Munoz failed to arrive
at the house, she assumed that he had not been allowed to
leave the Alamo. She set out on the mile walk at a brisk pace,
thereby warming herself and dissipating some of her frustration. Behind her, Esther's two daughters, each carrying a basket, struggled to keep up. As she fought the sharp gusts, the
cold air stung her eyes and tears blurred her vision. Winter
in San Antonio was decidedly colder than in Galveston, and
her outlook on life was as dreary as the weather.

The camel expedition had been gone for more than six
weeks, during which time she had seen none of her three
friends. Her sleep was troubled by imagined difficulties that
must confront Alex and Nate on their journey. She had seldom worried in her life, but now she was profoundly anxious.
She envisioned wild storms, water shortages, treacherous
landscapes, unappetizing food, and menacing Indians. She
tried to be optimistic, to sense the thrill of accomplishment
that her friends must feel when the camels performed well.
However, she was unable to hold those happy thoughts. She
wondered if her unusual perturbation was the inevitable result of caring for someone. Her affection for Alex was deep,
but Nate's friendship also mattered to her a great deal. As for
Hassan, if she could have spoken with him, she might have
withstood the waiting more easily. His mere presence would
have eased her disquiet and alleviated her fears. Although she
could not conceive a future with Hassan, she still missed him.

She was adrift, buffeted like the fallen leaves that skipped
across her path. Her life had taken too many unexpected
turns, starting with the move to San Antonio, then the
death of her father, and now her mother's strange behavior.
If only she could ask Major Babcock, his familiarity with
her mother's temperament might illuminate the situation.

Her misgivings about her mother had started the day
Elizabeth returned from Comfort, a day she remembered as

a milestone. Delighted to see her family safely back from Galveston and proud of what she and Zach had accomplished, Elizabeth was unprepared for her mother's reaction. Sylvia chastised them for going so far alone and criticized their choice to leave Agnes rather than bringing Precious home. Elizabeth was completely taken aback, deflated by these unexpected judgments. She wasn't used to her mother being so decisive, and there were decisions aplenty. The family would remain in San Antonio, the Brazos plantations were to be sold, and her mother was building a new house. Changes to the family's daily routine that Elizabeth had instituted in her mother's absence were quickly restored to the old ways. Her mother took action without explanation or consultation, making Elizabeth feel left out, undermined, and resentful. She tried to be patient, but her mother was short with everyone. The two women had even stopped brushing each other's hair in the evening.

Three weeks ago, Pvt. Munoz had appeared at her doorstep to tell her that Hassan was confined to Camp Verde and would not be allowed to come to San Antonio on supply duty. Pressed for details, Pvt. Munoz conjectured that Sgt. Bly was behind it and described Stacy's systematic harassment of Hassan and Ali.

"Miss McDermott, with Major Babcock away, there's not much any of us can do, but that's not why Hassan sent me. He promised Nate to keep the business going, and since he can't come to town, I said I would do what I could."

Elizabeth finished the thought. "He needs things to sell! Of course, I'll help."

Elizabeth had thrown herself into the task, dispatching Pvt. Munoz back to Camp Verde with a fine selection of articles for sale. She had urged him to convey her sympathies to Hassan and Ali and had promised to acquire more goods before their next meeting, which was scheduled for today.

Elizabeth sighed and trudged onward against the wind. As she came into view of the Alamo, she froze. Camels stood in the paddock, lots of them. Picking up her pace, she hurried toward the stately creatures, sure that she would find Alex or Nate or Hassan, or at the very least, Major

Babcock. A smile spread across her face, lighting up her cheeks that were already bright pink from the chill air. She skipped, almost running, as if a great burden had been lifted. Just outside the enclosure, Pvt. Munoz intercepted her, and she gushed her excitement.

"How wonderful! They're back! In time for Christmas! When did they get here? Who's with them?"

"I'm sorry, Miss McDermott. It's not our lot. It's the second shipment."

"Oh no." Disappointment buckled her knees, forcing Pvt. Munoz to seize her elbow.

"Thank you, I'm all right. It's just that I was hoping for Major Babcock's expedition. I wasn't expecting the second group yet."

"Neither were we. But it's here, and with a new commander."

"The camels came with their own commander?"

"Lt. Edward Beale. In from the East via New Orleans. He met up with the camels outside of Indianola. Rumor is he brought orders for Major Babcock to go back to Washington."

"Oh no! He will be completely disheartened."

"That's not all. They've come with their own camel men."

"What? What will happen to Abdullah, Hassan, Ali and Erdem?"

"No idea. The new ones are called Hi Jolly, Greek George, and Mico and there's a couple more."

"Those don't sound like Egyptian names."

"I'm not sure where they're from. Lt. Beale also brought three civilians. He calls them 'my boys', relations I think. From what I've seen, they behave like boys on an adventure."

"What could that mean for Alex? And what about Nate?"

"We won't know until the expedition returns, but they are in for one helluva surprise when they pull back into Camp Verde."

"Thank you, Pvt. Munoz. Oh, I almost forgot. Here are the items you asked for." Sally and Mabel handed over the two baskets. "And if you make it to Comfort, could you give these knitted baby booties to Mrs. Altgelt? They're for our slave, Precious."

Shivering and dejected, Elizabeth entered the house on Laredo Street through the front door, stomping her feet from the cold. Antoine quietly informed her that her mother had guests in the salon. She took a deep breath, arranged a pleasant expression on her face, and entered the room.

"Elizabeth, I'd like you to meet Lt. Beale of the US Army and his companions May, Ham, and Ed. They've come with the second camel shipment."

Unhappy to find these interlopers in her home, Elizabeth nevertheless was Sylvia McDermott's daughter. She smiled and curtsied before taking a seat near her mother. She listened quietly, trying to avoid the persistent stares from the three young men seated opposite. While her mind raced, assessing the newcomers and the implications of their arrival, she was shocked to hear her mother offer an invitation.

"We'd be honored to have you and the young gentlemen as our guests for Christmas dinner. It will be our first entertainment in the new residence. We won't actually move until after the New Year, so if you would like to sleep in a house, you may unroll your bedrolls in one of the empty rooms. It won't be comfortable, but at least you'll be warm and dry. I'm told the bunkhouse at the Alamo is rather drafty."

Lt. Beale smiled. "Why, thank you, Mrs. McDermott. We appreciate your kind invitation and accept most enthusiastically. As for lodging, I am happily settled at the Menger, but I imagine the young men would welcome a change of scene." The three nodded vigorously.

"Then it's agreed. We'll see you the day after tomorrow."

The moment Antoine closed the door behind their departing guests, Elizabeth flew at her mother.

"Mama, have you gone mad? Whatever are you thinking, inviting those people to our family Christmas?"

Sylvia sighed. Much as she was happy to see a spark of animation in her daughter, whose morose demeanor had infected the whole house, she was distressed to hear so much anger. "Elizabeth, I don't know what Lt. Beale really thinks about the camel project. Christmas dinner in a convivial atmosphere will give us a chance to praise the camels and Cousin Babcock. Those two will have to work together. We can set Lt. Beale on the right course."

"Oh Mama, Pvt. Munoz said that Cousin Babcock must go back to Washington."

Sylvia slumped into her chair. "How can the camel project go on without him? No one else believes in this as much as he does. No one else will give the same effort."

"I know, Mama. And more than that, Cousin Babcock has been so kind to us. What are we going to do without him?" Elizabeth burst out sobbing, and for the first time in weeks, allowed herself to be comforted by her mother. Wrapping her daughter in her arms, Sylvia wondered what would become of Elizabeth.

Antoine had come to recognize something about himself: he preferred constancy and predictability to change and upheaval. From the moment he had been sold away from his parents, he had craved stability. The last few months had been exasperating for him precisely because uncertainty had been his daily diet. Although he understood that a slave should not count on anything, in Galveston he had come to expect that one day would resemble the next. Now he knew the aching truth that his life could be upended at any moment. Miz Sylvia, so different without Massa Quentin, was changing everything, and rapidly. He longed for the mundane.

He had hopes that the new house would restore order to his life. For the past week he and Moses had been carting furniture south of the river. The new residence pleased him. He had never liked the house on Laredo Street, always feeling closed in by the thick walls of the adobe structure. The slave accommodations appended to the stable were cramped and airless. By contrast, the new house was spacious, open, with high ceilings and room to breathe. The two-story quarters out back were well built, with small but sufficient individual rooms. Anticipating the privacy he used to have in Galveston, he had his eye on a young woman he had seen near the Maverick place. He hoped he might be able to start a family. However, he understood that it could all go wrong at any point. Last night he had overheard a terrible row between Miz Sylvia and Missy 'Lizbeth.

"Mama, I have no desire to live in that behemoth that you have built. I won't move."

"Elizabeth, we need to be together as a family, especially after the loss of your father."

"What about the legal matter? Don't I need to stay here to preserve our property rights?"

"No, no. Everything is in my name now. We can sell this house and move to the new one."

"Mama, don't you understand? I don't want to go there! I like it here, close to town and the friends that I've made."

"Think for a minute! How would it look, you living here by yourself?"

"I *have* thought about it, Mama. Zachary also wants to stay here. I can keep Esther and the girls. You can take Antoine and Rebecca and Moses, and we can figure out what to do with Agnes after she gets back."

Sylvia raised her voice, showing unprecedented anger toward her daughter. "Listen here. You do not make decisions for this family, I do. You do not run this household, I do. And I will not have…"

Brazenly Elizabeth interrupted. "While you were in Galveston, I ran the household, and I ran it well. I can't go back to being a little girl again. I can't, and I won't!"

Antoine had peeked around the corner to see Elizabeth standing in the middle of the room, face to face with her mother. The girl was shaking, her tears welling. Sylvia stared at her daughter, then modulated her tone.

"My darling daughter, I am at a loss. It is so improbable for you to live here on your own. People will talk."

"I don't care one whit what people say."

"Well, I suppose it wouldn't be for long. You'll soon be finding a husband."

"Mama, I don't know about that."

"Nonsense. No fewer than four families have approached me since I returned from Galveston. And there are other possibilities. What about Alex, for example?"

Her mother's nonchalance made marriage sound like a commercial transaction. How could she talk like that, after marrying for love and abandoning her parents to come to Texas? What four families did she mean? And what about Alex? Elizabeth had bungled their last visit, but felt sure she would marry him. They had such good times together. She sniffled and kept still, lest she say something totally out of order.

Moved by her daughter's pathetic appearance, Sylvia relented. "All right, my child, light of my life. I will move to the new house after the New Year. Then you can decide when to move."

"Or if I want to move?"

Sylvia sighed. "All right, or if you want to move. We can talk about Esther and Rebecca later."

Elizabeth hugged her mother close. "Thank you, Mama, thank you."

This conversation had disturbed Antoine enormously. He could not imagine being separated from Esther, who was like an older sister and the closest thing he had to family. The McDermott women had discussed dividing him and Esther as cavalierly as if they were debating the distribution of furniture, and he had not one word to say in the matter. Every decision about his life would be made for him.

"Antoine, hey, Antoine! You with us? Grab ahold."

"Sorry Moses."

Antoine took one end of the table, helping to maneuver it through the huge doors, across the hall, and into the dining room until it rested beneath the crystal chandelier imported from New York. All the downstairs furniture was in place. Antoine only hoped that his place would become clear in the New Year.

By the following morning, the new McDermott house was resplendent with Christmas decorations: a tree strung with corn and cut-paper chains, an array of candles and candelabra in every room, and a table laid with the family's best china and crystal. Apprehensive about this first Christmas without her father, Elizabeth resolved to make the best of it. She hoped that her brothers, her mother, and Mr. Blackstone would temper her feelings of loss and distract her from the unwanted visitors. Two of Lt. Beale's boys struck her as incomparably arrogant when they exclaimed surprise at the array of food on the table. She profoundly resented their implication that Texas lacked refinement. The third lad was more agreeable, but he was called May Stacey, and Elizabeth couldn't help thinking of that toad Stacy Bly every time she heard his name. The boys' ignorance about camels and their disdainful attitude gave her the impression of privileged children on a lark. Although she supposed the meal was a success from her mother's point of view, she counted the minutes until it was over.

Unlike Elizabeth, the McDermott slaves rather enjoyed the day. Antoine, bedecked in his red jacket, ruled the entry, and Esther thrived in a real kitchen again, supervising a banquet the way she used to in Galveston. For the first time, Sally was called upon to serve, which she did proudly in a new pink uniform. The dinner went as planned, and Esther reveled in the overheard praise of her cooking. The only surprise was the black servant who accompanied Lt. Beale's three young men. At Miz Sylvia's suggestion, he took his meal in the kitchen.

"Y'all are welcome. I'm Esther."

"Abner, Abner Cannon. Pleased to meet you."

"Help yourself to whatever you want, Mr. Cannon, but please stay to the side here when I'm cookin' or servin'."

"Yes, Miz Esther, of course."

After the dishes were cleared and the guests were occupied with coffee and cigars, the slaves sat down at the kitchen table for a feast of the leftovers. Never having conversed with a free man from the north, they were endlessly curious. They learned that both Mr. Cannon and his wife worked for Lt. Beale's family.

Antoine was full of questions. "Excuse me, but what do y'all mean 'employed'? Can y'all choose to work or not? I mean, y'all had to come along on this trip, didn't you?"

"I guess so, but I didn't mind."

"If you said no, could they cut you loose?"

"I s'pose they could."

"So you gotta go where they say or else. Sounds a lot like slave life."

"No, no, not at all. My wife is a seamstress. We all read and write, and our three children are goin' to school. One wants to be a teacher. There's a whole community of our people, with our own lawyers, doctors, and preachers. We print our own newspapers and run our own churches."

"None of it run by white folk?"

"Nope."

"That's kinda hard for us to imagine."

Mr. Cannon hesitated. "From what I've seen so far, I'll say this 'bout slavery. Looks to me like it robs you of your imagination." Before he could elaborate, he was called upstairs to help the young men install their sleeping arrangements.

His comment disturbed Antoine. What good did it do to imagine another way of life if it was impossible to have it? Wasn't it better to accept your situation in peace rather than always striving against it? Perhaps if Samuel had been able to accept his situation he would be alive today.

Or, Antoine wondered, was his own craving for stability really a lack of imagination?

WITH THE EXPEDITION, CHRISTMAS DAY, 1856

H AVING COMPLETED MOST OF their circuit, the expedition approached the junction to Bandera, where they would turn north toward Camp Verde. Major Babcock reviewed his report, consisting of paragraph after paragraph of fulsome praise. The camels' fortitude, persistence, and stamina were noted. Special mention was made of their ability to carry feed for the mules and horses, all the while securing their own forage from local plants. The report acknowledged only two problems. First, a camel's footpads were susceptible to damage from sharp rocks, but they could be wrapped in cloth. Major Babcock compared this procedure favorably to shoeing a horse. The second problem he had not yet determined how to address. In spite of the camels' stellar performance, some soldiers remained inexplicably opposed to them. He must word that part carefully.

The trip had taken longer than Major Babcock had hoped, and he was anxious to submit his report. He surprised the troops on Christmas morning by announcing that he would continue straight to Castroville and on to San Antonio. This abandonment caused some consternation in the ranks, and Nate and Alex were no less discontented than the others.

"I hate to say it, Nate, but it seems like my uncle should've stayed with the camels."

"Yup. Christmas on the road, and our commander leaves."

"I can't stop thinking about Christmas dinner. Back in Philadelphia, the women cooked for days. We had roast turkey, cranberry sauce, and my mama's mashed potatoes with lots of butter. For desert, a big yellow cake with white icing, and if we were lucky, an orange for each of us kids."

"My grandpa and Hilde used to make a ham, corn bread, greens, and peach cobbler."

"Man, you're making my stomach hurt. I don't know if I can take one more day of Cookie's vittles. He sure can't hold a candle to your grandfather."

The air was cold, but the day blossomed blue as the expedition made good time. Unexpectedly, they came upon a wash full of water, probably the result of a faraway storm. One of the soldiers rode carefully into the stream, using a stick to poke around for obstructions and to check the depth. Finding no invisible holes that could break an ankle or tip a horse, the caravan set off slowly in single file. The camels had proven their ability to cross streams and even to swim in deep water, but when the banks were slippery, greater caution was indicated. Alex stood on the opposite side to help each camel up the bank, while Abdullah organized them after they made it across. Nate and Erdem stayed behind to urge the camels into the water, occasionally riding alongside if one became skittish.

Erdem coaxed a hesitant Perguida into the water. On the opposite bank, she lost her balance while climbing out of the creek. She tilted to one side. Her front legs folded up and she landed hard on her knees. Erdem barely managed to keep his seat. To escape being crushed, Alex jumped backwards, smashing his thigh against a rock. The pain was so intense that he nearly passed out. Rushing to his side, Abdullah inspected Alex's leg thoroughly and pronounced it badly bruised but not broken. For Alex, the remainder of the journey was a throbbing torment.

The day after Christmas, the caravan reached Camp Verde with a whoop and a holler. Neither horse nor camel could be restrained as all the animals picked up the pace, trotting or running into camp. Arriving near the end of the train, Alex was shocked to see the camel corral in disarray. The grounds had not been swept, feed was scattered about, and the animals appeared to be unguarded. Two camels standing in a makeshift enclave clearly had the itch. Alex dismounted and looked for Capt. Chisholm to make order out of their messy arrival. To his dismay, Sgt. Bly sauntered over with Pertag in tow. Other soldiers from their faction followed close behind. Alex took a deep breath.

"Howdy, Sergeant. Where's Captain Chisholm?"

"Fredericksburg. Can't say when he'll be back." Sgt. Bly chuckled.

"What about Lt. Halter?

"We wouldn't want to disturb Lt. Halter, would we? Not when he's napping after his lunch and brandy. Where's Major Babcock?" His sarcastic tone implied ill wishes toward the Major.

"San Antonio. He'll be here soon." Alex had no idea when Major Babcock might return, but it wouldn't hurt for Sgt. Bly to think it could be any minute. "Say, why don't you lend a hand?"

Watching this exchange, Nate noticed an ominous shifting of allegiance as some of the men from the expedition moved to stand with Sgt. Bly's group. He could hear them telling stories about the camels in a most derogatory fashion. Meanwhile Pvt. Munoz and several others arrayed themselves behind Alex.

Sgt. Bly struck an arrogant pose. "No, thanks. Y'all have a nice time. We've got other duties."

One of the soldiers laughed. "Yeah, like that card game we left. Let's get back to it."

Sgt. Bly sneered at Alex. "If you want help, call your lazy Ay-rab pals. They should be lolling about in their shack."

"I'll go." Private Munoz loped toward the lean-to.

Upset by the disorder, some of the horses started milling about and crowding the camels. Nate kept his hands on Ibrim's reins and his eyes on the jostling animals. Abdullah held Ayesha away from several horses being nudged too close. Neither man was in any position to help out in a scuffle.

Sgt. Bly pursued his advantage. "You boys need to know that some things have changed around here. But I imagine you'll learn soon enough."

Although he wanted to punch Stacy, Alex tried reasoning with him one more time. "Listen, Sergeant," he said, taking a couple of jagged steps closer.

"Whoa, what happened to you? See that gimpy walk there? You fall down and hurt yourself?"

One of the soldiers answered for him. "Hell no, a camel fell on him!" Guffaws spewed forth from Sgt. Bly's men.

A soldier standing with Alex shouted back. "That's a damn lie!"

When they saw Hassan and Ali running toward them, Nate, Alex, Erdem and Abdullah breathed a sigh of relief. The camel men started speaking a mile a minute in Arabic, and soon the camels were calming down. Hassan pitched in with the camels, nodded a greeting to Alex, and then stood at his side.

"Looky here, the Ay-rab riffraff got outta bed to do a little work. Tryin' to impress Major Babcock, maybe? Well, in case y'all didn't notice, he ain't here!"

"Hey," asked one of the expedition's men who now stood with Sgt. Bly, "what about some grub? You save us anything from Christmas dinner?"

"For you, sure. But there may not be enough to go 'round. First come, first served!"

Tired and worn out from their voyage, the expedition's soldiers had no patience for such provocation. "You'd best be sure there's enough for all of us, or there'll be hell to pay." The soldier advanced menacingly on Sgt. Bly, who unholstered his pistol and stepped forward.

A gunshot rang out, fired by none other than Lt. Halter, standing upright and appearing not the least bit sleepy. Though somewhat disheveled, he nevertheless had full command of his senses and looked as if he would not hesitate to aim at an unruly soldier.

"What a disgusting spectacle of incompetence and insubordination! You men are a disgrace to the military. There will no more of this conduct, or I will personally bring charges against you in a court martial. Offenders whose actions are more egregious risk being summarily shot."

"What'd he say?"

"If you don't shut up and get to work, he'll shoot."

Lt. Halter gave a series of precise orders that sent everyone scrambling. He then supervised an orderly distribution of the remains of Christmas dinner.

That night Nate and Alex joined the camel keepers around the fire outside the lean-to, sharing a bottle of whiskey that Hassan offered. They were astonished to learn that Ali and Hassan had not been allowed to go to San Antonio even once. Alex, gingerly stretching his sore leg, was secretly pleased that Hassan had not been able to see Elizabeth. He couldn't wait to do so himself.

"How'd you get the whiskey, then?"

"Pvt. Munoz brought it for me."

Nate took the bottle from Alex. "Thanks, Hassan. I appreciate y'all keepin' our business goin'. Mighty thoughtful of you, gettin' this bottle, especially since you fellas don't drink! I guess Alex and I'll have to take care of this by ourselves." He laughed heartily.

Tales of the expedition tumbled forth from Nate, Alex and Erdem, each one vying to impress Ali and Hassan. Only Abdullah was quiet, waiting for the moment to bring up rumors he had heard about conditions at Camp Verde. The mood turned sour when Ali and Hassan confirmed the stories. In detail, they recounted incidents of persecution from Sgt. Bly, collapse of the routine, and neglect of the camels. At the news that Ali and Hassan had not been paid, Abdullah reached for the half empty bottle, took a swig, and paced around the campfire muttering curses. No one even tried to restrain him.

The conversation ended abruptly with a clap of thunder. The group's rising temper was doused by a rainstorm that forced all six men into the lean-to together, where they endured a crowded and soggy sleep.

SAN ANTONIO, THE DAY AFTER CHRISTMAS

B ACK AT THE HOUSE on Laredo Street, Antoine responded to the bell, thinking that he must remind Miz Sylvia to install one at the new house. He opened the door cautiously, but flung it wide when he saw Major Babcock. "Come in sir. Good to see you. Let me call Miz Sylvia."

Sylvia and Elizabeth rushed to the Major. Taking one of the women in each arm, he held them close. "It's wonderful to see you. You both look beautiful."

"Thank you. We've missed you so much. Too bad you didn't make it yesterday in time for Christmas. Did the expedition go well?

"Very well. It was a remarkable success. Where are your brothers, Elizabeth?"

Zeke and Zach pushed past each other in their enthusiasm, nearly knocking their mother over.

"My goodness, boys, settle down. Cousin Babcock will tell us everything, but let him make himself at home. Antoine, ask Esther to bring hot tea and a plate of food." Sylvia paused, frowning slightly. "You've come just in time, you know. The second shipment of camels has arrived."

"I've seen them. A good-looking lot. They'll more than double the size of the herd. Much as I wished to come to you first, duty called me to the Alamo to dispatch my report. Imagine my excitement when I saw the camels."

Sylvia knew her cousin well enough to notice disappointment in a slight tilt to his mouth. Once he had eaten a little of the cold turkey and cornbread set before him, she gently probed. "Did you see Lt. Beale?"

"Indeed. He handed me orders to return to Washington."

"Oh dear, then it's true. Ever since we heard the rumors, I've been so upset. I assume you'll settle the camels first? And that we'll have the pleasure of your company at least until spring?'

"I'm afraid not. I'm to leave tomorrow."

"Why, that's cruel! Won't you go to Camp Verde first? What about your things?"

"As it happens, I have all of my reports and correspondence with me. Everything else can be shipped. For some reason my orders were not forwarded from Indianola. When Captain Van Steendam discovered the misplaced letter, he asked Lt. Beale to deliver it personally. Beale already knew the gist of it. Jefferson Davis wants me back east, sooner rather than later."

"What can this mean?"

"I fear the Secretary may be dissatisfied with my leadership."

"That's not possible."

"Perhaps not, but then again, the troops have had some difficulty responding to me. I'm not in their direct chain of command. Perhaps Lt. Beale will fare better. I must look on the bright side. In Washington, I can explain the camel cavalry to this new administration in person.

"The new administration. That must be it. Buchanan will put his own man in as Secretary of War."

"That could explain it. However, I find it shortsighted to play politics with something as important as defending the West. I believe my knowledge of the camels is crucial to the experiment's success. But for the moment, I must serve my country in other capacities."

Elizabeth listened to this exchange with increasing dismay. Finally Zachary asked the question that was troubling her. "Excuse me, but what will happen to Alex? Will he go back with you?"

"It's a damnable situation, excuse my language, ladies. I won't even be able to say goodbye to Alex. I would have preferred for us to travel together. I can tell you that his parents would like nothing better than to see him home in Philadelphia. But he's his own man and may do as he wishes."

"So he might stay?"

"Yes, but I fear his position may become less agreeable over time. He must choose his next steps carefully."

Elizabeth's conflicting emotions rendered her mute. Sylvia broke the silence. "Lt. Beale joined us for Christmas dinner. We spoke highly of both Alex and Nate. I hope that may help."

Jeremy Blackstone, having heard that Major Babcock was in town, slipped through the rear door of the McDermott house. He stopped in the hallway when he heard Nate's name.

Major Babcock continued. "I've recommended them to Lt. Beale. Both are civilians attached to my service. It will be up to him whether to keep them, assuming they want to stay on. He's brought along three young lads of his own."

"Yes, we met them, but they're nowhere near as useful as Nate and Alex, are they?"

"No, Beale's boys will be a long time coming to the knowledge that Nate and Alex have. But one of them is kin to Beale, so anything can happen."

Zachary was unquenchable. "What about Hassan and Ali and Abdullah?"

"They signed on for a year, and it's already been more than that, so I expect they'll be heading back to Egypt."

Elizabeth was overwhelmed with conflicting emotions. If Alex were serious about marriage, then certainly he would not go back east. How she wished she had been more encouraging at their last meeting! She hoped he would come to town soon so that she could convince him to stay in Texas. As for Hassan, in the past months, she had come to accept his impending return to Egypt. Yet, faced with the imminence of his departure, she felt disoriented as if standing before a confusing array of refracting mirrors.

Major Babcock was speaking again. "Lt. Beale told me his mission. He's to take the camels on an expedition to California."

"California? He didn't mention that at Christmas!"

Elizabeth felt faint. Alex might go back East and Hassan would return to Egypt. If Nate went to California with the camels, it was possible that she could lose all three friends at once, not just for a few months, but permanently.

Jeremy Blackstone, leaning against the wall in the corridor, suddenly felt sick to his stomach. He knew in his bones that Nate would join the expedition to California. He was equally certain that this time he could not accompany his grandson.

CALIFORNIA, MAYBE

ALEX LIMPED AROUND CAMP Verde, favoring his sore leg. He figured that it shouldn't still be bothering him. He must have slept on it wrong when they were all piled together in the lean-to. He resolved to take a careful look at it later.

Toward noon, a soldier raced into camp. "They're here! The second shipment's here!"

The bugler sounded assembly. By the time the first riders came into view, the men at Camp Verde were arrayed in proper formation. Expecting that Major Babcock would be bursting with pride, Nate and Alex wriggled into good position to see him leading the procession.

"Where is he, Nate? I can't see my Uncle."

"I can't either. Could be he's at the back."

"That isn't much like him."

"No it ain't. And who's that at the front?"

An unknown officer dismounted, saluted, and walked with Captain Chisholm toward the camel paddock. Scrounging for information, Nate and Alex were stunned to learn that Major Babcock was on his way to Washington and the camels were going to California. The immediate level of activity prevented them from thinking about the implications of this news. They led the new camels into a corral separate

from the acclimatized animals, set out feeding stations, unloaded the supplies, and found places in the shed for the
camel saddles. The new camel men, to their credit, jumped
to assist. Alex recognized Hi Jolly from Smyrna and was
pleased to be reunited with Gwynne Heap, who had been
left behind to acquire the second shipment. Nate watched
all of them from a distance, trying to figure out where Alex
stood with these newcomers. He noted that Pertag and Erdem rushed to greet Hi Jolly while Hassan, Ali and Abdullah had held themselves aloof, whispering closely together.

After the feeble winter sun dipped out of sight, Captain
Chisholm announced the lodging assignments. The bunkhouse addition, which had been completed while the expedition was away, would house the newly arrived soldiers as well
as the new camel men and Lt. Beale's boys. All existing sleeping arrangements were unchanged, meaning that Abdullah,
Ali, Hassan and Erdem would remain in the lean-to, which
leaked cold air like a sieve. The Egyptians were incensed that
the newcomers had been allocated better housing. Angrier
than ever, they decided that Ali must present their case to Captain Chisholm. Nate and Alex, also still in the lean-to, agreed.

The next morning, Ali donned a clean shirt while re-
hearsing and rephrasing his requests. When he was almost
prepared, a message came for Alex and Nate to report to
the officers' quarters, pre-empting Ali's plans.

"Come in, both of you." Lt. Beale spoke, but Capt.
Chisholm and Lt. Halter were also present.

"Yes, sir." They stood straight with as much military
comportment as they could muster.

"Mr. Babcock, I've had the pleasure of meeting your
uncle, a fine officer. The Major recommended you to my
service, as he did you, Mr. Wilkers."

Both Alex and Nate nodded.

"He described you as a fine pair, capable of handling
the camels under any situation. He commended your ability to teach the soldiers how to adapt to the peculiarities of
camel behavior."

"Thank you, sir." Inwardly, Alex flinched at the term
"peculiarities," fearing that this betrayed Lt. Beale's skepticism about the Camel Corps.

"I'm planning an expedition to California, to include at least half of the camels and a significant contingent of troops. There may be, and note I say, *may* be, a post for one or both of you, either with the camels who depart or with those who remain behind. In the next couple of weeks, I will make a decision. I am open to hearing your preferences."

"Thank you, sir."

"However, you should know that I am not fond of having civilians dangling around a military operation."

This Nate found ironic. He had met the three young civilians with Lt. Beale, and he certainly found them to be dangling. They had no idea what to do around camels. In addition, every aspect of their bearing triggered Nate's innate distrust of the privileged classes.

"If we find an appropriate assignment for you, you will need to enlist in the army."

Neither Nate nor Alex had considered this possibility.

"By the way, I dined on Christmas Day with Mrs. McDermott and her family. Mr. Wilkers, your grandfather was also present. They asked me to convey their fondest greetings to you."

"Thank you, sir," Nate and Alex answered in unison.

"That's all for now. Dismissed."

"Excuse me, sir," Alex interrupted. "Major Babcock promised us leave to go to San Antonio. I'm wondering..."

"Major Babcock is no longer in command. You are needed here. There will be no leave for anyone for the foreseeable future."

"Yes, sir." Enormously upset, Alex wondered how he could see Elizabeth. He had counted on being given leave within the next day or two. He was so distressed that he almost forgot his promise to Ali. "Excuse me, sir. I know you're very busy, but the Egyptian camel men really need to speak with you. Ali is waiting outside now."

"All right, send him in."

As they turned to go, Alex's leg gave way and he let out an involuntary groan.

"Mr. Babcock, are you injured?"

"No sir, sorry. A bruise from the expedition a few days ago. It's nothing."

"See the medic if it gets worse."

Under the giant live oak outside the officers' quarters, Nate and Alex, rather discomfited by their conversation with Lt. Beale, weighed their options. Both were skeptical about joining the Army and hoped that an alternative could be worked out that would let them stay with the camels. Although he didn't tell Nate, Alex would consider resigning altogether if it was the only way to see Elizabeth. He urgently needed to know what she was feeling.

While Alex brooded, Ali's meeting with Lt. Beale took longer than expected, and Nate began to worry that something was amiss. A soldier bounded out of the room and returned shortly with both Hassan and Abdullah. In a few minutes, Erdem and Pertag arrived from opposite sides of the camp. When the five camel keepers finally came out together, Pertag smirked in their direction and cut toward the bunkhouse. Ali's smile lit his face and Abdullah had a spring in his step. Erdem, too, looked satisfied, but Hassan's expression was inscrutable.

Ali was the spokesman. "It is decided. We are to go home. We leave tomorrow."

"Tomorrow? Ali, you must be kidding? How can you guys leave tomorrow? The new camels have just arrived. There's a ton of work to be done."

"I'm sorry, Alex. It is our chance. We have to take it."

"Didn't Lt. Beale ask whether you thought the camels would be all right? Doesn't he care about the mission?"

"He did ask. We told him the camels would be fine. We said that you could handle it along with Hi Jolly and the others."

"You don't honestly believe that?"

"I have my doubts. But you Americans have to do this on your own if you really want to have a Camel Corps. It should work, Inshallah."

"I'll be damned."

Nate spoke up. "Ease up a little, Alex. Things haven't exactly gone smoothly for these fellas, and I reckon it's likely to get worse."

"Shit, Nate, I guess you're right. But leaving tomorrow?"

"Alex, Nate, please understand. It is more than one year that we are away from home, and it is months that we receive no pay. Lt. Beale promised to write to Capt. Van Steendam in Indianola to pay us. It is our best chance. We must take it."

Alex continued to sulk, but Nate agreed. "If you can get out, you should go. But it's goin' to be rough for me and Alex. Y'all will be missed."

"Thank you, Nate. We will miss you too."

"Say, are all of you going?" Alex still couldn't believe that the men would leave tomorrow.

"Pertag will stay."

"That's not good."

Erdem had said nothing so far. "I will not go. I have no family. It is easy for me to stay here. I am friendly with Hi Jolly and Mico. The truth is, I have dreams of California."

"Well, if that don't beat all."

Alex couldn't fathom that the Egyptians were leaving. For him, the men and the camels were a single unit. He hadn't conceived of them as separate entities, had never imagined the Camel Corps without Abdullah, Hassan, and Ali. It dawned on him that he would probably never see Hassan again. After having worked, eaten, slept, and talked with Hassan for more than a year, Alex was not prepared for daily life without him. They had discussed every topic on earth, often speaking in their own hodgepodge of English and Arabic. They had laughed at each other's "foreign" ways, first in Egypt, then in America, and had come to appreciate each other's perspectives on life. Alex couldn't begin to guess how much he would miss him.

"Hey, Hassan, got a minute?"

"Sure." Hassan spoke first. "Alex, I want to thank you for your hospitality and your friendship. I wish you happiness, good health, and long life, and..."

"That's enough," Alex interrupted, laughing. "You're starting to sound like Ali." He laughed again. "Seriously, though, I'll miss you, too. Here, I want you to have this."

He handed Hassan the silver bolo tie that he had bought a few months ago in San Antonio and had worn every day since. Hassan choked up as he accepted the gift. He then removed the etched brass bracelet that had never left his wrist, and passed it to Alex, who thanked him profusely. They passed the rest of the afternoon walking along the creek, telling tales.

Outside the lean-to, a great roaring bonfire burned late into the night. Hassan was gratified that a number of the soldiers joined them for an evening of remembrance. Private Munoz presented Hassan with a belt that he had made himself, decorated with designs of camels burnt into the leather. Hassan admired the workmanship and artistry. Ali insisted on making a speech of thanks. The soldiers drank prodigious quantities of whiskey, laughed extravagantly, and mocked the camels as often as they praised them. In its roughness and its genuine spirit of friendship, the evening struck Hassan as quintessentially American.

The three Egyptians set off on horseback just after dawn under a blanket of gray clouds. Astride horses instead of camels, they looked strange and unnatural, as if they had been stripped of some vital part of their being. No one would have taken them for foreigners. Abdullah proudly displayed the star-shaped belt buckle that Nate had given him. Ali sported a fringed leather vest bartered from one of the soldiers. Hassan wore the wide-brimmed hat that he had purchased in Jamaica, the red bandana that he had received from a kind bystander when the camels landed at Indianola, his new belt from Pvt. Munoz, and Alex's bolo tie.

Alex, Nate and Erdem accompanied the Egyptians to the top of the first rise, still somewhat incredulous that they were really going. The six men lingered together, shaking hands and bidding each other safe journey. For Hassan, it was a deeply moving moment. Planted in his soul, these friendships could grow no further, but their roots remained. These people and their country had changed him. He would carry their memory for the rest of his life.

At the top of the second rise, Hassan looked back one final time to see his three friends still standing there. Everyone waved again. Then Hassan, Ali and Abdullah turned toward San Antonio, leaving behind them the great American camel experiment.

San Antonio, two days later

T HE WIND HAD BEEN blowing so stiffly all morning that
Antoine barely heard the bell. He had to lean against the
door to prevent it flying open with a bang. With his shoulder
pressed against the wood, he twisted his head around to see
who was there. His carefully neutral expression broke into a
smile at the sight of Ali, Abdullah and Hassan.

"Hello! Come in and get warm."

"Thank you. We would be most grateful for an audience with Mrs. McDermott."

Antoine smiled at Ali's formal English. "You're lucky
she's here. She's been out a lot, gettin' ready to move to the
new place. You gotta see it on your next visit. It's somethin' else."

"We are happy for her new home."

Baffled by Ali's bland response, Antoine looked quizzically at Hassan, whose gaze was mysterious. Abdullah seemed
oddly more contented than Antoine had ever seen him.

Sylvia whisked into the salon, curious about this unusual visit. "Gentlemen, please sit down."

Following right behind her mother, Elizabeth took a
seat and began desperately scanning Hassan's face. She had
not seen him since that day in Comfort almost three months
ago. The men kept their eyes lowered out of respect, making it difficult for her to know what anyone was thinking.
Zeke and Zachary barged into the room, excitedly shaking
hands and peppering their guests with questions. Seeing
that the Arabs were touched by her boys' enthusiasm, Sylvia let them carry on a bit before reminding them of their
manners. They retreated to stand behind Sylvia's chair and
waited impatiently while Esther served refreshments.

Abdullah chewed the delicious pastry slowly, taking in
every detail of the room. He had not been inside this house
before, but agreed with Hassan that it resembled the architecture of the Mediterranean. Knowing he would never
meet these people again, he looked closely at each one, including Antoine, who stood scarcely out of view in the corridor. He realized that he was fond of this family.

After a few more pleasantries, Ali took a deep breath and sat straight in his chair. "Madam, we have come to bid you farewell. We will return to our own country. It has been an honor to know you and your family. We have appreciated your gracious welcome. We will carry your memory on our journeys and in the stories we tell at home."

Sylvia was surprised, but also moved. "Oh my, thank you. We heard you might be going home. I confess that when we first encountered the camels, I had no idea that we would come to know you as we have. It has been a pleasure. You will be missed."

"You honor us with your kind words, Madam."

Elizabeth sat rigid, afraid that if she moved so much as a little finger, she would collapse in a puddle of tears. Her breathing came in shallow bursts. She remained watchful, content to let her brothers inquire after the details. She thought she was prepared for Hassan's departure, but in the moment, she was filled with sadness. Her spirits lifted upon learning that both Nate and Alex had returned safely from the expedition, but sank again when told that both had been refused permission to come to San Antonio. She had no way of finding out what either one intended. Everything was frustratingly uncertain. The only unalterable fact was that she was seeing Hassan for the last time. Boldly she stared at him, trying to memorize every feature of his face.

A shift in her mother's tone signaled an end to the visit. "We hope you have a safe and easy journey home. Please accept our best wishes for your future."

"And we thank you again for your hospitality and for showing us the warmth of your country. May Allah bless you and your family. May every success and happiness come to you, and may you live in good health, Inshallah."

As they rose, Zeke and Zach plunged forward, once more shaking hands all around and reminiscing about the trip from Indianola to San Antonio. Elizabeth locked eyes with Hassan, and, overcome, left the room.

As Sylvia turned to go, leaving her sons to banter awhile longer, Ali approached her. "May we give our regards to Esther and her daughters?"

"Of course. Antoine, show the men to the back."

Though the weather was cold, the high adobe walls protected the courtyard from the wind. A pale noonday sun illuminated the small group gathered around the fountain. Elizabeth watched from her bedroom window as the Arabs said their farewells to Antoine, Esther, Sally and Mabel. Seeing Hassan glance repeatedly in her direction, Elizabeth summoned the courage to step into the courtyard. Hassan immediately went to her, standing a respectful distance apart.

"Eleezabet." Never had she heard her name spoken with such emotion.

"Hassan, oh Hassan. I can't..." She started to choke up and turned away.

"Eleezabet, wait please. I have something for you." From his pocket he pulled out a leather thong the length of a bracelet on which were strung three round glass beads, separated from each other by knots. Similar in design, but of different sizes, each was colored in concentric circles: white, light blue, and indigo. "These are to protect someone against the evil eye. They bring luck. They were given to me by my family. I would like you to have one."

He untied the knots, selecting the middle bead and polishing it with his bandana. He held it a moment next to his heart and then lovingly placed it in her hand. "This one was a gift from Auntie Fatima."

Tears coursed down her cheeks as she accepted the bead, letting her fingers graze lightly against his hand. "Thank you, Hassan. I will cherish it."

"May it protect you and keep you well."

A million replies came to mind but none were able to find their way to her voice. She stood, trembling slightly, consuming him with her eyes. "Hassan, I have nothing for you."

"It's not necessary. I have built a room in my heart where you will live always."

She gasped. "Oh, Hassan." She turned abruptly. "I insist. I'll be right back."

Frantically she searched her room for something to give him, a token of her feelings. It had to be something that he could keep forever, something that would not upset his new wife, something useful that he might employ often. Finally she found it.

"Please accept this letter opener. It is part of a matched set, a gift from my father. I will keep the pen and inkwell, and I want you to have this. Whenever I take up my pen, I will think of you." Following his example, she shined the silver letter opener with her handkerchief, held it next to her heart, and then gave it over to him.

"Thank you. When I hold this, it will be like holding you."

Elizabeth sobbed. "Hassan, I will pray every day for your safe passage home. And for your happiness."

Ali crept over quietly. "Hassan, we must go."

Hassan put his hand over his heart, then extended it toward Elizabeth and turned away.

Although the Arabs could easily have slipped out the rear entrance, Antoine insisted on escorting the men back through the house and out the front door. He had learned much from them about respect. Following them outside, he closed the door behind him.

"Hassan, I want to give you this." In his hand he held his leather talisman of African origin.

"Thank you Antoine, but I cannot take it. You told me it was made for your father by your grandfather. You must keep it."

"I learned from you that my father and his father were followers of Mohammed. I follow Jesus. It doesn't seem right for me to keep it."

"But it is a gift from your father."

"I've thought about this a lot. My father loved the place in Africa where he was born. He always wanted to go home. I'll never know where he came from, but Egypt is in Africa. I think it would honor my father and grandfather to send this home with you. It might ease my father's soul."

Hassan looked to Ali, who nodded approvingly.

"I will do this. I will wear it close to my heart during the voyage." He slipped the amulet's leather string over his head and tucked it inside his shirt. "When I am home, I will ask my grandfather Alhaji Mustafa how to remember your father and your grandfather. He will pronounce the correct prayers. I will also speak to my grandmother Ara, who knows the proper way to respect ancestors. Your grandfather and your father will become adopted ancestors in our family, and we will honor their memory."

Camp Verde, Texas, December 31, 1856

My dearest Annabelle,

My spirits are so low it is difficult to lift a pen. The expedition returned in good order, and a few days later the second shipment of camels arrived, earlier than expected. Although both facts should have occasioned rejoicing, I am absolutely dejected. Major Babcock has been summoned to Washington, while once again there were no orders concerning myself.

Even more distressing, Lt. Beale, the new commander, plans to depart with the majority of the camels for California by springtime.

Please convey this information to your father and plead with him to secure my reassignment posthaste lest I be transferred to California along with the camels.

Your devoted husband,

Winston

SAN ANTONIO, JANUARY 1, 1857

NEW YEAR'S DAY WAS celebrated with a lavish meal of roast pork and black-eyed peas, dishes designed to ensure good luck for the coming year. Elizabeth consumed ample helpings, hoping to fulfill her wishes, the most immediate of which was to avoid moving to the new house. The plan was for Sylvia to move first, followed by Zeke, who wanted to stay in the old house for a short while. Then she and Zachary would have the adobe house to themselves, and she could once again feel that she had some control over her life without her mother supervising every tiny detail.

So far the necessary steps were unfolding as she hoped. Almost all the furniture had been cleared from the courtyard, either taken to the new house or rearranged inside the adobe house. Tomorrow her mother's bedroom would be dismantled and her mother would sleep at the new house. Nevertheless, Elizabeth took nothing for granted, especially after the conversation she had overheard between her mother and Jeremy Blackstone.

"I swear she is stubborn. Maybe I should issue an ultimatum. We are one family. We should live in one house!"

"Sylvia, she's been through a lot. She's still hurtin' from her father's death."

"I know, but she's a child!"

"She's growin' up."

"Of course she's growing up, Jeremy. But, as you said, she's been through a lot. She's so vulnerable. I should watch over her."

"Maybe she needs to feel that somethin' is hers to decide."

"But she's so young!"

"How old were you when you left your folks to come to Texas?"

"That's not the same thing. I was married."

"You were clear across the country from your parents. You and Elizabeth are in the same town."

"All right, I'll leave it be for now."

"It'll be all right. I've watched her. I think she needs to be by herself for awhile."

As she wished for luck and contemplated her New Year's resolutions, Elizabeth fervently prayed that nothing would happen to upset her mother's exodus.

Moving day dawned unseasonably warm and cheerful, a good omen. After breakfast, Elizabeth dutifully helped her mother to fold the remaining clothes and fasten the last valise. Impatiently she waited for Moses to bring the carriage. When at last her mother, Zeke and Zach were ready to climb in, she begged to remain behind.

"I'll come to see the new house soon, Mama. There's some things I want to do here. Zeke and Zach can tell me all about it when they come back here tonight."

"Elizabeth, I don't understand you these days, but all right."

The instant they turned the corner, Elizabeth strolled from room to room, touching the walls and furniture, visualizing how she would reconfigure the house to her taste.

Across town at the Menger house, Jeremy filled a borrowed cart with his belongings. After Sylvia returned from Galveston, he had settled back into his little room to think. Nate was a huge worry. Although Nate was safely returned from the expedition, he was stuck out at Camp Verde. Jeremy's only eyewitness account of Nate's situation had come during a surprising visit by the Egyptians, who had stopped to pay their respects on their way home. He had been tickled at their effusive praise of his cooking, but their stories of hostility at the camel camp distressed him. Their assurance that Alex always backed Nate assuaged his concerns a bit. But he believed that Alex would stay in Texas for Elizabeth, leaving Nate to go to California alone. Nate probably wouldn't even be able to say goodbye.

Jeremy's other problem was Sylvia McDermott. He had developed feelings for her, profound and compelling and unlike anything he had known before. With his first wife, Melissa, the relationship had been youthful exuberance, intense but intermittent, due to his constant rambling. His second wife, Hilde had provided a practical way to care for Nate while Jeremy's affection for her developed over time. With Sylvia, it was another matter altogether, completely unexpected. A thousand small, inescapable attractions bound him to her. The ardor of his feelings caught him unprepared, overcoming his unease with the difference in their stations and convincing him that the two of them were right for each other. Most surprisingly, Sylvia professed the same devotion to him. He was at a loss to explain how two such mismatched people could be so comfortable together. To Jeremy, it bordered on the miraculous. For now, he had no choice but to put aside his worries about Nate and give rein to his fondness for Sylvia.

The handcart held a few clothes, some pots and pans, the rug that Melissa had made him, his pistol and rifle, an old family Bible, his herbs, and his medical kit. Lastly, he squeezed his rocking chair out the door of the tiny room and balanced it on top. Deliberately he turned south across the river.

In the middle of the afternoon, Sylvia's new house loomed as a foreboding edifice, standing by itself and backlit by the lowering sun. He wondered again what had possessed her to build it. Unable to picture a future neighborhood surrounding it, he saw only stark loneliness. This house struck him as anything but homelike, at least not yet. However, he had a lot of faith in Sylvia. If she wanted a thriving community here, it would certainly grow. The woman seemed capable of altering almost anything that she touched. She had transformed herself, and she had certainly remade him, rejuvenating him and giving him a new purpose.

The double doors to the new house stood open. When he saw Jeremy approach with his handcart, Antoine rushed down the wide front stairs to meet him. "Hello, Mr. Blackstone. May I help you with these things?"

"Thanks, Antoine. Could you call Miz Sylvia please?"

Sylvia tripped lightly down the stairs, waving and smiling. "Hello, Jeremy."

"Howdy, Sylvia. You look to be feelin' fine today."

"Very fine. How are you?" In spite of the fact that she had been waiting for this day, a sudden awkwardness gripped her. "I see you've brought your rocker."

"Yup. You know what it means if this rocker goes up on that porch."

"I'm counting on it." She said, smiling shyly but looking him in the eye.

Antoine unloaded the cart and piled Jeremy's things in the dining room for want of clear instructions where they should be stowed. Jeremy carried the rocking chair up the stairs and set it carefully next to Sylvia's.

"Antoine, could you return that cart to town for me?"

"Yes, Mr. Blackstone."

Sylvia added, "And Antoine, take Rebecca with you. You both are dismissed for tonight. Stay at the old house and we'll finish moving tomorrow. Come back at noon."

"Yes'm." Antoine turned his head away to prevent her from seeing his expression.

Sylvia and Jeremy rocked in companionable silence after Antoine and Rebecca were long gone. A deep contentment descended along with the sun until a wintry chill robbed the day of its unseasonable warmth.

"Let's go inside." At the threshold, he scooped her up and carried her over.

Laughing like a girl, she grabbed his hand and led him upstairs. Having known only her husband, Sylvia had no idea what to expect from another man. She was apprehensive about this new experience, uncertain how she would respond. Above all else, she hoped that her nervous anticipation would not ruin the moment. To her great delight, Jeremy made her feel at ease. Moreover, he knew his way around a woman's body. He kissed the hollow of her throat, the inside of knee, and the small of her back. Every inch of her received his attention. He caressed, licked, stroked, and hugged. He guided her from giggling to gasping, until her body was aflame with an urgency that demanded deliverance.

Her screams of joy echoed around the empty house, filling it with life and christening it a home.

CAMP VERDE, JANUARY 2, 1857

A FTER THE EGYPTIANS LEFT, Alex, Nate and Erdem were in constant demand to help the newly arrived men and camels integrate into Camp Verde. The increased workload was especially taxing for Alex, whose leg continued to annoy him. For a few days he had been healing well and walking more evenly, but recently his limp had worsened again, due to recurring pain in his leg. He wondered absentmindedly how he could be so banged up from a fall that had been almost ten days ago. He had probably bruised it during the recent frenzy, bumping up against camels and hefting all sorts of gear. He found it hard to think clearly. The ache in his leg kept him from focusing properly. At times, all he could do was complete the chore in front of him and then sit down to rest.

Nate, too, was overworked and grumpy, partially because he still wasn't sure whether or not to go to California.

Around the campfire with Alex and Erdem, he launched another complaint.

"New Year's Day comes and goes without any celebration. At least they gave us black-eyed peas. Otherwise pretty meager. Not such a great year, judgin' from the start of it. Look at us, still sleepin' in the lean-to."

Erdem took a deep breath. "I must say something, Nate. I am invited to join Hi Jolly in the bunkhouse."

"What the hell? They invited you, but not us? Those assholes."

"Sgt. Bly controls the soldiers, and he will never ask you. But Hi Jolly is leader of the camel men. If I go to California, I must get along with him."

"Goddamn it."

"I am sorry, Nate, but I must do this."

Nate could not keep the sarcasm from his voice. "You go ahead. Alex and I will take over these high-class lodgings. We'll be fine sleepin' here."

Alex had been uncharacteristically silent. "Yes, sleep."

Startled, Nate noticed a sheen on Alex's face.

"Sleep," Alex said again, his voice slurred. Then he toppled over.

Nate jumped up and touched Alex's forehead. "He's burning with fever. Erdem, go and get Lt. Halter. I don't care if he's havin' dinner. Tell him it's urgent."

Carrying a lantern, Lt. Halter arrived flanked by Corporal Watkins, the closest thing the company had to a medic. "I hope you gentlemen have a good reason for dragging me away from my evening meal." When he saw Alex, his tone shifted. "Good Lord, he's blazing. Get those clothes off and bring some water."

Erdem ran for water, while Nate unbuttoned Alex's shirt and removed it. Lt. Halter commanded, "Trousers, too. You must cool him everywhere. A bathtub would be best, but this will have to do."

Nate noticed that Alex's leg was swollen. "Sir, he had an injury a few days ago, but the skin wasn't broken."

"Cut the clothes off!" ordered Lt. Halter.

Nate took a knife and made a slit down Alex's leg. Alex moaned, and at mid-thigh, he screamed. The leg was grossly swollen, with black, dead-looking skin sloughing off, and there was a putrid odor. Gagging, Nate turned away.

Lt. Halter was horrified. "Corporal? Your recommendations?"

"I'm sorry, Lieutenant. I don't rightly know what to do with something like this."

"Wipe him down with the cool water. Lots of it. We have to break the fever. Corporal, get hot water and strong soap. Wash that leg to see what's under there. On the double!"

Alex shivered, moaned and mumbled incoherently. While the corporal cleaned the wound, Nate pinned Alex to keep him from thrashing about. Lt Halter, holding a perfumed handkerchief over his nose, leaned in close.

"This tissue is necrotic. It must be cut out before he develops blood poisoning or gangrene. Corporal, can you perform such a surgery?'

"Sir, I ain't been trained on this, but I have a special knife. I can give it a try."

"Give it a try? Corporal, do you know the location of the artery in a man's leg? Can you be sure you won't sever it causing him to bleed to death?" For once, Nate appreciated Lt. Halter's imperious tone.

"Artery, why no sir. I guess not."

Capt. Chisholm and Lt. Beale joined the scene, and Lt. Halter briefed them on the gravity of the situation. "There's no one in Camp with that kind of skill," Capt. Chisholm confirmed. "The corporal can do amputations but not something this precise."

"Amputation? Did you say amputation?" Nate's voice was tremulous.

"Calm down, Mr. Wilkers." Lt. Halter was surprisingly authoritative. "Young master Babcock is not going to perish this night, but it would be best to get him to a doctor. Captain, I recommend that he be transported to Comfort. They have a qualified surgeon there who will know what to do."

"All right, let's get going." Nate jumped up. "Sorry sirs, permission requested."

"Granted, Mr. Wilkers. Fit out the wagon."

"Excuse me, sir. The road is terrible for wagons. We can rig a stretcher onto one of the camels. We'd make better time."

"Fine, if you can make it work. In the meantime, Corporal, get this man cooled down."

Nate, Erdem, Pvt. Munoz, and the soldiers from the *Supply* soon rigged up a stretcher attached to Massanda's packsaddle on one side and balanced on the other by a full water barrel.

"We think this will do it, Captain, and we'll also have a good supply of water to keep him cool."

"Good. Pvt. Munoz, accompany Mr. Wilkers and Mr. Babcock to Comfort. Report to Mr. Altgelt, and let him direct you to the surgeon."

Erdem stepped forward. "Lt. Beale, please."

"No, Erdem, I need you here."

Blessed by clear skies and a full moon, the three camels made reasonable time in the night brightness. Strapped into his stretcher, Alex drifted in and out of consciousness. When awake, he moaned or babbled incoherently, making Nate increasingly anxious. Once when Nate stopped to give him water, Alex, though delirious, spoke distinctly, "Elizabeth, don't leave me, please. I want to marry you."

In Comfort, the surgeon laid Alex on a table and began his examination. "I don't understand this. There is a large bruise here."

"Yeah, he smashed against a rock over a week ago."

"But look at the color of it. This side is fading, but down there it's livid. And here, the tissue is black." He probed the area. Alex woke to a crashing pain and let loose a yell.

"Sorry, young man. I must look." Alex gritted his teeth. "Ah, see, there's a deep hole. Dead tissue everywhere. This looks like a completely different wound that has joined the first one. Was he bitten by a snake?"

"No, no, I've been with him every day for the last three months. Nothing like that."

"I will do what I can. Hold him. He must be very still."

Alex gulped a glass of whiskey before they tied him to the table, stretching a piece of cloth across his torso to bind his arms. Nate held his ankles to keep the legs quiet.

"The doc says you've gotta chew down on this. It's gonna hurt."

"Shit, Nate. Already hurts like…" His voice trailed off as he bit down hard and his eyes widened in pain. Then, mercifully, Alex passed out.

The first rays of dawn slipped into the little room. Alex lay asleep on the table, his leg sporting a brand new bandage. Nate slumped on a chair in the corner while Pvt. Munoz dozed on the floor. The surgeon, having spent a sleepless night, sat in the kitchen taking coffee with his wife. When Nate began to rouse, the surgeon's wife extended a warm cup.

"Thank you, ma'am. Well, Doc, what do you think?"

"I have cleaned the wound and removed the dead tissue. But I do not understand the cause. If whatever is killing the tissue continues to do so, it could become blood poisoning. The safest thing would be to cut off the leg now, but I am not sure."

"Cut off his leg?" Nate said this a little too loudly.

"I heard that," cried Alex, who reflexively tried to move. "Aaah!"

The doctor repeated his explanations. "I recommend that you let me amputate."

Alex surprised everyone with his lucidity. His fever was in temporary remission. "How much time do I have to decide?"

"You might be safe for a day or two. Perhaps."

"That's enough for me. Nate, can you get me to San Antonio? I have to see Elizabeth. I can't decide this on my own. If she's gonna marry me, she should have a say."

The surgeon intervened. "San Antonio? It will take too long. It's too dangerous."

Alex insisted. "Not on the camels. If we leave now, we'll be there tomorrow, right Nate?"

"Yeah, maybe sooner if you can stand it. The camels can go without resting. We'd have to trot or gallop sometimes. You'll be bounced around. It could hurt like the devil."

"It's what I want. Bounce me to hell and back, but get me to San Antonio."

While his wife tore strips of muslin into neat strips, the surgeon showed Nate how to clean the wound with carbolic acid and wrap it tightly with a clean bandage. Frau Altgelt brought a basket of food.

"The wound must stay clean. Use each bandage only once and burn the used ones when you get to San Antonio. I will give him laudanum to help him sleep and ease the pain. Keep him cool and give him lots of water. When you reach San Antonio, go to my friend Schuler in La Villita. We wish you a safe journey."

"Thank you sir."

As they were about to depart, a woman's call stopped them. It was Agnes, running from a nearby house. "Massa Alex, Massa Alex!"

Frau Altgelt gently took hold of Agnes. "There, there, Agnes. He is hurt, but Nate will take him to San Antonio."

Agnes remembered Nate well enough and still blamed him for Samuel's death, in spite of everything Esther and Miz Sylvia had explained. Her face darkened. She was afraid of Nate, and she didn't like seeing Alex hurt. Already strapped into his stretcher on Massanda and beginning to feel the woozy effects of the laudanum, Alex startled when Agnes grabbed his hand.

"You be careful, Massa Alex. You get well now. Go home to Missy 'Lizbeth." From her belt, upon which were suspended her usual assortment of odd objects, Agnes untied a rabbit's foot. "Here, you take this. It lucky. Keep you safe." She wrapped his hand around it. Then, as he faded out and lost his grip, she stuffed it into his shirt pocket.

Nate and Pvt. Munoz, with Alex lying in the stretcher, left Comfort at a trot, determined to make as much time as they could while the day was new. They nibbled on the sandwiches, sausages, and apples that Frau Altgelt had prepared, stopping only to relieve themselves and to tend to Alex. When the winter night fell early, they simply kept going. Fighting their own fatigue, they took turns dozing in the saddle. The gibbous moon illuminated their route until they recognized the environs of San Antonio. They had covered 50 miles in a single long day.

Nate's pounding on Doc Schuler's door roused half of La Villita. Nate and Pvt. Munoz carried Alex into the surgeon's reception room, where again he was laid out on a table. While Pvt. Munoz went to the Menger to find Jeremy Blackstone, Nate leapt back onto Ibrim to go for Elizabeth.

The household on Laredo Street had not yet settled into a rhythm since Antoine had decamped to the new house. Elizabeth wasn't used to answering the door and often didn't hear the bell. This night, she woke to an intense battering sound. Throwing on a robe, she shuffled to the front to find Zach already opening the door for Nate, whom she had not seen for months.

"Oh Nate!" She ran right into his arms and wrapped herself around him in a great hug. He let his arms close about her for a second, shocked at how natural this felt and terribly guilty that he should be holding her at a time like this.

"I've missed you so much." She stepped back. "Let me look at you. How are you? Did you come alone? Where's Alex? Come in and let me get you something warm."

Zachary interrupted. "Nate, what's wrong? Why are you here?"

"Alex is sick, real sick. I left him with the surgeon over at La Villita. Elizabeth, he's askin' for you."

"Oh no! Let me dress. Esther, prepare food for Nate and take it to Doc Schuler's."

While Elizabeth tossed on some clothes, Nate told Zachary what had happened. "Hey, Zach, where's your mama?"

"She and Zeke are already livin' at the new house. So's your grandpa, by the way." Nate raised an eyebrow at this.

Elizabeth raced out the front door. Grabbing her waist, Nate gave her a boost as she tossed her leg over and swung onto Ibrim. He jumped on behind, already commanding the kneeling camel to rise. Wordlessly they dashed to Doc Schuler's, where they met Jeremy. Nate lifted Elizabeth from the camel and watched as she ran into the house. Jeremy noticed his grandson's gaze following her up the steps.

"Nate, my God you're a sight for sore eyes."

"You, too, Grandpa." Jeremy embraced his grandson with a force that Nate thought would crack his ribs. "It's all right, Grandpa, I'm all right. Let's go to Alex."

Alex, who had been resting with his eyes closed, brightened considerably when he heard Elizabeth's voice. "Elizabeth!"

"Alex, what happened?"

"A little mishap that got kinda complicated. I have to make some decisions. They might have to amputate."

Elisabeth flinched visibly. "Oh, Alex." She didn't know what to say.

Jeremy peered over Doc Schuler's shoulder as he summarized his assessment. "My friend in Comfort did a good job. The wound is clean. The boy looks healthy. Maybe he can keep the leg."

"What's this, Doc?" Jeremy pointed to the odd coloration.

"I'm not sure. Alex, did you get a snakebite?"

"No, but it's funny, they asked the same question in Comfort. Why?"

"The depth of the hole, the dead tissue. It seems like a reaction to some kind of poison."

Jeremy pursued the point. "Nate, Alex, both of you, think! Did anything happen on the trail besides the accident with the camel?"

"No."

"What about when you got back to Camp Verde? Anything unusual?"

"No, Grandpa we worked our butts off, but nothing unusual. Except maybe we didn't get enough sleep because six of us had to sleep in the lean-to."

"Alex, where did you sleep? I mean what part of the lean-to?"

"Over in the corner, Mr. Blackstone. We had to rearrange some stuff. It was dusty, and then damp from the rain, but nothin' else."

"Hell, I bet it's a spider bite."

"I don't remember being bit by a spider."

"You might not have noticed. The one I'm thinkin' of is small, brownish, a recluse. You probably disturbed it squeezin' everyone into the small space. It's poisonous. That would explain the dead flesh and the fevers."

Doc Schuler pronounced his verdict. "Let's watch it for a few days."

Pvt. Munoz felt obliged to return to Camp Verde with the three camels. After composing a brief note of apology to Capt. Chisholm and Lt. Beale, Nate settled himself to stay with Alex and Elizabeth for as long as it took. Alex went in an out of consciousness, while Elizabeth and Nate refused to leave his side. Seeing Elizabeth dozing with her head on the foot of his bed and Nate curled up on his bedroll on the floor, Mrs. Schuler moved a daybed into the room for Elizabeth and found a cot for Nate. Jeremy checked in frequently and stayed for long stretches, as did Sylvia, Zeke, and Zach. From time to time Mrs. Schuler found Antoine on her back step waiting for news. On the third day, Alex became feverish, the edges of the wound once again inflamed and dark. A red streak, tender to the touch, had started down his leg.

"Mr. Blackstone, do you want to tell him, or shall I?"

"I'll do it." Jeremy went over to Alex, who saw at once what was coming. "We gotta take the leg."

Alex was unable to prevent a single tear from trickling down his right cheek. "Elizabeth?"

"Alex, what's a leg? Let them do it, please. You have to survive this."

"Elizabeth, I'll always remember the night we danced at Mrs. Eberly's place in Indianola. You were so beautiful in that yellow gown." Sitting up, he downed the whiskey that Jeremy thrust at him.

"Think of that night," Doc Schuler ordered, as he put a chloroform-soaked rag over Alex's nose and mouth.

Jeremy dragged Elizabeth from the room, urged her into the carriage, and bade Moses take her to Laredo Street. As she turned the corner, Elizabeth swore she heard Alex scream. Less than an hour later, Nate appeared at the door.

"It was surprisingly quick. Alex is out cold, but they think he'll wake up in an hour or two. Let's eat somethin', and then I'll take you back."

After the first few days of agonizing pain, Alex rebounded. The cauterized amputation scabbed over nicely. He was awake more often, eating better, sitting up, and even standing with the help of crutches. One afternoon when Alex was feeling especially strong, Nate left him and went to meet the supply detail at the Alamo to get news of Camp Verde. Alone together, Elizabeth and Alex watched dust motes dancing in the afternoon light. Alex shifted to a sitting position.

"Elizabeth, I want to ask you something. Er, I want to ask you the most important question of my life. I need to get down on my knees, but as I only have one knee, I don't know how to do that." He laughed, breaking the nervous tension. "Seriously, I can't picture my life without you. I want to stay here with you, but without my leg, everything has changed. I don't know what kind of life I can offer you."

For Elizabeth, every detail in the room came into sharper focus: the glint of light off the surgical instruments, the crisp white bandage on Alex's stump, the faint medicinal aroma hanging in the air. Her mind captured every nuance of expression that passed across his face, every inflection of his voice. Years later she could recount this conversation in minute precision. Listening with extreme attention, she was determined to handle this discussion better than the last one.

"Alex" she said, taking his hand. "No one knows what life will offer us. I mean, who would have thought I would be in San Antonio? Or that I would come here with a train of camels?" They both smiled. "Or," and she paused, because it was still hard for her to speak of it, "or that my father would die."

"I know. But I have only one leg, and that makes for all kinds of problems. I don't even know if I can ride a horse, let alone a camel."

"Alex, a horse does not make a man."

"Maybe not. But how will I get around? Will I live my life in one of those wheeled chairs? Will you have to push me all over, help me do the simplest things? For the rest of your life? I can't ask you do to that."

"Of course you can ask. And the answer might surprise you, Alex Babcock. What exactly are you asking?"

"A while ago, I asked you to wait."

Elizabeth interrupted. "I know, and I want to apologize. I was very rude and I'm so sorry."

"It doesn't matter. The point is, you did wait. You're here with me now. And I want to ask you to wait a bit longer, until I can move around, until I have a chance to think about things more. But as soon as I feel up to it, I'm going to ask you something else."

This time she did not hesitate. "Of course I'll wait. I will do so cheerfully, here by your side!"

Elizabeth smiled as he reached his hand behind her head, pulled her toward him, and kissed her. He tasted different from Hassan, but his kiss was delicious. More promissory than passionate, this kiss was tender and full of feeling, offering a future that could make her happy. Elizabeth kissed him back, warmly and gently.

Returning to find Alex and Elizabeth gazing into each other's eyes, Nate knew that something monumental had occurred. He had been wavering about California, but now he knew he would go. He was sure that he could not live near Elizabeth, watching her happily married to Alex. After spending so much time in close company with her these last days, he felt very attached to her and wanted an intimacy that he could never have. It would be pure torture to be around her while she belonged to his best friend.

"Howdy, Alex."

"Hi, Nate." Alex smiled. "Elizabeth, why don't you take a break? Nate's back, and you two don't have to be watching over me all the time." When Elizabeth left the building, Alex leaned back with his hands behind his head.

"Whoa, Alex, you're grinnin' like a 'possum eatin' shit. What happened?"

"I think she will marry me."

"What do you mean, you think? Did you ask her or not?"

"Well, I sorta did."

"Damn it, Alex, I swear you told me somewhere near Howard Springs that you 'sorta' asked her a couple months ago. Did you or didn't you?"

"I asked her to wait and she agreed. Then I kissed her." Alex grinned more broadly, and Nate struggled to maintain a veneer of camaraderie.

"Good for you, Alex. I guess you're feelin' better."

"Yeah, really better. Without my leg, you know, I've been, uh, worried, uh, you know, about how everything else might or might not be working. After that kiss, man, I can tell you, everything is working!" He laughed out loud, causing Nate to laugh along with him.

"I hadn't thought of that."

"Yeah, a big relief. Hey Nate, what did you learn at the Alamo?"

"I'm pretty near to losin' my position at Camp Verde. The Captain's complainin' that I've been away too long. Lt. Beale doesn't know me, and Lt. Halter, well, who knows if he's stickin' up for me. Or if he is, if that even helps. I gotta get back. The supply detail's leavin' in a couple hours, and I need to see my Grandpa first."

"You thinking of signing on for California?"

"Maybe. I'll be back in a week to check on you, even if I have to break the rules to get here."

"By that time, I hope to be long gone from this place. I'm tired of the smells around here. Look for me at the Laredo house." Alex struggled to stand up on one leg, leaning against the table, and the men embraced. "Nate, you're the first person I met in Indianola. We've been through all this together, and now you've saved my life." His voice caught briefly.

"Now Alex, don't go gettin' sentimental on me. Anyone would've done it."

"No, not anyone. Thanks, Nate."

"See you in a week. Don't start runnin' around and makin' trouble before I get back."

From his rocking chair on the front porch of the new house, Jeremy Blackstone spotted the horseman and knew it was Nate. He sat squarely, a strong, healthy young man. Although Jeremy took no satisfaction in Alex's misfortune, he was abjectly grateful that Nate was not lying in Doc Schuler's reception room with an amputated leg. Seeing Alex injured, Jeremy had been forced to confront the reality that he could no longer protect Nate. This helplessness struck a nerve of terror.

"Howdy, Grandpa."

"Howdy." Jeremy climbed down the stairs to meet Nate at ground level. Nate dismounted, hugged his grandfather, then lost his words.

"You wanna see the house?"

"Sure."

By the time they had toured the main hall, salon, small sitting room, dining room, kitchen, and library, Nate was overwhelmed. Upstairs he counted six bedrooms, and noted that his grandfather's gear was installed in a room that connected to Sylvia's through an interior door.

"This place is somethin' else."

"Yeah, takes some gettin' used to. Wanna talk outside?"

Nate was relieved. Although he felt at home in the adobe house, this mansion was intimidating. Jeremy led him down to the river where two stone benches and a palm tree formed the beginnings of a garden.

"Sylvia has plans for scads of flowers and bushes. It's a good place to watch the sunset."

Nate noted the familiar way his grandfather spoke about Sylvia McDermott. "You like it here, Grandpa?

"Well enough. It's good for me. I can't explain it. This thing with me and Sylvia, well, it's the best I've ever had."

"Really, Grandpa?"

"Yup, I've been blessed with two good women, as you know. But with her, it's somethin' unusual."

"So you gonna marry her?"

"Nope. I've buried two wives already. Somethin' about this…" He hesitated. "I can't risk it."

"That's a little superstitious, ain't it?"

"Maybe."

"You're not worried about what people will say?"

"I ain't never been, but I did ask her that. She's feisty, says she can't be bothered. So I'm takin' her at her word. Maybe later we'll get married. Not now."

A couple of longhorns came to drink on the other side of the river. A turtle slid off a log making a gentle splash while a blue heron strutted delicately along the bank.

"Grandpa, I've got some big decisions to make. The camels are goin' to California."

"I've heard."

"I'm thinkin' I'll go along."

Although he had been expecting this, Jeremy felt a tightening in his stomach and a tension in his jaw. He made himself say what he had resolved to say. "Whatever you decide, I'll back you. Completely."

This unexpected, unequivocal support from his grandfather loosened Nate's tongue. He confessed his doubts and misgivings. Would Lt. Beale accept him? What if he had to join the Army in order to go? What kind of commander was Lt. Beale? Would Sgt. Bly be going, and if so, who would keep him in check? What about Lt. Beale's three young companions? How dangerous was crossing the desert? If he didn't go, what would he do? What about the possibility of going out to California and then coming back?

Jeremy listened to every idea and argument, pro and con, but held his peace unless asked a direct question. Then he offered brief, simple suggestions. The effort to keep from begging Nate to stay was causing a slight throbbing at his temple. But there was one thing he felt duty-bound to ask.

"You gonna tell her?"

"Who, Elizabeth?"

"Yup."

"No, Grandpa, not now. When I finally decide if I'm goin', then I'll tell her."

"That's not what I mean. You gonna tell her how you feel about her?"

"Grandpa!"

"I got eyes, son."

"Ain't no point. She's gonna marry Alex."

"You sure about that?"

"He's pretty much asked her. I couldn't go after her now anyway, tryin' to take his girl when he's so banged up. It would be like kickin' a man while he's down. I wouldn't do that to an enemy, let alone a friend."

"If you skip out for California without sayin' anything, you might spend the rest of your life wishin' you had."

"Even if I said somethin', and even if she didn't laugh me right out of the room, don't you think it would be too peculiar, you takin' up with her mama and me makin' advances to her?"

Jeremy spoke sharply. "Now you listen here, Nate. What's between me and Sylvia has nothin' to do with you. You work this out for yourself, and you pay no mind to other people."

"Sure, Grandpa. It's late. I gotta go. I promised Alex I'll be back in a week. See you then."

"You keep well, Nate, and listen around you. The answers will come."

CAMP VERDE, LATE JANUARY 1857

NATE WONDERED WHERE HE would sleep this night. Erdem had moved to the bunkhouse, but no one had yet offered Nate a place there. He didn't relish sleeping in the lean-to alone, especially if it still harbored the spider that bit Alex. Although his grandfather had assured him that the spider would be long gone, he planned to brush out every corner and crack. Riding straight to the new officers quarters, he found Capt. Chisholm, Lt. Beale, and Lt. Halter together just before dinner.

"Reporting for duty, sirs."

Capt. Chisholm responded first. "Good evening, Mr. Wilkers. How is Mr. Babcock?"

"His leg had to be amputated, but he's comin' along."

"They had to amputate? Because of a bad fall?"

"Not exactly sir. Blood poisoning from a spider bite." Mrs. Chisholm, who had stepped into the room, let out a little shriek and returned to the kitchen.

Lt. Beale gave Nate an appraising look. "Mr. Wilkers, Capt. Chisholm and Lt. Halter have recommended you for the expedition to California. We plan to depart in several weeks. In the interval, I'll be watching you. Dismissed."

"Yes, sir, thank you, sir."

Lt. Halter sipped his whiskey and added, "Mr. Wilkers, your personal effects are in the custody of Private Munoz in the bunk house. And, when you have a chance, check on Ibrim."

"Yes, sir." Before his foot hit the bottom step, Nate broke into a run toward the camel paddock, where he found Ibrim separated from the others. Erdem was bent over the camel's foreleg, wrapping a bandage around it.

"What the hell happened to Ibrim?" he called as he leapt over the fence. He patted Ibrim's side and nuzzled the animal.

"Nate! Welcome back. How is Alex?" Erdem stood up and shook Nate's hand, smiling eagerly. Nate had to remind himself how important politeness was to these foreigners. "Good to see you, too, Erdem. Alex lost the leg."

"I am very sorry. May Allah the Most Merciful protect him. I have been praying for him, but I am not as pious as Hassan and Ali. I will pray harder. I hope he will recover well?"

"He's much better. Already trying to figure out how to ride a camel now that he has only one leg."

Erdem smiled. "Ah, good. That sounds like Alex."

"Yeah. How 'bout you? How are things goin'?"

"Many stories to tell you, but first Ibrim."

Some of the soldiers thought it would be amusing to see if "Nate's camel" was really as fast as its reputation. At first Ibrim had obeyed, tearing across the countryside and giving the riders a thrill. But a couple of the men were rough with him, and he refused first one then another. Confronted with the worst offenders, he spat at them, bellowed horrifically, and even kicked. Someone got the idea to set Ibrim against a newly arrived male with the goal of "taking some of the spunk out" of Ibrim. The fight had been vicious, with both camels receiving deep bites on their necks before Hi Jolly and Erdem stopped the fight.

"Nate, it was terrible, but Hi Jolly knew it was wrong. Lt. Beale, too. He was very angry. Anyway, you can see that the neck is almost healed.."

"What about the leg?"

Nate could scarcely contain his fury as Erdem's story continued. Bragging as usual, Sgt. Bly claimed to be un-afraid of any camel, so one of the new men dared him to ride Ibrim. Among the seasoned soldiers it was widely known that Ibrim had taken a dislike to Sgt. Bly ever since he had mistreated the camel in Indianola. They tried to help him save face, but he refused to back down. In front of witnesses, Ibrim spat at Sgt. Bly, letting loose the slimy goop of a partially digested meal. With his lower body covered in a putrid mess, he responded to this public indignity by whacking the camel's foreleg with his rifle.

"I swear I'm gonna kill that man. How's the leg? Is it broken?"

"No, but it's bruised. You can see that it pains him. The skin is scraped, so I oil it and keep it covered. It should be all right to leave it open by tomorrow."

"Thanks, Erdem, really. Thanks a lot. Damnation. How are we gonna build a camel cavalry if this kind of shit goes on? I hope Lt. Beale figures out what's happenin' around here."

"I think maybe he will. There is a rumor that Sgt. Bly will not go to California."

"Great. What other news?"

"We are back in the lean-to."

Much to Nate's surprise, all the camel men now inhabited the lean-to, which they had been obliged to build larger. Lt. Beale found it more "natural" for the foreigners to make their own lodgings in a style that would suit them. Nate was to sleep in the bunkhouse after all.

"What do you think of the new camel men, Erdem?"

"They do not know as much as Abdullah, but they do well enough. Hi Jolly's English is good, and the others are learning. One interesting thing. Like me, they do not want to go home. They plan to make their lives in America. Maybe this is best for the camels."

Nate continued his efforts to understand the changes at Camp Verde. He played cards with the new men, volunteered for extra duty with the camels, and patiently explained camel behavior to anyone who showed even the slightest interest. He paid special attention to Hi Jolly and his crew, assessing their skills, seeing how they interacted, and letting them tell him things he already knew. This required far more patience than he had expected. He came to realize how smoothly every operation used to go. Working with Alex, Hassan, Abdullah, and Ali, every man knew what to do, often without speaking. Nate missed them terribly. It was hard not to start every sentence with "Abdullah said" or "Hassan used to" or "Ali would always." Now, even the simplest chore required explanation, and he had to concentrate on everyone else's work to be sure it was done right.

He spent lots of time with Ibrim, feeding him, combing him, examining his wounded leg and the bite on his neck, and though he wouldn't call it such, keeping guard. He was pleased to see Ibrim put weight on the leg without flinching. By week's end the camel was walking normally, and Nate felt comfortable taking him to San Antonio.

"Yes, Mr. Wilkers, permission granted. You've conducted yourself to good report this week. You may go with the supply detail. And, yes, please do take Ibrim. I do not want that animal left untended. Without your hand, it seems to be a troublemaker."

Nate refused to rise to the bait. There was nothing wrong with Ibrim. The fault lay with Sgt. Bly and the soldiers.

"Please give my regards to Mrs. McDermott and her family. As for Mr. Babcock, I hope you will find him in full recovery. While it's out of the question for him to go to California, tell him he may have a post here at Camp Verde if he wishes."

Nate compelled his mind to accommodate to the excruciatingly slow crawl of the supply detail. Because Lt. Beale wanted the camels to remain at Camp Verde in advance of the expedition, supplies were now fetched with mule wagons that inched around pits and rocks in the rough road. Due to recent rains, they mired easily. Nate pitched in, helping to place boards under the wheels and using Ibrim to pull the wagons free. At least the agonizing pace gave him time to think. California intrigued him, not for the gold rush mentality, but for its wide-open possibilities. If you could think of a thing, in California you could do it. He might go with the camels, but only if Lt. Beale accepted him as a civilian. Under no circumstances, not even to get to California, would he accept a subservient position to Sgt. Bly or anyone like him.

He dreamed of a relay system of fast camels carrying mail between the West Coast and San Antonio. He would supplement a government contract with private correspondence, specializing in short messages that could be carried at a reasonable price. In San Antonio, the new telegraph service could relay the messages further east, cutting weeks off the normal delivery time. The more he analyzed, the more potential he saw. He could manage the service from California and Alex could run the San Antonio end of the operation. He would call it the Camel Postal Express. He couldn't wait to hear what Alex and Elizabeth would think of his plans.

At last he reached San Antonio. Full of excitement, he left Ibrim at the Alamo and walked briskly to Laredo Street. Several carriages stood before the house. His heart stopped when he saw the front door draped with black bunting. His anxiety increased when Antoine opened the door.

"Thank God you've come. Wait here, please."

Fear that something had happened to Elizabeth slapped him in the face, bringing to the fore his repressed feelings for her. When she appeared, he was so relieved that he stepped forward to embrace her. She remained at a bit of a distance and took one hand, trembling. Only then did he notice her puffy red-rimmed eyes and her plain black gown. He inhaled sharply.

"Oh, Nate. Alex is dead."

"No!"

His single shout echoed throughout the house, causing the dull murmur of sympathetic voices to cease and propelling Sylvia to the entry hall. Nate crouched over, his hands to his head, while Elizabeth stood apart, blinded by a new round of tears. Zach caught his sister, who looked pale as if to faint. Sylvia put her arm around Nate's shoulders, ushering him gently past the prying eyes in the adjoining rooms and into the back courtyard. This simple gesture of maternal kindness soothed Nate and helped him regain his composure.

Nate sniffled. "Tell me."

Alex had been recovering well. The amputation, kept clean with fresh bandages, was healing. Doc Schuler administered quinine to fight the blood poisoning and syrup of orange peel for strength. Then one day the stub was tender and red streaks signaled the return of pyaemia. Whether the blood poisoning was due to the spider bite or an infection, Doc Schuler couldn't say, but nothing could be done. In forty-eight hours, Alex was dead.

Seated with Nate on the bench by the fountain, Sylvia did all the talking. Elizabeth sobbed intermittently, and Zach stared off into space.

"Nate, the funeral is tomorrow. We're so glad you came to town in time."

"Where's my grandfather?"

"He's been sent for. We'd like you to be one of the pall bearers, along with Zeke, Zach, your grandfather, and two of the church elders."

"Of course, Miz McDermott, anything."

"Zach, take Nate to your room, and let him wash up. Have Esther bring him something to eat. I'll send your grandfather to you as soon as he returns. Elizabeth?"

"I'll stay here, Mama. I want to sit outside by myself for awhile."

A few minutes later, Elizabeth saw Nate charge out of Zach's bedroom, cross the courtyard to the opposite corner without coming near the fountain, and duck into the stables. She heard the clatter of objects being thrown against the wall. Swear words punctuated the crashing sounds. She rose once to go to Nate, then hearing a sharp clang followed by a deep groan, thought better of it. She sat down, her ears attuned to the shed. In an odd way, she felt comforted that Nate shared her grief and anger. Not long after, she glimpsed Jeremy entering through the back gate. She raised her hand and pointed at the stables. With a nod, Jeremy turned and went in. The banging stopped, and the conversation became too muffled for her to hear. She sat for a long time, reminded of the vigil she had kept at this very spot after her father's death. Then all at once she was full of resolve. She sent Mabel to call her mother.

"Mama, I have a favor to ask."

"Of course, child."

"I want you to move the official mourning to the new house."

"But these people have come to comfort you."

"I know, Mama, but listen. Most of the people are your friends, not mine, and the new house is much better for large groups. I would like you to go there now and take everyone with you. Take most of the food, too, and all the servants."

"Well, it's most unusual." Sylvia was amazed by the determination in Elizabeth's voice.

"I'd like Mr. Blackstone and Nate to stay, along with Zeke and Zach. I want the house to be more like it was when Alex used to visit, as if we could picture him arriving any minute."

"Are you sure?"

"Yes, Mama, please. This would really help me, and I'll be grateful, ever so grateful."

Somewhat stung, Sylvia led a bizarre procession of nonplussed mourners south of town, across the river, and into the isolated but splendid McDermott mansion.

That evening in the Laredo house, the salon was warmed by a burning brazier around which sat Elizabeth, her brothers, Nate, and Jeremy. A large bottle of imported whiskey, now two-thirds empty, made the rounds, and Elizabeth partook along with the men. Zachary, although far too young, allowed himself a few tastes, and no one objected. Their silence was interspersed with remembrances and stories: Alex announcing the camels in Indianola, Alex giving camel rides to the children, Alex standing in the chaparral trying to chase down a wayward Tullah. Zachary recalled Alex teaching him how to tie knots. Zeke spoke of slipping away from camp with Alex to indulge in a camel race. They remembered Alex telling stories, always Alex telling stories. Elizabeth contributed the image of a surprised Alex covered with mud, arriving at Mrs. Eberly's hotel to find the family sitting on the veranda. One image from Indianola she held to herself: Alex dancing with her in a swirl of rhythm, rapid heartbeats, and radiant smiles.

"Didn't he want to be buried back east?" Nate still couldn't quite grasp that Alex was dead.

"No, Alex insisted that he wanted to be buried here. He asked me to visit his grave and said he'd like me to keep his memory by telling him our news from time to time." Elizabeth sobbed again. Nate reflexively reached over and patted her arm, noting that she looked at him appreciatively and did not recoil.

"Yeah," Zach added. "He wants us all to visit. He doesn't know whether people who've passed on can hear

us, but he sure would like for us to try." The bottle made
another round during the ensuing silence.

"So tell us, Nate, what have you decided about California?"

Jeremy twisted in his seat, wondering how his grandson
would respond to Elizabeth. Whether it was the booze or
the intoxicating pull of Elizabeth's gaze, Nate couldn't say,
but he told all about his plans: California, a camel express,
acquiring a fleet of camels, everything. After explaining
how he had figured Alex could run the San Antonio end of
things, he abruptly stopped. Elizabeth sniffled, and when
she spoke, Jeremy noticed a slur to her pronunciation.

"That's a grand vision, Nate. Alex would have loved it.
You were his best friend, you know. He told me to be sure
you knew that."

Nate stood up so quickly he spilt his drink. "Thanks,"
he choked, then disappeared into the hall, his muffled
sobs audible in the empty house. A few minutes later he
returned. "Pass the bottle, Grandpa," he said with a bit
too much bravado.

Jeremy opened a second bottle, and another round of
memories began. When Zach fell asleep on the settee and
Zeke looked about to pass out, Jeremy nudged the two boys
out of their seats and ushered them to their room, leaving
Nate and Elizabeth seated side by side, staring blankly at
the flickering coals.

"I'll have to go back to Camp Verde right after the services."

"I guessed as much."

"I've got somethin' to say to you, Elizabeth." He turned
his chair to face her, and took her hand. "There ain't no good
way to do this, and this ain't the time, but…" He hesitated.

Elizabeth stared, dumbstruck, wondering what was on
his mind. "Go on."

"The plain fact is, with Alex gone, you're my best friend.
We talk easy. You're smart, honest, and kind. You put others before yourself, but you don't take no nonsense either. I
like all that. And you're beautiful."

"Nate?"

"Don't interrupt. I gotta do this now or I never will." He
had thought about how Alex had "sorta" asked Elizabeth to
marry him. If he were to state his case, he would do it plainly.

"All right, I'm listening."

"With me goin' to California, there's a lot of things we can't predict. I could decide that California holds my future and stay there, or I could come back."

Elizabeth smiled involuntarily. Nate was such a planner. He reminded her of her father in that way. Nate was always figuring how things might turn out.

"Anything could happen," he continued. "Whatever happens, I want you to be part of it. Tonight might be the worst time to say this, but I gotta do it, so here goes." He dropped to one knee. "Elizabeth, will you marry me?"

By now quite tipsy, Elizabeth started to giggle softly and couldn't stop. She clapped her hand over her mouth to contain herself before replying, "Why Nathaniel Wilkers, I am honored!" She stood to curtsy, lost her balance, and fell back into the chair.

Gripping her shoulders, Nate looked directly into her eyes. The gesture and his earnest tone returned her to some semblance of sobriety.

"Elizabeth, I'm serious. I don't need an answer today, or even for a year if it takes me that long to get to California and back. Everything can change. I know that. You might fall for someone else while I'm gone. But I want to marry you. I'm askin' you proper and I mean every word of it. Just remember that you've been asked."

"I, I don't know what to say."

"Don't say anything. Let's turn in. We have to be ready for tomorrow. Tomorrow is for Alex."

He helped her up. Unsteady on their feet, they leaned on each other for support as they went to their respective bedrooms. He kissed her on the cheek at her door before stumbling into the guest room where his grandfather lay snoring loudly. He flopped onto the adjacent bed, a satisfied smile pasted on his drunken face. In an instant he was asleep.

The next morning, Elizabeth awoke with a pounding headache, certain that something important had happened the night before but not quite sure of the specifics.

The funeral failed to comfort. Elizabeth had expected something intimate. Instead, the church was overflowing. Suspecting that a majority were there merely to be seen by her mother, she was grateful to be seated in the front pew, unable to observe the throng extending behind her.

The formulaic pronouncements of the pastor, intended to ease the bereaved, only annoyed her. The acute grief lurking at the base of her neck was unmoved by his talk of the afterlife. She didn't care one iota about the state of Alex's soul. She wanted him in the flesh, alive. She fantasized a scenario in which he would open the church door, march boldly up to her with his characteristically loose-limbed stride, and slide next to her on the pew. He would whisper something to make her laugh and they would watch this charade together. She smiled. An instant later, confronted by the finality of his absence, she grimaced, relieved that her black veil hid the ravages on her face.

The mourners proceeded from the church to the cemetery where Alex was laid to rest in a brief service. Then the crowd drifted to the new house. Many among them were curiosity seekers anxious to step inside the McDermott mansion. The chattering crush of sycophants disgusted Elizabeth, but had the opposite effect on her mother, who seemed oddly revived by the jumble of people. Sylvia glided from person to person, accepting their condolences, expressing her gratitude, and welcoming each one. Elizabeth tried to follow suit, but after making the rounds once she could no longer tolerate the insincere comments. Escaping into the library, she found Jeremy sitting alone with the book of Audubon prints.

"Excuse me, Mr. Blackstone. I was trying to slip away."

"Too much, ain't it?"

"Indeed it is. I miss Alex so much, and I don't want to hear condolences from people who didn't know him, who don't even know me for that matter."

"Yup."

"But last night was good, wasn't it? We remembered him together, we who loved him." She started to weep quietly. "Sorry. I seem to be crying a lot lately."

"You just go on."

"Has Nate left for Camp Verde?"

"Right after the service."

She sighed. "I'm all alone now. Alex, Major Babcock, Hassan, Nate, all gone. At least Nate may come back, but then again, maybe he won't."

"I know."

"I'm sorry, Mr. Blackstone. It must be very hard for you to imagine Nate so far away."

"Yup."

After a few moments, Elizabeth rose. "If my mother asks, tell her I've gone to the cemetery. Moses can take me in the carriage."

"Let me take you. I'll tell her where we're going."

The old cemetery on Commerce Street had been full for some years, so Alex was buried in the new City Cemetery two miles east of town. For the next few days, Elizabeth visited every day. Feeling responsible for Elizabeth's care, Esther insisted that one of her daughters join these outings. The first day, Mabel reported that Elizabeth stood whispering to the grave until she tired and sat down on the grass. Distressed, Esther sent chairs the following day. When Elizabeth lingered at the cemetery the entire day and Sally came home famished, Esther prepared a picnic basket and a jug of water for the next visit. Because Elizabeth was undeterred by weather, Esther added a blanket and an umbrella. It was like outfitting an expedition.

By the second week, Elizabeth had established a routine. She departed after breakfast, sometimes staying until sunset. If she came home for lunch, she often went back again. Esther's daughters informed her that Elizabeth talked, talked, and talked. Sometimes she wept quietly. Often she sobbed until she was spent. She shouted, gesticulated wildly and paced back and forth in front of the grave. Occasionally she laughed. Once they saw her swaying as if she were dancing. Esther was overcome with worry. It wasn't natural, going to the grave like that.

Esther's life these days allowed plenty of time to ruminate on her problems. Ever since Miz Sylvia had moved, taking with her Zeke, the other slaves, and the family social

life, the house had been unnervingly quiet. There were almost no callers. Even Miz Sylvia seldom visited, instead
sending for her daughter to come to her. Esther objected
to the family living in two places. She missed Antoine and
Rebecca as well as Agnes, who had not yet returned from
Comfort. This new loneliness augmented her daily heart-
ache for her Henry who was still in Galveston. Esther could
in no way fathom why the McDermott family would vol-
untarily live apart when she would give anything to be reunited with her own.

Nevertheless, Esther accepted the need to stay with
Elizabeth. She felt sure that Massa Quentin would want her
watching over his daughter rather than following his wife
to the new house, especially since Miz Sylvia had taken up
with Mr. Blackstone. She liked Mr. Blackstone, but it was
against the Bible for him to be carrying on with Miz Sylvia.
They hadn't behaved like that when they lived under her
roof. She was glad that she didn't have to see it in front of
her face.

Esther lived each week longing for Sunday, a day that
was almost normal. The McDermotts attended church as
a family before dining at the new house. Esther supervised
the cooking for a large gathering while Moses handled the
arriving carriages. Antoine in his finest costume was restored to his role as butler, greeting the guests and ushering
them into the parlor. It was like the old days, the one time
of the week when Esther felt secure. It was also the only day
that Elizabeth could not go to the cemetery.

Increasingly anxious about Elizabeth's behavior, Esther
debated what to do. She felt guilty not telling Miz Sylvia,
but she very much wanted to maintain the fragile peace between mother and daughter. Afraid of the repercussions of
a misplaced remark, Esther held her peace. One morning
after breakfast, Elizabeth took her aside.

"My mother wishes me to be more active socially. I have
agreed to resume my piano lessons, and we will accept callers between three and five in the afternoon."

"Yes, Missy 'Lizbeth."

"Esther, you must understand that I am in charge now.
My visits to the cemetery help me. There is nothing to worry

about, but I do understand that people might find it unusual. So let me be clear: I forbid you to tell my mother."

"Yes'm."

After that conversation, Esther made a simple plan. She directed her loyalty to Elizabeth. She would see the girl married and help her raise a family. This vision made sense. Esther could picture living and dying like her mother, a faithful member of a reconstituted McDermott household. But her own daughters, when they reached maturity, would be free! She counted the days until their eighteenth birthdays, doing her best to keep their lives as unruffled as possible. She would take care not to upset Elizabeth or her mother and endanger her daughters' futures. Thus, although she fretted, Esther said nothing to Sylvia about these daily trips to the gravesite. Helpless to do anything else, she prayed that Elizabeth would soon come to her senses, stop spending so much time at the cemetery, and move back in with her mother at the new house. She feared that everything of importance to her depended on Elizabeth returning to sanity. She prayed that it would happen soon.

WITH THE CAMELS, MARCH 1857

C AMP VERDE THRUMMED LIKE a flock of birds preparing for migration, and Nate was in the thick of it. Having negotiated a civilian post attached to Lt. Beale's command, he set about becoming invaluable, an easy task because only Erdem and two soldiers from the *Supply* remained from the original mission. These three deferred to Nate's judgment, thereby setting an example for many of the new arrivals, including Gwynne Heap, Hi Jolly and his crew. When it was announced that Sgt. Bly would remain in Texas, his ability to cause problems diminished. Nate's influence increased, and he became the de facto authority on the camels.

The constant demand on his time helped Nate battle his loneliness. Although the Egyptians had been gone for weeks, he still kept expecting Hassan to walk around the corner, caught himself scanning for Abdullah's silhouette among the camels, or thought he heard Ali's lilting voice.

Over everything lay his grief for Alex, whose absence tormented him. He had suffered losses before, especially the death of Hilde, who had been like a mother to him, but this was worse. He vacillated between profound sadness and unfettered rage. The absurdity of Alex being slain by a spider bite was beyond the pale. His friend's death smacked of an arbitrary randomness that offended him deeply. He railed against the injustice of Alex dying while people like Sgt. Bly were allowed to live, oblivious to having been spared. When he considered that it could as easily have been himself instead of Alex who slept in the corner of the lean-to, Nate caught a first glimpse of his own mortality. The notion chilled him to the marrow.

Nate became more sympathetic to his grandfather's loss of two wives and a daughter. He developed a new comprehension of his grandfather's vigilance over every move that Nate had made in his entire lifetime, a constant monitoring that he had long found stifling. He understood that his grandfather needed to protect what was left. Appreciating that the intention had not been to constrain but to nurture, he wished he could talk things over with his grandfather. His inability to do so made Nate feel even more alone.

However, he was determined not to allow his desolation to transform him into a cautious, hesitant replica of Jeremy Blackstone. Instead he channeled his anger and loss toward his future in California. In those moments when melancholy threatened, he clawed away from the abyss by dedicating his efforts to the memory of Alex. Above all else, he realized that his plans had to include Elizabeth. Whether he would send for her when he reached California or go back to Texas could be decided later. First he had to know whether his vision for the camels would materialize into something solid.

Nate was encouraged by Lt. Beale's efforts to build an effective Camel Corps. Lt. Beale instituted a strict discipline of camel care and a training program for packing and handling the animals. His penchant for action and practicality pleased Nate. Major Babcock's preference for breeding the animals now seemed misplaced. Although he felt somewhat traitorous to the Major, Nate favored Lt. Beale's plan to give the camels a real assignment. A successful mission could inspire the importation of more camels, increasing their numbers faster than breeding. When he learned that the intrepid commander had already crossed the continent more than once at the head of successful expeditions, he became confident that Lt. Beale was the right man to lead the trek to California.

At last they were ready to set off. Lt. Beale's expedition made Major Babcock's venture look puny. The departure was a spectacle on a monumental scale. Hundreds of mules and horses, more than thirty-five camels, and a train of soldiers and wagons extended for more than a mile. This would be a historic mission, without doubt, and Nate Wilkers was glad to be in it. He couldn't help thinking how much Alex would have wanted to take part.

After a day or two, Nate settled into the rhythm of the expedition. Riding Ibrim exclusively, he became so attuned to the came that he could signal Ibrim with the slightest touch. The camels, even the new ones, performed well, and Nate studied them closely in order to think through the details of his new camel express. The first part of the trip followed the same route as Major Babcock's outing, and the days were relatively uneventful, except for routine problems like wagons breaking axles, horses throwing shoes and mules escaping. Beyond Comanche Springs lay new terrain for Nate. Although rougher going, Nate found the higher hills, limestone mesas, and wide vistas wildly beautiful. Despite an occasional rain, the spring weather was pleasantly warm, and overall the trek was agreeable.

He made friends with Gwynne Heap, about whom Alex had spoken so favorably. Gwynne knew camels, cared deeply about the mission, and was a most amazing artist. Nate spent much of his spare time watching in fascination as Gwynne Heap sketched the camels. To look at one of Heap's drawings was to see the camels moving, to hear the sound of their soft pads on the trail, and to feel the breeze on your skin. In addition to the action scenes, Gwynne drew camel portraits, capturing their individual personalities in ways that astonished Nate. When Gwynne presented Nate with a drawing of Ibrim, so realistic that Nate imagined he could feel the camel's fur, he was overcome.

Although Hi Jolly was no substitute for Abdullah, he was friendly and competent. Somehow he managed to keep Pertag in line, an accomplishment for which Nate was extremely grateful. Nate even made peace with Lt. Beale's boys after he observed them willing to work. One of them, May Stacey, proved to be sensible and good company. Although Nate sometimes teased him about the daily journal that he kept, he nevertheless thought it clever to make a record of this once-in-a-lifetime trip.

One day, Nate and Hi Jolly, riding Ibrim and Mahomet, joined a group of four soldiers sent to search for water. While the soldiers descended into a valley, Nate and Hi Jolly proceeded up a ridge to scout the terrain on the other side. The landscape, consisting of multicolored rocks, dusty flats, and sparse vegetation, was the most barren that Nate had seen thus far. When he scanned the horizon, he saw nothing alive, neither man nor animal, only a lone bird high in the sky. He wondered where they would find water, but knew that the errand was not urgent. The camels carried plenty of water for both the men and the mules. Even in this environment, the camels didn't need to drink very often.

As Nate and Hi Jolly started their descent, a gunshot sent them careening back toward the soldiers. Coming over the ridge, they saw the soldiers bunched together in the valley, surrounded by a small band of Indians. Despite all the descriptions he had heard, Nate had never seen real Indians before. Their exotic face paint was every bit as bizarre as he had been told. Bareback astride their multicolored ponies, the Indians circled the soldiers, raising a ruckus of dust and preventing any possibility of escape. They held their rifles in the air, firing them periodically. Whatever they were crying out in their own language, it had a terrifying effect. Nate was dumbstruck. He grabbed his Colt, uncertain what to do next. The soldiers were outnumbered, the situation dire.

Hi Jolly, however, had no such inhibitions. He goaded Mahomet into a run and tumbled down the hillside, riding hard toward the Indians. The camel knocked loose rocks that hit others, unleashing a cascade that caught the attention of the Indians. That day Hi Jolly had chosen to wear a turban that covered his hair and face as protection from the sun. The startled Indians confronted a man without a face charging toward them on an ethereal beast. When Hi Jolly waved his scimitar in the air and screamed in Arabic, the Indians must have been convinced that they were fighting an apparition of the devil. They promptly vanished over the horizon.

Nate still laughed to think of it. He wished Alex and Hassan could have seen it, especially Alex, who would have told the story better than anyone.

San Antonio, April 1857

T HE TENOR OF ELIZABETH'S visits to the cemetery changed over time. After her initial grief and rage dissipated, she remembered Alex's last wishes and began to tell him the news. As days dragged into weeks, every routine occurrence became a potential subject to discuss with Alex. She recounted even the tiniest scraps of information. She described how the crops were faring in the unusually dry weather, what Esther had prepared for breakfast, and how Zach had made her laugh with an amusing remark. She gave details of the latest soiree on her mother's social schedule, both beforehand, when she would express her reluctance to attend, and after, when she complained of having done so. She reported daily on everyone that he knew, although she had frustratingly little to say about the doings at Camp Verde. Private Munoz was the only one left who brought her news since the caravan had left for California.

One afternoon, Elizabeth made an extra trip to the cemetery to tell Alex that Lt. Halter had been seen passing through town. The Lieutenant had not visited anyone, so no one could say for certain whether his orders had finally arrived or whether he had simply abandoned his post.

She talked at length about her mother and Jeremy Blackstone as she tried to understand this odd pairing. Although she was very fond of Jeremy, he was so unlike her charismatic father that she was at pains to grasp her mother's romantic attraction. But as she talked it out with Alex, she gained a new perspective. Her mother had always lived in her father's shadow, but Mr. Blackstone's quiet ways allowed her mother to shine on her own. Also, his peaceful constancy must be soothing after the upheaval of the past year. Seeing it that way, Elizabeth resolved to accept them as a couple more graciously.

Elizabeth often speculated about the camel caravan, wending its way to California. Nate had not returned to San Antonio after the funeral, although he had sent a note to his grandfather that included a greeting to her. She tried to calculate how long it might be before they received word that Nate had reached the west coast. One day she took a map to the cemetery and spread it out upon the grave. Studying it with Alex, she asked him whether he thought Nate's Camel Postal Express would succeed. She imagined Alex enthusiastic, but in her view, the distances were too grand and the project too unwieldy. She wondered what Nate would decide.

She told and retold every camel tale she could remember. During his recuperation, Alex had regaled her with countless images: acquiring the camels in Egypt, life at Camp Verde, the expedition to West Texas. His stories were so vivid that she felt she had been there with him. Now, sitting by his grave, she repeated them to embed them in her memory. "Alex, do you remember the story you told me about how you first met Hassan at that reception? Can you still picture the lightering, with Tullah swinging in the air?"

On one occasion, Elizabeth admitted how much she missed Hassan and how hard it had been for her to let him go. Then she fell silent, pondering what would have happened if she had gone to Egypt with Hassan. She imagined being married to Hassan, laughing with Auntie Fatima and doting on Grandma Ara. But that was impossible. How could she talk with them when she spoke no Arabic? Speaking out loud, she reminded Alex that her affections had long since solidified in his favor.

She talked of her brothers. When Precious delivered a baby boy, Zachary and Antoine went to Comfort to fetch Agnes. Zach's absence for more than a week had upset her mother, but Elizabeth knew that her brother would prolong his visit if possible. He returned full of devotion to the lifestyle of the German freethinkers and talked her ear off about moral philosophy. He was so passionate about abolition that he had even discussed the subject with Antoine! She told Alex all this, knowing that he would have agreed with many of Zachary's new opinions.

She described the array of families making social calls on her mother with the obvious intention of acquainting their daughters with Zeke. Even though he would only be sixteen in the fall, he was so tall and handsome that everyone thought he was older. Toughened by the trip to Galveston, he was aggressively involved in his mother's financial dealings, and Elizabeth thought that he might marry before she did. She complained of an incipient arrogance in Zeke, which she felt sure Alex could have helped to correct.

She confessed to Alex that her mother and half the town knew that she frequented the cemetery. There was talk that she had become odd and "peculiar". In spite of this, she had no shortage of suitors, especially with her seventeenth birthday coming up. Every Sunday, one or another young man appeared at her mother's dinner table. Although they were sons of the best families in town, she criticized them roundly. Every Monday at the gravesite, she ruthlessly sized up each contender, comparing him unfavorably to Alex. She often laughed out loud, assuring Alex that she was quite content to visit him.

"Anyway, Alex, I'm not interested in that boy. He's only after the family business."

She often imagined Alex's side of their conversations. "Elizabeth, don't you think you need to be more willing to consider one of them? You ought to find a husband. I don't want you to be alone."

"I know, Alex. You said that before you died."

"I meant it. I want you to be happy."

"Really, I'm happy here with you. You know that."

"Yes, but this can't last. Has no one has asked you to marry?"

"Nope. I fear one of them will, but so far, you're the only one who's asked me."

"Well, I didn't really ask you, did I? I sorta asked you."

"Haha, Alex! You certainly did that. You 'sorta' asked me twice!"

"Yeah, Nate used to tease me about that. He said you don't 'sorta' ask a girl to marry."

She laughed out loud, then paused. "What was that again?"

"Nate said you can't 'sorta' ask a girl to marry. You either ask or you don't!"

"That's it, Alex. That's it!"

As if coming out of a dark forest into a clearly lit meadow, Elizabeth remembered for the first time her drunken conversation with Nate the night before Alex's funeral. Nate had asked her to marry him. For real. Nothing "sorta" about it.

All at once she understood what she was doing here talking with Alex every day. She was waiting for Nate.

EN ROUTE TO CALIFORNIA, LATE APRIL 1857

NATE GREW UNEASY WHEN he came to understand that the Army had no real plans for the camels in California. No one could say whether they would remain there, be distributed to forts along the route, or go back to Texas. It was one thing to reach your destination, but vitally important to prepare for what would happen afterward. Vague answers were not sufficient for Nate.

Equally worrisome, disharmony had crept into the caravan. The southern soldiers voiced increasing animosity to being commanded by a Yankee, and Lt. Beale had developed a mercurial quality that didn't help. A few of the new men from the North talked openly of politics and abolition, augmenting regional division among the troops. Some of the Yankees had seen the recent violence in Kansas and predicted more of the same. If war broke out, something that Nate had not before considered as a possibility, he could be stranded in California without a way to get back or worse yet, he could be conscripted into the Army. He had no desire to fight.

Nate's greatest disquiet came from a profound intuition that he was going in the wrong direction, that some internal compass was urging him to turn around. The prospect that he might never again see his grandfather gnawed an empty place in his soul. Leaving Elizabeth seemed more and more to have been a bad idea. He felt as if he held one end of a rope that stretched back to San Antonio, gripping it for dear life. But what if it snapped and left him alone? For the first time, he understood that he was not much of a rugged individualist. He needed his family.

Nate had to abandon his musings as the caravan approached a steep arroyo where two wagons were mired. Finding Gwynne Heap struggling to dislodge them, Nate immediately jumped down to help. Surprisingly, clearing the wagons turned out to be a difficult, time-consuming effort that caused them to arrive in camp late. For reasons that neither man could grasp nor accept, Lt. Beale lost his temper and roundly criticized Gwynne Heap in front of everyone. Offended, Gwynne shot back a sharp retort and was discharged on the spot. Before dawn the next morning, he was on his way back east.

Nate was shocked. If Gwynne Heap, a stalwart member of the troop, could be dismissed in such a fashion, then Lt. Beale was capable of anything. Nate's trust was seriously undermined. He waited two days to be sure of his decision. Then he confronted Lt. Beale.

"Sir, I must resign my post."

"Mr. Wilkers, what makes you think you can quit?"

"I'm a civilian, and I'm leavin' your service." Nate held his ground and declined to explain further. "I think it best if I take the camel called Ibrim. As you've said yourself, he can be unruly."

"Now you've gone too far. These camels are the property of the US Army."

"Excuse me, sir. Perhaps I have not made it plain enough. This particular camel most probably will cause trouble for the mission. I propose to take him off your hands."

"I am not authorized to give away one of our camels, even a bad one."

"I will purchase him then."

Lt. Beale named an exorbitant price, which Nate whittled down to a lesser but still excessive amount. Much to everyone's surprise, Nate unrolled a wad of bills and paid cash for Ibrim on the spot. He waited calmly while Lt. Beale wrote out a bill of sale.

Nate let Ibrim stroll at an easy pace. He wanted to remember the sight of the camel caravan on its way to California. He was confident that they would make it, despite whatever hardships or adventures they might encounter en route. Although he wished keenly that he might witness their historic arrival in California, he was absolutely convinced that he belonged back in Texas.

SAN ANTONIO, MAY 2, 1857

E LIZABETH SAT COMFORTABLY NEXT to Alex's grave in a semi-permanent enclave that she had constructed over the last several weeks. On two sides, a portable wall of woven grass blocked the wind. Her wooden chair, softened with brightly colored cushions, had a parasol attached, muting the spring sun that threatened to overheat the day. A pitcher of water rested on the small table and a book of Walt Whitman's poetry lay in her lap.

Wistfully, she reminisced. Last year at this time she had made her debut into society at the Galveston May Day celebrations, surrounded by a group of admiring young men who might have had an interest in her hand. Trying to recall every sensation of the day, she told Alex about it in great detail. She sniffled when telling him how her father had escorted her into the room, how the warmth of his pride had made her stand tall. She couldn't imagine what her father would think of her now, coming every day to talk to a gravestone four months after Alex had died. People gossiped that she had lost her mind. But she knew she wasn't a mad woman, merely a patient one. She had no idea how long she must wait, but wait she would.

Refreshed by her visit with Alex, she returned to the house on Laredo Street to entertain her guests. To keep her mother at bay, she scrupulously maintained a social life, minimal but appropriate to Sylvia's wishes. This afternoon she sat sipping tea and playing cards with a young woman and two young men. An older woman knitted in the corner, chaperoning the party.

When the front bell's tinkle announced another visitor, little Mabel answered the door. Lacking Antoine's finesse, she squealed. "Massa Nate!"

Heedless of protocol, Nate strode right past Mabel into the salon. Elizabeth flushed as she rose to greet him. "Nate, oh my goodness! Is it really you?" She stared at him in disbelief.

Barely acknowledging the guests, Nate stepped forward and took her hand. "Howdy, Elizabeth, may I have a word?"

She left her guests open-mouthed and led Nate out back under the shade of the veranda. "Nate, what's happened? Is everything all right? Are you back from California already?"

"I've quit the expedition. I'm stayin' here, and I'm gonna ask again. If you need time to think, I'll go see Grandpa and come back later. Elizabeth, will you marry me?"

"Yes, yes, and YES!" Then the tears came. "Nate, it's been so hard waiting."

"No more waiting now! We'll get married as soon as we can arrange it."

He lifted her up, swung her in a circle, and set her down. In a single smooth motion, he leaned forward and kissed her. A calming relief washed over her, slowing her breathing. As the kiss lingered, her body lit up. From then on, she would be especially aroused whenever Nate smelled of sweat and camel.

"Let's go tell Grandpa and your mother."

"Yes, Nate, but first let's go tell Alex."

"No, Elizabeth, we'll see to the living first."

Her eyes widened slightly. "Of course, you're right. Alex would want it that way. I'll ask for the carriage."

"Let's go on Ibrim. I bought him. He's mine!" Nate beamed.

"That's wonderful!"

Elizabeth ran toward the front door, and as she passed the salon, composed herself enough to address her gawking guests. "My apologies. I must see my mother immediately. Esther, please show our visitors out."

Nate swung Elizabeth onto the camel saddle and leapt up behind her. He set Ibrim to a trot, heedless of the disruptions they caused. As soon as the road became less crowded, he urged the camel into a run. On the sparsely populated south side of town, noise carried easily. When he heard the thundering, Antoine hurried to the front door and opened it in time to see a camel kneeling. The laughing couple ran up the stairs hand in hand, shouting the news. Sylvia and Jeremy came to greet them, engulfing them in a surfeit of hugs, tears and congratulations.

With a date less than two weeks away, the wedding plans unrolled at a frantic pace. Elizabeth chose two of the Navarro girls for her maids of honor and Nate asked his grandfather to be best man. Without Quentin McDermott to walk his daughter down the aisle, Sylvia proposed Zeke for the job. Zachary objected.

"Mama, I think I should be the one to escort Elizabeth. I looked after her while you were in Galveston. I went with her to find Precious. I live in the house with her. And besides, just because Zeke is the eldest doesn't mean he should get to do everything."

"Mama, I think Zachary will do a wonderful job. Zach, I would be honored." Later Elizabeth would be immensely grateful for this choice.

Her daughter's impending marriage sent Sylvia's thoughts to Quentin. He had been leery of Elizabeth marrying one of the Galveston elite, as it turned out with good reason. Nate was not the man Quentin would have imagined, but he would have appreciated Nate's industriousness and would have rejoiced in his daughter's happiness. Quentin would have been satisfied with their move to San Antonio and the shift of their assets to land and cattle. Much of what he had foreseen had reached fruition. Only his prediction for war had not yet come to pass, and Sylvia prayed fervently that for once her husband might be wrong.

Elizabeth became less drawn to the cemetery, and when she did go, Nate usually went with her. He couldn't quite bring himself to converse with his deceased friend, but he stood patiently while she spoke of their plans to marry.

Increasingly certain of Alex's blessing, Elizabeth started to rejoin the world.

Invitations were sent to Elizabeth's personal friends for a betrothal party at the adobe house on Saturday before the wedding. Lit by flickering lamps, tables dotted the courtyard amid the palms and potted plants. Under a starry canopy, the evening temperature was perfect for al fresco dining. For the first time in months, Elizabeth enjoyed entertaining. Nate, unused to this style of socializing, was reticent. Nevertheless, he did his best to move from table to table, learning the names of these new acquaintances, even finding a few who were interested in his business ideas. Elizabeth had never seen Nate more handsome, with a fresh haircut and new trousers. His future bride was ravishing in her lemon yellow gown, and Nate approved of her wearing it in homage to Alex.

Nate began at once to revive his trading activity, which he could now pursue full-time and without encumbrances. He got reacquainted with his suppliers and former clients, making a few quick transactions that brought in enough cash to increase his available merchandise. After the wedding, he planned to follow Elizabeth's suggestions for new markets in Boerne and Comfort. If he could buy additional camels from the Army, they could carry their commerce to Austin, Fredericksburg and beyond. In the meantime, he and Jeremy were occupied with a secret project. Elizabeth and Sylvia knew they were working with Moses in the shed behind the new house, but the men refused to say a word about it.

The night before the wedding, the two families assembled around the dining room table at the new house. Sylvia announced that she had signed over to Elizabeth full ownership of the adobe house on Laredo Street along with the rights to Esther and her daughters. For a personal gift, she bestowed her emerald ring and for Nate, a pair of onyx and diamond cufflinks. Jeremy presented the couple a wooden plaque beautifully carved with the words "Bless This Home."

The sound of horses, loud conversation, and feet stomping up the stairs sent Antoine scurrying to the door. Concerned by the raucous noise, Jeremy rose to investigate.

Antoine had scarcely opened the door when in tumbled Amos Prudeau and Drew Johnsville.

"Well, I'll be," said Jeremy. "Look who's here."

"Look at yourself, you old codger. Come up in the world, ain't ya?"

"Yeah, took us forever to find this place. Where the hell is Nate?"

"Mind your manners, boys." Jeremy said.

Sylvia stood at the entrance to the parlor, her eyes twinkling, not the least put out by their rough appearance. "Welcome, gentlemen."

Nate rushed into the hall, embracing Amos and receiving backslaps from Drew. "Howdy. What are y'all doin' here?"

Amos chuckled. "What are we doin' here? What do y'all *think* we're doin' here? You gettin' married, ain't ya? Didn't think we'd miss it, did ya?"

"How'd you find out?"

"A telegram! Can you imagine that? A telegram tellin' us you was about to get married without so much as a word."

Drew added, "Nice telegram too. Invited us to come along. And here we are. Amos figures you need someone to stand up with you."

Nate was overwhelmed. "Great. It's great that y'all have come. But, well, Grandpa …."

Drew piped in. "Hell, Jeremy, at your age, you should be happy to sit in the front row and watch the show."

Amos shook his head. "Damn it, Drew, it's up to Nate. If he'll have me, and if Jeremy don't mind the company, I'd be proud to stand up with y'all."

Drew added, "Y'all better agree. He spent half a month's wages on new clothes."

Nate stammered and looked at his grandfather.

"Always room for Amos." Jeremy replied.

"Both of you together. It'll be an honor." He was thrilled beyond words for Amos to join the wedding. "So who sent the telegram?"

Drew guffawed. "Ain't you guessed, Nate?"

"Grandpa? Or maybe Elizabeth?"

"Hell no, it was sent by the bride's mama herself! Ain't that right Miz McDermott?"

Sylvia's melodious laughter filled the room. "We couldn't have this wedding without you boys, now could we? Come on, let's get you something to eat. Y'all are welcome to sleep here tonight. You can have a bath, too."

"Guess we need that. Thanks, Miz McDermott. Give us a minute to grab our gear."

Sparkling weather dawned after a thunderstorm had washed all dust from the air and all sadness from Elizabeth. The church was incomparably beautiful. Sylvia, with her love of flowers, had tied bouquets at the end of each pew, laid sprays at each windowsill, and placed three large arrangements upon the altar. That morning Elizabeth and her mother had brushed each other's hair, as they had not done in months.

After the ceremony, Nate and Elizabeth marched out of the church, ducking under a shower of rice. Expecting to see the carriage that had brought her, Elizabeth was thrilled to see Ibrim. The camel had been outfitted with a custom-built two-person seat covered with red velvet cloth and bedecked with flowers. His bridle was festooned with golden tassels strung with bells that pealed delicately when he moved his head. His tail had been braided with red ribbons. A small set of stairs made it easy for them to climb in. Sitting side by side they waved to their well-wishers while Nate gave Ibrim the signal to rise. This had been his secret present. Elizabeth was overcome with joy.

The reception took place at the new house. Champagne flowed, along with the finest whiskey from Ireland and Kentucky. Soon everyone was in fine spirits, especially the guests from Indianola. Drew, already inebriated, approached Nate and punched his arm playfully.

"Say, why were you in such a rush to get married? We barely had time to get here. Elizabeth ain't knocked up, is she?"

"Hell, Drew!" Amos never could get used to Drew's bad manners.

Nate took offense. "Goddammit, Drew, that's my wife you're talkin' about! It's none of your business, but no she ain't."

Coming up behind Nate, Elizabeth slid her arm into his and smiled. Even Drew's rudeness couldn't dampen her mood today. "I heard what you said, Drew Johnsville, you rascal."

Amos, embarrassed beyond words, shook his head, but Drew was undeterred.

"But seriously, why the rush? Why'd it have to be today? I mean, it's kinda odd gettin' married on a Thursday, if you don't mind my sayin' so."

Elizabeth laughed. "Well, I do mind your saying so! But I'm happy to explain. It's the date. It had to be today's date."

"Yeah, but why?"

Nate smiled at Elizabeth, who grinned back at him. "We wanted to be married on May 14, one year exactly after the camels set foot on Texas soil."

EPILOGUE:
EIGHT YEARS LATER

SAN ANTONIO, JUNE 30, 1865

I N ONE HAND, SYLVIA McDermott clutched a damp hand-kerchief that she raised from time to time to dab her eyes. Jeremy Blackstone cradled the other. They sat side by side, rocking in the shade of the covered porch at the new house. The family still called it new, even though this house had long since become a fully established home and was now at the center of noisy activity. Nearby hammering promised new construction and an influx of residents, including Mr. Altgelt from Comfort, who planned to move to San Antonio to practice law. He proposed to name the neighborhood the King William District, after the King of Prussia. This choice struck Sylvia as somewhat unpatriotic, but she kept silent. During the war years, the definition of patriotism had been so fluid that she felt it prudent to refrain from criticism. At last the pounding ceased, and the usual quiet returned. Sylvia picked up the letter that lay in her lap.

"He's coming home. Thank God, Jeremy, he's coming home." She read the letter again.

Dear Mama,

I am a prisoner of the Yankees. I am allowed to write this letter, but I am not permitted to say where I am being held. The war is over, and we shall be released. I'll return to you as soon as I can.

With deepest affection, your son,

Ezekiel McDermott

She sobbed. "He doesn't say whether he's been wounded, but thank God, he's alive. I couldn't bear to lose another child."

"Nothing worse than losing a child."

"Oh, Jeremy. I'm so sorry. I can't imagine how it's been for you all these years, the grief you've carried after Linville. But when I think about Zachary...."

"A parent never stops thinking about it. Only consolation is time. Only thing that can smooth the edge of pain."

"It's been almost three years since we lost Zach, but it still feels sharp to me. Why, oh why, was he so stubborn?"

Squeezing her hand tenderly, Jeremy made no reply.

Sylvia conjured a mental image of Zachary as a teenager, grown mature but still slight of build. In appearance he resembled her more than his father, but he was every bit Quentin McDermott's son, willful and pigheaded, especially once he had set his mind to something. She could still hear his voice the day he had announced his decision.

"Mama, war has come as Papa predicted. I don't believe in slavery, and I sure as hell won't fight to preserve it. I'm goin' to join Mr. Kleinhart. We plan to sit this one out. I don't mean to hurt you, and I know that Zeke is determined to fight for the South. But as God is my witness, my conscience won't let me do any different."

So he had gone to Comfort, branded a traitor by many, including his brother Zeke. The community there held lengthy discussions about how to respond to the war. While some members flatly declined to participate, others, including Mr. Altgelt, eventually wore the Confederate uniform. However, even those who dressed the part often refused to fight. Most Texans, unable to accept Comfort's pacifist tendencies, took them to be pro-union sympathizers, and thus enemies. The community's elders feared for their safety. In the summer of 1862, sixty-five men from Comfort headed to Mexico to arrange a haven for their families.

The Confederate soldiers perceived this trip to Mexico as a pro-Union action. When the Comfort men camped without choosing a defensive position or posting guards, the Confederates launched a pre-dawn attack. Nineteen Comfort men were killed and nine others wounded, among them Zachary. The soldiers executed all the wounded. The newspapers described the event as a "military action against insurrectionists," but to Sylvia, the only appropriate term was massacre.

"I thought at least he would be safe in Comfort. But he was murdered. Murdered!"

Hearing the rage creep into her voice, Jeremy leaned over and put his arm around her shoulders "Dwellin' on it won't help. Besides, Zeke is comin' home."

"Yes, you're right. Zeke is alive. We must send word to Elizabeth and Nate."

"We'll do that, but you sit a spell first. It's a lot to take in."

"You know, Jeremy, we're lucky we didn't lose Nate, too, with all that back and forth to Mexico. It was so dangerous!"

"I worried myself sick."

"I remember. Many a night you didn't sleep a wink."

"Yup, but the planters were grateful. Gave 'em a livelihood."

When the Union forces quit Texas, the Confederate army had no idea what to do with the camels, so Nate was able to buy a few animals at a good price. Then the Union blockaded Galveston and Indianola, killing the cotton trade. But if a planter could get his cotton to San Antonio, Nate would buy it and transport it to Mexico on the camels. Selling the cotton there, he made a handsome profit.

Sylvia smiled, "Yes, and I was happy to have the coffee he brought back. Real coffee, while most people were making do with chicory."

"Elizabeth was good about suggestin' things for him to cart home. That girl has an eye for what people want. Nate always said the camels were his future. Took me a long time to see it."

"They've done all right, in spite of the war. And those adorable babies!" Talking about Nate and Elizabeth and their two children cheered Sylvia. "Zeke will see his niece and nephew for the first time. To think, I'm a grandmother twice over and you're a great-grandfather!"

"It's somethin', ain't it?" The sun's descending angle lit the underside of the puffy white clouds a brilliant copper. They rocked quietly until the sound of multiple footsteps disturbed the peace.

The war had sharpened Antoine's hearing. A sufficient number of unknown and unsavory types had visited during the war years that hyper-vigilance had become second nature to him. Able to hear people coming up the half dozen stairs, he often reached the door before the callers could ring the bell. He had opened the door to announcements of life and death, war and peace, success and ruin. He had developed an acute ability to assess the person standing before him, and his talent for response had evolved into a high art. He knew when to be deferential in the face of insult and how to be haughty to those who demanded more than their due. An audience with Sylvia McDermott was not granted to just anyone. Antoine walked quickly toward the front hall, admiring once more the double mahogany doors. As he pulled them open, he had the surprise of his life.

On the top step stood Henry from Galveston, the father of Esther's girls, accompanied by Malvina, Mrs. Eberly's slave from Indianola. He had seen neither one in eight years. Henry had aged, a bald patch spreading over the back of his head. Dressed in a suit that appeared new, he held himself straight, grinning. Malvina looked unchanged except for a hint of wrinkles about her eyes. Her tawny skin was still creamy, the color enhanced by the goldenrod hue of her simple but well-cut cotton dress, also new. Antoine noticed that the style highlighted her curvy figure. Both wore new shoes. Malvina looked him up and down.

The commotion drew Rebecca to the front window. When she caught a glimpse of Henry, she cried, "Lord have mercy! I'm goin' for Esther!"

As Antoine looked from one to the other, his confusion was so evident that both Henry and Malvina burst out laughing. He stepped out onto the porch, closed the door behind him, and lowered his voice. "Henry, Malvina. What's goin' on? Let's go 'round back to the quarters, I'm powerful curious to know why y'all are here."

"We're free, Antoine. We'll stand right here if we want to."

"What, Henry? You finally buy your freedom? You come to see Esther?" Such an explanation made sense, but Antoine still couldn't figure out Malvina's presence.

"No, it ain't like that." Henry spoke with determination. "I ain't come to *see* Esther. I come *for* Esther. We all free now."

Malvina fixed her gaze on Antoine. "And I come for you." Antoine was flabbergasted. Malvina handed him a piece of paper. "I know you can read. Here."

June 19, 1865, General Order Number 3, Galveston

"The people of Texas are informed that in accordance with a Proclamation from the Executive of the United States, all slaves are free. This involves an absolute equality of rights and rights of property between former masters and slaves, and the connection heretofore existing between them becomes that between employer and free laborer."

Antoine trembled. "Is it true?"

"True as the risin' sun!"

"Hallelujah!" He hugged Henry and Malvina. They danced a jig on the porch, thudding so loudly that Sylvia and Jeremy came to see what was happening

Malvina passed Sylvia the newspaper clipping. Sylvia scanned it quickly, handed it back, and turned to go inside without saying a word. Jeremy placed his hand gently on the small of her back and followed her in. Behind their backs, Malvina's solemn expression changed into a self-satisfied smile.

"Henry!" It was Esther's voice. Henry spun around to see Rebecca and Esther speeding up the street as fast as Esther could go. She was plumper than Henry remembered, but her face was aglow. Agnes loped alongside, calling "Henreeee!"

Henry leaped off the porch and ran to them, staring so hard at Esther that he paid no mind to Agnes and scarcely noticed the two beautiful young women at Esther's side. Breathless, Esther called out, "Henry! Praise the Lord, it is you!"

"We're free, Esther! All of us are free!"

Esther and Henry clung together. "Henry, here's your babies, all grown up. Sally already free by Massa Quentin's will. Mabel soon. But what you sayin'? We all free?" Henry hugged his daughters, his eyes filled with tears.

Agnes stood to one side, rocking back and forth, murmuring. "Henreee, Henreee. Freee? Freee?" She reached out and patted Henry's shoulders with both hands. "It really you? We really free?"

"Hush, Agnes. Henry, you remember Agnes?"

Nodding, Henry gently removed her hands. "We really free. President Lincoln freed the slaves two and a half years ago! Can you believe it? They kept it from us."

"Two and a half years? Lord Almighty."

"When the Union army got to Galveston, they announced it first thing. I'll never forget that day. June 19th, not even two weeks ago."

"That's sure gonna be a feast day from now on."

Henry laughed. "You bet. They already call it 'Juneteenth' and we gonna celebrate every year. Juneteenth! The day my whole family was set free."

From up on the front porch, Antoine watched Henry's reunion with his family, overcome with emotion. Malvina, who still stood beside him, began what sounded like a prepared speech.

"I only gonna say this once. I always figured I'd be one of them New Orleans placées, settled with a white father for my babies and a house of my own. I had the looks, and my mistress coulda worked it out for me. Where I messed up was, I didn't count on her husband, that son of a bitch, who sold me to Texas. Don't get me wrong. Miz Eberly treated me good and she passed up some good money to keep me instead of sellin' me off to some cigar-stinking cracker. No sir, no whisky-soaked redneck, neither."

Antoine stared at her.

"So now we free and I gonna say my piece. I ain't never wanted me no husband after I seen you. Oh, I ain't been pinin' all these years. I had me a baby girl and a baby boy. They died of fever couple years ago. A fair number o' men come for me. But I ain't never wanted nuthin' fixed and final. I told 'em, ain't no way."

Malvina took a deep breath. Antoine didn't move a muscle, but watched every flick of her eyes, which were overly bright. "This is how I sees it. You upright, you strong. I watched you plenty durin' your short spell in Indianola. I'm still young enough, and I come all this way. Well?"

Antoine had trouble taking it all in: Esther, Rebecca, Agnes, Henry and the girls at street level, crying and hugging; Malvina standing in front of him making incredible pronouncements; the thrilling yet shocking revelation that he was free. He had never been impetuous and he had no intention of making a decision on the spur of the moment. Still, his response surprised him.

"Well, Malvina. You gotta know this: I have me three sons. When Miz Sylvia settled here, I took up with a fine woman. I never felt for another woman like I did for my boys' mama. Four years ago, she died givin' life to the last born. After she died, Miz Sylvia bought my boys from their mama's owner. Miz Sylvia lets 'em stay with me in the quarters and she feeds 'em, so I figure she might have somethin' to say about this."

Malvina shook her head. "Ain't you heard nuthin' I said? We free now. Y'all don't need to be lookin' to Miz Sylvia. Just decide."

"I ain't that kinda man. Me and my family, we owe her."

Malvina looked miserable and embarrassed. Esther called out. "Come to the other house. These folks been travelin', and they gotta eat!" The group was already headed back, skipping and laughing, arm in arm, a radiant joy filling the street. Malvina turned to join them.

"Wait a minute." Antoine went inside. "Miz Sylvia."

"I heard. Go along, but Antoine, think about staying on as an employee. You would earn real wages. Think about it, please."

Coming through the back entrance to the adobe house, they met Elizabeth and her two young children in the court-yard and told her the news. "Oh, Esther, surely you won't leave me now? Not after so many years?"

Henry stepped forward. "Missy 'Lizbeth, you had your time with Esther, and now she gonna be with her own family. We gonna talk about our plans. I been thinkin' 'bout it all the way from Galveston."

Elizabeth was stunned. She retreated to the front salon where she sat silently, feeling a stranger in her own house.

Henry explained to the others. "The day after June-teenth, I took my saved money. Bought a ticket to Indiano-la. Met Malvina while I was tryin' to buy a wagon, so we threw in together. Indianola had only just heard the news."

Esther and Agnes looked askance at this. Their recol-lections of Malvina were not particularly pleasant, but if Henry vouched for her, they would keep an open mind. They listened to her closely.

"Meetin' Henry was a blessing. Before we left Indiano-la, I took him to Pastor Yates. You ever hear of Pastor Jack Yates?" No one had.

Henry continued. "He came to Matagorda County a couple years ago and started preachin'. The man's got a true callin', a vision from God. He says we gotta go to Hous-ton, make us a strong community. First thing, buy land. Land roots a man and lets him support a family. We gonna build houses and schools and gardens and businesses, and of course, a fine new church. Pastor Yates can read and write and figure. More than that, he's wise. We gonna fol-low him."

Everyone waited for Esther to reply first. "I been away from my man too long. Even if the journey's hard, I'm goin'. Mabel?"

"I'm goin'!"

"Sally's workin' as a seamstress. Donald here is good with her." She indicated the young man who had joined them on the way to the house. "Maybe y'all need to talk it over?"

"No need, Mama, we're goin'! We'll get married in that new church!"

Henry embraced his daughters. "Who else? What about Precious?"

"She had a baby boy." Much was known but not spoken about that baby. "Then she took up with a white man in Comfort and had two more babies. After the Comfort killings, they left for California."

No one had yet asked Agnes. Rocking back and forth in her seat, she had listened to everything. Suddenly she stood up and shouted, "I'm goin', too!" Then she plunked back down and asked sheepishly, "Ain't I?" Esther took her hand. "You most definitely goin' too."

Only Antoine struggled to make up his mind. That night he tossed and turned, agonizing over this new uncertainty. He kept hearing the voice of the free man they had met years before, the one who said that slavery stole a man's imagination. When Antoine tried to picture life as a free man, the limitless possibilities overwhelmed him. When he thought about leaving San Antonio, he found it immeasurably difficult to conceive what might lie ahead. Too much choice seemed as hard as no choice. He questioned his ability to make the right decision. Whatever he did now, he would have to accept responsibility for what happened after. The opportunity exhilarated, but the potential consequences terrified.

After a sleepless night, the morning sunshine clarified his decision. He would free his mind to imagine. He would open his heart to Malvina to see what feelings might grow there. He would give up his comparative security to strike out for Houston and make a future for his three sons.

Two days later, he walked out the front of the McDermott house, opening that grand, imposing door for the last time. From now on, he would open doors of his own.

SAN ANTONIO, ONE MONTH LATER

"WELCOME HOME." ELIZABETH WAS in the courtyard playing with the children when Nate entered through the rear gate. "Good trip?"

He kissed her lightly on the cheek. "Very. Had the camels movin' some lumber from Bastrop into town. Faster'n easier than a wagon."

"It's a good thing that Moses decided not to leave with everyone else. He really is best with the camels, isn't he?" Elizabeth enjoyed sharing Nate's pleasure when work was going well.

"Really good, yeah, and he's trainin' some of the Mexican boys, but it ain't sure that he'll stay."

"I know. I've been helping him write letters to look for his wife and children. Maybe if he finds them, he'll bring them here."

"Maybe. But I think as soon as he's saved enough wages, he'll go lookin' for them himself."

"Oh, Nate, speaking of letters, I almost forgot." She stood up quickly. "A letter came addressed to you in care of the Army Depot. It's from California!"

"Well, I'll be." Nate opened the letter and read it aloud.

Hello Nate,

This is Erdem. I am called Ed now. As you see I can read and write English. I live in California. I am full American. I make saddles and sell them. I use my old ways with leather to make new American saddles. Many people buy my saddles. I am married but no children yet. Life is good.

I was afraid to write you during the war. I did not know if my letter would find you. The camel caravan had problems with Indians and the desert, but we made it. I remember you were angry with Lt. Beale, but he wrote a good report about the camels. I heard that the government would bring more camels, but we have not seen them.

"Yes, Nate, we knew that part. Remember that letter we got from Cousin Babcock? It must have been a year after Lt. Beale left. He said that Beale's report was positive and that

Secretary of War Floyd had recommended the purchase of a thousand camels. I wonder what happened."

"Congress never did anything about it. Then the war broke out. Nothing will happen now. The railroads will get all the attention."

"What else does he say?"

When the war started, Lt. Beale took the camels to his ranch. At first I thought it was not correct for him to do that. But he protected them and fed them through the war. Now the Army wants to sell them. Some will go to circuses. Some will work the mines. Life in the mines is not good. It is very sad to see our camels used like that. I am glad you kept Ibrim.

"Oh no, Nate." Elizabeth interrupted again. "Do you think they would do that to the Camp Verde camels? Sell them off? I mean after the Union takes them back?"

"Probably."

"Can't we buy them?"

"There's over a hundred of them now. We could try to buy them, but we'd have to sell some of them on to circuses ourselves. Will you let me finish reading this?"

"Sorry."

On the trip, some camels got lost. They must be alone in the desert now. Perhaps they will survive. I hope so.

You won't believe it. We saw that old Yaqui woman and her grand-daughter somewhere in Arizona. One of the new men went off to marry the girl. The grandmother said he will be President of Mexico one day. I wish you could have seen it!

Hi Jolly went to Arizona with a few camels. Mico is a farmer, and Greek George is very rich. The newspaper says he is an outlaw.

I had one letter from Ali a few years ago. He works for the Americans in Cairo. Abdullah returned to his uncle's camels. Hassan is a businessman. (Maybe he learned from you, Nate?) They are all married. Hassan already had a son. Have you heard from them? How is Elizabeth? Did you marry her like you said you would? How is her mother and brothers? I hope everyone is well.

Fond greetings from your old friend,

Ed

Nate read the letter several times over. It was true, then, that the camel experiment had evaporated like rain in the desert. So many things had conspired against it: political disinterest, the war, the railroads, and the reluctance of many soldiers to work with the camels. Jefferson Davis's vision of a camel cavalry escorting wagon trains across the continent, fighting the Indians, and carrying Gatling guns into war would never come to pass. Still, Nate owed everything to the camels and could not conceive what his life would have been without them.

Elizabeth's thoughts drifted an ocean away, imagining Hassan married with a child. He probably had more than one by now. She wondered what his life was like, what hers might have been.

Nate put the letter down and exhaled. "Honey, what do you say we go for a ride?"

Elizabeth snapped out of her reverie. "Of course, let me change."

She called their new German housemaid to watch the children and quickly donned her riding skirt. Pausing to reach under the bed, she lifted out a metal box, opened it, and gazed fondly at its contents. A warm nostalgia washed over her while she studied the daguerreotype of Ibrim with herself, Nate, Alex and Hassan. As she examined every feature of the faces, she was astonished at how young they all looked. Replacing the photo, she pulled out other items. She fingered the glass bead that Hassan had given her and held Alex's rabbit's foot to her cheek, smiling ruefully.

Nate called her. "Let's go before it gets too late!"

"Coming. Say, could we stop and visit Alex for a minute? Seems the thing to do after getting Erdem's letter."

"Sure."

They mounted horses and rode toward the cemetery. Elizabeth still visited Alex whenever she had something important on her mind. Long accustomed to this ritual, Nate held back a little while Elizabeth approached Alex's grave. He heard her murmuring and then she laughed, turned, and strode toward him with determination. Her eyes moist, but her face smiling, she kissed him warmly. "Let's go."

At Nate's camel paddock on the edge of town, Moses helped them to saddle Ibrim and Adela. In short order they were out in the countryside ambling toward Castroville, reveling in the evening breeze and the camel's gentle rhythm. They allowed the camels to nibble a particularly large mesquite bush and chatted about Erdem's letter. In another mile, they came upon open rangeland, where cattle had trimmed the natural vegetation, making it easy going. Nate shouted to Elizabeth.

"You wanna race?"

"Catch me if you can!"

Elizabeth urged Adela forward until she was galloping across the plains. Nate on Ibrim joined the race enthusiastically. As Elizabeth's bonnet fell back from her face, her ebony hair flew around her, glistening in the afternoon light. Peals of laughter filled the air as Nate guided Ibrim in circles and zigzags, outrunning Adela and keeping the chase going. When he came up beside Elizabeth, the camels slowed to a walk. Still breathless, he took her hand and kissed it. She flashed him a deliriously happy smile. Under her breath she whispered, "Thank God for the camels!"

H ASSAN PACED ANXIOUSLY WHILE he waited for Sula to deliver their fourth child. He preferred to be alone when she was in labor, shunning the company of his male comrades who would have distracted him with gossip and entertainment. It was the least he could do, praying and sending his strength to help his beloved with her task.

Today his joy at the coming of a child was mixed with a wistful longing for his grandfather Alhaji Mustafa, who had died a year ago. Hassan's memories drifted eight years earlier to the time when he returned to Egypt from the United States. Never had he been so confused, feeling a foreigner in his own land. On the surface everything was familiar, but his perspective had changed, as had his daily habits. For a while he wore his foreign clothes, until, faced with ridicule from his friends, he hung his hat and bandana on the wall. Thrilled to eat the food he grew up with, he suffered odd cravings for hush puppies and fried catfish. He began to question things he had always accepted, everything from small habits to grand inequalities. In doing so, he was too blunt, insufficiently diplomatic in a culture that valued politeness. Even his posture carried a confidence that smacked of superiority. In short, he had become too American.

Alhaji Mustafa had explained that most people did not wish to have their world view challenged. As the returning traveler, Hassan had been transformed by his experiences and wished to share them. Those who had never left home could not envision what he spoke of and therefore could not appreciate the wisdom of his foreign ideas. Alhaji Mustafa had known this apathy, when he had returned from his travels south of the Sahara and had found that few were interested in his tales of the rest of Africa. He cautioned Hassan to choose his stories wisely because some people might think he was immodestly bragging. He taught Hassan to share his observations in small portions that people could digest. Hassan would be forever grateful for the ways that Alhaji Mustafa helped him to incorporate his new persona into the expectations held by others. Also, it had been enormously comforting that, unlike most everyone else, Alhaji Mustafa was ravenous for Hassan's stories. The two men had spent hours together. By first listening to Hassan and then recounting his own youthful adventures, his grandfather had deepened Hassan's understanding of what he had lived in America. Hassan had never loved his grandfather more.

His grandfather's friend Alhaji Ibrahim Muhammad engaged him in his business, using Hassan's language skills to expand his trading with Europeans and Americans. The arrangement brought Hassan success. He met quite a few Americans in Egypt over the years, but he knew he would never go back there. Although he might have been able to arrange it, he sent no correspondence.

Overjoyed to be reunited with Sula, he nevertheless yearned for Elizabeth in those first few weeks. He was somehow disappointed by Sula's quiet, submissive ways that others so admired. She was still a wonderful confidante, and they continued to pass many of their best moments outdoors in the courtyard. But she seldom asserted her own views, was reluctant to contradict him, and rarely engaged him in banter. Strange as it seemed, he missed Elizabeth's independence. Not quite sure how his grandfather would react to these feelings, Hassan had been circumspect. Somehow his grandfather had uncovered the truth.

"Sometimes the most beloved must be left in place and can live with us only in the ways that they have changed us."

Hassan was speechless. "How did you know?"

"I have lived a long time, grandson. Do not grieve, and do not feel guilty. You will make an excellent husband for Sula, and she a fine wife for you. It is not a betrayal of Sula to appreciate this love you left behind. You must let it enrich your ability to love others."

And so it had been. His marriage to Sula satisfied. He and Sula had moved in with Alhaji Mustafa to care for him and Grandma Ara while raising their family. His first child, now six, was named Mustafa to honor his grandfather. Happily, Alhaji Mustafa had lived long enough to walk with the youngster, once again prompting Grandma Ara to say that Alhaji Mustafa, Hassan, and little Mustafa moved with the same stride. His daughter, Fatima, was four and aptly named. She naturally appeared anywhere there was a conversation, listening to every detail, asking endless questions, and repeating what she heard. Abdullah, though only two, already showed an affinity for animals.

A baby's wail informed him that he was a father again. When the little girl's umbilical cord was cut, Grandma Ara whispered the call to prayer in her right ear. Sula's mother recited an appropriate sura from the Qur'an, and then Grandma Ara brought the baby to Hassan.

"Blessings be upon you, my son. Allah has bestowed upon you a beautiful daughter."

"Praise be to Allah."

"Hassan, this child has a will of her own. She pushed forcefully into the world. I wonder what she has in store for us!"

Hassan laughed. "I heard her yelling to announce her arrival."

"Look, my grandson, your daughter has blue eyes, like my husband Alhaji Mustafa and your Auntie Fatima, the only ones in our family with such eyes. Perhaps this one should have been called Fatima. Alas, you'll have to choose another name for her."

Hassan stared at the tiny hands, the full head of curly dark hair and the luminescent blue eyes, open wide and curious. Moist, fresh, and dazzling, these eyes transported him to another time and place, when he had lost his heart to a deep azure gaze and midnight hair. His recollection released intense love for this tiny girl.

"Grandfather was lucky to bring you home."

"What, Hassan?"

"I mean, we are fortunate that Grandfather brought you here, so that you could be my grandmother and now great-grandmother to these beautiful children."

"Thank you, Hassan. It has been Allah's greatest blessing to me." Grandma Ara was perplexed by the emotion in her grandson.

"The eyes and hair. She shall be called Badia."

"Excellent choice, Hassan! Badia, meaning unique, unprecedented."

"And for the happiness that she brings us, Aleeza, meaning joy."

"It's a most auspicious name, my son. BadiaAleeza."

"No, Grandma, let her be called AleezaBadia."

Cradling the baby tenderly, Hassan smiled at his own miniature Elizabeth.

AUTHOR'S NOTE

This is a work of fiction based on historical events. So, how much of it really happened? The broad outline of the camel experiment is accurate: Congressional appropriation, acquisition, Indianola, Camp Verde, the second shipment and on to California. As Secretary of War, Jefferson Davis promoted the project from the beginning. Key dates, such as the camels' arrival at Indianola on May 14, 1856, are correct, but other chronologies and events have been modified for the sake of the story. For example, the camels did not stop in Galveston. Many of the camel antics are based on incidents recorded in official documents and in eyewitness reports. Descriptions of the lightering, the hay bales, and the fence are elaborated from actual accounts, and most of the camel names are taken from government reports. The camel born on ship was indeed called Uncle Sam, and Mrs. Mary Shirkey did knit socks for the President from the camel's wool.

All of the main characters are imaginary: the entire McDermott household, Major Babcock and Alex, Lt. Halter, Nate, and Jeremy. Official reports list three Egyptian camel handlers who came with the first shipment and subsequently returned home. This brief mention inspired the characters of Hassan and his extended family as well as Ali, Abdullah, Erdem and Pertag, all of whom are fictional.

Several real people make appearances, but their words and actions are entirely fictitious. Angelina Eberly did own a hotel in Indianola, and a statue of her stands in downtown Austin today. The presence of Ernst Altgelt, Gail Borden, Jefferson Davis, Sam and Mary Maverick, Jose Antonio Navarro, Jack Yates, and other historical figures is plausible, but invented. The camel handlers from the second shipment, Hi Jolly, Mico, and Greek George, appear in historical accounts that are often illustrated by Gwynne Heap's marvelous sketches. Lt. Beale's expedition to California with the camels is documented in his own report and in the journal of May Humpreys Stacey.

Indianola, once the second most prosperous port in Texas, was destroyed by hurricanes in 1875 and 1886, and abandoned by 1887. Saluria was flattened by the same two storms. The Matagorda Island lighthouse has been moved, but still stands. Camp Verde changed hands between Union and Confederate troops, before ceasing military use in 1869. The remains of the Officers Quarters are on private land.

The original reports, ship's logs, and correspondence are archived in the US Library of Congress. Other references for the Camel Corps include:

Emmet, Chris, *Texas camel tales: Incidents growing up around an attempt by the War department of the United States to foster an uninterrupted flow of commerce through Texas by the use of camels*, Steck-Vaughn, 1933; reissued 2011

Faulk, Odie B. *The U.S. Camel Corps: an army experiment*, Oxford University Press, New York, NY, 1976

Fowler, Harlan D. *Camels to California; a chapter in western transportation*, Stanford University Press, Stanford, CA, 1950

Lesley, Lewis Burt (ed.). *Uncle Sam's Camels: the journal of May Humphreys Stacey supplemented by the report of Edward Fitzgerald Beale*, Huntington Library Press, San Marino, CA, 2006

For more about Texas cities, see:

Malsch, Brownson *Indianola, The Mother of Western Texas*, State House Press, Austin, TX 1988

McComb, David *Galveston: A History*, University of Texas Press, Austin, TX 1986

For seemingly endless and fascinating information about people and places in Texas, check out the *Handbook of Texas*, from the Texas State Historical Association. This fountain of anecdotes and ideas is searchable online at *tshaonline.org*.

Although I consulted the above sources as well as biographies, journals, and travelogues of the period in order to set the novel in context, the result is a product of my imagination. All errors are totally my own.

A final note: For me, discovering this story was sheer fun. If you have shared that joy even a little, then I am truly happy.

ACKNOWLEDGMENTS

Completion of a work like this depends on help from many people. Marjorie Blair, Barbara Bell, and Kay Pierce motivated me to finish the story by asking repeatedly when the next bit would be ready. Anne Czarniecki also encouraged me to keep going, then slogged through the first ragged version and made many valuable suggestions. Cynthia Sulaski shared her skills with punctuation and grammar by editing, correcting, and making notes. Larry Yarak lent his professorial eye to the final proofs. Silver Feather Design (silverfeatherdesign.com) created the layout and cover designs, and Ibex Strategies (ibextstrategies.com) handled logistics and business matters. Thanks also to Marcus Liwag for assistance with the cover. A number of other people read early drafts and made helpful comments. Many thanks to all of you! And an extra special gratitude to close friends—you know who you are—who helped me to think of this as more than a dream.

My deepest appreciation goes to my husband, Larry Yarak, who cheered and supported me in every way possible and to our sons Steven and Jonathan, who always believed in their mother.

CPSIA information can be obtained at www.ICGtesting.com
Printed in the USA
LVOW07s1333090816

499654LV00002B/111/P